BALMORROW'S BRIDE

Judith A. Lansdowne

Zebra Books
Kensington Publishing Corp.
http://www.zebrabooks.com

To Kelly and Joseph
and special thanks to
Joan Overfield

ZEBRA BOOKS are published by

Kensington Publishing Corp.
850 Third Avenue
New York, NY 10022

First Printing: July, 1998
10 9 8 7 6 5 4 3 2 1

Printed in the United States of America

Chapter 1

Clarissa Beresfont peered apprehensively from the coach window at the rugged landscape that clawed threateningly toward her. Northumberland. The very word sent shivers down her spine. Northumberland. Savage. Feral. A ruthless wilderness of angry crags, murky forests, frenzied waterways. From the very moment Clarissa's little party had departed the inn at Cardmore on Dobnan early that morning, sign after sign of civilization had faded one by one until now only monstrously gnarled trees, beastly outcroppings of bare rock, and surly waters that overflowed the lowlands met her eyes.

Northumberland. Well, it is certainly everything I expected, Clarissa thought with a sigh and a grim smile. It must be the most hideous place in all of Great Britain. I do hope *he* is not equally as hideous. She sighed again and turned her gaze from the window to the young woman who sat dazed upon the seat beside her. "It is very wild, is it not, Charis?" she asked with only the merest tremble in her voice. "Can you imagine what it must be like to actually live in such a place?"

The Viscountess of Halliard raised frightened eyes and gulped. "I have never seen anything so beastly in my entire life," she whispered, almost as if she feared the landscape would hear her and wreak vengeance upon her for such blatantly negative words. "I am so very sorry, Clare. We ought to turn about and go directly home. I had no idea he lived in such a vile place as this. If I had, I would certainly have told you so and not at all encouraged you to accept his offer. I am certain we ought to go home. I shall call out to Malcolm and tell him to turn us about this very moment."

Clarissa wished heartily to support her sister-in-law in this decision. With each roll forward of the carriage wheels her mind sank farther into melancholy and her once determined optimism quivered and quaked. But she could not allow herself to agree with Charis' longing to turn back. It was necessary that she, Clarissa Beresfont, continue forward, down this most portentous and intimidating path—a path that she had chosen not for her own benefit, but to provide for the happiness and security of the brother she loved.

Not once since that dreadful Monday evening when she had strolled into the library at Halliard Hall to discover her brother, Malcolm, with an empty brandy decanter beside him, a drained glass in one hand and a loaded pistol in the other—the pistol already cocked and pointed at his head—not since that very moment, when he had stuttered out to her with a stiff lip and tears standing in his eyes, the exact depth of the pit into which they had fallen, had Clarissa given the least thought to her own needs and wishes. And she would not fall prey to them now. She would not allow herself to indulge in self-pity and despair. She would not surrender to the terrors rapidly sprouting in her vivid imagination nor allow her fear of the unknown to gain precedence over the grim reality of Malcolm's despair. She absolutely would not go scuttling back to Newbury in a panic because of mere trees and hills and streams. She was not such a coward!

She would do anything—anything—to save Malcolm, to keep him from a suicide's grave and to provide him with an opportunity to rebuild a life for himself and his wife. And if marriage to a nobleman who dwelt in a place as foreign to her as the wilds of Africa was the only means that presented itself of assuring her brother's well-being, it was little enough for her to do.

"I am certain that Castle Balmorrow cannot be near so monstrous a place as the landscape that surrounds it, Charis," Clarissa said with a forced smile. "And you, yourself, have assured me that the earl is as fine a gentleman as you have ever met. No, we shall not turn about. Malcolm has already sent Lord Balmorrow word of my acceptance and Lord Balmorrow has sent this grand coach and coachman to fetch us to him and I shall not be so fickle now as to change my mind and cry off because I cannot like the scenery of his homeland."

Those words took great effort to speak and though they sounded exactly as they should, Clarissa could not help but hear in them a most desolate echo. What perverse imp of fate had taken her so in dislike? Why had her life taken such a strained and distasteful path? In all of her twenty years she had never been forced to take one step that had not been planned and thoroughly considered. And now, of a sudden, here she was tooling up a rutted road through the forests of Northumberland on her way to marry a gentleman she had never once set eyes upon.

A mere hour's ride from the Scottish border, upon the ramparts of Castle Balmorrow, Alexander St. John Sinclair paced slowly, his dark locks blowing in a rising wind. His broad shoulders, covered only by the cambric of his collarless shirt and a long-sleeved waistcoat, seemed to sag somewhat as he pondered. He clasped his hands tightly behind his back and stared at the granite beneath his feet ignoring the wild beauty that spread unfettered below him. He was buried so deeply within himself that he did not even notice when a pair of much smaller top boots began to pace directly behind his own, following him step for step around the fluted rooftops.

Zander, flushed with the excitement of having gained the ramparts for the first time in his seven years, rejoiced in going unnoticed and trailed his father in silence, his own hands clasped firmly behind his back, his head lowered, his young shoulders sloping a bit in proud imitation of his hero.

Balmorrow's brow furrowed; his mouth twitched at one corner; he sighed so low that it could not be heard above the wind. Well, but I have done the thing, he told himself silently. And no matter what, I shall not undo it. Clarissa Beresfont will be my bride and I must make the best of that, though the mere thought of it sends shivers through me.

Balmorrow had held out hope for the longest time that

the rumors of Malcolm Beresfont's penury had been greatly exaggerated. But at last he had been forced to conclude that they were not. Somehow, in some quiet and unobtrusive way, the present viscount's father had managed to divest himself of all of his considerable fortune and run deeply into debt besides, bequeathing his heir nothing but havoc and heartache.

For over a year the Earl of Balmorrow had prayed that the new Viscount Halliard would somehow come about, somehow discover a way to restore his family finances. Balmorrow had even gone so far as to add to the expediency of his prayers by seeking out and paying all of the old viscount's debts that he himself could locate before those who were owed the sums should appear upon the front steps of Halliard Hall. But the Beresfont family had taken such an incredible hit that even Balmorrow's considerable secret contributions had not been enough to bring them about.

No, Balmorrow thought with another sigh, Malcolm Beresfont definitely stands upon the very edge of the cliff of disaster or has already slipped into the slough of despair. Otherwise he would never have accepted so readily the settlements I offered in return for Miss Beresfont's hand in marriage. "Marriage! Aye, there is considerable rub!" he mumbled, rubbing his hand against the back of his neck.

Balmorrow had planned never to marry again. He had promised himself, no matter how limpid the eyes or glossy the curls or piquant the face, that he would never again repeat the vows that had condemned him to ten teeth-rattling years with Madeline. But he had been able to think of no other way as expeditious and acceptable as this proposed marriage to rescue Halliard and his sister. And surely Miss Beresfont was as much in need of the protection and security he offered her as a husband as her brother was in need of Balmorrow's money. A sister of a penniless viscount, after all, stood not much chance upon the marriage mart or in the world in general.

Balmorrow groaned and ran his hand through his windblown hair. He could not, without shirking his responsibility, allow Malcolm Beresfont to go under, no more than he could allow that young gentleman's sister to be forced into the life of a poverty-stricken spinster. As much as he longed at this moment to deny the truth of the matter, he could do no such thing. The Sinclairs owed the Beresfonts an enormous debt. And if the time to repay that debt happened to come upon his watch, as it so obviously had, then he would see to it that it was repaid honorably, even if it meant that he had to marry Miss Clarissa Beresfont, sight unseen.

The mere thought that he had never so much as laid eyes upon Miss Beresfont brought him to an abrupt halt. The little shadow behind him paced straight into the back of his legs.

"Zander!" he exclaimed, turning to see what had thumped against him. "What the devil are you doing up here?"

"P-pacing, Papa. This is the place for pacing, is it not?"

"Well, yes," smiled the earl, stooping to tug his son's coat more tightly about his shoulders, "but you ought not to be up here. It is dangerous, Zan. One great gust of wind and, whoosh, off you go over the ramparts and into the moat."

A most innocent and serious little face, dominated by exact replicas of Balmorrow's own great blue eyes, peered up at the earl doubtfully. "We do not have a moat, Papa."

"We do not? Well, we must get one then, eh? What kind of respectable castle does not have a moat?" Balmorrow took the boy by the hand and went to gaze down over the ramparts. "We shall speak to the men about it tomorrow, eh, Zan? A nice wide moat right there and a drawbridge to go over it as well. Duncan and Leopold and John will not mind to dig us a moat, do you think?"

The little boy giggled. He knew perfectly well that each of the men his father had mentioned would mind very much and say so, too, in no uncertain terms.

"And look there, Zan. Is that not Sylvester searching for you? Now why would he be out searching for you? Perhaps you have not quite finished with your lessons for today?"

"No, I am finished, Papa. I have learned everything."

"What? Everything?"

"Uh-huh."

"Well," grinned the earl, "perhaps I had best dispense with Sylvester's services then. A boy who knows everything certainly has no use for a tutor."

"Well, per'aps I do not know *everything,*" amended Zander, who was most fond of his tutor and had no wish to lose that gentleman's company. "Per'aps I need Sylvester to teach me some things, Papa. I am not very good at sums."

"You are not? Well, perhaps I shall not send Sylvester off quite yet, then. Why are you wanting to pace, Zan? Are you worried about something?"

"Uh-huh."

"Tell me."

"I am worried 'bout having a mama. Are you certain I need to have one, Papa? Brandy says perhaps she will be cruel and send us off to school and we shall never see you ever again."

"Oh, I rather think not," drawled the earl, his eyes sparkling with mirth. "I am a good deal larger than she, I believe, because I am larger than almost everybody, am I not? Yes, and I expect I can best her should it come to a mill over something of such import as sending you two away. Besides, it was I decided to send Brandy to school."

"Yes, but you changed your mind."

"Brandilynn was never made for Miss Prinkton's School for Young Ladies. Still, you will go to school one day, Zan. The time is drawing near. Another year or two and you will be at Eton."

"Don't want to."

"Nevertheless, it will happen. You do not wish to be thought an illiterate barbarian from the hinterlands, do you?"

"Yes, that is 'zactly what I wish, Papa. I have heard Uncle Jack call you that and I wish to be just like you."

Balmorrow roared into laughter and, turning from the ramparts, swung his son up onto his shoulders and carried him through the door in the east tower and down the winding staircase into the corridor that led to the east wing.

In the kitchen of the castle, which lay at the rear of the central keep, a blue-eyed, dark-haired young lady of nine was busily smearing butter across a thick piece of freshly-baked bread. "Do you think Papa actually means to do it, Duncan?" she asked thoughtfully. "I never thought to see the day myself."

"Oh, ye din't, eh?" replied Balmorrow's cook, his great craggy face beaming down upon the raven-haired vixen who had invaded his kitchen and pulled up a chair as if she meant to spend the day. "In all yer years of knowin' him, ye never oncet suspected as how yer pa might crave t'be married again?"

"Uh-uh. He has never said a word about it, Duncan. Has he ever said a word about it to you?"

Duncan chuckled and settled himself into a chair opposite the girl, buttering himself a slice of bread and taking a great bite out of it. " 'Tain't somethin' The Balmorrow be like to confide to his cook, my lady, nor his childer. 'Tis a personal matter what a man ain't like to lay upon the dining table for open discussion."

"Yes, but he might well have mentioned the likelihood before he made the offer, do you not think, Duncan? I mean, to simply declare one day that Zander and I are to have a new mama without asking whether we desire one or not does not seem quite the thing to me."

Duncan grinned and took another bite of the bread. He chewed thoughtfully, his bushy brows rising and falling along with the movement of his jaws. Lady Brandilynn was a scamp, she was, and a joy to his heart! "I reckon," he mused, "that yer pa has reasons fer wantin' a wife that ain't got a great deal to do with you and Master Zan, milady."

"What kind of reasons?"

"Well, reasons what a man understands but don't like to go about explainin' to his childer."

"Oh," replied Brandy thoughtfully, "man things."

"Indeed," grinned Duncan. "Man things, an' ye'll do well not to question the earl too diligently about 'em. A gentleman has a life that must be lived, whether he be havin' childer er not. Ye ain't downright opposed to yer pa takin' a wife, are ye, milady?"

"Oh, no. I think it will be interesting to have a new mama if she is not cruel and proud and does not wish to send me back to Miss Prinkton's School for Young Ladies. Do you think she will put up with Papa, Duncan, this Miss Clarissa Beresfont? Papa is a considerable handful."

"I believe she might, milady," Duncan nodded, "if she can be brought to love him well enough."

"Well, of course she loves him, Duncan," Brandy asserted impatiently, finishing off her bread. "She has agreed to marry him. She would not do so if she did not love him."

Duncan was inclined to enlighten the little lady to the fact that not all marriages—especially not those between members of her papa's class—were love matches as they inevitably turned out to be in the little fairy tales the earl told her from time to time. But he thought better of it, hoping that perhaps, at last, The Balmorrow had discovered someone who actually did love him and would share in his joys and sorrows and be a true helpmate to him as a wife ought to be.

"She must love Papa very much, this Miss Beresfont, to come all the way to Northumberland to be married at our castle," whispered Brandy with a most romantic gleam in her eyes. "I think it is a good sign that she is so eager to have him that she does not insist upon being married in London, do not you, Duncan?"

"Oh, my goodness," murmured Charis as the heavy traveling coach swept up a rise and presented its occupants with their first sight of Castle Balmorrow. It was a most intimidating spectacle in the valley below them, set as it was against the wilderness of AllCatch Spinney with the Roiling Hills rising to its east and the genuine mountain of The Likely Run, afire with the colors of the setting sun, soaring into the distance at its western gate.

Clarissa could not believe her eyes. She blinked and blinked again. Surely this was not to be her home. Surely this could be no one's home. The great granite structure rose a full five stories into the air. With rounded towers at all four corners it hunched, an ugly, oblong, brute of a building amidst the newly greening grass of a small park. There was nothing to save it, nothing to make it appealing to the eye, nothing to give it architectural grace or sophistication. "It is utterly barbaric," she murmured to herself. "A bastion of stones piled high by savages."

Castle Balmorrow did not improve upon closer study. As the coach drew to a halt before the main gate, it became all too clear to Clarissa that the outer walls of the repulsive structure were deeply pitted and pockmarked in places and literally crumbling in others. Great gouges of granite had tumbled to the ground and been left where they had fallen and never replaced.

Is he clutch-fisted then, this Lord Balmorrow? she wondered, nibbling distractedly at her lower lip. He certainly did not appear to be in the proposed terms of the marriage settlements. Malcolm had been overjoyed to read them.

The mere thought of the marriage settlements set Clarissa's heart to pounding. The Earl of Balmorrow, according to Malcolm, had been more than generous. He had, in fact, proposed to bestow upon her brother a sum which would set Malcolm and Charis firmly back upon their feet. And he had indicated his intent to set aside a separate five thousand pounds in Clarissa's name alone, without one string attached to it. She might manage or invest the sum in anyway she cared to do. Still, all of this he had offered by way of his man of business, never once approaching either herself or Malcolm personally in the matter. She had thought it the oddest thing at the time, but it had not mattered. Nothing had mattered, for the earl's proposal had come immediately upon the heels of Malcolm's thwarted suicide attempt.

Malcolm, who had ridden beside the coach the entire way, dismounted upon the circular drive at the foot of the entrance to the main keep and, staring in awe at the structure before him, backed his way toward the coach to assist his wife and sister to descend onto the graveled circle. One of the outriders Balmorrow had sent to accompany them lowered the coach steps and then rushed to ply the knocker upon the enormous brass-bound doors.

"Perhaps the inside is not so unwelcoming as the outside," Malcolm offered quietly.

"Or perhaps it is much worse," declared Charis. "Malcolm we must not allow Clare to do this thing. Certainly we cannot condemn her to live in such a place as this simply to improve our own comfort. We shall draw our purse strings a bit more tightly and I will not so much as *think* to travel to London for the Season this year. That will put us on a better footing and I will not mind in the least to do it, I promise you."

Viscount Halliard blanched. Even in the decreasing light of the sunset Clarissa could see the whitish tinge about his lips as the color drained from her brother's face.

So, even to this day Malcolm had not had the heart to explain to Charis how deeply in debt they stood. He had not told her that they were only one jump ahead of the bailiff's man and total disgrace. Well, I should have known he would not, Clarissa told herself. He is so madly in love with her that he cannot bear for her to think badly of him. He would rather die than to bring disgrace upon her. "Do not be such a peagoose, Charis," she said then in the most confident tone she could muster. "Certainly it is not the sort of home I am accustomed to, but I shall undoubtedly *grow* accustomed to it. And I shall like to be a countess," she added, a wobbling smile upon her lips which she aimed encouragingly at her brother. "I never thought to look beyond a viscount at the very most, you know. It is a great privilege to be chosen to be the bride of the Earl of Balmorrow. Reverend Mr. Hobright and Mrs. Hobright said as much when I told them the news. They were both overcome with joy for me."

"Are you certain you would not rather marry Lord Parkhurst?" Charis eyed the ediface before them distrustfully. "Lord Parkhurst has the most delightful residence near Portsmouth they say. It is a very gentlemanly farm with horses and cows and fields of corn."

Clarissa shook her head slowly from side to side. Obviously Malcolm had not told Charis about Edward, Lord Parkhurst either. Well, but it was none of Charis' business that Lord Parkhurst had withdrawn his suit once he had discovered the true state of the Halliard finances. No, nor was it Edward's fault that he could not afford to align himself with a woman who had no money to bring to the marriage and whose brother's holdings were about to be put upon the auction block. Such a state of affairs would give any gentleman pause, would it not? Most certainly it would.

The thought of Edward, Lord Parkhurst with his bright hazel eyes and golden hair, his handsome countenance and easy manners, brought a strange stuttering to Clarissa's heart. Oh, how she could have loved him! He was everything delightful, her ideal of a true gentleman. She had made his acquaintance early in her Season—that dreadful Season which had been cut short by her father's death—and she had fallen immediately under his spell. He was everything desirable in a gentleman—comely, sophisticated, courtly and gallant. When he spoke he sent her pulses racing and when he smiled his most amused and knowing smile, her heart fluttered upward into her throat. And she might well have married him, too, had her father not died so unexpectedly and the true state of the Halliard finances come so devastatingly to light.

But Lord Parkhurst would not have her now and the unknown Lord Balmorrow would. And there, she told herself, lies the crux of the matter. Not only will Lord Balmorrow have me, but he has offered to pay well for the privilege. Though why he has chosen me above all others, I cannot imagine. We have not once met. Why he has never even been pointed out to me across a crowded room. But perhaps I have unknowingly been pointed out to him, she thought hopefully. And perhaps he saw in me an indefinable something that at once attracted him.

Oh, good heavens no, she thought with a secret laugh at herself, that is highly unlikely. He is an earl, after all. He would have requested an introduction if he had been attracted to me in such a way. Perhaps he has simply heard of me and my circumstances and thinks I will be a thankful and therefore biddable wife who will not be likely to thwart his will. Or perhaps he merely wishes someone to raise his children and has offered for any number of young ladies, and I am the only one to acquiesce. A widower with two children might well be desperate for a wife and might well find a young woman willing to take on a ready-made family hard to come by.

Indeed, that must be it. Lord Balmorrow must at some point have become aware of the state of Malcolm's affairs and taken hope that at last he could buy himself a wife of good family who would not hold out against him because of his children. That he would expect her to be beholden to him for rescuing herself and her family from penury, Clarissa did not doubt. The Earl of Balmorrow would expect gratitude for his offer and expect her to strive to be a comfortable and conformable helpmate and to take a large part in the raising of his family.

And there is nothing at all wrong with such expectations on his part, Clarissa counseled herself silently as she took her brother's arm. After all, I agreed to marry him only because his money will save Malcolm from total despair. I am in his debt. And I shall strive to be everything he wishes me to be because of it. There is nothing at all wrong in that. It is a business dealing—and one highly in my own favor for I have already seen my brother restored to his senses and I shall have my own home and the protection of a husband besides.

In grim silence Malcolm Beresfont escorted his wife and his sister toward the now open doors where an elderly butler dressed appropriately for his profession in a spotless black coat and striped pantaloons, awaited them amidst the dank, dark, and cavernous shadows of the Great Hall. The man relieved Malcolm of his hat, his whip and his gloves, took the ladies' bonnets and traveling cloaks and, with a most impassive face, informed them that Lord Balmorrow had only just returned from the village of St. John with his cousin, the Bishop of Leeds, and that both gentlemen would be pleased to receive Miss Beresfont and her family in the chapel of the west wing.

"In the chapel?" asked Charis, puzzled.

"Indeed, my lady," replied the servant. "His Nibs—that is to say—His Grace, the bishop, must set off this evening for London. Has an appointment with the Archbishop of Canterbury that cannot be changed. I am to escort you directly to the chapel."

Clarissa's mouth opened, closed, opened again. What on earth had the Bishop of Leeds' trip to London to do with anything? And why would any sane gentleman think to welcome his bride-to-be and her relatives in a chapel? Unless—but no, not even a Bedlamite would expect a young lady—a perfect stranger at that—to marry him the moment she arrived upon his doorstep without so much as offering her a cup of tea and a chance to change into clean clothing and the opportunity for a brief respite from a most arduous journey—not even a Bedlamite would do that.

Chapter 2

"Well, since you refuse to seek my opinion in the matter, coz, I shall be forced to overstep the bounds and provide it without your request." The Bishop of Leeds lowered himself into the only chair in the tiny antechamber beside the chapel. "You have lost your mind completely, Lex. How could you have offered for a woman you have never seen before in your life?"

"I could and I did," mumbled the earl, leaning one hip against the sill of the chamber's only window and gazing studiously down at the toe of one brightly polished half-boot. "She is the daughter of Thomas Beresfont, Alden, and her situation, as well as her brother's, is desperate. You know how much our family owes Thomas Beresfont and his father. I am simply repaying a debt at a time when its repayment is crucial. Your involvement in the matter is simply to do the marriage up right and proper so it cannot be undone. You may keep your opinions to yourself."

"But you have not the vaguest idea what sort of person this Miss Beresfont is, Lex. Perhaps she is a virtual shrew and detests children. Have you thought of that?"

"Yes, but it is of no account. If she detests children I shall see that Brandy and Zander are kept far from her and she from them. This is a huge old wreck of a place, Alden. A person may wander about in it for days on end without once encountering the rest of the occupants. And I will take her to London with me for the Season. That will give her some respite from my imps."

"That is not at all what I mean," replied His Grace, with a tinge of frustration. "A wife has duties to her husband, Alex, and to her children. Relationships must be formed regardless of her feelings in the matter."

"Brandy and Zan are not her children. They are Madeline's."

"Yes, but—"

"Cease and desist, Alden! I have the special license. I have the prelate—if you do not abandon me, that is—and I shall do the thing as soon as Miss Beresfont arrives! It will be over and done with in the blink of an eye and you may rush off to London without once looking back."

"And that is another thing," sighed His Grace. "Are you mad to bring the woman to stand before me without even going down to welcome her into your home? Do you actually expect her to marry you in her traveling dress and without so much as a glass of ratafia or a cup of tea to wash the dust from her throat?"

"Yes."

"Yes?"

"Yes. Parsons will welcome her, and Brandy and Zan too. Brandy has even picked her a bouquet of wildflowers from the flutterby room. It is expected, Brandy informs me, that the bride should have a bouquet."

"Well, it *is* expected, Alex. And a good deal more is expected, as well. I shall return from London in a month. Why not postpone the wedding until then? Get to know the girl. Give her an opportunity to know you. Her brother and sister-in-law make the journey with her, you say. They will be expecting to play chaperon to the two of you for a time before the wedding."

The sound of children giggling and hesitant footsteps upon the marble floor of the chapel interrupted the two and Balmorrow, with an indecisiveness most uncharacteristic to him, made his way slowly to the connecting door. He peered for only a moment into the chapel then spun back to face his cousin. "Do it now, Alden. She is here and she is holding the bouquet. I am here with the ring in my pocket. Do not insist upon prolonging my agony. Nothing in our situations will change within a month. I am duty-bound to have her if she is willing, and she is forced by circumstances to be willing, and all else is irrelevant."

The Bishop of Leeds rose from the chair with his scarlet and ermine robes flowing about him and strolled over to put an arm about his cousin's shoulders. "All this rush is because of Madeline, is it not, Alex? You have had to fight to screw your courage to the sticking place and now you fear that if you wait for one more moment the pain of your first marriage will come too clearly home to you and you will cry craven."

"Yes, something like that. Whatever you say, Alden. Think what you like, but I have offered and Miss Beresfont has accepted and you must do the thing—now."

"Now? Certainly you are going out to introduce yourself to her at the very least."

"No. You are going out to bid her welcome and to show her where to stand and then I am coming out to stand beside her and we will say the words, and then I am leaving this pile of stones to escort you back to the village and your post chaise to London."

"You are a Bedlamite, Alex! And if the woman marries you under these circumstances, she is a Bedlamite as well and the two of you deserving of whatever you get!"

"Yes, exactly so," nodded Balmorrow anxiously. "Exactly so, Alden, and you have no need to feel guilty about any of it."

Clarissa stood, petrified, before the Bishop of Leeds in the candlelit chapel on the third floor of the west wing of Castle Balmorrow. In her gloved hands she clutched a bouquet of tug-at-hearts, violets, jonquils, and daffodils. She was spastically twisting their poor little stems into stringy shreds. Beside her, the Earl of Balmorrow, who had appeared only after she had already taken her place before the tiny altar, stoically repeated the marriage vows in a deep, resonant voice. As far as she was able to notice, the gentleman had not so much as glanced at her from the corner of his eye. When her turn came, Clarissa, haltingly and in need of prompting at several points, repeated the vows as well.

It was not until Balmorrow took her hand into his great paw and slipped a plain gold ring upon her finger that Clarissa was privileged to see more of him than his rugged profile. She had a quick glimpse of large and extraordinarily deep blue eyes nestled amongst lush black lashes, a nose of acceptable length with an odd angle to it at the tip, and apparently average lips that appeared to turn up quite naturally at the corners. But he turned back toward the bishop before she could gather much more about him.

Behind her in one of the three little pews that had likely served the family for centuries, she heard Malcolm sigh and Charis stifle a sob. There was a rustling, too, and a soft giggle. His children, she thought. My stepchildren. I am barely a bride and already a mama. That thought terrified her almost as much as did the gentleman beside her. But at least she had met the children. They had come running to greet her and to escort her through the maze of corridors and stairwells and chambers to the chapel. She had not, however, met the earl. Never met him, she thought with a shudder. I have married the man and we have yet to be so much as introduced!

The ceremony at an end, Balmorrow, without so much as a nod to his new wife, escorted the bishop out through the side door by which the two men had entered and left his bride to stand alone and open-mouthed before the altar.

"We will show you how to get down to the little dining room," announced Brandilynn, slipping from one of the benches and starting toward the door opposite the one through which her father had exited. "Duncan will be certain to have everything ready by now. And there are chambers prepared for all of you. But you would like to eat first, would you not? Zander and I are starving."

Malcolm, in a state of utter disbelief, went to the altar and took his sister's arm and led both Clarissa and Charis from the chapel in the children's wake. He chewed his lower lip as they descended through a warren of corridors and staircases to the first floor of the main keep. "I cannot believe it," he mumbled at last. "That he should escort the bishop from the chamber rather than his bride! Lord, what have I done, Clare? And just look at this abominable place. It is exactly as it must have been when it was first built. At any moment I expect to see knights gathered 'round a table drinking and cursing and throwing near raw meat to enormous wolfhounds drooling at their feet."

"It is a wretched old pile of stones!" exclaimed Charis on a little sob. "Oh, Clarissa, if we had only known. And for the man to marry you in such a rush as though one moment to reflect and you would have run away! Malcolm, we should not have allowed Clare to do this thing. We shall have it annulled."

Clarissa, dazed, said nothing at all but followed where Malcolm led, the little bouquet of flowers still clutched in one hand.

What the children called the little dining room proved to be much less intimidating than the parts of the castle they had wandered through to reach it, but it was daunting nonetheless. Its ceiling, from which three small chandeliers bestowed the light of fifty candles apiece, rose two full stories above their heads. But, unlike the rooms just traversed, here the thick granite walls had been covered by glistening wood paneling and watered silk. Several Tintorettos, a Rubens, and what Clarissa absolutely knew to be a da Vinci had been hung rather nonchalantly about, interspersed with brightly polished gold wall sconces, hanging crystals, and shining mirrors.

At the far end of the chamber, near a hearth picked out in gold-veined marble, an oval mahogany table with sleek, bowed legs positively glowed. It was draped in lace, and golden covers had been laid upon it for five. Clarissa could not believe her eyes. The covers were truly gold and the cutlery as well and the crystal sported golden rims and stems. In the center of the table a low, gold-rimmed crystal bowl filled with wildflowers sat within a slightly lower but wider bowl filled with sparkling clear water in which tiny golden fish swam gaily about.

On the back wall a mahogany sideboard sported golden urns. Two matching china cabinets displayed sparkling plates and platters and cups and saucers of fine Dresden. But the dining area occupied only one portion of the entire chamber. Lush Aubusson carpets divided the beautifully patterned hardwood floor into two other separate and distinct sections, each of which held a grouping of sedate furniture gathered about separate and very pretty little hearths. Settees in rose and gold and white, and armchairs of cherrywood upholstered in watered silk, made a pleasant display amidst footstools and cricket tables and long, low, svelte tables of glistening cherry. Malcolm and Charis appeared as much overcome by the unexpectedly refined decor as Clarissa herself.

"Now this is more like it," murmured Malcolm. "This is what it is like to be truly rich, my dears, to be able to refer to all this as the little dining room."

"Well, we cannot possibly eat in all our dirt," Charis pointed out. "It would be most unacceptable."

"Uh-uh," answered a little voice from the right side of the table. "We don't never dress for dinner in the little dining room. But if you are wishing to wash up, you know, it is right through there." Zander, his blue eyes shining, was kneeling upon the seat of his chair and pointing shyly to a small door in one of the paneled walls.

"What is right through there, my lad?" asked Malcolm, wandering toward the door. "Egad, Charis, Clare, it is a water closet with sink and towels and—"

"You turn those gold things an' water comes right out," offered Zander, climbing down off the chair and going to stand beside Malcolm. "At least most of the time it does. And sometimes, when it is summer an' the sun has been shining all day long, it is even warm water. Papa made it! And there is soap, too, right on that dish there. For washing your hands," he added, noting the wonder in Malcolm's eyes and mistaking it for confusion about the soap.

"Let me take your bouquet," a small voice murmured very near Clarissa. "I shall put it in that little vase and it will still be pretty in the morning. Zander and I did not pick the flowers until very late this afternoon so they would still be fresh and pretty when you came."

"Th-thank you."

"Oh, you are very welcome. I told Papa you must have flowers. All brides have flowers. Papa was so very nervous that he forgot all about them."

Malcolm, Charis and Clarissa all had a turn at refreshing themselves in the unique and quite pretty little water closet. By the time Clarissa emerged, the butler and a bevy of footmen had entered the chamber and waited only for her to be seated before they began to serve the meal.

"What?" Malcolm asked as the first dish, a warm turtle soup, was placed before him. "Does the earl not join us?"

Brandilynn, who occupied the chair closest to Malcolm, shook her head. "Papa promised to take Cousin Alden back to the village so that he could post to London before the night was out. Cousin Alden has an appointment with the Archbishop of Canterbury and should have set out yesterday—but seeing it was Papa who wished to be married, he stayed on to do the thing. Cousin Alden is the Bishop of Leeds, you know, and a very busy man."

"H-how far is it to the village?" Clarissa queried softly, wondering if Balmorrow intended to return at all this night.

"It takes forever to get there," offered Zander, peering at her around the centerpiece. "And even longer to get back."

"Oh, it does not," put in Brandilynn. "It is merely ten miles or so if one must go by the road—which one must when escorting Cousin Alden. He does not ride, you know. His silly robes would get all caught up in the horse's hooves."

"Unless he rides side-saddle, like a lady," giggled Zander.

"But Papa left Donadee at MacGivern's stable when he went to fetch Cousin Alden, so he will leave the coach for Kerry to drive home and ride cross-country himself. But he does not wish us to hold dinner for him. He says he will not be here in time."

"He does not never hardly eat dinner anyway," interjected Zan. "He hates dinner."

"No, he does not, Zan. It is only that sometimes he is not hungry."

Whether Balmorrow was hungry or not, the children proved correct. By the time the last of the sweetmeats had been disposed of and the table abandoned, the earl was still absent from the gathering. Balmorrow's butler, however, reappeared a short time later and whispered in Malcolm's ear and Malcolm, rising, followed the man from the room. A few moments after that, a most becoming lady of indeterminate years entered the chamber, introduced herself as Mrs. Beal, the housekeeper, and offered to show Charis and Clarissa to their chambers. "For ye must be exhausted after bein' three days on the road an' all, an' his lordship says as how he'll be closeted with Viscount Halliard for the remainder of the evenin'."

"He has returned?" asked Clarissa in wonder.

"Oh, yes, my lady. But he is wishful of finalizing the marriage contracts an' such and says as how the childer ought ta be in bed an' your ladyships as well. Your trunks, my lady," she added with a gracious nod at Clarissa, "have all been unpacked for you and if you wish tea, it shall be served in your sitting room. You need only request it."

The children dashed away and Mrs. Beal led Clarissa and Charis through another warren of corridors and staircases, explaining that guests were usually apartmented in the east wing of the castle along with the family. "For 'tis a terrible large place, ye know, and confusin'. 'Tis much easier on guests to have the family nearby."

Charis was shown to her chambers first and introduced to a red-headed, freckle-faced young woman by the name of Mary who was to act as her abigail for the remainder of her stay, and then Mrs. Beal proceeded down the same long corridor to the very end and ushered Clarissa into a most remarkable apartment.

Decorated in wedgewood blue and creamy white, with delicate chairs, settees, and window seats upholstered in floral-patterned silks, the sitting room boasted a set of well-stocked bookshelves that traveled at shoulder height all the way around the room. Draperies of soft blue adorned the mullioned windows and a fire flickered in a small, white marble hearth.

The bedchamber was dominated by an oversized creamy white sleigh bed with a quilted coverlet. Two gleaming hearths faced with tiles of white and blue set beneath mantles of marble sparkled in the light of five glass-shaded oil lamps. Beyond the bedchamber lay a dressing room, softly lit and inviting Clarissa's inspection. She moved toward the open door and was met by a young woman in a respectable blue round gown, who curtsied as Mrs. Beal introduced her. "Kate will see to your every need, my lady. And I'll be going if it please ye, an' see the childer are tucked up an' safe."

"Oh, yes, of course, Mrs. Beal. I thank you," murmured Clarissa, gazing disbelievingly about the dressing room.

"Be there somethin' wrong, m'lady?" Kate asked, moving to help undo the tapes of Clarissa's dress. "His lordship said as how if ye were to find anythin' amiss, ye must just say so an' 'twould be attended to."

"He did?"

"Oh, yes, m'lady."

"Tell me, Kate, whose apartments were these? They are so—so delicate and beautiful and—and feminine. Did they, perhaps, belong to his lordship's first wife?"

"Oh, no, my lady. They was belonging to 'er Majesty. Kept special, ye know, fer when him and her come ta visit. But they don't come now. Not since His Majesty grew ill, so to speak."

"The Queen? Her Majesty the Queen slept here?"

"Indeed. Though there's been many an argol-bargol between the Balmorrows and the Hanovers, Her Majesty was always fond of Castle Balmorrow. Liked the solitude, she did. An' here she was always allowed to be herself. Now, let me be takin' down yer hair, my lady. 'Tis exhausted ye are and who to blame ye."

Clarissa allowed herself to be coddled and cooed at and tucked up into bed and found the entire process extremely comforting. She had not had the services of an abigail since her father's death. Kate, with a smile, bid her new mistress goodnight, extinguished the lamps, and left Clarissa to close her eyes beneath the pretty flowered quilt. Which, with a sigh, Clarissa did.

And then she opened them again with a little gasp. This was her wedding night! That giant of a man who had not so much as spoken directly to her as yet, would he be expecting to—oh, no, most certainly not! Why he had not even had the graciousness to dine with her or to come sit with her after dinner. He had sent for Malcolm and that was all. Certainly he could not expect—Clarissa flushed in the darkness and a little shiver ran up her spine. Charis had spoken to her, of course, about what a man expected—had a right to expect—of his wife on their wedding night. But surely, surely, this Lord Balmorrow who had effectively ignored her even during the rushed marriage ceremony would not now come wandering into her bedchamber expecting—Clarissa felt tears rising to her eyes and a sob caught in her throat. She knuckled at the tears angrily and pushed the sob away. What on earth had she done? She had bought Malcolm's and Charis's and, yes, even her own security by marrying a savage, uncivilized brute who cared not a lick for her! Why, she had been exhausted and dazed and he had rushed her to the altar in such a state that she had had no time for second thoughts. But she was having second thoughts now. Second and third and fourth thoughts. She lay, tense, on her back in the darkness and swiped at silent tears that insisted upon dribbling across her cheekbones and into her ears.

Balmorrow, his head resting against the leather of his favorite chair, sat before the sputtering fire in his library, a glass of brandy in one hand, his feet propped upon a footstool, a full decanter of tax-free cognac on a cricket table beside him. He had calmed Halliard's considerable fears on his sister's behalf and had sent him off to bed smiling and in possession of a bank draft that would put an end to the worst episode so far in the young viscount's life. And both Halliard and his wife would be out of Balmorrow's hair first thing in the morning. Of course, Balmorrow had apologized for sending them off so soon, but Halliard had been quickly brought to acknowledge that a gentleman certainly could not wish to have his in-laws fluttering about during the first days of his marriage.

The first days of his marriage. Balmorrow took a sip of the thick, golden liquid and frowned at the fire before him. The first days of his marriage. But who the devil was he married to? She had looked worn to a frazzle but passably pretty from what he had allowed himself to see of her. She had long reddish brown hair tied back into some sort of knot and interesting green eyes. Her nose was short and upturned and had a sprinkling of freckles upon it. And she had looked to him like little more than a child though he knew her to be twenty—merely twelve years his junior.

He had been a brute to force her to take the vows within a quarter hour of her arrival, but it had proved an excellent excuse that Alden had had that appointment with Canterbury. The children would have let that slip. She would accept that much, he told himself. A man must surely have the right to be married by his cousin, even if it did prove a hurried affair.

Well, and she did not run screaming from the chapel, he told himself silently. She agreed to marry me and she did, no matter how shabby an affair it must have seemed to her. That is admirable, I think. She keeps her promises. That is something to build upon. Madeline used to make scads of promises and never keep a one of them. But then, I loved Madeline. I do not love Miss Beresfont.

Which does not matter a bit, he scolded himself angrily, taking another sip of the brandy. For I do not intend to make a complete fool of myself for love ever again. Miss Beresfont is now my wife. I am her husband. We may not love each other, but we shall contrive to exist together amicably.

Still, it took him the entire decanter of free-booted cognac before he reached a point where he no longer cared that he had married a perfect stranger. And it was nigh onto four in the morning when his pounding brought Parsons, his butler, in nightshirt and cap, and Mackelry, his valet, in similar attire, to the still room just beyond the servants' quarters to lead him off to his own chambers.

"I jush got los'," Balmorrow mumbled, as Parsons tugged off one boot and Mackelry the other. "Thought was m'room. Closed the dabable door an' 'twouldn't open again."

" 'Twould have opened had ye turned the knob," muttered Mackelry. "Did ye once think to turn the knob, my lord?"

"Uh-huh," replied the earl with a nod of his tousled curls. "Couldn't fine it."

"The knob? Ye could not find the doorknob?" asked Parsons disbelievingly.

"Dark," mumbled Balmorrow.

Mackelry, his lips twitching upward despite a strong determination to remain angry, stood the earl up, tugged him out of his coat, pushed him down upon the bed and tossed a blanket over him. "Sleep," he ordered. "I ain't tugging ye out of no more clothes. Ye do not deserve it."

Balmorrow buried his head in his pillow and was snoring before Parsons shut the door.

"Dark," Mackelry sputtered on a gasping laugh as the two began the trek back to their own quarters. "So dark he could not find the doorknob. Found the door, though, did he not?"

"Likely dents in't now from all that pounding," mused Parsons. "Ain't seen his lordship that disguised since—well, not for a long while. Hard on him getting leg-shackled. Not up to't he weren't."

"Aye," nodded Mackelry. "His heart were not in't, but he will come around, Parsons. Always makes the best of what presents itself, does his lordship. Never seen a man for landing on his feet like what he always does no matter how dangerous the leap."

When Clarissa awoke at five, the first rays of sunlight were beginning to rise above the crags to the east of the castle and slip weakly between the draperies of her room. For a moment, having forgotten where she was, she luxuriated between the fine satin sheets and rubbed at sleepy eyes. Why on earth had she awakened so very early? She was not accustomed to rise until well past eight and it was certainly much too dark to be anywhere near that hour. And then she remembered and sat straight up in the bed. She looked around her anxiously, peering into the lingering shadows. No, thank goodness, Lord Balmorrow was nowhere to be seen. He had not, then, thought to disturb her after her long journey and the shock of the hurried wedding. Clarissa gave a long sigh and, feeling much more relaxed, settled back down between the sheets. At least the man had been considerate enough not to plague her with all that business of the wedding night and a husband's needs and—

Clarissa's eyes popped back open. Why had he not come? she thought perversely. Why had he not so much has scratched upon her door to bid her a goodnight? What sort of gentleman was he to marry a woman and not speak to her afterward? Hugging herself and whispering, Clarissa drifted back toward sleep plagued by visions of strong, broad shoulders turned away from her and dark, long, raggedy curls. "He did not even bother to cut his hair," she muttered sleepily. "He did not so much as bother to have his hair cut."

At six Balmorrow shuddered into wakefulness. His mouth tasted like dirty stockings and his head felt like a great melon about to burst. He groaned, rolled onto his side, got his foot tangled in the blanket, yanked at the poor abused material and tore a gaping hole clear through it. He would have cursed, but his actions had proved severely daunting and sent him scrambling over the side of the bed in search of the chamber pot. It was a mere second after he stuck his long arm under the bed that he remembered the newly installed water closet, in deference to which the chamber pot had been eliminated.

He gained his feet, clasped a hand over his mouth and stumbled dizzily toward the dressing room and the door to the water closet which opened at its far side. In the semi-darkness he clunked his big toe against the leg of one of the armoires, spun away groaning and caught the side of a clothespress with his knee, careened away in agony and knocked his shaving mirror to the floor with an elbow, brought his bare foot down upon a sliver of the silver-backed glass and lurched forward into the water closet, groaning and spattering blood, to gain the convenience just in the nick of time. He fell to his knees and cast up his accounts until his skin was cold and clammy, his curls clung to his forehead and neck in sweaty ringlets, and his stomach seemed likely to follow its contents into the facility. But at last the need to retch receded and, with a sigh, he sat down on the hardwood floor and buried his head between his knees.

What in heaven's name was wrong with him? Had someone attempted to poison him again? Had he contracted some vile disease? He rolled his tongue around in his mouth and thought about trying to stand to get himself a glass of water, then groaned and dispensed with the idea.

And then he remembered. Stupid! he thought. Wasn't no vile disease you contracted, Lex, it was a marriage, and you downed an entire decanter of cognac in response to it!

He waited a good five minutes with his head tucked between his knees, sitting on the cold floor, shivering, until he thought that at last he could stand again. He leaned heavily with one hand upon a counter and pulled himself to his feet. Thank goodness I can manage that much, he thought. Now if I can only maneuver myself back through the dressing room and safely into bed. Or at least onto the bed, he readjusted his thought, noticing for the first time that he still wore breeches and shirt and waistcoat.

He managed on his return trip to avoid most of the hazards of the dressing room, only knocking one small vase from a cricket table, and climbed unsteadily back onto the immense four poster. He closed his red-rimmed blue eyes and sank wearily toward oblivion, mumbling to himself that he would feel better soon. And then his eyes popped open of their own accord and his brain stood at instant attention, abruptly rattling out words—Marriage! Wedding! Bride! I do!

"Oh, damnation," Balmorrow muttered, pulling the torn blanket over his head in shame. "I do. I did. But then I got completely foxed and—and—I did not—I did not even go to welcome her. I did not even introduce myself. I did not do so much as bid the young woman goodnight!"

Chapter 3

"Papa sent them off first thing this morning," Brandilynn replied cheerily as she and Zander helped themselves to shirred eggs and bacon from the sideboard in the breakfast room.

"We told 'em goodbye," added Zander helpfully. "But we waited to break our fast until you came down."

"You, Zan," Brandilynn pointed out, setting her plate upon the pristine linen tablecloth, "had three muffins and an orange with Lord Halliard and Lady Halliard."

"Yes, but that was just t'be polite. 'Tweren't breakfast. I am seven," the boy added, climbing up into a chair on Clarissa's right and bestowing a dazzling smile upon her. "How old are you?"

"Zan," hissed Brandilynn, "one does not ask how old ladies are. It is not at all mannerly."

"But how else are you s'posed t'know?"

"You are not s'posed to know."

"Ladies' ages are secret?"

"Yes."

"I shall be twenty-one in July," offered Clarissa, bewildered by the children's presence and the earl's absence. "Though

Brandilynn is correct. A gentleman ought not to ask a lady her age. Does your papa not come down for breakfast?"

"Sometimes," supplied Brandilynn around a bite of biscuit. "I expect he will come this morning because you are here."

"Yes, an' he willn't want to miss you," nodded Zan enthusiastically, " 'cause it would not be polite."

"He will not miss her, Zan. She is not going away. She is our mama now."

"I forgot," replied Zander, swallowing an enormous bite of bacon.

"Shall we call you Mama?" Brandilynn continued, her blue-eyed gaze fixed upon Clarissa. "Or would you rather we did not? We could call you Stepmama, but Zan does not wish to do that."

"You have discussed it?" asked Clarissa, sipping at a cup of hot chocolate.

"Oh, yes. It is exceedingly important. But Papa said most strictly that we are not to pester you about it and that we are to let you decide."

"Your papa does not care one way or the other?"

"Uh-uh," Zan grunted around a mouthful of eggs.

"Zan, do not grunt like a little pig. Swallow before you speak," came a quiet voice from the doorway.

Clarissa turned immediately to discover Balmorrow's bewilderingly blue eyes staring dazedly at her. Her heart, which had been behaving quite properly up to now, began to pound and she gave a quiet little gasp. The Earl of Balmorrow's countenance, impossible though it seemed, wore an even more distant and unapproachable look this morning than it had in the chapel last evening. And he limped, she noted in dismay. He limped quite noticeably as he made his way to the sideboard. Had she, in her effort to save Malcolm, married not only a dour, unapproachable giant, but a cripple as well?

"Morning, Miss Beresfont," the earl murmured, turning his back on her and searching the sideboard for something he obviously could not find.

Clarissa stared at him open-mouthed.

"I thought she is not Miss Beresfont any more, Papa," said Zander, jumping from his chair and going to stand beside his father. "I thought she is our mama now."

"Do not shout, Zan, m'head ain't up to it. Where the devil did Nancy put my ale this time?"

"Right there, Papa, behind the eper-thing. She don't like you drinking ale in the morning."

"Yes, I realize that," grumbled Balmorrow. "But the last time I looked I was the master and Nancy the maid." Balmorrow reached behind the silver epergne, produced the pitcher of ale and poured himself a large tankard full, then he limped to the table, Zander limping in perfect imitation directly behind him.

"What happened, Papa?" Brandilynn asked.

"Huh?" The earl settled himself at the head of the table and stared questioningly at his daughter.

"Why are you limping?"

"Oh. Accident. Broke a mirror. Cut my foot. Hard to get your foot into a boot when it is bandaged and difficult to walk once it is in there."

"Seven years bad luck," sighed Brandilynn.

"Balderdash."

Feeling incredibly guilty about his behavior of the night before, Balmorrow turned his gaze upon his bride. He was determined to welcome her to his family with some semblance of decorum but he found the frowning countenance that met his gaze dismaying. Well, and why should she not frown, he told himself. I practically forced her to marry me. I gave her not the least opportunity to reconsider. And then I ignored her completely the rest of the evening. I did not even have the good grace to dine with the girl or to bid her goodnight.

"We are privileged to have you with us, Miss Beres—I mean, Clara."

"Clarissa," hissed Brandilynn.

"Yes, Clarissa," her father corrected himself on the instant, forcing himself to maintain eye contact with his bride.

Clarissa glared back at him, determined not to lower her gaze lest he think her frightened of him—which she was beginning to be she noted with a tiny gulp. He seemed even larger and more terrifying this morning than he had last evening.

Balmorrow, receiving no reply but determined not to look as sheepish as he felt, continued to study her. Her green eyes were frozen and the grim line into which a perfectly delectable pair of lips had been drawn proved excessively daunting. "You have met the children, eh?" he asked.

Clarissa blinked in disbelief. Well, of course I have met the children, she thought. Did I not dine with them last evening? Am I not sitting here breaking my fast with them now? Are you daft as well as a brute? But she said nothing, only nodded.

Of all the stupid things to ask, Balmorrow chided himself silently. Of course she has met the children. It is myself she has not met! He raised his tankard and took a long, deep draught, then set it down before him again. "Do you ride, Clara, uh, Cara, uh, Clarissa?" he stuttered into the sober silence that pervaded the room. Even the children had ceased to babble.

Great heavens, the man could not even remember her name! "No," Clarissa replied bluntly because she was angry with him.

No. No. The girl did not ride. Balmorrow could feel the back of his neck growing warm along with the tips of his ears. Of course not. It was his favorite pastime, riding through the forest and along The Likely Run and up into the hills. Why should he be lucky enough to have married a woman who could share in the sheer joy of it? "Perhaps you would like me to teach you?" he suggested without much hope.

"I rather think not," replied Clarissa, who knew perfectly well how to ride but had determined to be obstinate. "I am not fond of horses," she added, responding to an odd glint in the earl's eyes. "They are so—smelly—you know."

"Smelly!" giggled Zander, wiggling in the chair beside Clarissa's own.

"Smelly!" giggled Brandilynn as well.

"Are not the two of you required somewhere else?" grumbled the earl abruptly. "Is Sylvester on holiday? For what precisely do I pay the man?"

Clarissa was amazed to see both children scramble from their seats and scamper for the breakfast room doorway. "Smelly!" Zander giggled again and then they were gone.

"Well, you need not have frightened them off," she snapped in exasperation.

"Frighten? Those two?" Balmorrow's sleek black brows rose in surprise. "I should have to wear a sheet and go clanking chains about in the middle of the blackest night to get merely a squeak of fear out of either one of them. It is merely that at times when you wish them gone, you must indicate it clearly."

What an ogre she must think me, Balmorrow mused, his eyes growing cold at the thought that anyone should accuse him of frightening his own children. The devil!

Clarissa watched uncomfortably as the earl downed the remainder of his ale and got up to pour himself another tankard full. This time, she thought, he will at least eat something with that dreadful stuff. But he did not, reseating himself with only the tankard before him. Good heavens, what was wrong with the man? Even Malcolm did never drink himself into a stupor at breakfast! "Are you mad?" she sighed before she could stop herself.

"Mad? As in Bedlamite?" he asked, his eyebrows rising. "Why do you ask?"

Clarissa felt her cheeks flush. "I—I did not mean—it was merely a thought that slipped out unbidden."

"Why did you think it?"

"Well, I have never seen a gentleman attempt to drink himself under the table at breakfast before."

"It is only ale, Miss Beres—m'dear."

"Do not call me your dear," spluttered Clarissa. "You do so just because you cannot remember my name. I realize that I agreed to a marriage of convenience, but I did expect—I did expect—a modicum of civility would be involved in it. And civilized gentlemen do remember their wives' names and do not drink ale for breakfast—at least not two whole tankards full without eating something to nullify its effects. You are determined to drink yourself under this table, my lord, and if such is not your usual manner of beginning the day then I must assume that it is because—because you already regret having married me."

Balmorrow set down his tankard and stared at her in wonder. She was twisting her napkin around her fingers in agitation and she came near to tipping her cup of chocolate onto the linen, but grabbed it in the nick of time and pushed it out of danger. Berating himself in silence, the earl stood and limped to the sideboard, filled a plate with whatever was nearest to hand and carried it back to the table where he set it down in the place Zander had vacated at Clarissa's right. He then returned to the sideboard, poured himself a cup of coffee and carried that to the table as well. He then sat beside his bride and forked cold shirred eggs into his mouth. He was certain even before he choked them down that they would come up presently, but it seemed the least he could do to set the young lady more at ease.

"There," he mumbled, "now I shall not get foxed, do you think?" He raised the coffee to his lips and sipped carefully. He set it down and glanced at Clarissa out of the corner of his eye. "I think you are a most beautiful and desirable young woman, Miss Beres—Clarissa—and I do not regret having married you."

"You do not?"

"No, I do not. What I do regret is my boorish disregard for your sensibilities. What a villain you must think me for having rushed you into that wedding so frantically."

Clarissa turned in her chair to study the gentleman beside her. His eyes now met hers with startling earnestness and repentance. She had never before realized that a gentleman's eyes could reveal emotions more clearly than his words, and for a moment the Earl of Balmorrow took her breath away.

"If you have finished, would you care to walk about the place with me? You ought to know where it is that you live and be introduced to your staff at the very least. And it will give us an opportunity to come to know each other a bit." Balmorrow took a deep breath and downed a muffin in three gulps. That, too, he was positive would rise again. "You are mistress here now, you know. And if there are things you require that are not available to you, you must only tell me. I wish you to be happy, Clarissa."

Clarissa studied the rugged profile as he choked down the muffin, followed it by another sip of coffee, and then rubbed a napkin across his lips.

"I—I should like to see the castle and meet the staff," she murmured, gazing down at the table. "If it would not prove troublesome for you, my lord."

"It will be a privilege," Balmorrow responded. "But one thing we must settle between us now. I am Alexander St. John Sinclair, Earl of Balmorrow. There are several lesser titles, but they are not of any import. You may call me Balmorrow if you wish, or Alex, but you may *not* call me my lord because you are not a servant and it makes you sound like one. And I must call you something. Is it Clarissa you prefer?"

Clarissa looked at him, looked away, looked back again. "Sometimes," she replied softly, "I am called Clare. It is what I like better than Clarissa."

"Then Clare it shall be. And what is your wish with the children? Have you settled it amongst you? Zander, I know, wishes to call you mama. Madeline died when he was born and so he has never yet had a mama. But Brandy will not say what she wishes to do. I told them they must abide by your decision."

"You did?"

"Indeed."

"The three of us will discuss it," Clarissa declared with a nod. "We were only beginning to broach the subject when you entered, my l—Balmorrow."

The castle proved to be at one and the same time an ugly pile of stones and a richly furnished, comfortable home. Balmorrow escorted his bride through great halls hung with ancient tapestries, bracketed by hearths wide and high enough to burn whole trees. And through small cozy chambers as well, paneled and wallpapered and furnished in the height of fashion. He urged Clarissa up and down staircases of marble, polished oak, granite, and pine. Her arm tucked possessively through his, he led her up one corridor and down another. One moment Clarissa could peer out through a mullioned window hung with velvet draperies upon a large deer park and in the blink of an eye gaze in awe from an open balcony at great forested hillsides and mountainous crags.

When at last he declared that they were near the end of their tour, he led her through a gallery of his ancestors and into a room beyond. Clarissa gasped. With two outside walls entirely of glass and tremendous skylights four stories above their heads, the room glowed with sunlight. Their entrance through the gallery had set them on a wide balcony that traveled around the entire room at the level of the second story with staircases that descended to the ground floor at either end.

"Oh!" Clarissa cried, leaning over the balcony rail. "It is

the most beautiful thing I have ever seen! Oh!" she cried again, as a cloud of bright colors floated toward her. "Balmorrow, it is a fairyland!"

The earl held out his arm and a portion of the cloud of color descended upon it. "Flutterbys," he grinned. "My great-grandfather collected them from all over the world but would not have them dead and stuck up with pins so he built this room. Now they breed here and come and go through the skylights as they please once the weather is warm. But the skylights remain closed this early in the spring. We keep fires blazing yet to keep it warm enough. That makes all the flowers bloom early."

Clarissa gazed downward again. Below her grew a forest of fruit trees and flowers, exotic and common, of all sizes, colors, and varieties. Amongst them fountains bubbled and tiny streams flowed. She could see that places had been set aside for tables and chairs on small platforms. Cobbled paths twisted roundabout. Even some birds fluttered and sang. But the most numerous residents were, indeed, butterflies. Clouds and clouds of them lifted and lowered like living, breathing rainbows.

Enchanted, Clarissa had not the least wish to leave the remarkable chamber. A pensive Balmorrow watched as she extended her arms and some of the flutterbys came to settle on them. Tenderly he coaxed two of them onto his hand and placed them gently in her hair. "There," he whispered. "God's own little tiara for you alone. If only there were a looking glass so that you could see yourself. You are bedecked in glory."

When at last Clarissa could be urged to leave, they returned to the east wing to discover the entire staff congregated in the long drawing room, each with a glass of champagne in hand, each waiting to drink to the new mistress of Castle Balmorrow. The earl accepted a glass from Parsons as well and then allowed the butler to voice the toast. Clarissa noted with some satisfaction that Balmorrow nodded in agreement with the compliments bestowed upon her by the head of the staff and then raised his glass high in her honor.

Parsons offered Clarissa his arm and escorted her through a plethora of servants, introducing each by name and position. I shall never be able to remember all of them, she thought with some trepidation. There are so very many! Even the lowliest little pot boy was there, scrubbed and beaming and bowing with tiny elegance before her. And then with a nod from Parsons, they all scattered and only Mrs. Beal remained. "Ye must only inform me, m'lady," smiled the housekeeper, "what are your wishes and all shall be as you like it."

Clarissa blanched at the mere thought of taking hold of the reins of such an enormous household.

Mrs. Beal's smile widened. "Perhaps ye would care to wait a while before taking command, m'lady? I shalln't mind to go on as I have until ye accustom yeself to such an enormous responsibility as this household be. If something particularly displeases ye, however, ye must tell me at once. His lordship will not like for ye to abide with something that displeases you, not for one moment."

With a tiny bob of a curtsy, Mrs. Beal then departed, leaving Clarissa to stand bewildered in the drawing room, having heard for the third time since last evening that all at Castle Balmorrow was to be as she wished it. She looked around for Balmorrow and discovered him leaning against the door frame, his arms crossed upon his chest and a glimmer of mirth in his great blue eyes.

"Do not be intimidated, Clare," he offered quietly. "No one actually expects you to take over the reins at any time soon. You are new here, and young, and running an entire castle is an enormous charge."

"It is not that," murmured Clare, her gaze meeting his directly. "It is that Parsons and Kate and now Mrs. Beal have all said that if there is something I do not like, I must simply tell them and they will see it is attended to."

"Yes?"

"Is it true?"

Balmorrow's lips twitched upward in a most engaging grin. Clarissa nearly gasped to see just how engaging a grin it was.

"Of course it is true—depending."

"Depending?"

"Upon what it is that displeases you. If it is Zander, for instance, Sylvester is *not* allowed to toss him out with the bath water no matter how much you may wish it. If you detest your chambers, however, you must only say so and others shall be provided. And now I must leave you to entertain yourself for awhile I am afraid. There is pressing work to be done while the sun still shines and I must see to it."

Balmorrow straightened, bowed, and limped from the room. Clarissa strolled to the pianoforte at the far end of the chamber and took a seat upon the stool before it, trailing her fingers carelessly over the keys. Perhaps, she thought, this gentleman and I *shall* deal well enough together. He is certainly not the knave I thought him to be last evening. And though he has not the elegance and sophistication of Edward, Lord Parkhurst, he is—not unhandsome. And—and the children and the servants are very nice. Perhaps it is not such a great sacrifice that I have made on Malcolm's behalf. Perhaps it will not prove to be much of a sacrifice at all.

The sun set and the fire boys lit the fires and the children popped in to bid Clarissa goodnight. With Kate's help Clarissa donned her best gown. She was to join her husband for a private dinner. She worried that the gown was a year old, but it looked quite lovely still. She meant to please Balmorrow this evening. Nervously, she allowed Kate to arrange her hair in a most becoming new fashion, high on her head in a Grecian knot with long tendrils of shining chestnut curls floating against her cheeks. She studied herself critically in the looking glass and then followed Kate apprehensively through candlelit corridors to a room at the rear of the ground floor of the east wing, wondering each step of the way what Balmorrow would think of her.

In comparison to the rest of the castle this room was positively tiny. The ceiling was barely eight feet high. The walls were all within ten feet of each other and not one chandelier hung anywhere in sight. The twin sets of windows were hung with rich burgundy draperies and the walls were papered in cream silk with thin burgundy stripes. A fire blazed cheerily on a small hearth surrounded by tiles of cream with burgundy etchings. Before the fire sat a small, round table covered in crisp Irish linen, with a candleabra and a vase of roses at its center and two covers laid. The room did much to ease Clarissa's anxiety. It would be her first dinner with her husband and he had chosen to share it with her alone in this most pleasant atmosphere.

"I did not see this room when Lord Balmorrow showed me about today, Kate," Clarissa smiled, captivated. "How cozy it is."

" 'Tis his lordship's sitting room, my lady. The rest of his lordship's chambers be right through that door."

There was a small armchair near one set of windows with a table beside it holding an oil lamp, a miniature, and a small, leatherbound volume. Clarissa made her way to the chair as Kate departed and settled into it to await Balmorrow's presence. A tiny clock upon the fireplace mantle chimed eight in a delicate little voice. He is behind that door at this very moment dressing for dinner, Clarissa thought. How quietly he goes about it.

She lifted the miniature from the table and studied it in the light of the lamp. It was a portrait of Brandilynn as a tyke and Zander a babe in her arms. She thought it a precious rendition of the two innocents and replaced it carefully. She picked up the volume and glanced at its cover. There was no title. She flipped it open to the first page and found it filled with numbers and letters and words scribbled in a most senseless fashion. She turned page after page and stared in amazement at the incomprehensibility of it. Just as she was about to set it aside, she turned one more page and recognized her own name scrawled across the page with an exclamation point behind it.

What on earth, she wondered, and flipped to the next page. There began more numbers and letters and senseless scribblings, many lined out with broad, violent strokes. With a shake of her head she closed the volume and set it aside. The ormulu clock on the mantle chimed very prettily the half hour and she sighed. Whatever Balmorrow was intending to wear, it was taking him forever to get into it and that was a fact. At the very least he might poke his head out the door and say he would be with her presently.

Nine o'clock arrived and Parsons appeared in his best formal attire at the entrance to the chambers. "Beg pardon, my lady, but I must speak to Mr. Mackelry for a moment." Parsons stepped lightly past her, gave one knock upon the door to the earl's room and entered. Thence commenced a degree of exasperated whispering and a good deal of shuffling and stomping about.

"He did what?" Mackelry gasped.

"Fell off of Duggan's roof. Foot slipped, you know. Hard to balance on a slope with your foot all bandaged up and stuffed into a boot."

"But what was he doing on Duggan's roof at all?"

"Well, it was clouding up and the men not near done, so he was bound to help them, not wanting Mrs. Duggan and the new babe to get a drenching this evening. At least he did not fall until the last bit of thatching was in place."

"Was he dire hurt?"

"No, not dire. But when he regained his senses he rode on to see about hiring more men to help drain the marsh and knowing he was late, he came riding back neck-or-nothing down Tealy Bens Slope and—"

"Do not tell me," murmured Mackelry. "He set Donadee at some obstacle, lost his seat, and broke his danged neck."

"He did not break his danged neck. But he did set Donadee at the old wall and then discovered that the other side had washed out. Come down hard I reckon for Donadee came up lame and his lordship had to walk him the rest of the way home."

"How did his lordship come up?" asked Mackelry with a sad lack of concern for the horse that Parsons could not understand.

"Well, he came up bruised from one end to the other, I imagine, though I have not seen him as yet. He is in the barn fretting over Donadee's leg."

"He would do better to be in here fretting over her ladyship who has been waiting upon him since eight o'clock," groaned Mackelry. "You'll need to tell Duncan to set dinner back again."

"Duncan claims dinner was ruined thirty minutes ago and is stomping about the kitchen wielding his knife in all directions attempting to make pheasant pie out of what is left."

A tap at the window interrupted the groan that was emanating from between Mackelry's lips. "Your lordship!" he exclaimed, drawing aside the curtains and unlatching the pane.

"Been a devil of a day, Mack," grumbled the earl, swinging over the sill and into the room. "Is she waiting?"

"Yes, your lordship," replied Parsons, hoping he was correct.

"Go and explain that I will be with her in a moment then, and tell Duncan to begin sending things in."

"Oh, sir," sighed Mackelry, surveying the sorry sight that was his lordship, "you will be hours."

"No I will not, Mack," replied Balmorrow with a significant lift of his eyebrow. "I will be a moment. You will contrive."

Parsons exited the chambers and in a matter of five minutes an approximation of the dinner Duncan had planned began to arrive. The Earl of Balmorrow arrived as well, dressed informally in breeches, half-boots, a blue silk shirt and a burgundy smoking jacket. He seated Clarissa at the table, apologized profusely for having kept her waiting, did not make mention of her gown nor the way her ringlets curled becomingly beside her cheeks and groaned when he sat down across from her.

Clarissa took note of the dark shadow that stained his cheeks and chin—for even Mackelry at his best could not shave him in so little time—and she wondered at how gingerly he sat on the very edge of his chair.

"Are you not feeling just the thing?" Clarissa ventured to ask as his soup departed untouched and the turbot appeared.

"I am fine, splendid," the earl replied, flicking at his portion of the fish with his fork and moving flakes of it about on his plate but never bringing any of the thing to his mouth. "And you, did you have a pleasant day?"

Clarissa stared as the turbot disappeared and a hurriedly prepared pheasant pie was set before them. Balmorrow served her and then himself and then pushed that about on his plate much as he had done with the fish course.

"Zander was correct, I see," Clarissa stated. "You do not like to eat dinner."

"No, I do," replied the earl, hurriedly stuffing a piece of the pheasant pie between his lips. He chewed more slowly than Clarissa had ever seen anyone do and when at last he swallowed, he shuddered the slightest bit. "So tell me what you have been doing." His voice sounded odd and wavering to Clarissa's ears.

She parted her lips to say that she had tried out his pianoforte and played at spillikins with the children and gone out to sketch the castle, but her narrative came to a stuttering halt as the earl turned pale, rose hurriedly from the table and practically dove for the door to his bedchamber.

"I fear his lordship will not be returning, my lady," advised Mackelry several minutes later. "He fell, you know, and is not feeling quite the thing."

"He fell? I thought he cut his foot?"

"Yes, my lady, he did cut his foot. But that was this morning. 'Twas this afternoon he fell."

"From his horse?"

"Well, first from Duggan's roof, then from the horse as I understand it. His dinner is not sitting well, my lady."

Clarissa sighed and rubbed at her temples. What kind of a man had she married? She had thought him a great boor and a Bedlamite last evening. Now she wondered if he were not merely a clumsy simpleton with more hair than wit. "Is there anything I can do to help him, Mackelry?"

"No, my lady."

Clarissa seized upon an entering Parsons to escort her back to her own chambers where she settled upon the settee before the hearth in the sitting room and gazed perplexedly into the flames. Could all of this be true? Or was it some Canterbury tale to be rid of her for the remainder of the evening? She had begun to think, during that pleasant tour of the castle, that Lord Balmorrow intended this marriage to prove a congenial association for the both of them. But now—

Truthfully, though, the poor man had not looked at all well when he had dashed from the table. And he had chosen to dine with her in that lovely little room rather than in the formal dining room surrounded by servants. And the dinner, had it reached the table on time, would have proved sumptuous, she was certain. All these things bode well for his intention to please her and for the honesty of his sudden illness.

Still, it would most certainly be in character for a man who had ignored her throughout her wedding night to wish to be rid of her at an instant's notice. And, she thought, this sudden indisposition is also a thundering good excuse for him not to visit my chamber again tonight. Why *did* the man marry me, she wondered, if he cannot so much as abide the thought of our marriage bed? Am I meant to be merely stepmother and mistress of his house and nothing more?

"Well, and he need merely tell me if that is so," Clarissa whispered aloud. "He has paid a very high price for such minor services, but if that is all he desires of me, he need only make it clear. I shall not hold it against him. I owe him Malcolm's life whether he realizes it or not." A tear glistened upon Clarissa's cheek as she thought how differently the evening would have gone had it been Lord Parkhurst whose bride she had just become, but she swiped the tear away with one finger and took a very deep breath. "I am not Edward's bride," she told herself stolidly. "I am Balmorrow's bride. I have made him a bargain and I shall keep it. But he must tell me clearly what it is that he expects of me. At least he must tell me that much."

Chapter 4

Balmorrow tossed uncomfortably between the sheets unable to find a position in which some part of his body did not ache. He mumbled and groaned the entire night away and when Mackelry appeared to draw back the draperies it was to find the earl partially dressed in his sitting room, his legs thrown over the arm of his favorite chair, a pout on his face, and his feet bare.

"My lord," Mackelry murmured, "you will catch your death of cold. There is not even a fire."

" 'Tis laid, Mack. I was merely too exhausted to bother setting it alight. I have been awake most of the night. Ugly, drafty old castle! Always we must light the fires if we are not to freeze to death. The only warm place in this despicable pile of stones is filled with flutterbys."

"But you have done wonders, your lordship, with your attempts at remodeling. 'Tis not near so chill as it was used to be in the chambers you have completed."

"Yes, well, but it is still dastardly cold and I cannot think of what more to do to warm it. Castles are the devil, Mackelry. I would give my eyeteeth to have been born Duggan and live in a snug little cottage."

Mackelry, a grin playing softly across his face, knelt to light the fire. He had been in service at Castle Balmorrow since the age of six when the old earl had taken him off the parish roles and made him a fire boy. He had seen this truly amusing heir and his sisters born and raised. He had worked his way upward through the ranks, and surprisingly, had been asked by Master Alex if he might consider taking on the responsibilities of becoming his personal valet. Which, of course, Mackelry had done with joy, because by the time Master Alex had reached the age of fifteen, everyone knew beyond doubt that that young gentleman was bound to become the best entertainment the area would have for years to come.

"You are in queer stirrups is all, your lordship," Mackelry offered as the kindling caught. "Aching all over, are you not? Well, but one must expect to ache when one falls from rooftops and horses and such. You are not a stripling any longer. We feel things more intensely when we age."

"Thank you, Mack," mumbled the earl, "for reminding me how old I have grown. *That* is bound to improve my humor."

"Bosh!" Mackelry replied, going to open the draperies and let in the sunshine, "you are barely thirty—in the prime of your life."

"I thought I had grown old."

"Not so old as to be worth grumbling over," laughed Mackelry. "Even I am not so old as that!"

"Do you think I am a fool, Mack?" Balmorrow sighed, righting himself in the chair.

"Never, your lordship. You are a thatchgallows and a rapscallion and are given over to peculiar starts and vagaries, but never a fool."

"Then why do I feel like one, Mack? I swear I have never felt so foolish before in all my life. I cannot seem to do anything right of late."

"A temporary aberration, my lord. It will pass."

"It will?"

"Oh, undoubtedly, my lord. It must, for there are a goodly number of people depending upon you to come about. It is simply that you are a bit tense over—over—"

One elegant eyebrow rose slightly and Mackelry stuttered to a halt at sight of it.

"No, do go on, Mack. I am simply a bit tense over—?"

"B-being caught in parson's mousetrap, your lordship."

"Yes, indeed. Over being caught in parson's mousetrap with a very pretty little mouse of whom I know nothing."

"Nay, the lass has not a thing to do with it," protested Mackelry. Immediately his hand clamped over his mouth and his ears burned a brilliant red.

Balmorrow rocked back in his chair and laughed. "You never did know when to cease and desist, Mack. I love when your ears blaze like that. But you are quite right. It is the mousetrap itself sends terror through me. I am a gentleman who has learned his lesson about marriage but has been forced to ignore it and that makes me considerably apprehensive. But I shall come about, shall I not? I have always come about."

"Indeed, your lordship."

"Is it very early, Mack?"

" 'Tis not yet seven, my lord," replied the valet, preparing to lather the earl's face, but stopping to peer suspiciously at the mantle. "Now where has that clock gone?" he murmured perplexedly.

"I have not a clue."

"But, 'twas on this mantle last evening."

"T'ain't there now. I do not understand it, myself. They never move the clock in my sitting room—only this one."

"*They* do not move anything," Mackelry replied with some asperity. "There are no such things as ghosts, your lordship."

"Yes, there are, Mack," Balmorrow grinned. "I have been attempting to convince you of that for some twenty years. There are ghosts in this place and they plague the life out of me. And now, they will not let my clock alone. Is seven too early to send word to Kate to pack up her ladyship's trunks do you think?"

Mackelry, shaving brush lathered and in hand, stared open-mouthed down at his employer. "Her ladyship's trunks packed? Packed?"

"I have business in London, Mack. You do not think that perhaps my countess would like to accompany me?"

Mackelry, giving a sigh of relief as visions of the new bride being sent back to her home faded, smiled and nodded. "Indeed. Business and a bridal trip together, eh, my lord?"

"Well, London does not seem like much of a bridal trip. But I thought since I must go to Town—I did take time to discover some things about my countess before I offered for her, you know. She has never had a real Season, for instance. Her father died right in the midst of her introduction into Society and so she was forced to withdraw and go into mourning. I thought she might enjoy the Season. Most ladies enjoy London, do they not, Mack? Even those who are already married? Madeline always enjoyed it immensely."

"Quite right, your lordship. Exactly so. I shall speak to Kate as soon as you are presentable."

"Yes, and you might advise her as to what she must pack for herself, Mack. I do not believe Kate has ever been to London and she is to accompany the countess."

The Earl of Balmorrow, shaved and presentable in buckskin breeches, riding boots, a bright cambric shirt and nankeen hunting jacket, with a Belcher kerchief tied rakishly around his throat ignored his breakfast and went straight to the stables to check on Donadee. He was taken aback to discover his new bride patting the gelding's nose. "Good morning," he called, making his way to the box stall. "I thought you were not fond of horses."

"Well, I am not," fibbed Clarissa, surprised to see him about so early. "I merely thought—well, you did say—no, it was not you. Perhaps it was Mr. Mackelry said—that your horse had been injured last evening."

"And you cared so about it that you came to see what you might do?"

Clarissa flushed and cast her gaze to the stable floor. "N-no, not exactly, m'l—Balmorrow."

The truth was that Clarissa had become so suspicious that Mackelry's words of last evening had been lies designed to dismiss her from the earl's presence that she had come to see for herself if his horse showed even the slightest sign of harm. She had meant to assure herself of the horse's well-being and then to confront the earl on his dishonesty and to explain to him that lies and subterfuge were not in the least necessary, that she would much prefer him to simply explain what he desired of her as his wife and she would do it. But now her suspicions and determination were wavering because the animal was definitely limping and sporting a poultice.

"I—I only thought, perhaps, I might pet the poor thing a bit. To—to cheer him, you know."

Balmorrow smiled down upon her in the most disturbing way. He was truly a good-looking man when he smiled, with those great blue eyes beaming and those sensuous lips curving gently upward. And even a dimple, she noted, appeared shyly in his left cheek. Though he was not nearly so refined, and certainly not as gallant and sophisticated as Edward, Lord Parkhurst, and though she did prefer a gentleman of light coloring with glorious blond curls, still, when Balmorrow smiled, she could not find any great fault with his appearance.

One of his hands reached up to stroke Donadee's nose while his other arm went gently about Clarissa's shoulders. "Have you been properly introduced then? No? Clare, this is Donadee, the most obstreperous beast ever to bear a saddle. And Donny, this is my lady, Clare, whose every wish you are to obey, you stubborn old mule."

"Oh, is he old? He does not look it."

"Very old," grinned Balmorrow. "Nearing seventeen years, but still the finest bit of blood and bone ever breeched. I was there when he was born. Breathed life into his nostrils myself."

"You did?"

"Indeed. It is why he owns a large part of my heart. It was unforgivable of me to set him at that wall, and in the dark, too. If he had broken his leg—well, but he did not, did you old man, and I thank God for it, too."

"*You* might well have broken your neck," Clarissa pointed out as Balmorrow's hold on her tightened.

"And deserved it. But Donadee did not deserve it. If it were not for his great trust in me he would have refused that jump. Have you had your breakfast?"

"Yes, I woke early."

"Very early for it is only now come up on eight."

"I was not—not very sleepy." Clarissa blinked, confused, as the light in Balmorrow's eyes dimmed at her words.

"I am a wretched man," he mumbled, turning away from the horse and escorting Clarissa from the stable, "and a worse husband. You would be sleeping late else."

Clarissa had not the least idea what he meant and stared up at him with a most perplexed look upon her countenance. The true naivete it implied made him chuckle. "Never mind, Clare," he smiled, escorting her from the stable. "You will gather my meaning soon. I have been thinking. It is already April and I ought to be in London."

"For the Season?" asked Clarissa eagerly.

"Well, for other reasons but, yes, the Season will begin as well. You will not mind to remain behind here and take charge of the staff and the children for me?" His blue eyes studied her with a teasing glint, but she did not note it, for Clarissa had turned away in disappointment at his words.

So, now she knew. He had offered for her for no other reason than that he wished a wife to look after his children, his castle, and his servants while he was on the Town. Well, and what of it! She had married him for no other reason than his money. It was a fair and equitable bargain. If he had not offered the sums necessary to save Malcolm, she would have rejected him out-of-hand. Clarissa came to a halt and swung around to face him.

"Yes? What is it?" he asked with a cock of a perfectly arched eyebrow. "What have I said to send you so suddenly into a brown study?"

"I—"

"Yes?"

"I had been wondering, my lord, why you wished to marry me and now I know. That is all."

"Well, and am I to be my lord for the rest of our lives now, because I do not offer to take you with me to London?"

"No. Not at all, Balmorrow. It was a slip of the tongue merely."

"Am I to understand that you wish to accompany me to London, Clare? But what would you do there? Young ladies have Seasons in London for the purpose of bringing a gentleman up to scratch and you have brought me up to scratch already without any of that nonsense."

"I did never attempt to bring you 'up to scratch' as you so rudely put it, my lord," glowered Clarissa, taken aback by his words. "I did never once think of you in such a manner! In fact, I did never once think of you at all for I never heard your name until you offered for me!"

"Still, m'dear," grinned Balmorrow, "I am a devil of a good catch for all that. You could not have done better if you *had* set your cap at me. I am rich, titled, and reasonably good-looking. You are beyond belief fortunate to have gotten me."

"Oh!" exclaimed Clarissa, teased into laughter by the mirth in his eyes. "Such unmitigated conceit, sir!"

"Yes," Balmorrow laughed, taking her hands in his and drawing her close. "And there is a good deal more where that comes from, let me tell you. You have married into the most conceited, arrogant, audacious family upon the face of the earth, my Lady Balmorrow. I know it to be true. We have been informed of it in writing by no one less than King George himself."

And then Balmorrow's laughter died and for a very long moment he stared down into Clarissa's eyes.

He is going to kiss me, she thought, suddenly and inexplicably petrified. He is going to kiss me right here in the stable yard.

But he did not. Instead he gave her hands a squeeze and a pat and then set them free. "I have forgotten," he said with a most unreadable gleam in his eyes. "Kate has need of you. She awaits you in your chambers. You had best go see what the problem is. This abigail business is all new to her and she is quite like to panic. Run off and see to her, do."

Why had he not kissed her? As she hurried toward the castle, all Clarissa could think was: Why had he not kissed her? Certainly he had intended to do so. Edward, Lord Parkhurst had kissed her once in the Manchesters' rose garden and Balmorrow had had the same look in his eyes this morning that Lord Parkhurst had had that afternoon. But where Lord Parkhurst had swooped down upon her lips swiftly and confidently and with not the least hesitation, Balmorrow had chosen instead to send her away.

Clarissa's nerves pricked at her. Doubts assailed her mind and yearnings she had never known nibbled at her insides. Did he think her ugly then or somehow unworthy of his kiss? Or had he noted the unaccountable fear that had come over her? Perhaps that was it. He had divined her anxiety and had had pity upon her. Oh! But she had not wished for his pity! What a fool she was! To allow herself to appear to him a squeamish miss when she was his wife and truly desired to please him if she could! A man ought to desire to kiss his wife and ought to go ahead and do it, too! Why had he not?

Why had he not overlooked her slight hesitation and gone ahead and placed his lips upon her own? Tears of frustration rose to Clarissa's eyes as she reached her chambers to discover Kate repacking the trunks she had unpacked only two nights before.

"Oh, my lady," cried Kate noticing Clarissa's tears at once. "Whatever has happened? Have you hurt yourself? Shall I fetch the master?"

"No! No! Do not dare fetch Lord Balmorrow. It is mere silliness on my part. I shall be just fine." Clarissa took a muslin handkerchief from a drawer, wiped angrily at the tears and blew her nose mightily. "There. Now all the drama is at an end. Kate, what are you doing? Why are you packing my trunks?"

"Because his lordship sent word, my lady. 'Pack up everything she owns,' Mr. Mackelry said. 'And everything you own as well, Kate. We are bound for London.' "

Clarissa could not believe her ears. "Are you certain you understood correctly, Kate? That you and I are to accompany his lordship to London?"

"Oh, yes, my lady. And we are to leave directly after luncheon."

Clarissa was about to ask again if Kate were certain she had understood the message correctly when Brandilynn scratched upon the open door. "Papa said I was to be of help," she announced with a wide smile. "And I am to give you these to pack because you will be expected to wear them in Town."

"Oh!" gasped Clarissa, opening the long, black velvet box that Brandy handed her. "How beautiful!"

"They are the Balmorrow sapphires and were a present from Charles Stuart to my great-great-grandmama," Brandy explained as Clarissa glanced up. "Papa says there has never before been a Countess of Balmorrow with green eyes and that he wishes now that they were emeralds, but he thought you might force yourself to wear them for one evening—for his sake—because all the Countesses of Balmorrow have worn them at Court since they came into the family."

"At Court?" Clarissa plopped down upon the little bench before her vanity. "At Court? Your papa attends the Court of St. James?"

"Well, he says it is a great bore and overflowing with excessively silly twits, but he is expected to appear at least once every year. It is because he is The Balmorrow and required to pay public homage to the King—except now it will be the Prince he must bow to I expect."

"If he don't, everyone will think there is to be a war between us an' them," offered Zander, clomping noisily into the room in a pair of oversized Hessians. "Look, Brandy, what Papa gave me. He says they pinch his feet."

"Well, they certainly do not pinch yours," giggled Brandy.

"No, an' I have got m'own boots on right inside of 'em too! Papa says I am goin' to be big as him someday. An' maybe bigger!"

"Bigger?" cried Clarissa playfully. "Oh, good heavens! Bigger than your papa? What a giant that would make you! A regular Goliath!"

"Uh-huh," nodded Zan, standing as straight and proud as any soldier. "An' then his boots will not even fit me at all. They will be too *small.* What do you want us to do, Mama? Papa said we were to help you get ready for goin' to London."

"Oh!" breathed Brandy on a little gasp. "And we were s'posed to apologize for him. He said he teased you about not going to London an' we were to say he was sorry for it."

Balmorrow bestowed a wet, noisy kiss upon each of his children, bid them mind Sylvester and Mrs. Beal and most especially Duncan, who would cook them up into stew if they proved the least bit recalcitrant, and climbed into his traveling coach, choosing to sit with his back to the horses, across from Clarissa. He waved for quite as long as Brandy and Zander were in sight, encouraging Clarissa to do the same, then settled back into one corner and stared across at her in silence.

"What?" Clarissa asked after a minute or two under his steady scrutiny.

"Hmmm?"

"Why are you staring at me so?"

"Well, I have seen all this scenery before, so I thought to feast my eyes upon my lovely bride instead."

Clarissa felt a blush rise to her cheeks.

"Are you pleased to be off to London?"

"Indeed."

"Did you truly believe that I would go to Town without you a mere two days after our wedding, Clare?"

"Yes."

"Yes, because you have not the least experience of me. I ought to have thought of that. I could have kicked myself when the words left my mouth and you turned so suddenly silent. And then when you said so clearly that now you knew why I had married you—I do apologize for it, Clare. I did never marry you simply to gain a glorified upper servant. You must believe that. I was merely teasing is all. I should say I will never tease you again, but I cannot, you know, because I have been a tease for all my life and quite likely I cannot stop completely."

"Were you—were you teasing when you held my hands in the stable yard as well?"

"When I held your hands?"

"I thought for a moment that you were going to—to—kiss me, my lord. But then you did not, you know. Was that teasing as well? Because I thought—I thought surely it must have been my fault that you did not. Kiss me, I mean."

"Your fault? Your fault? Why on earth would you think—? I was going to kiss you, madam, but I turned craven. It occurred to me that it would be better for you to discover that you *were* going to London first, and then you would be much more likely not to despise being kissed."

"What an odd idea," murmured Clarissa, one eyebrow cocked questioningly. "Why should you think I would despise being kissed?"

"Well, not despise being kissed exactly. Despise being kissed *by me.* I have behaved abominably toward you from the first in this affair. Do not deny that you think so, Clare, because even I think so. And then just when I was determined not to do anything further to make you dislike me, I went and teased you about London! I do truly apologize for all of it. And I intend to set everything on an even keel between us."

"You do?"

"Indeed. We spend tonight at Larchmont Abbey. My godmother is the Duchess of Larchmont and she will be disappointed if we do not stop."

The abrupt change of subject left Clarissa speechless. How

had the man gotten from setting things upon an even keel to spending the night with his godmother?

"You are not to let her frighten you, Clare. She is an intimidating old lady, but she will take you in disgust if you display the least fear of her."

"Is she very old?" asked Clarissa, attempting to readjust her thinking to this new topic.

"Very old. Hundreds of years old. Thousands even!"

"Thousands?" Clarissa giggled.

"Well, perhaps not thousands. I seem to recall that she is in her seventies. But one year spent with Her Grace seems like a century. I know. I spent a whole year with her when I was a child. I thought I should never live free again!"

These words might have evoked a twinge of sympathy in Clarissa if they had not been accompanied by a quiet chuckle and eyes brimming with mirth.

"I give you fair warning, m'dear. She has a gold-headed cane with which she jabs at people who do not pay her the proper attention, and she has a cruel wit when she is not pleased with one. And if you get upon her nerves just once too often, she will send you to bed without your dinner."

"Oh my goodness, no!" exclaimed Clarissa playfully, entering into what were obviously treasured reminiscences of his boyhood. "And what will she do, do you think, if I should escape my chamber by climbing down a trellis?"

"She will march you directly to the chapel and make you read five whole chapters of Leviticus aloud. Five! And no getting out of it either, not even if you stutter and it takes you forever to get the words out."

"Did you?" Clarissa asked softly, her eyes studying him with a warm sympathy.

"Stutter? Yes. Abominably. But my godmama cured me of it."

"My lady don't know about The Balmorrows," Kate sighed, gazing out from the window of the coach that followed slowly in the wake of the earl's. "I could see as she was taken by surprise that she should be expected to appear at Court."

"Aye, a great many gently bred ladies lack an acquaintanceship with—history," replied Mackelry, stretching his legs out before him. "Wrapped 'round in ignorance of anything the least unpleasant, most gentlewomen are. But now she is The Balmorrow's wife, this young lady will learn history, Kate. As things stand at present, she will not be able to avoid doing so."

"Is the master in deep waters then?"

"Extremely deep, Kate. But that is not for you to fret about. He will gain safe ground as he always does."

"My lady thought the sapphires beautiful," Kate offered, knowing Mackelry would discuss his lordship's danger no further.

"He has given them to her already? That bodes well. He has set it in his mind to please her then. Though she is not like to be pleased easily if he does not soon cease drinking himself into oblivion and falling from rooftops and horses and begin to perform his husbandly duties."

Kate blushed becomingly and Mackelry chuckled. "I was not referring just to those duties that make you color up, Kate. I refer to the fact that his lordship has not as yet so much as joined the mistress for a proper dinner. That, however, will be attended to tonight. He will not dare deny his presence at the duchess' table."

"And he will eat," nodded Kate knowingly, having many times been present in the Balmorrow kitchen when the earl's dinner had been returned course by course in the same state as it had been served him.

"Indeed he will eat, for Her Grace will call it to his attention directly if he does not."

"Is he never going to get over being poisoned?" Kate asked with a worried frown. "It's been near eight months."

"I do not know, Kate. He's fit enough. 'Tis simply his appetite disappears when dinner reaches the table."

"It sets Duncan's teeth on edge. That it does," sighed Kate.

Mackelry, well-aware that Kate had a strong personal interest in Duncan's peace of mind, grinned and nodded and then turned his gaze out the window.

The Duchess of Larchmont peered at the hastily scrawled message and then at Franklin. "Do you know, Franklin, what is happening with Balmorrow?"

"Yer Grace?"

"Do you know why he has sent you galloping neck-or-nothing across country to inform me of his imminent arrival upon my doorstep when most times the only notice he sees fit to advance me is a knock upon my door?"

"Why I reckon—don't he say, Yer Grace, in the writin'?"

"The only thing my godson writes, Franklin, is to expect him in your wake."

Balmorrow's head groom raised an eyebrow. "That's all what he says, Yer Grace?"

"Indeed. What is it that he does not say, Franklin?"

The groom stared down at his mud-splattered boots—evidence that he had taken a shortcut through Sputterin Marsh—and rubbed thoughtfully at the back of his neck. "Well, Yer Grace, I reckon as 'ow maybe his lordship might mean ta surprise ye, then."

"I detest surprises, Franklin. Speak to me."

"Well, his lordship be on his way to London, Yer Grace."

"Yes, he generally is when he passes this way."

"Yes, Yer Grace. An' he be takin' her ladyship with him."

"Her ladyship? What ladyship? Franklin, do cease studying the mud upon your boots and look at me and tell me what sort of scrape Balmorrow has gotten himself into now," demanded the duchess, tapping her cane upon the floor, which instantly brought Franklin's eyes to meet her own. Franklin had been introduced to that cane once before and did not care to make its acquaintance again because he could barely think a clear thought with the urge to guffaw coming over him every time the wretched thing jabbed in his direction.

"His lordship, Yer Grace, has got hisself leg-shackled," Franklin stated without batting an eyelash.

"He has what?" roared the duchess, rising to her full height of four-foot-eleven.

"G-got hisself leg-shackled, Yer Grace. Two nights ago at the castle. With a special license and his nibs doin' the honors. An' he be bringin' his bride to meet ye on their way to Lunnon."

Chapter 5

"Alex, I have allowed that since no one but you and your bride visit, we shall not dine formally, but that is all I have allowed," declared the duchess, imperiously tapping the edge of her spoon against a fine porcelain bowl. "Cease fidgeting about at once, sir, and address yourself to your soup."

Balmorrow's brilliant blue eyes sparkled and flashed into Clarissa's bemused green ones across the dining table. The corners of his lips twitched upward and he winked at her.

Now why does he do that? she wondered. And then she knew.

"Good evening, soup," the earl drawled lazily. "Fine weather we are having, no?"

Clarissa came near to choking on a spoonful of the chowder at his perfectly polite words. She clutched her napkin quickly to her lips, smothering a giggle behind it.

The duchess, a sparkle in her eyes quite equal to the sparkle in her godson's, took a bit of her own soup and then set her spoon aside. "Very well, Alex, I misspoke. Please do not address yourself to your soup."

"No, Your Grace, not if you do not wish me to do so. Are you certain you do not wish me to do so?"

"Indeed. You will however taste the soup, sweet boy, or

none of us shall go on to the next course. Truly, Alex, I will not have you insult Andre as you do Duncan. A chef cannot bear to have his artistry go unappreciated."

"Well, but Duncan is not a chef, Your Grace. He is a simple cook with no upward leanings."

"He is a most excellent cook," Clarissa inserted. "And he works extremely hard to please you. Kate says so."

The duchess nodded. "I do believe Duncan is the most unappreciated talent in all of England. The mere thought of how he must constantly stretch his imagination to tempt my godson's appetite sends me into a tizzy. For you must know, my dear, that Alex is a monster to please when it comes to dinner of late. And it is past time you ceased to be so," she added with a glare at her godson. "It was months ago you were poisoned and it is over and done with. Wipe the thing from your mind, Alexander. You will waste away to nothing, else."

Poisoned? Clarissa's jaw dropped and she stared across at her husband in amazement. Poisoned?

Balmorrow merely winked, spooned a modicum of the chowder between his lips, then set aside the spoon and smiled complacently at his godmother.

"Very well," the duchess sighed. "You need not eat all of the soup. But you will do justice to the remainder of Andre's dinner. For if you do not, Alex, I shall allow him to come up here and—"

"And what, Godmama?"

"And—lop off your ears with his carving knife!"

Balmorrow burst into whoops. "My ears?" he cried, slapping a hand over each of them with laughing abandon. "My ears?" The merry roar of his laughter rumbled through the room infecting both the duchess and Clarissa and driving the puzzlement about poison from Clarissa's mind.

"My ears?" cried the earl again. "Really, Godmama, what sort of vile threat is that? I thought at least you would let him cut out my heart or my gizzard or my—well, never mind," he finished, his free-hearted laughter winding down to a chuckle. "Lop off my ears—I should have a fine time keeping my hat upon my head then, let me tell you."

Clarissa noted, however, that Balmorrow did attempt from then on to do justice to every course, and though she could see he had to literally force himself to chew and swallow when it came to a perfectly delectable lobster pie, he nonetheless ate most of what was set before him and graciously sent a word of appreciation to Her Grace's chef. He then sat back and grinned expectantly at the duchess.

"One glass," that imposing matron declared in response.

"Two, please," pleaded Balmorrow with the most innocent and beguiling look upon his face.

"One," responded the duchess, "and an extra splash which Bentley will pour. Come, Clarissa, we will withdraw to the winter parlor and leave Alex to enjoy my late husband's prize. If you are going to smoke one of those vile Spanish cigar things, however," she tossed over her shoulder, "you will do me the courtesy to open the window, Alex."

"Most certainly, Your Grace," grinned Balmorrow, "all of the windows."

The duchess' butler lost some of his starch as the ladies departed and setting an exquisite Venetian snifter before Balmorrow, opened a matching decanter and poured the late duke's coveted one-hundred-year-old Amantillado slowly down the side of the glass.

"Will you join me, Bentley?" Balmorrow asked with a cocked eyebrow.

"I rather think not, your lordship. 'Twould be highly irregular."

"You joined me last time."

"Ahh, yes, but—'twas your birthday, my lord."

"Well, two nights ago I got myself married, Bentley. Does that not require you to unbend a bit?"

"Indeed, sir, if there were to be a toast—"

"Pour yourself a glass then," urged the earl, "for I most certainly intend to make a toast."

In the winter parlor the duchess settled herself upon a most impressive powder blue brocade sopha and patted the seat beside her. "Come, sit, my dear, and we shall have a word or two before that rascally godson of mine reappears. So, you are Thomas Beresfont's daughter. I knew your father when he was young."

"Did you, Your Grace?" Clarissa had never once heard her father speak of the Duchess of Larchmont.

"Oh, yes, Halliard and Larchmont were bosom beaux. You could not know one without knowing the other. And you could not marry one," she smiled, "without having the other run tame about your residence."

"My papa ran tame here?"

"Indeed, and in Larchmont House in London, though we did not see so much of him after he married. I did wish to attend his funeral, my dear, but I was ill and could not." The duchess studied Clarissa with a most disconcerting gaze. "I cannot fathom why Alex should marry you without the least hint to anyone. You are not increasing, are you, girl?"

"What?" Crusty old duchess or not, Clarissa could not believe her ears. "I assure you, Your Grace, that Lord Balmorrow and I had never so much as laid eyes upon each other before our wedding!"

"No, no, you mistake me. I do not for one moment suggest that you and Alex—Alex would never involve himself in such a way with an innocent. I only wish to be assured that some other buck did not dandle you upon his knee and Alex come to your rescue, eh?"

"No!" exclaimed Clarissa. "I have never—how could you think—of all the—"

"Shhh, shhh, settle down, girl. You will have half the household upon us if you do not lower your voice. It was merely the first reason that sprang to my mind. Had you been increasing, Alex would have had good excuse to marry you out of hand without one word to any of his family. And it is a piece of whimsy I would not put past him—rescuing a young lady from certain shame—especially if the young lady is also the daughter of a Halliard. It was the money, then? I had heard rumors, but I gave them no credence. That Thomas Beresfont should cut up so very cold that it must be solved by marriage settlements? I found the notion inconceivable."

"It is a marriage of convenience on both our parts," murmured Clarissa, silently seething at the duchess' offhand trampling of her reputation and at what she considered the old woman's prying into her family's affairs.

"Oh, most certainly not, my dear," chuckled the elderly lady. "Never a marriage of convenience on both your parts.

I am certain that you are the most *inconvenient* thing that has happened to Alex in years. However could your father have run through his fortune to such an extent? He was never a gamester."

"He—Why do you say I am inconvenient to Alex? I shall be stepmama to his children and mistress of Castle Balmorrow. I shall take Master Alexander and Lady Brandilynn under my wing and see to the household and the accounts and—"

"—get generally under Alex's feet and in his hair," laughed the duchess with great good humor.

"That is not at all correct, Your Grace. It is true that I accepted his lordship's offer because—well, because of the marriage settlements he proposed—but I am perfectly willing to be of whatever service to him that I can be. And I certainly have no intention of disrupting his peace. We have made a bargain, you see, and I do intend to abide by it. He need only tell me what it is he requires of me and he shall have it."

"Oh! Oh!" gurgled the duchess. "Young and beautiful and innocent and honorable to boot! And don't it serve that boy right! Yes, and it is about time, too. But I ought not laugh so, my dear. Surely you think me a madwoman. Has Alex explained to you exactly what he considers to be your end of this bargain? Was it he who spoke of the children and the accounts?"

Clarissa gazed at the elderly lady and shook her head.

"No. No, I thought not. Have you asked him what it is he expects of you? What has he said?"

"Only that he wishes to set things upon an even keel between us—but then he turned the subject aside and began telling me about you."

"He has not given it one thought," announced the duchess, attempting to quell the small chortles that still lingered in her tone. "He has not so much as considered what ought to be your side of this supposed bargain. That is why he changed the topic I have no doubt. Do not press him upon it, Clarissa. He will think of something to tell you and when he does, he will raise the discussion of your bargain himself."

"But—but he offered for me, Your Grace. Surely he required a wife for some reason."

"Only give him time, my dear, and he will think of one. Meanwhile, it is highly likely that your mere presence upon his arm in London will rip up Alex's peace no end. Your marriage will come as a shock, you know, to any number of people. The gossips will stir it into the scandal broth at every tea, attempting to understand how such a thing could happen and not one of them have the least suspicion in advance. And Alex's cronies will no doubt roast him over it for weeks. And with the added responsibilities you present him, there is no telling what notions will enter the boy's head or what he will do. I shall be sad to miss it. I have no doubt London will be most entertained."

"He is a bit odd, is he not?" mused Clarissa aloud, sending the duchess into another round of chuckles.

"Not for a Balmorrow, dearest. The Earls of Balmorrow have always been a most unorthodox lot. Alex is the soul of propriety compared to his ancestors."

"I am the soul of propriety compared to your ancestors as well, Godmama," the earl drawled from the doorway. "Whatever this discussion is about, you must at least admit that. Between the two of us, you and I own the blackest villains in all of history." Balmorrow ambled into the room and lowered himself into a sturdy chair facing the two ladies.

"I keep that chair expressly for him," the duchess explained to Clarissa with a glance that warned her to change the topic of conversation immediately. "It is the only one on this floor that does not collapse when he goes to sit in it."

"That is merely because every other piece, Godmama, is built for tiny ladies and man-milliners." The earl stretched his long legs out before him, stretched his arms mightily above his head and yawned. "I am sorry, but I have not had a decent night's sleep in weeks. Clare," he added, smiling upon her, "there is a pianoforte. Do you play, perhaps?"

Clarissa nodded.

"Would you be kind enough to give us some music then? The duchess does not play any longer because of the ache in her hands and I am nothing but thumbs myself. I have been out here in the hinterlands for what seems an eternity and I miss music more than anything. At least in London there is always music."

"Does Brandy still not play?" asked the duchess.

"No, nor Zan, which I cannot understand. You would think at least one of them to have inherited Madeline's talent.

But no, they are both as fumble-fingered around musical instruments as I am myself. A pox on them! They are determined to take after the Sinclairs and not the Howards. Come, m'dear," he added, rising and offering Clarissa his hand. "I will gladly escort you to the thing, see you seated and turn your pages with a beaming smile if you will be so kind as to play for us."

Clarissa had allowed Kate to help her into her nightrail and now sat before the mirror as the little abigail brushed her hair into long, shining waves. She had played the pianoforte until tea and enjoyed each moment of it. Never before have I felt so appreciated, she thought happily. Balmorrow had stood beside her turning pages the entire time and he and the duchess both had listened—actually listened—to the music and applauded her and urged her to play another composition and another until she thought her poor fingers might actually fall off on to the keyboard. And Balmorrow had smelled so wonderful! Clarissa gurgled at the thought and Kate looked at her suspiciously in the mirror. But he *had* smelled good—a sweet, dusky smell like fine old wood and tart apples. It had been the wine and the cigar, of course.

"Will there be anything else, m'lady?" Kate asked, setting the hairbrush aside. The lovely old four poster bed had already been turned down and a spritely fire danced low, though merrily, in the grate.

"No, Kate, thank you." The fine linen sheets were inviting and Clarissa longed to snuggle down between them. She was so very tired suddenly. The journey to London would be a long and exhausting one, especially following as it did upon her journey from Newbury all the way into Northumberland. But she did not care in the least. She was not such a poor spirited thing as to let a bit of traveling bother her. And she wanted to see London again. She wanted to spend an entire Season in London. She wanted it with all her heart. Clarissa climbed up into the bed and reached to extinguish the candle that stood flickering on her bedside table. "Goodnight, then, Kate," she said as the abigail curtsied and started toward the door. "And pleasant dreams to you."

"And to you as well, my lady," murmured Kate, closing the door softly behind her.

Mackelry, in high good spirits, met Kate in the hall and offered to escort her to her own chambers. "Bless the old gal," he chuckled.

"Who?" Kate asked in wonder.

"Why the duchess, Kate. Give 'em two sitting rooms with but one bedchamber shared between 'em. Man and wife, you know."

"Oh, and my lady not even realizing it!" Kate giggled and flushed most becomingly, and Mackelry thought that if he were a bit younger, he would have a go at winning that maiden's heart away from Duncan. He offered her his arm and, each with a candle in hand, they started off down the long corridor toward the servants' quarters.

Balmorrow, divested of all but his breeches, a silk smoking jacket tied loosely around his heavily-muscled torso, paced the brightly-colored carpeting of his sitting room, his bare feet soundless upon the Turkish design. There was a decanter of brandy on a cricket table and a glass waiting beside it. It was always there, whenever he came. Bentley saw to it. Bentley was one of Balmorrow's favorite butlers. But Bentley truly should not have set that decanter at the ready tonight. It was throwing Balmorrow into a dither. He wished to go directly to it, drink a few glasses and slip into oblivion. But he knew his obligations lay in another direction.

He called himself a number of amazingly descriptive names, ran his fingers mercilessly through his hair, stomped over and tossed a log onto his fire, and then muttered more expletives in regard to his father, Clarissa's father, Malcolm Beresfont, the duchess, and fate in general. All in all it took a full ten minutes before his feet propelled him across the carpet and his knuckles rapped gently upon the door to the shared bedchamber. He waited patiently but when no one answered he swore softly and rapped a bit more loudly. When still no answer came, he took the china knob in his hand and turned it slowly, easing the door quietly open.

Shadows flickered and dimmed and flickered again in unison with the rise and fall of the fading fire on the hearth. Balmorrow waited for his eyes to adjust to the dimness of the room. Then he took a step forward and another and another until he reached the side of the big four poster. He gazed down silently at the sleeping Clarissa, her long tresses flowing across the white satin pillow case from beneath a most fetching beribboned cap, her face deep in shadow. His heart began to beat in the most unorthodox manner and, quite suddenly, he found it hard to breathe. By Jove, but she was beautiful. He had thought it from his first glimpse of her at the wedding. He had thought as much again yesterday and today, but he had not been certain he was seeing aright until this very moment.

Balmorrow lowered himself to the edge of the bed and touched a strand of her hair—gently, carefully. His breathing became labored and his pulses raced and he knew for a fact that an incredible passion was rising within him. He ceased to touch the soft, thick hair and moved his finger caressingly down her cheek instead, thrilling to the velvety texture of it.

Clarissa's eyes popped open and she gasped. "What—who—?" she stuttered, striving to see him more clearly in the dim light. "Balmorrow, is it you?" she asked, shying from his touch and pushing herself upward into a sitting position.

"Indeed."

"What—what do you want?"

"Only to know your name."

"My name? To know my name?" Clarissa stared at him wide-eyed. What was wrong with the man? Certainly he knew her name. Perhaps—perhaps he is asleep, she thought suddenly. I have heard that people sometimes walk in their sleep. Perhaps he has done just that and wandered into my room by mistake. He does look rather dazed.

"I am Clarissa," she said quietly. "I am your wife."

"Are you? Or are you some wraith come to steal my soul? My eyes tell me that you are real, but my mind whispers that you cannot be."

Clarissa could not believe her ears. Some wraith come to steal his soul? Charis had explained to her, as best she could bring herself to do so, what a man expected of his wife on their wedding night and on many nights thereafter, but none of it had had to do with wraiths and soul-stealing. None of it, in point of fact, had had to do with a gentleman sitting upon the edge of her bed in the firelight and waking her by the lightest touch of his finger against her cheek. She could still feel it—his touch—though his finger had long since departed. And his eyes—his eyes in the shadows—seemed to burn with fever. "Are you not well, my lord?" Clarissa asked.

"No," Balmorrow murmured. "No, not well. Deuced uncomfortable in fact. Burning."

"B-burning?" Clarissa's hand almost went to feel his brow, but abruptly she pulled back. Why the man was practically naked! How could she have sat there not noticing his bared chest for such a length of time? And, my goodness, she thought and gave a little gulp, it is such a wide, hairy chest! She had the most unaccountable urge to tangle her fingers in that odd pelt. Would it be rough or smooth, warm or cool, thick or thin? And did it curl like the hair on his head? She could not tell, quite, for the firelight had grown dim and it was hard to see clearly.

Balmorrow, for some inexplicable reason, began to chuckle and Clarissa ceased to gape at his chest and returned her gaze to his face. "What?" she asked. "First you are ill and burning and raving about spirits and now you are laughing? Are you completely lunatic, my lord?"

"No, only experiencing an odd taste of reality. Would you like to touch it?"

"T-touch?"

"My chest. You may, you know. It now belongs to you."

Clarissa's eyes widened. The man *was* mad. "It—I—n-no, most certainly not! It does not belong to me. It is your chest, Balmorrow."

"And do I not belong to you, Clare? Did I not vow to be your husband? Or was that all a dream?"

"Well, but, you—I—"

Balmorrow chuckled again and caught Clarissa's witlessly flailing hands between his own. He raised them to his lips and kissed her palms tenderly. Then he placed them against his chest and held them gently there.

Clarissa's eyes widened. It was like silk. Exactly like fine, soft, silk. Beneath his hands her fingers grew brave and twisted among the alluring spirals of downy fleece, but then the impropriety of such action reached her mind and she ceased, flustered, her jaw dropping at her own audacity.

"By Jove, but you are the most enticing gudgeon," Balmorrow murmured, transferring both her hands into one of his and leaning slowly toward her.

Clarissa, mystified, leaned slowly away.

"No, do not move back, you heartless waif. I only mean to kiss those charming lips."

"Ch-charming lips?"

"What? Do you not think your lips are charming, Clare?"

"Well, no, for goodness sake! They are lips, after all, like chicken beaks, ugly but useful."

Balmorrow gulped back a crack of laughter. "Chicken beaks? You compare your lips to chicken beaks?"

"Not merely my lips," scowled Clare. "Everyone's lips. They are merely objects to be used for eating and speaking and—"

"Kissing," whispered Balmorrow, placing a finger lightly upon those alluring lips of hers and tracing them.

Clare shivered at his touch. It was a delightful feeling and her shiver somehow delightful as well.

"Have you ever been kissed, Clare?"

"Well, of course I have. Edward, Lord Parkhurst kissed me once in a garden."

"He did? Caught you unawares, did he? Well, I should like to kiss you now, Clare. This very moment. Husbands sometimes grow fond of kissing their wives. I should like to give it a try and see if I will grow fond of it. Do you know about passion and love, Clare? Have you perchance read about it somewhere? Have you felt it yourself?"

"I know about husbands and wives," Clarissa announced. "Charis explained it to me."

"Charis?"

"My sister-in-law."

"And what did she tell you?" His finger had ceased to trace the outline of her lips and moved to caress the long line of her neck. It paused to feel the pulse beating rapidly at the base of her throat. "Did she tell you that I would wish to make love to you, Clare?"

"Y-yes."

"And did she tell you what that would involve?"

"Y-yes, but—"

"But what?"

"Well, I think she certainly must have been mistaken, or

I misunderstood, for it sounded quite nonsensical to me. Goodness gracious, how could any two people possibly—"

Balmorrow's finger went back to her lips, silencing her. Then his hand roamed to the back of her neck and held her firmly while he leaned forward and pressed his lips against her own. She could feel the tickling of his tongue as he moved it gently but insistently, and her lips parted slightly in surprise. Balmorrow took advantage and slipped in and in a moment Clarissa's surprise became a most incredible urge to keep his tongue exactly where it had most illogically gone. She closed her eyes and was lost to all thought, letting herself be guided solely by the perfectly delectable sensations his kiss was arousing in her. Her arms went around his neck; her fingers entwined themselves in his curls. Her breathing grew ragged and her head spun as the earl's kiss went on and on. When at last he disengaged himself from her, he found it necessary to disentangle himself from her embrace and push her back a little way from him. Clarissa opened her eyes and gaped at him.

"You *are* a wraith sent to steal my soul," sighed Balmorrow with a sad shake of his head.

"Glory be!" gasped Clarissa, finding her tongue at last. "Whatever sort of kiss was that? It was not at all like Edward, Lord Parkhurst's."

Balmorrow pulled her to him again and bestowed a chaste peck upon her brow. "Do not say that you enjoyed it, sweetings?"

"I—I—may we do it again?"

"Indeed," smiled Balmorrow. "But first I shall put another log on the fire, shall I? It is going to be a rather long night, I think."

Chapter 6

Balmorrow's entourage departed Larchmont Abbey at an unconscionably early hour. The dew still lay thick upon the newly-sprouting grass. The sun barely flickered through the mist. A bleary-eyed Clarissa settled into one corner of the coach with a tiny smile upon her face and one arm possessively through Balmorrow's, compelling him to sit directly beside her with the length of his body pressed gently against her own. Several beaming smiles, including Mackelry's, acknowledged and approved of this arrangement.

The Duchess of Larchmont waved them off with a good deal of energy for such an elderly lady and stared after them until they disappeared from sight. "I think, Bentley," she murmured as she turned back into the abbey, "that my godson is going to have a very interesting and adventurous Season in London. It is like to be even more interesting and adventurous than last year."

"Indeed, Your Grace," nodded Bentley.

Balmorrow stretched and placed the heels of his boots upon the seat across from him. He then disengaged himself from Clarissa's grasp, untied the bow of her bonnet, removed that little confection, and then placed his arm gently around her, drawing her to rest her head upon his shoulder. "Nap," he said quietly. "You have gotten not a wink of sleep. Close your eyes, Clare, and nod off for an hour or two. There is not much to see at any rate."

Clarissa, marveling at the sense of safety and comfort that flowed through her this morning as she snuggled into Balmorrow's embrace, closed her eyes without protest and was soon into dreams. The earl, himself weary to the bone, closed his eyes as well and, with half an ear attuned to the pace of the horses before and behind him and the consistent clomping of the outriders to each side, swayed into a semi-consciousness that, if not quite sleep, was at least restful. He was jolted from it two hours later by the sudden lurching of the coach and the increased rumble of the wheels. His own team and the team behind had broken into a run; the outriders had moved out of position. Balmorrow's arms tightened around Clarissa and he lowered his head to bestow a tender kiss upon the top of her head. "Wake up, Clare," he whispered. "Come, sweetings, open those lovely eyes."

"Wh-what?" Clare replied sleepily.

"You must wake up, my dear. Just for a few moments. We are about to be robbed, I think."

"What? Robbed?" Clarissa jerked into awareness. "Robbed?"

"I rather think so," nodded Balmorrow, releasing his hold on her and moving to the far window.

Highwaymen! Robbed and murdered on the Great North Road! And just when she had discovered the sheer ecstasy of wedded life, too! And the secrets that no woman could possibly describe to another! And the truly wonderful tenderness of her new husband! "Where is your pistol?" Clarissa asked Balmorrow with a tiny gasp. "Have you two? I have never shot a pistol, but I shall attempt to do so. They shall not take us without a fight!"

"What a brave bantam you are," Balmorrow chuckled, glancing over at her as she hurriedly tied her bonnet upon her curls at a most disreputable angle. "But I hardly think pistols will be necessary, Clare. We are crossing Little Biggers Heath. It will be Mad Jack chasing us, certainly. And believe me, my dear, I have no wish whatsoever to frustrate Mad Jack. "Enough, Neville," he shouted, opening the trap. "Bring us to a halt just beyond the next turning and wave off the outriders. We will stand and deliver."

Clarissa stared at him in disbelief. "But they are highwaymen! Balmorrow, they will murder us!"

"No, m'dear," he replied as their coach and the one behind them drew to a halt. "They will not murder us."

As soon as the coach wheels ceased to spin Balmorrow opened the door and swung down into the road meeting a small group of riders as they came to a halt beside the vehicle. The earl turned his back upon them, lowered the coach steps and assisted a flustered Clarissa in descending to the road.

"Damnation! What did ye think to do, Balmorrow, outrun us all the way inta Lunnon?" bellowed one of the men as he dismounted and stomped forward, a horse pistol held loosely in one hand. His face was so effectively shaded by a wide-brimmed hat and the collar of a drab surtout raised high against his stubbled cheeks, that try as she might, Clarissa knew she would never be able to describe him effectively to a magistrate.

"Well, not all the way into London. We have another three days of traveling to make London in this rig. I swear, Jack, you are daft to be chasing down coaches in broad daylight," Balmorrow drawled with a quick and telling look and a glance in Clarissa's direction. "Get yourself killed if you keep at it."

"Things been abominable slow," the man growled, his eyes coming to rest in some amazement upon Clarissa. " 'Ere now, who's the flash mort?" he asked gruffly.

Balmorrow's arm, Clarissa noticed, went immediately and protectively around her. Who on earth was this person? And why had her new husband chosen simply to stop and face him without so much as a shot fired? "I am Lady Balmorrow," Clarissa announced in the bravest voice she could muster. "And you are a villain and a thatchgallows to molest innocent people upon the public road!"

"Ssshhh, Clare," protested Balmorrow, his lips actually twitching upward into a smile.

"I will not shush," Clarissa declared, not understanding in the least why her husband should find anything at all amusing in the situation. "This person is a—a—bridle cull and I will call him such!"

The highwayman's eyes, which had widened a moment, at

once grew squinty again. He glanced at Balmorrow, then back at Clarissa, and then without another word, pushed past them and climbed into the coach while his two associates sat their mounts with pistols trained upon the travelers, the two coachmen, and the outriders who had gathered at the head of the earl's team.

Clarissa could not at all see what the highwayman was doing inside the coach. Perhaps searching for jewels hidden in some secret compartment. Well, good luck to you, she thought. The only jewels are the Balmorrow sapphires in one of my trunks on the coach behind us. And no matter what power you wield over him, Alex will not stand by and smile and allow you to take the Balmorrow sapphires. He will certainly not do that.

After the longest time, the highwayman backed clumsily out of the coach muttering to himself and spun to face the earl and Clarissa. "Gi' me yer purse," he ordered, raising his pistol to an even level with Balmorrow's nose.

Balmorrow took his arm from around Clarissa, reached into his pocket and produced a small leather bag which he tossed to the man.

"Aye, that's the ticket! An' you, lady, unbuckle that thar falderol and gi' it me. The trinket, lady, on yer wrist there. An' them thin's what's in yer ears, too."

"What?" Clarissa had completely forgotten that she wore her mother's rubies. There was a bracelet with matching ear bobs only, but— "No, most certainly not," she protested, amazed at herself for forgetting she wore them. "They are from my mother who is dead. They are all I have to remember her by."

The villain glared at her and without a word cocked the weapon that still pointed steadily at her husband's nose.

"Well, for goodness sake! Do you mean to tell me that you will shoot Alex for nothing but—but—these pieces of red glass?"

"Aye," muttered the man.

"Right here in the middle of the road?"

"Aye."

With an angry sigh, Clarissa fumbled with the clasp on her bracelet, entangling it in the buttons on her glove. But at last she got it off and placed it into the villain's outstretched hand.

"I reckon ye kin keep them whatcheemacallits in yer ears," the man grumbled, closing his fist around the rubies and removing his pistol from before Balmorrow's nose. "Wouldn't want ye ter fergit yer ma. G'day ter ye, ma'am, Balmorrow."

"Do not pout, m'dear," Balmorrow murmured once they were underway again. "I am exceedingly sorry about your bracelet, but I am exceedingly grateful you gave it up for my sake. I realize I cannot replace it, but I shall buy you a new one nonetheless."

"No, you cannot replace it," sighed Clarissa, pulling away as he attempted to place an arm once again around her shoulders.

"You are angry with me. Why?"

"No, I am not angry."

"No?"

"Well, perhaps I am. You might at least have attempted to outdistance them, Alex, if you would not fight back. You did not once protest anything. You let him take your purse and my bracelet. And you called him Jack! And—and—you smiled when I gave that miscreant a set-down. Why did you do that?"

"Because you did it so charmingly, my dear. I could see Jack was most impressed with you."

"Do you actually know this villain, Alex?"

"Oh yes. Know him quite well."

"How do you know him?" Clarissa queried, allowing Balmorrow to put an arm around her once more and pull her close.

"How? Why I—that is to say—the other two riders, they are his brothers, you know."

"No, I did not know."

"Of course you did not. Well, but they are, and the youngest only eighteen, I think, by now."

"That is very interesting," murmured Clarissa. "But it does not answer my question. How do you come to know a highwayman on a first name basis, sir? And why did you allow him to rob us?"

"Well, I did not wish to oppose him, Clare. He might well have gotten hurt. Especially had the outriders begun firing. Might have gotten himself killed."

Clarissa frowned. "And why should that worry you, sir? He is a highwayman."

"Yes," sighed Balmorrow, once again relieving her of her bonnet and then planting a kiss upon her upturned nose. "But he is my highwayman, Clare, and I do not wish to see him injured. It is a long and boring tale, my relationship with Mad Jack Docker, and not one that I have the patience to relate at the moment."

"Mad Jack Docker? *That* was Mad Jack Docker? The most notorious villain since Captain Blood? Why Malcolm and Charis and I were warned of him even before we left Newbury."

"What? Someone has heard of Jack as far south as Newbury? No, he cannot be so very notorious as all that," chuckled Balmorrow, finding his wife's wide and curious eyes most captivating and placing a soft kiss beside each of them. "You must certainly have mistaken the name. Highwaymen's names are incredibly alike, you know. Are you not tired anymore? Would you not like to nod off for a while again?"

"So you might avoid telling me about yourself and this rogue?"

Balmorrow grinned. "No, for I shall not say any more about him regardless. If and when I decide that it is something you must know, Clare, I will explain it to you. As for now, if you are not sleepy, I shall just go and sit over there and give you room to move about and look out at the scenery, shall I?"

"I can see the scenery very well, thank you," Clarissa responded quietly, hoping he would not remove his arm from around her as he had threatened. "I shall be perfectly content to simply sit as we are and watch the world go flashing by."

The world flashed by for two more nights and three more days during which Clarissa found herself the object of every kindness and consideration on Balmorrow's part. His every word, his every action, proved that he had set himself to care for her and to please her. And though he would not discuss any further his acquaintanceship with Mad Jack Docker nor say more than that he had gotten some bad fish at a dinner when Clarissa questioned him about being poisoned, he nonetheless showed himself to be delighted with her companionship and regaled her with stories of London and the people she would meet there, bringing her to laughter time and time again.

When at last Clarissa stood before the mirror in the dressing room of her chambers at Balmorrow House in Leicester Square, she could not help but wonder what sort of silly gudgeon she had been to have dreaded her marriage to Alex, to have looked upon it as a sacrifice, an offering for Malcolm's life. Oh, she had been such a fool! Whatever the reason Alex had first offered for her and however awkward their wedding had been, certainly his intentions toward her had always been noble and honorable.

I am the Countess of Balmorrow, Clarissa thought. I am *his* countess. She allowed Kate to put the final touches upon her upswept hair and then wandered down to the parlor in search of her husband. She found him gazing intently out the front window. "There you are," she said softly, her eyes betraying the happiness in her heart. "It is almost time for dinner, is it not?"

"Indeed," murmured Balmorrow, turning to welcome her. "You look grand," he added. "It is a most becoming gown."

"But it is old and not at all the thing."

"Oh? And I thought it to be just the thing. It makes you look young and innocent and—and—delectable," he added, seeing her nose wrinkle in distaste at his first two adjectives.

He offered his arm and escorted her into a most intimate chamber just off the main dining room where covers had been laid for two at a small table and a rosebud in a silver holder rested across her plate.

"How beautiful," Clarissa smiled, lifting the rosebud to her nose and inhaling the faint, sweet scent of it. "And how thoughtful of you, Alex." Her eyes surreptitiously sought his to see if he were watching as she elegantly set the rose aside. To her chagrin he was not, having turned to speak in low whispers with Jonson who butled at the townhouse because Parsons could not be spared from the Castle. Whatever it was they discussed, she thought, certainly it annoyed her husband. His broad shoulders heaved several times and he shook his dark curls vehemently. And then the both of them, butler and earl, wandered off, still conversing, down the main corridor. When, nearly five minutes later, Balmorrow returned, his scowl had completely disappeared and with a smile, he seated her personally at the table.

They were served more exquisitely at the townhouse than at the castle. Here the meal was laced with sauces and spices and most extraordinary herbs. The number of courses and the number of removes had increased. The table was ladened with side dishes. Three kinds of wine accompanied the dinner. And still, Clarissa noted, Balmorrow ate little of it. Merely a taste of this and a bite of that. When it came time for her to withdraw, Balmorrow stood and crossed to her and drew her arm through his. He escorted her to the withdrawing room, settled her into a perfectly grand wing chair with plum and cream striped cushions, and poured himself a glass of brandy from the sideboard. He had not sat alone over his brandy since they had left Larchmont Abbey and Clarissa could not help but feel wonderful because of it. She knew perfectly well that it was a time-honored tradition for the gentleman of a house to spend this time after dinner in solitude. But Balmorrow did not. Clarissa's eyes glowed with love because of it as she gazed up at him.

Balmorrow's heart lurched the merest bit when he noted that glow. He took a deep breath, turned away, sipped his brandy and turned back again. She was still looking up at him and that quite noticeable glow lingered. He studied her silently. Of course it was not the light of love that made her eyes simmer so alluringly and he was a fool to have thought it for so much as a moment. She was merely relieved that he had not turned out to be an ogre and pleased with the attentions he had so far bestowed upon her. And that is fine, he told himself with an unconscious shake of his dark curls. That is wonderful, in fact. I want her always to be pleased to be my wife.

"Clare," he said, hooking a footstool with the toe of his shoe, tugging it over beside her chair and sitting down upon it. "I am afraid I must leave you for a brief time tonight. Something has come up which must be attended to immediately."

"Oh, is that what made you scowl at Jonson so before dinner?"

"Yes. It was a summons I did not in the least wish to acknowledge. But since I have received it, I must respond to it."

"Can it not wait until morning, Alex?"

"No. It came from Carlton House."

"From the Prince?"

"Indeed. And I am afraid he will not be put off. If I do not appear within the next hour or so, he, himself, will come stomping up our front steps and banging upon our door and then there will be the devil to pay. I have sent a note 'round to Cavendish Square. My sister Maggie is in town. She will come and spend the evening with you."

Clarissa's jaw dropped a bit. "Your sister, Maggie?"

"Uh-huh."

"But I never knew you *had* a sister."

"I have two. The elder is Margaret and the younger, Michaela. But Michaela is not in town, so it will need to be Maggie. She is the Duchess of Corning now, but if I am summoned to Carlton House, so Corning will be, too, and Maggie left to diddle her thumbs. London is shy of company as yet."

"Your sister is a duchess?"

"Ummm."

"Your godmother is a duchess and your sister is a duchess?"

"Ummm."

"Is no one in your family ordinary?"

Balmorrow grinned around his brandy glass. "Me," he offered. "I am merely an earl."

"And what is Michaela?"

"A minor princess," he laughed. "Married the ruler of a tiny principality in some godforsaken place on the continent. Infinitessimal place. Barely worth noticing. But he is a pleasing gent, Archie. Makes a decent brother-in-law. 'Course, Corning does as well when he is not out of humor. You shall spend the evening with Maggie discussing whatever it is ladies discuss, eh? And I will return as soon as I can break free."

Clarissa nodded.

Standing, Balmorrow set aside his glass and bent to place a kiss upon her lips. "I shall not be very long. You have my word on it."

Clarissa could not think what to do with herself once Balmorrow had departed. She wandered about the townhouse from room to room inspecting it more thoroughly than she had done upon her arrival. At last she came to rest in the library which, she found, was filled with brightly bound volumes, some of ancient vintage, some less than a year old. They covered every conceivable subject from agriculture to philosophy to stargazing.

"There is an entire section, right there next to the window, of nothing but horrendously unacceptable novels," offered a husky voice from the doorway. "A number of them French."

Clarissa turned on the instant.

"You will excuse my being so forward, but I would not have Jonson announce me. I wanted to catch a glimpse of you while you were unaware. You are quite beautiful. Alex's note says you are his new bride. Are you?"

Clarissa's mouth opened and closed and opened again like a gasping fish.

"It truly was evil of him to marry you out of hand and not once mention to his family that he might do so. I am Maggie," added the very tall, slender woman in the doorway. "And you are Clarissa but prefer to be called Clare, or so Alex wrote."

Clarissa nodded. She could not think of a thing to say. Well, she might have thought of something to say if once she could take her eyes from Alex's sister, but she could not pry her eyes away. Were they all giants? The entire family? Maggie possessed the same dark curls, several of them softly framing her face beneath a most becoming chapeau which she was presently removing, and she had the same brilliant blue eyes as her brother and she towered over Clarissa in much the same way Balmorrow did.

"I admit I am a long Meg," smiled the Duchess of Corning engagingly, "but Corning does not care in the least. He is six foot himself and since I am merely five foot, nine inches, we match quite admirably. It did take me forever, of course, to discover him. And I was forced to dance with the most amazingly short men in the meantime. If Alex had not dragged David into Almack's one Wednesday evening, I should have grown stoop-shouldered by the end of the Season."

"I—you—I am most pleased to make your acquaintance, Your Grace," stuttered Clarissa finally. "Will you join me in the drawing room? I shall ring for tea, shall I?"

"No, I shall not join you in the drawing room nor share your tea if you refer to me so formally. I am your sister now, after all, and I am called Maggie. And besides, the drawing room is much too stuffy—we shall have our refreshments upon the ballroom balcony if you please."

"In the middle of the night?" Was this sister as mad as she had thought Alex at first to be?

Maggie, grinning, stepped forward, took Clarissa's arm and ushered her gently from the library, down the long hall, and up the staircase to the second floor. "To tell the truth," she whispered conspiratorially, "I have already told Jonson to see to our refreshments on the balcony. I expect Alex has not taken you out there as yet. He will. It is one of his favorite spots."

Clarissa noted that the ballroom doors stood wide and candles were lit throughout. Jonson must have sent footmen scurrying indeed. The pretty French doors to the outside stood open as well, and Maggie drew her through them to the balcony where a small table flanked by two chairs sat waiting. On the table stood a decanter and two glasses glittering in the flame of one remarkably pretty oil lamp fashioned in the shape of a little tea pot and decorated with glass roses. The duchess led Clarissa first to the balcony rail and pointed out to her the twinkling street lamps in the distance. "Right over there," she said, "Alex and David are busily getting disguised with the Prince and his cronies, and in that direction—do you see the little blaze of lights—lie the infamous clubs to which most wives lose their husbands of an evening. White's, Boodles, The Guards, Arthur's, and Graham's, all right there in St. James's. Watier's is in Bolton Street and not quite visible from here. But is it not a pretty picture with the lamps and the torch boys and the stars twinkling through the haze?"

Clarissa nodded. It *was* pretty. How wonderful that the townhouse balcony should face upon such a lovely scene. She gazed on it with delight then followed the duchess to the table where she took a seat in one of the chairs, the lovely scene yet visible through the widespread bars of the railings.

"I hope you do not mind that I have asked Jonson to set out brandy rather than tea," murmured the duchess, and laughed to see Clarissa give a startled jump.

"Brandy?"

"Did you never taste it, then?"

"No, never."

"You will," chuckled Maggie. "And you will like it, too. I do. It is a secret the gentlemen keep from us. Something they wish to enjoy all on their own. Gentlemen are most selfish about some things. It pays a woman to look into what they guard most dearly, for some of their secrets are wonderful!" Maggie poured the golden liquid into the glasses and demonstrated how it was to be swirled and sniffed and sipped and rolled about on one's tongue before swallowing.

Clarissa was aghast at the thought of it, but she had no wish to appear less than perfect in the eyes of her new sister-in-law, so she listened and watched attentively and then sampled the brandy before her in the acceptable manner. A sweet smile lit her face. "Oh, it is so warm and wonderful!"

"Yes," grinned Maggie. "And it makes all one's nerves settle so nicely. I always wondered why the gentlemen were drawn to it. Now, of course, I know. And I have brought with me something equally as marvelous. If you had not agreed to try the brandy, of course, I should not have mentioned these." Thereupon, the Duchess of Corning rummaged through her reticule and at length produced two small, slim cigars. "They are called cheroots and come from the Peninsula. All of the officers who have returned are smoking them. David and Alex have managed to procure some as well. They are much nicer than those great, ugly fat things and millions of times better than snuff."

"Snuff?" asked Clarissa wide-eyed. "You have tried snuff?"

"Oh, certainly. I find it disgusting myself. But these—these are heavenly." Whereupon Balmorrow's sister produced a pair of tiny silver scissors, clipped the end from one of the cheroots and putting it between her lips, lit the other end. She puffed at it and a most delicious aroma spread upon the night air. With a quiet smile she offered the scissors and the second cheroot to Clarissa who clipped one end as she'd been shown, then put that end between her lips and allowed Maggie to light the other. Clarissa inhaled and burst into coughs.

"Oh, I forgot to tell you," grinned Maggie quite as endearingly as her brother was wont to do. "You are merely to puff upon them and roll the smoke around in your mouth, not inhale the blasted stuff. It is wicked if you inhale it. Try again, carefully."

Clarissa tried again and this time managed not to strangle on the smoke. In fact, she thought, it is rather nice. And it smells so—so—dusky. It occurred to her that this was part of the smell that so pleased her about Balmorrow—not all of it, of course, but a subtle portion. "I like it," she confessed with a most innocently delighted smile. "And the brandy, too!"

They sat for a good long while gazing off into the night, smoking the cheroots Maggie had swiped from her husband's private cache and drinking Balmorrow's brandy. Maggie shared a number of hilarious stories from her own and Alex's childhood and Clarissa, feeling splendidly relaxed and uninhibited, related a story or two of her own. As the evening deepened, Clarissa was even coerced into confessing the unexpectedness of Balmorrow's offer and her anger and confusion at the oddness of her wedding and wedding night and, indeed, just what she had thought of the Earl of Balmorrow at the very first.

"But I was very, very wrong," she added as her tale reached the end. "He is not at all the great Bedlamite I thought him to be. He is—superb! I believe I am most truly falling in love with him."

"Oh," murmured the duchess quietly.

"Oh what?"

"Hmm? Oh, nothing, I just thought—" The duchess rose and went to look down over the balcony railing. "I thought I heard a carriage. David has driven the curricle as far as the mews and Alex is up beside him. We had best go down, Clare. It will not do to let them discover us out here with the brandy and cigars. We will receive them in the drawing room, shall we? Here, dearest," she added, rummaging through her reticule again and producing a snuff box filled with tiny candies. "Put two of these in your mouth and let them melt there. It will keep the gentlemen from smelling the smoke and brandy upon your breath. Most likely they will not notice anyway, you know, because they have been smoking and drinking all evening as well. But it is better not to take the chance. We do not wish them to know that we are privy to the secrets of their after-dinner indulgences."

Clarissa placed two of the candies upon her tongue as did Maggie, and then, arm in arm, they hurried from the balcony through the ballroom and down the stairs to the first floor. Giggling like naughty schoolgirls, they decided upon poses to take in the drawing room, dropped into them and prepared to act surprised when the gentlemen entered. Jonson, who himself had heard the carriage, appeared like magic and set a tea tray on the table before the ladies. "I rather think you ought to pour some, Your Grace," he murmured conspiratorially. " 'Twill augment the image you wish to display." He then hurried out amidst whoops of laughter from the duchess and giggles from Clarissa.

Chapter 7

"Clarissa, you are foxed!" Balmorrow declared vehemently once he had got her alone in her bedchamber.

"Am not," giggled Clarissa.

"Indeed you are and in front of Corning, too. And do not think he did not notice. It is extremely difficult to avoid noticing a young lady who giggles at one's every word, and more so when she insists upon kissing your ring and falls flat on her bottom while striving to do it."

"I slipped," responded Clarissa with a prim pout which twitched into a girlishly guilty smile despite her attempt to remain serious. "Anyone might slip, Alex."

"Yes? And I suppose anyone might spill an entire pot of tea upon Corning's new buff pantaloons and then giggle as she chases him about the room attempting to sop it up."

"Well, he would not stand still for a moment," Clarissa declared righteously.

"Because he did not wish you dabbing and poking and swiping at—ah—various portions of his anatomy with that silly little serviette."

"Oh, was that why he kept running away? Oh dear, and I followed him everywhere and would not desist."

"No, you definitely did not desist. And Maggie kept urging

you on, too! Of all the muttonheaded pairs of minxes! I have never, ever, seen Corning's ears so blatantly red in all my life—and the two of you continuing to harass him until his tongue tripped over every word he tried to utter and he was finally forced to seize Maggie by the arm and flee the house stuttering!"

"He w-was f-funny," giggled Clarissa.

Balmorrow turned away from her for a moment, struggling to keep himself from bursting into whoops at the thought of Corning rushing into the night, red-eared and stuttering, dragging a laughing Maggie behind him. "Which is not at all the point," he managed at last, his lips twitching upward despite his resolve not to allow them to do so.

"Oh, I know it is not at all the point," agreed Clarissa, seating herself primly upon the edge of the bed, her white muslin nightrail gathered about her. "But even you must agree that he was. Funny, I mean."

"Yes, madam, Corning was extremely humorous," replied the earl, coming to stare down at her, his knees very nearly touching her own. "And you were and are extremely disguised."

"No, am I? What does that mean, Alex? Disguised?"

"It means that you are in your cups, chirping merry. Foxed, Clare! It means that you are foxed! What have you been drinking? Certainly not the tea you spilled all over Corning."

"I—we—" Clarissa stared up at him, her eyes as big as saucers. He took a step forward. She leaned back and tumbled down upon the mattress, still staring up at him.

Balmorrow burst into laughter. "How *can* you look so innocent and be so guilty?" he chuckled, bouncing down beside her on the bed and pulling her atop him.

Clarissa snuggled happily and comfortably into his embrace and hiccoughed. She felt him shake with laughter beneath her.

"Was it wine?"

"Br-brandy."

"You drank my brandy?"

"Uh-huh. Maggie said we should. She said it was a splendid secret that you gentlemen did not wish we ladies to share. And it is splendid, too! And so are those little, puffy things."

"Little, puffy—"

"The share—share-o—?"

"My cheroots?" Balmorrow's eyebrows rose and his eyes widened, and Clarissa felt her heart beat increase at the sight of those lovely blue orbs gazing so amazedly up at her. "You drank my brandy and smoked my cheroots? You and Maggie both?"

"Uh-huh. Well, no. It was your brandy but they were the Duke of Corning's share—cher-oots. Please do not be angry, Alex. I merely wished to discover what it was that gentlemen liked so much about them."

Balmorrow rolled her gently down beside him and reaching up, grabbed a pillow and placed it beneath her head. "Cease apologizing; cease giggling; and cease to move, sweetings, until I return," he murmured in her ear, then launched himself from the bed and padded out of the room, his bare feet all but soundless on the thick carpeting. Clarissa could not imagine where he was bound. He is not angry, she told herself, relieved. If he were angry, he would not have called me sweetings and placed a pillow beneath my head. Perhaps, she thought foggily, he has gone to fetch us more brandy. Now he knows that I have drunk it, perhaps he wishes me to join him in some. Oh, but I am so weary of a sudden, she thought, closing eyes that were beginning to ache just the slightest bit.

Clarissa turned on to her side and gave the slightest lurch. For a moment she had felt as if she were falling right off the mattress and on to the floor. But that was silly. She was nowhere near the end of the mattress. Clarissa opened her eyes to check. No, of course not. She was nowhere near the end of the mattress. But—but—it was moving. The mattress was moving! Clarissa gasped and grabbed the coverlet with both hands. The room, she noticed, was moving as well. Dipping and spinning as if it were a tiny boat being tossed about on great waves. "Oh!" she squeaked quietly and closed her eyes again, tightly. It did not help in the least. She could feel the room spinning around her and it was beginning to make her very queasy. Very, very queasy—as though she were about to suffer the *mal de mer*. She had only suffered the *mal de mer* once, when Malcolm had taken her rowing in a tiny boat upon a very wavy lake. The thought sent shivers through her. She remembered how dreadful each moment had been and how she had wished to die—right there on the spot! "Oh, please, no," she murmured in a tiny voice. "Not that. I have *not* been upon any boat. I have not!"

"No, my dear," whispered Balmorrow, and Clarissa was amazed to see him there beside her. Why, she had never even noticed his return! "You have not been upon any boat but you have drunk far too much brandy to be good for you, and smoking the cheroots will not have helped either. Here, sit up like a good girl and hold tight to my arm," he urged, lowering himself to the bed beside her.

"I—I am n-not feeling j-just the thing, Alex."

"No, sweetings."

Balmorrow placed a basin in Clarissa's lap and put one arm around her slim shoulders and with his free hand, smoothed the hair from her brow. He stayed with her, soothing her and supporting her and holding the basin and emptying it and holding it and emptying it while she cast up her accounts again and again and again.

"Am I—am I going to die?" Clarissa gasped plaintively, her eyes big with nausea and fear.

"No, little one. It is simply a part of the splendid secret we gentlemen refuse to share. You will not die of brandy and cigars." When the nausea at last ceased, Balmorrow washed her face and neck and hands with a cloth soaked in cool lavender water, gave her a posset to drink and tucked her into bed.

"Close your eyes now," he whispered as he bent down to place a kiss upon her cheek. "You will feel much more the thing come morning. Only your head will ache a bit."

He extinguished the lamps and closed the door softly behind him, carried the basin down into the kitchen and then returned to his own chamber where he collapsed, chuckling upon the bed. It occurred to him that chuckling while the poor girl suffered was most unacceptable, but he could not dismiss her antics with Corning from his mind. She had been such an appealing little minx—and even more so when she had confessed to him what she and Maggie had done. Certainly it would be more proper to take her to task over the matter, but how could he cut up stiff over something he had done himself many a time? Besides, she had undoubtedly learned her lesson. She would not sneak his brandy and cigars again. "Maggie, however, needs a switch applied to her bottom," he chuckled. "Of all the unorthodox ways to welcome my wife into the family!"

Corning was of a like opinion about the unorthodoxy of such a welcome when Maggie confessed why the new Countess of Balmorrow had acted so oddly toward him, but he did not mention it to his wife. "Well, at least *you* are not totally disguised," he conceded instead with a wink in her direction as he untied his cravat. "Only a bit merry, ain't you, Mags?"

"Yes, David, I am only a bit merry. Do you like her?"

"Lord, how should I know? I have not actually met the chit yet, only the impish part of her. She is young for Balmorrow, is she not?"

"Perhaps." Maggie helped the duke out of his jacket and sat upon the bed watching as he slipped out of shoes and shirt and into a red silk kaftan and slippers.

"So, what makes you frown about her?" Corning asked quietly as he led her out into the sitting room and settled onto a sopha before the fire.

Maggie, already in her nightrail, settled comfortably against him and stared thoughtfully into the blaze. "Clare believes she is falling in love with Alex," she murmured after a brief silence, "and he with her."

"Nothing to frown about in that, Mags. She is married to him after all. I know it ain't the thing for wives and husbands to be living in each others' pockets, but thunderation, I do not see anything wrong with them being in love with each other. It would make the world a deuced sight less complicated if all married people loved the person they were married to. You would not have to be so careful about admiring a man's children for one thing."

"Oh, David? Did you slip up again?"

"Uh-huh. Ran into Lady Gresham in Picadilly. Mentioned the brat she had with her was a good deal more robust and handsome than Gilley had ever been. Meant it as a compliment, you know. 'Course when she blushed and bumbled about I saw my error. 'Twas not Gilley's brat at all."

"No," giggled Maggie. "Most of them are not. Only Lawrence, I think."

"Yes, well, but I did not remember in time. What do they call them?"

"The Chaucer Children," grinned Maggie, "because she fed Lord Gresham a Canterbury Tale about each one of them."

"Well, there you are though. If she actually loved Gilley, she would not let him be cuckolded like that, over and over again. Have they all different fathers?"

"I am sure I do not know, David. The Polite World appears to think so. Would you like me to ask Lady Gresham for you?"

"Gawd no, Maggie! Do not you dare!"

Maggie gave him a peck on the cheek and cuddled more closely, resting her head upon his shoulder. David was tall and fair and broad-shouldered, with the most lovable face and a tendency to come up adorably stiff-rumped at times. "I do love you, you know, David," she whispered, slipping her hand inside his kaftan and caressing his bare chest.

"Yes, and a regular fiend you are about it, too," he chuckled, playfully slapping at her teasing hand, "and have been from the very first. I shall never forget our wedding night, Mags. There I was attempting to remember all the things m'father had told me about how my bride would be and how I must be kind and patient and understanding, and then in you walked—not even waiting for me to come to your chamber—in that wonderfully flimsy negligee and planted the most delicious kiss upon my lips!"

"How red you turned," giggled Maggie. "Your ears looked as if they had caught on fire."

"That was not all that had caught on fire."

"No, certainly not. But I was determined to please you, David, for I loved you with all my heart. That was why I asked Alex for advice. It was he told me what I should expect of you and how to please you in return."

"Balmorrow? By thunder, I expect he picked out that negligee, too, did he not?"

"No, he did not. He did, however, suggest what it might look like. I had no mama to ask, David, and Michaela was even more innocent than I. And Madeline had been dead for two years."

The duke bestowed a chaste kiss upon the duchess' brow and marveled at the sheer beauty and boldness of his lady.

His mother had thought him nicked in the nob to wish to marry one of the Sinclairs, but his heart had ruled his head when it came to Maggie, and he was glad of it. "So tell me, Mags, why do you frown over the little countess loving your brother?" he asked.

"Because Alex loved Madeline with all his heart, David, and she did everything to crush him. He vowed he would never give his heart to any woman ever again. And he meant it, too. And Clare will suffer if she comes to love him and he does never love her back."

"Alex will treat her with understanding and goodwill no matter what, Mags. You know he will. And perhaps he will come to love her despite his determination not to do so."

"Apparently all the rumors about the Halliard fortune having dissipated were true and Clare and her brother in a great deal of trouble. Alex was duty bound to save them. I expect this marriage was the only way," Maggie sighed.

"It was," the duke nodded, smoothing a wisp of hair from Maggie's cheek, "the only way that would allow Malcolm to save face at least."

"You knew?"

"That the sister had accepted? No, I did not know that until this evening. But we did speak of it, Alex and I. Months ago."

"Well, he is on unsteady ground, my brother. He wishes to please the lady and to make the best of this marriage. Everything she told me points to that. But Clare mistakes his efforts for love. Oh, David, she knows nothing about Alex or his dreadful union with Madeline. I will lay you odds that she has not the least suspicion how much inner strength and determination Alex had to muster just to propel himself to their marriage bed. And she is a complete innocent, David, besides."

"Then it would be kind of you to let her innocence linger as long as possible, m'dear," whispered Corning. "Mayhap Alex will be drawn to it and let himself fall head over heels in love with the girl."

"Do you truly think so?"

"No, but it is not an impossibility. Lady Sarah arrived in town two days ago, by the way, and already she has been asking after Alex or so Hanger says. The Carlton House crowd were all agog, m'dear, to hear that your brother had married again, though Alex refused to describe Clarissa to them and would only say she was old Halliard's daughter."

Maggie giggled. "The gentlemen at Carlton House are worse than a pack of old spinsters."

"Indeed, gabblemongers beyond compare."

"Why were you summmoned, David?"

Corning coughed and said nothing.

Maggie pulled away from him and sat so she might look him directly in the eye. "Was it something dreadful, David? Tell me."

"It was nothing, Mags. It will be handled."

"What will be handled?" Maggie's dark blue eyes demanded an answer and Corning could not stand against their silent insistence.

"Apparently the unrest amongst laborers is accelerating, Mags. The Luddites have rioted in Leeds and Bolton and there is evidence that the nonconformists are supporting them and urging them on."

"Oh, no!"

"Yes. And the Presbyterians and Methodists and Roman Catholics and even the smaller reformist groups have increased their call for equal rights. They want the Test Act completely obliterated, Mags."

"Well, but the Test Act ought to be obliterated. It ought never to have been enacted."

"Yes, I know you feel that way. You cannot help but feel that way. You are a true daughter of the Balmorrows and you have been raised to recognize the injustice of the thing from your first breath. But the Prime Minister will not admit any injustice in it. And now that a connection between the Luddites and the nonconformists has been established, Perceval has come shouting to Prinny of sedition and conspiracy against the Crown. And he is pointing his finger, Mags, declaring that a gentleman of power necessarily stands behind and organizes the rebels."

"Alex!" Maggie gasped.

"Yes, my darling," the duke murmured, catching at her hand and pressing a kiss into her palm. "Perceval stood before us tonight in Prinny's presence and shouted Balmorrow and conspiracy in one breath."

"Alex is not a conspirator in treason!"

"I know. And so he declared to everyone present. 'Balmorrows,' he said with that insufferably smug look of his—you know the one I mean, Mags. 'Balmorrows do not sneak about in the dark of night coercing preachers and shopkeepers and laborers to fight their battles for them. Balmorrows placed two Stuarts on the throne of England with their own hands, restored a third to it as was his right and attempted to oust a Hanover all in plain sight of every English gentleman and under the glaring light of day. And when I fight for the nonconformists—as I shall continue to do—I do so before all of you upon the floor of the House of Lords. I do *not* hide in the shadows threatening revolution through the mouths of the Great Unwashed!' "

"Quite right," nodded Maggie enthusiastically. "Good for Alex! The Balmorrows have always been open and explicit about what they believe. And everyone knows so, too! That is precisely the reason that Alex appears at Court every year, to reassure the Hanovers that his loyalties have *not* been withdrawn from them as yet."

Corning chuckled and drew her back into his arms. "Proud little peagoose! And didn't it set Prinny's teeth on edge to hear that Alex intended to continue the debate over the Test Act and Catholic Emancipation in the Lords! But Prinny respects your brother for all that. And though Alex has a tendency to drive poor Prinny into apoplexy I, for one, am exceptionally grateful for the sheer audacity that has surged through every Earl of Balmorrow's veins. It is the honest and sheer brilliance of it that has kept their heads from rolling off their shoulders," he murmured, kissing Maggie's ear. "Still, your brother, Mags, has an excess of the stuff."

"Aye," giggled Maggie. "Enough for twelve Balmorrows."

"Precisely. You are not to worry. We all of us know that if Alex decided to turn against the present government he would bellow and rage about it up and down the corridors of Westminster and then stalk off to Castle Balmorrow and arm for war, most likely pulling all of the Scottish contingents out of the battle against France and carrying them with him."

"He could, you know," declared Maggie softly.

"Indeed, we all know he could. The Scots love him. But never a *secret* conspiracy, Mags. No one will believe that—

which is exactly what Prinny told Perceval in no uncertain terms. Rumors may take wing, however. You must be prepared for it. It was only last year Brummell was suspected of leaking secrets to the French."

"Yes, and that was proved a total farradiddle!"

"Exactly so." Corning bestowed a kiss upon the tip of Maggie's nose then stood and swept her up into his arms and carried her wiggling and giggling to his bedchamber.

It was well on toward three o'clock in the morning when Balmorrow, dressed in black kidskin riding breeches and a collarless cambric shirt, wearing Bluchers which were much more suitable for riding than the fashionable Hessians, a set of silver spurs, a dark cloak that hung merely to his thighs, and a low-crowned, wide-brimmed hat pulled low over his brow, closed the kitchen door quietly behind him and strode silently across the kitchen garden and into the stables. In a matter of moments he emerged leading a remarkable black of near fifteen hands and walked it slowly across the cobbles and into the street at the front of the house before he mounted and cantered out into the swirling fog and broken moonbeams of a near deserted London. He was not in a great hurry. The note he had passed to Jack inside the leather bound volume secreted inside the coach had not set a precise date, merely the meeting place and a time—at the base of London Bridge between three and five in the morning. Both men would continue to make the outing when they could until they came upon each other. It was the best way. There was no telling who might be keeping an eye upon Jack. And since this latest bombshell of a conspiracy between the Luddites and the nonconformists had finally come to light, no telling who might be keeping an eye upon Balmorrow either.

He pulled the black up once or twice to listen for following hoofbeats and gazed nonchalantly back over his shoulder after he had turned one corner or another, but as near as he could make out, he was alone as he approached the Thames. The bridge was shrouded in fog and where Balmorrow dismounted, it was barely possible to locate one's wiggling fingers before one's eyes. He tied the black's reins to a tree branch far enough from the road to keep the horse safe from discovery and made the rest of his journey on foot, coming upon the bridge abutment in virtual silence.

"Hey, Lex," hissed a voice almost in his ear.

"Jack?"

"Aye." The highwayman emerged from a bit of brush to Balmorrow's right. "I come bearing thanks from Liverpool. He was delighted with your translation of the message, though how you got all that from a list of numbers, he cannot fathom."

"Yes, well, it was not easy, Jack. Codes were much easier to translate in my father's day. It appears our stew is beginning to boil, does it not? Word of that little message has evidently reached Perceval. He stomped into Carlton House tonight and all but proclaimed me a traitor."

"You don't say?"

"I do say, Jack, and do not be laughing about it either. Prinny's entire entourage was present at the time."

"What? All of 'em?"

"All. And the only three who dared breathe during Perceval's none too subtly cast aspersions were Corning and Brummell and Prinny himself. I thought the rest would die from lack of air. Perceval was so angry that I blanched at the news myself even though it was I who deciphered the thing and sent it to Liverpool and therefore was expecting to hear it."

The man called Mad Jack Docker leaned his shoulders against the bridge abutment and chuckled. "I can see you now, Lex, turning appropriately pale and cringing with fear."

"Cringing?"

"You mean you did not cringe, Cuz? Not a bit? For effect?"

"You loon," Balmorrow grinned. "Balmorrows never cringe. And thank you, by the way, for being so vigilant upon the road. I had doubts that we would meet. I knew you would not be expecting me quite so early in the month."

"Parsons sent word to Duggan and Duggan's eldest boy rode to Seaford to tell my brothers. And they, of course, came riding like hellions to inform me. There ought to be a better way to pass messages, Lex, than for me to be continually riding down upon coaches pretending to steal peoples' purses and the like. I could very well get myself shot, you know, if I mistake and attempt to halt the wrong vehicle. I shall need to speak to Liverpool about that. Alden got here safely, by the way, but I have not been in touch with him as yet. Who was that young lady, Lex, called herself Lady Balmorrow?"

The earl smiled in the darkness. "She was Lady Balmorrow."

"No, really, who was she?"

"She was and is my wife, Jack."

"Your wife? But—but—"

"She is old Halliard's daughter. The one I spoke to you about."

"You spoke to me about her, yes," nodded Mad Jack Docker in confusion, "but you did not say a word about marrying the girl. And hellfire, Lex, the bracelet is a perfect match!"

"A perfect match to what?"

"Was it always hers? I mean, it was not just a clanker about it having come to her from her mother? She did not just receive it, say, as a—a—wedding gift?"

"No. Came to her through her mother. A perfect match to what, Jack?"

"Well, damnation! I thought it looked familiar, so last evening I went and presented myself upon The Summarfield's doorstep and begged to view the ruby necklace. Caused some lifted eyebrows, but I told a whopper about wishing to have one like it made for the duchess, for her birthday. Lex, you have gone and married the enemy! Your wife's bracelet is a perfect match to The Summarfield's necklace."

Balmorrow sighed and ran one hand through his hair, losing himself for a long period in thought. "Well," he mumbled at last, "bracelet or no bracelet, Clare is no more our enemy than Zander, Jack. She is a complete innocent. I am certain of that. And she has never been to London but once in her life and then for no more than a month or so. I doubt she would be any use as a conspirator in Newbury. I doubt there are any nonconformists in Newbury. I know there are no Luddites there. But it is puzzling that her bracelet and The Summarfield's necklace should make a set. And Clare has earrings to match as well."

Balmorrow sighed again and rested his shoulders against a tree trunk. "If the bracelet and earrings did come to Clare from her mother and they are a perfect match with The Summarfield's necklace, then the necklace once belonged to Clare's mother as well," he murmured thoughtfully.

" 'Zounds, Jack, but that's part of the answer to what happened to Halliard's fortune! Our villains somehow got themselves a hold upon that old gent. He gave them the necklace that ought to have gone to his daughter as a payment to stave them off. But it was not sufficient. Eventually, they drained him dry."

"Blackmail?"

"Indeed. I could not believe, you know, that Halliard could possibly have run through his entire fortune and then some in a space of two years. But if these villains of ours had gotten some sort of hold upon him, they might well have taken everything."

"No, he would have come to you, Lex. Halliard and your father were steadfast friends. The Sinclairs and the Beresfonts have been standing up for one another since old King Charlie lost his head on the steps at Whitehall. Halliard would have known he could depend upon you."

"Unless—unless what they held over his head was something so terrible that he dare not even attempt to shake free of them. He knew I would not let his son and daughter go under, Jack. He must have counted upon that. And so he paid whatever the fiends demanded until the very day he died."

Chapter 8

The elegance of the modiste's shop was enough to set Clarissa's heart aflutter, but the deference with which she was received by Madame de Bonnette and assisted to a lovely Louis IV chair beside a table covered with pattern books and hand-drawn designs and copies of all the best fashion magazines impressed her even more. Maggie laughed to see her new sister-in-law preen under all the attention.

"Do not get too uppity, dear sister," she whispered as Madame strolled into a back room to procure a silk just the exact shade to set off the remarkable clarity and brilliance of Lady Balmorrow's eyes. "Suzanne knows to a farthing how much blunt Alex is willing to expend to fit you out in proper style and is fawning all over you because the sum is extravagant."

"But how could she know? I do not even know. Alex simply said I was to purchase whatever pleased me."

"I expect he told her. They have known each other for ages. It was Madeline's patronage that built Suzanne's reputation and Alex's blunt that built this extraordinary establishment for her. And it is not merely the money Alex is willing to spend that will have Suzanne catering to your every wish. It increases her consequence, you know, to have the Duchess of Corning and the Countess of Balmorrow both displaying her creations."

"I expect it does," Clarissa murmured. "I had no idea that she was modiste to—to—Alex's first wife."

"Actually, she was Madeline's dresser. But she despised having to spend any time whatsoever at Castle Balmorrow and so once they were married, Madeline petitioned Alex to set Suzanne up in a little shop of her own."

"And he did so."

"Indeed. Alex would have done anything for Madeline."

It was a simple statement and quite a lovely comment upon her husband that Balmorrow had loved his first wife to such a degree as that. But Maggie's comment induced a most uneasy ache in the very pit of Clarissa's stomach. Clarissa was so amazed at the sudden feeling of distress that she fell into a pensive silence which ended only when Madame reappeared with a gorgeous emerald silk draped tenderly over her arm. "How beautiful!" Clarissa exclaimed then, pretending more excitement than she felt in an attempt to subdue the unwarranted ache. "It will make a perfect ball gown, will it not, Maggie?"

"Indeed," Maggie nodded, relief flooding through her. The sudden dimming of Clarissa's enthusiasm had not gone unnoticed. It had been an atrocious *faux pas,* Maggie had seen at once, to mention Madeline. I am not usually so muddleheaded, she thought angrily, and I will take care not to be so again. From this moment on, I will guard my tongue when it comes to anything at all concerning Alex and Madeline.

The two young matrons spent three hours and more selecting patterns and fabrics and being measured at the sumptuous little shop in Mayfair and then proceeded to spend another two hours in search of stockings, gloves, fans, slippers, bonnets, undergarments and negligees. The time flew by. The Duchess of Corning and the Countess Balmorrow laughed and giggled like school girls as they wandered through the shops, trying on this bonnet and that shawl and oohing and aahing over these stockings and those gloves. And bit by bit the two footmen Balmorrow had sent to fetch and carry for his wife and his sister grew hotter and more weary than they had ever expected to be in all their lives.

It was not until Maggie had been taken home and Balmorrow's carriage, filled to overflowing with purchases, arrived at the house in Leicester Square that Clarissa developed even one qualm about the enormous bills she had contracted in her husband's name. Had she gone mad? she wondered as she looked around her. Never in her life had she owned so many pairs of gloves—and at such a price! And most certainly she did not require fourteen pairs of silk stockings! And the slippers! She had ordered a pair of slippers to accompany each ensemble she had ordered from Madame de Bonnette. Assuredly such extravagance was uncalled for. She gulped as one of the footmen—she thought his name was Drury—assisted her to descend from the coach, and gulped again as the front door opened and Balmorrow himself stood gazing down upon her.

"Need I ask how you spent your day?" he queried as he descended the steps, put an arm around her shoulders and stared with a cocked eyebrow at the heavily-laden carriage. "There were not any shops that you and Maggie overlooked, do you think?"

"I do not think so," murmured Clarissa.

"No, neither do I. I cannot remember the last time I saw a vehicle so stuffed to overflowing. Well, let the footmen see to it. Come inside and pour my tea for me and we will have a moment or two to ourselves, eh?"

Clarissa took the arm he offered with some hesitancy. "I am certain I do not need every bit of it," she said softly as he led her up the steps and into the house. "No one actually needs six bonnets."

"Six bonnets? And each one, I expect, looks adorable upon you in its own special way."

"Y-yes. At least—that is what Maggie said."

"My sister is infallible in regard to bonnets," nodded Balmorrow, giving the pelisse and bonnet she wore into the butler's care and escorting her up the staircase to the first floor and into the small parlor where tea and cakes were just being placed upon the long, low cherrywood table before the over-stuffed sopha. He settled her upon the sopha and took a seat across from her in a large wing chair. He crossed one knee over the other and sat staring at her, a smile playing around his lips. "Why so quiet, Clare? Did you not have an enjoyable time?"

"Oh, yes," replied Clarissa, her eyes downcast as she poured his tea. "I had a wonderful time. It is just—I am so sorry," she murmured, handing him his cup.

"Sorry?" Balmorrow's eyes were beginning to sparkle with mirth. "About what, m'dear?"

"About—about—" Clarissa looked up, her own teacup in hand, to meet his amused gaze. "It is not funny!" she exclaimed with some indignation. "I shall feel a fool having to send things back to the shops!"

"What things were you thinking of sending back?" asked Balmorrow pleasantly. "The packages stowed in the boot? Or those in the carriage itself? Or those that covered the coachman's feet on the floor of the box?"

Clarissa gazed up at him, the most contrite look upon her face. He reached for a tart, popped it into his mouth, and chewed thoughtfully. The smile flickered across his face again. "How many gowns did you chose, Clare, at Madame de Bonnette's?"

"I—several."

"Several?"

"Well, there were three ball gowns, and two carriage dresses, and a riding habit—"

"I thought you despised horses. You said they were smelly."

"I—well—I was angry with you when I said that. I wished to displease you."

"I see. So you do ride?"

"I ride quite respectably though I have not done so since Malcolm sold up father's stables lock, stock, and barrel."

"I shall have to buy you a mount then."

Clarissa's eyes lit with excitement. "A horse? Truly?"

"Well, I cannot have you donning a riding habit and then strolling on foot about the park, can I? You would look a nodcock."

"Oh," sighed Clarissa, her attention suddenly refocused upon her purchases, "and an opera gown, four morning gowns, two garden dresses—"

"Enough," laughed Balmorrow.

"Yes, more than enough," nodded Clarissa. "I cannot think what got into me. I have cost you a fortune. But I shall send word to Madame to cancel most of the gowns immediately and I shall see that the falderols are returned. I promise, Alex."

"No such thing," Balmorrow said, rising and placing his empty cup upon the silver tray. "I want you to be all the rage, Clare, provided, of course, you do not send me to the ten-percenters along the way. And you will not, for I shall warn you well in advance of that event." He held out his hands to her and tugged her to her feet. "Your packages ought to be in your chambers by now. Come and show me what treasures you have acquired."

All of Clarissa's qualms over her purchases, all of her guilt over the amount of money she had spent upon herself dissipated within the next half-hour as she displayed her purchases to her new husband. She had never guessed that a gentleman would be at all interested in his wife's wardrobe. She was amazed at the laughter and delight that bubbled from him as she unwrapped first one package and then the next and posed before him in her new finery.

Balmorrow adjusted her jockey cap at a most rakish angle, teased her into plying each of her fans most flirtatiously at him. Then he helped her to tie the strings of the blue silk bonnet with the cream rucking beneath her chin and nibbled at her ear. And when he placed the luscious Kashmir shawl of deep reds and golds and blues about her shoulders, he bent to tickle at the nape of her neck with his tongue. He urged her to sit before her dressing table and knelt before her, tickling her feet playfully as he slid first one pair of stockings and then another onto them. His every word, his every touch, the very glint of appreciation in his eyes and each provoking tilt of an eyebrow induced a breathlessness in her, brought a warm flush to her body, and made her pulses race.

Why, he is attempting to seduce me! she thought suddenly. How very odd!

Just as Charis had not adequately informed her of the wonder and enchantment of the marriage bed, so she had failed to mention that a husband might entice his wife and tempt her and seduce her through such marvelous teasings and attentions as these.

How odd that Charis should not mention it!

"What are you thinking of so seriously, little one?" Balmorrow murmured, his arms coming gently around her as she stood before her looking glass. "Are you dreaming of how beautiful you will look in Madame de Bonnette's creations?"

"Beautiful? Me? But I am not, Alex. I am merely passably pretty."

"No, do you think so?"

"Yes. My eyes are plain old green."

"Wide, and clear, and fine, with a most dangerous gleam to them."

"And my hair is reddish and ugly and has no style to it at all."

"A burst of flame flickering about your smooth, unblemished brow and dangling temptingly," he chuckled, pulling the pins from her hair, "down across your silken shoulders."

"And my nose is abominably short."

"Impertinent," he amended, and turning her to face him, bestowed a tender kiss upon that offending appendage.

"You *are* attempting to seduce me!" Clarissa exclaimed despite her every intention not to let him know of her surprise.

"Yes, indeed," grinned Balmorrow. "I wondered how long it would take for you to tip to it." He swept her up into his arms and carried her, her heart fluttering wildly, into her bedchamber and deposited her in the middle of her bed.

"But, Alex, it is the middle of the day!"

"A much more exciting time for love than the dead of night."

"But the servants."

"The very reason for locks upon the *inside* of chamber doors," he grinned, moving to throw the bolt upon Clarissa's.

"But, Alex—"

Balmorrow turned to look down upon her and one eyebrow cocked questioningly. "Am I mistaken? Do you wish me to go away and cease plaguing you?"

"Oh, no!" Clarissa's hands fluttered excitedly in the air as she sat upon the bed. "I just did not—Alex, are you certain it is the thing for a husband to dally with his wife in the very middle of the afternoon? Are you not expected to be at one of your clubs or—or—wherever it is gentlemen go?"

Lady Sarah Summarfield glared at Miss Gonnering in angry disbelief. "Surely you are mistaken, Aunt Grace. Lord Balmorrow married? And to a little nobody? What a banger someone has told you!"

"It is truth, dearest. I had it from his cousin, the Bishop of Leeds, who married them at Castle Balmorrow less than a fortnight ago."

"Preposterous! Alex would never—"

"To hear the bishop tell it, it was a hasty affair. Married the gel with a special license and no one but his children and her family in attendance. But they are properly wed nonetheless, Sarah, and you must resign yourself to the fact."

"Resign myself? I should say not! There is something havey-cavey in it. Why, Clarissa Beresfont was only on the town for a month before her father died. And most certainly Alex never made her acquaintance."

The Summarfield began to pace her drawing room, her hands clasping and unclasping angrily at her breast. Her guinea gold curls glimmered in the afternoon sunlight that flowed through the mullioned windows, and her changeable hazel eyes simmered with outrage. "He will be at the Hoggs' soiree this evening if he is, indeed, in town. He would not think to miss it. I shall confront him and get directly to the bottom of this appalling news. Surely there is something, some reason, that he gets the bishop to set this absurd story about!"

Miss Grace Gonnering, a rotund lady of near sixty years, with gold-gray hair and eyes of a hazel as bewitching and changeable as her niece's, decided against further discussion. Obviously Sarah was not in the mood to accept the sad news. And it was sad, Grace thought, picking up her embroidery and setting a fine stitch along the leaf of a rosebud. Sad because her niece had come very close to disgracing herself last Season to gain Lord Balmorrow's attention and now had lost him entirely.

Sarah had flung herself at that gentleman from the very moment that she had come out of black gloves for Summarfield. She had chased Lord Balmorrow from one entertainment to another, constantly dangling upon his arm, forever clinging to him like an ivy vine. And now he had gone and married someone else. Well, it served Sarah right. Grace had warned her time and again that her constant plaguing of Lord Balmorrow could give him nothing but a disgust of her. The man was a widower after all, with children to whom his next wife must needs be a stepmother. And he would seek for them an exemplary woman of good, substantial character, not a hoyden who flashed her wares about as though she were some prize at a local fair.

Still, it was odd. Miss Gonnering sighed as she selected a deep red silk for the bud of the rose. Why would the wealthy and powerful Earl of Balmorrow wed a virtually unknown young woman when he had his choice of all the ladies on the marriage mart? Perhaps Sarah was correct. Perhaps there was something havey-cavey about it.

"If he truly is married to this—this—person," muttered Lady Sarah into the silent room, "you may lay odds upon it that Alex's heart is not engaged."

"It makes no never mind," Miss Gonnering replied. "If he is married, he is married, and there is an end to it."

"No, never!"

"Sarah!" Miss Grace Gonnering's hazel eyes widened considerably above her chubby cheeks. "You would not even think to—to—form a—a—misalliance with the man?"

"This marriage of his is the misalliance, Aunt Grace, and I shall not let it keep me from him."

"But, my dear—"

"No, I want to hear nothing further on the subject until I hear directly from Alex's own lips exactly what that chit did to force him into such a travesty. For you may place a wager upon it, Aunt Grace, he was entrapped."

Lady Sarah's anger had brought a flush to her lovely heart-shaped face and a fire to her eyes and even her Aunt Grace could not deny that the effect was stunning. One look at her niece in such an aroused state and, married or not, Lord Balmorrow would be hard put to resist the young lady. Miss Gonnering only prayed that the earl would not offer Sarah a slip on the shoulder, for she was not at all confident that Sarah would scorn the position of Balmorrow's mistress. "You realize, of course, that you must do nothing exceptional at the Hoggs, Sarah. If Lord Balmorrow appears with his wife, you must be everything that is polite to him and gracious to the young lady."

Lady Sarah glared at her aunt, but nodded abruptly. "If you will pardon me, Aunt," she said, turning on her heel, "I think I shall go up to my chamber and decide what to wear this evening. You, I collect, will wear your best gray touille?"

"Indeed," nodded Miss Gonnering with a sad little sigh. What else was there for her to wear? For going about in Society, Miss Gonnering possessed only an ugly gown of putrid brown dimity, another of staid black bombazine, a rather faded lavender brocade that was ages old and the grey touille that had seen two summers even before Mr. Summarfield had succumbed to the fever. It was the dream of Miss Gonnering's life to consign them all to the flames and to have instead an evening dress of bottle green taffeta with carmine piping and a small, just a very tiny, flounce at the front—and perhaps a matching turban.

But that was by far too much to expect and well Miss Gonnering knew it. Mr. Summarfield had been a fine gentleman and kind to her for all the five years that she had lived with him and Sarah, but the gentleman had cut up very cold. And though Sarah had somehow contrived in the past year to bring some monies into the establishment, still, a person could not actually expect her niece to spend what little she had upon a new gown for a poor relation—not when there was food to be purchased and coals and the house to be kept in repair. Why Sarah could not even support a competent staff.

"At first I could not imagine it happening," murmured Clarissa sleepily as she snuggled in Balmorrow's arms. "But I have come to love you, Alex. You are the most wonderful husband."

Balmorrow kissed the top of her head and then, sighing, rested his own head against the headboard of the bed.

"You are supposed to say 'I love you' back, Alex."

"No, am I?"

"Indeed."

"I can see we need to have a discussion, my dear. I knew

we would. I only hoped to postpone it until—well—for a while longer at least."

"A discussion?"

"Yes." He kissed the top of her head again and again leaned back. "You do not love me, Clare. And I don't love you either."

"What?" Clarissa sat straight up with a start and turned to face him with a most amazed look upon her face.

Balmorrow's gaze wandered lazily from her eyes to her lips to the tiny pulse at the base of her throat.

"You—you do not love me?" Clarissa stuttered disbelievingly.

"No, sweetings, and you do not love me either," he responded, raising his gaze to meet hers and trailing one finger along the edge of her ear. "You merely think you do. It is a most unaccountable phenomenon. It happens with most females. They invariably mistake passion, desire, and extreme lust for love."

"They do not!" protested Clarissa, slapping his finger away. "I mean, I do not!"

"Shhh, not so loudly, Clare. I can hear you perfectly well. I am not clear across the house, you know."

"No, but you are gone far away somewhere in your mind and your brain has become all turned about and ruckety."

"Ruckety? Do you mean rackety, perhaps?" Balmorrow grinned.

"How can you say that I do not love you? How can you? Did I not just give myself to you body and soul?"

"No, not truly. You only think you did."

Clarissa opened her mouth to protest vehemently, but his great clump of a hand covered her lips. "Listen to me, Clare. I do not love you and you do not love me. We have known each other less than a fortnight. We cannot possibly love each other. Love is more than pretty words and soft touches and a lusty roll between the sheets."

"Well, of course it is!" Clarissa exclaimed, having finally disposed of his hand by biting his middle finger. "I am not such a peagoose as to think that! I love you, Alex St. John Sinclair, with every inch of my being."

"Less than two weeks ago you were frightened of me and detested me, too."

"I was not. I did not."

"Yes, you were and you did. And perhaps now you will detest me again—which is perfectly all right. I do not mind if you detest me from time to time, Clare. Sometimes I do and say perfectly detestable things."

"Is there someone else owns your heart?" Clarissa mumbled, staring downward, avoiding his studious gaze. "Is that why you do not love me?"

Balmorrow tilted her chin upward and stared for what seemed an eternity into her eyes. His very touch sent a warmth surging through her and the place where his finger rested beneath her chin blazed. Clarissa could feel tears rising and attempted to blink them back, but they would not be refused and overflowed. He brushed some of them aside with one gentle finger. "No, do not cry, Clare," he whispered, drawing her into his arms and stroking her back. "There is no other woman owns my heart. There is no other woman wishes to own it."

"Th-there is not?" she asked, pulling away.

"No, sweetings. There are a plethora of belles who wish to own *me*—because they long to be the Countess Balmorrow—but I doubt any one of them has designs upon my heart. And now that you are the Countess Balmorrow they will all abandon the chase. Mine is a stubborn, thorny heart at best, Clare, and not a very great prize. Even Madeline did not care to possess it."

"M-Madeline? But she was your wife. She bore your children. You would do a-anything for Madeline. M-Maggie told me so. Surely she possessed your heart and held it precious."

Balmorrow drew Clarissa to him again and wrapped his arms tightly around her, so tightly that she could barely breathe. He cradled her against his chest and rubbed his chin softly across the top of her head. For a very long moment he was silent and Clarissa could feel the steady beat of his heart.

"I loved Madeline with all my heart and soul," he breathed at last. "There was a time I would have soared up into the sky and gathered all the stars in heaven to adorn the sheer wonder of her if only she had cared to have me do so. But she did not care to have me do so. No, and she did not care to have my love either, or to possess my heart, though I was not keen enough to know it then.

"I did never intend to make you so sad, sweetings," he sighed, kissing her ear with a whisper. "I only meant to be plain with you about our relationship because it is the very worst thing in the world to imagine love where it does not exist. I know that to be true. It is because you are an innocent, Clare, and I the gentleman who introduced you to intimacies and pleasures and passions you have never imagined. That is the reason you think you are in love with me. That is all it is, and it will pass."

"It will not pass."

"Well, perhaps not. Perhaps someday you will grow to love me and I will grow to love you as well."

"I love you now, you—you—great clunch!" Clarissa's tears had ceased to flow and she freed herself from his grasp with an energetic tug. Turning to face him, she studied the doubt written across his face with wonder. "Oh, you are such a lack-wit, Alex! How can you have grown so very old and not know when you have engaged a woman's heart?"

Balmorrow shrugged his shoulders. "Perhaps because I have never done so before? And I am not so very old," he mumbled with a charming pout. "I know you think me ancient, Countess Balmorrow, but I am merely thirty and in the very prime of my life. But if the time should come, Clare," he added, his hands reaching for her and caressing the soft skin of her upper arms, "that you discover yourself in love with a gentleman more your own age—you must only be kind enough to tell me, eh? And I shall help you to be—most discreet—about the matter."

Clarissa could not believe her ears. She opened her mouth to protest that her heart was his and her love was true and she would never be so ramshackle as to form a tendre for any man but her husband, but he stopped her saying a word by placing his lips upon hers and drinking in her very soul.

"Enough," he said when he pulled back, leaving her breathless, her whole body aching for him. "We are to attend a soiree tonight at Lord Hogg's. You will like Artemus and Diana. They are Zander's godparents."

"This is not the time to change the subject, Alex."

"It is precisely the time. Lord and Lady Hogg will be delighted to make your acquaintance, I assure you."

"But I have nothing at all to wear," protested Clarissa,

frustrated, as he rose from the bed. "Not one of my gowns will be ready until next week at the soonest."

"You have an entire armoire full of gowns that we brought with us from the castle."

"But they are all so—so—"

"Old?"

"Childish."

"No, do not say so. Even that pale gold with the puffed sleeves and the white bow?"

"Well—"

"It is quite pretty, Clare. Honestly. And besides, I have bought you something to wear with it." Balmorrow reached beneath one of the pillows on the bed. It was obvious to Clarissa that he had stowed the thing there well before she had returned from her own shopping. Had he been so certain, then, that they would end the afternoon in her bedchamber? "For you, Lady Balmorrow," he said, placing a long, slender black velvet case in her hands.

She opened it slowly and cried out. On a bed of white satin lay a brilliant emerald and diamond pendant set in gold filigree and suspended from a wide braided gold chain. Beside it sparkled matching eardrops. "Oh!" Clarissa gasped. "Oh! Oh! Alex! They are the most beautiful things I have ever seen!"

"To replace the rubies that Mad Jack had the audacity to confiscate," he said, brushing a strand of hair behind her ear. "You will accompany me to the Hoggs tonight, will you not? Even if you must wear the gold muslin?"

"Yes," Clarissa replied, noting the anxious look in his great blue eyes and reaching up to stroke his cheek tenderly. "Of course I will accompany you. And I will do so whether you buy me presents or not. I am your wife, Alex. I will accompany you anywhere you wish."

And I will prove to you, somehow, that I do love you, you great Bedlamite, she added silently as the grin she had come to hold most dear flashed into view. And I shall make you come to see that you love me as well. You may lay odds upon that, Alexander St. John Sinclair!

Chapter 9

The Hoggs' soiree proved to be a sad crush; there was barely room to turn around without stepping on someone's toes. Clarissa was astounded at the number of fashionable gentlemen and richly gowned ladies who surrounded her, filling the air with their senseless chatter. Though she had been to any number of entertainments in that one month of her only Season, she had never been thrown into the midst of such a tremendous gathering as this.

"It will be in all of the papers tomorrow," Maggie announced, tugging Clarissa's arm possessively through hers and leading her sister-in-law across the crowded drawing room and through the wide open pocket doors into the adjoining chamber where there was a bit more air blowing in through the open windows. "The less room to stand, sit, or fall over in a fit of the vapors, the more successful the party. *The Times* will hail it as a triumph. Diana is already in alt. Of course, a good deal of the success is due to you, my dear."

"To me?" Clarissa could not believe she had heard correctly.

"Yes, indeed. Word has got 'round, you see, that Alex has taken a bride and most of these people have come to see just what sort of a bride he has taken."

"Stuff," replied Clarissa a bit breathlessly. "Why they could not even be certain that we would attend."

"Alex always attends. Every year. So does David. They are great friends of Lord Hogg and do their best to pander to Lady Hogg's every whim—so that when hunting season arrives, she will not oppose Lord Hogg's inviting them to the estate. The Hoggs live in the midst of Quorn country. It is some of the best hunting to be had," she added as she noticed the puzzled look upon Clarissa's face. "Your father did not hunt, I gather."

"No. That is, I do not think so. He went for visits now and again, but he never mentioned hunting."

"No, well, Alex loves to hunt and will most likely drag you off at the first invitation to do so."

"He will not expect me to—to—ride to hounds?"

Maggie chuckled and shook her head. "No, he will not expect that. It is not a pastime designed for ladies and most of the gentlemen frown upon a woman joining the chase."

"What chase?" Balmorrow asked, drawing up beside them.

"I was explaining about you and David and how you both toad-eat Lady Hogg because of the hunt."

"Oh. Well, I would not refer to it as toad-eating exactly."

"You would not?"

"No. Allowing her to walk all over us and stomp our faces into the ground if she so desires is not toad-eating, Maggie. It is extreme desperation. The day I am not invited to hunt with the Belvoir and Cottesmore packs is the day I shall most likely place a loaded pistol to my head and pull the trigger. Oh, damnation," he added on a small groan.

"What?" Maggie and Clarissa looked at him in wonder, but only for a moment.

"Double damnation," muttered Maggie, following Balmorrow's gaze.

"Alex! Alex!" called a husky voice, and Clarissa watched as one of the most beautiful women she had ever seen came hurrying through the crowded drawing room toward them, a path parting before her with her every step. In a matter of moments she was upon them, or rather upon Balmorrow, for she had hurled herself at him and thrown both arms about his neck. Although he was forced to catch her, Balmorrow lowered her immediately to the floor where she stood quickly upon her toes and pressed her pretty bow-shaped lips up against the earl's with a resounding smack.

"Sarah, please," Clarissa heard her husband mumble in a most harassed tone. "This is neither the time nor the place."

"But Alex, I have missed you exceedingly," protested the incredibly gorgeous blonde, with a charming giggle. "You have been at that dreadful castle for ever so long. I thought you might never return to London."

Clarissa noticed that Balmorrow's ears were tinged with just the slightest red as he reached up to untangle the beauty's fingers from the curls at the nape of his neck. "Stop it," he hissed. "You are acting the hoyden."

"But I am a hoyden," smiled Lady Sarah flirtatiously, releasing him from her grasp and taking both his hands in hers instead. "It is one of the things you like most about me, my lord, my disdain for propriety." She turned her back into him and drew his arms around her. "Good evening, Your Grace," she said, dismissing Maggie with a brief nod. "And is this your new wife, Alex? You must introduce us immediately. I know I shall like her. She looks a most beguiling little chick. I am Lady Sarah," she added, drawing Balmorrow's arms more tightly beneath breasts which had been threatening without that added pressure to come bursting right out of the meagre bodice of her gown. "And you are Miss Halliard—no, Miss Beresfont."

"No. Lady Balmorrow." Balmorrow's voice rumbled like distant thunder as he disengaged himself from Sarah's grasp and stood glowering down at the back of her head.

"Oh, but of course! How stupid of me!" exclaimed Sarah. She made a slight curtsy and smiled charmingly at Clarissa. "A slip of the tongue merely. It will be difficult for all of us to grow accustomed to Lord Balmorrow's new state, I vow. He has been the gay, romantic widower for so very long. La," she giggled, retrieving the gilt edged fan that hung from her wrist and snapping it open to play it before her pink and white porcelain face, "we did none of us expect Alex to return to us leg-shackled! What a remarkable huntress you must be, my dear."

"I hear music," Balmorrow growled, bending to whisper in Lady Sarah's ear but his words audible to Clarissa as well. "Come dance with me, Sarah, for old time's sake, eh?" And he spun the lady gently around, placed her arm through his own, and without so much as a backward glance led her out into the corridor.

"Well, of all the—" Clarissa choked out angrily, but was stopped from completing the sentence by Maggie who caught her wrist in a grip of iron and tugged her away into a far corner of the room.

"Sit down here and catch your breath, do. And attempt to look less like a cat about to spit," Maggie hissed, urging Clarissa into a chair behind a large potted rhododendron.

"Of all the—" began Clarissa again.

"No, do not say a word. Just sit still and calm yourself. You are reacting exactly as she wishes and everyone is watching you do so. Even David!" she added with a glare over her shoulder. "I have no doubt there are bets written in White's betting book about the outcome of this encounter, and most of the money will be riding upon that—unscrupulous jade—to win him back!"

"W-win him back?"

"Yes, win him back. All last Season the betting ran that she would be the next Lady Balmorrow."

"Oh," muttered Clarissa, her hands balled into fists in her lap. "Oh, no. She—he—"

"Do not make a cake of yourself over it," Maggie sputtered. "She is nothing but a trollop despite her antecedents and she stood not the least chance of capturing my brother. He might well bed The Summarfield, but he would never make her stepmother to his children."

"B-bed her? Maggie, is she—are they—"

"I have not the least idea. Alex is devilish discreet about his affairs. He does not go flaunting his ladybirds on his arm all over town. But that deuced ace of spades has been after him ever since Summarfield stuck his spoon in the wall. Summarfield was still warm in his grave when she set her hooks for Alex."

"Ace of spades?"

"Oh my goodness, I am so angry I am speaking in cant! It merely means that she is a widow, my dear. That is all."

"A widow—and a most beautiful and alluring widow, too. And he has gone off to dance with her." Clarissa's anger faded as rapidly as it had flared. Her fists unclenched and the flush upon her face was replaced by a peculiar paleness. "And why not," she murmured soulfully, "when his wife is virtually a child and his mistress is so—so—voluptuous and sophisticated."

"Oh, pooh," Maggie grumbled. "You refine too much upon the thing. He took her off to dance simply to diffuse the situation. Alex married you, my dear, not Sarah Summarfield. And you must not call her his mistress. It is not at all the thing for a gentleman's wife to take any notice at all of such things. And besides, no one actually knows that Sarah and Alex—that they—I personally think that it is all a load of cow dung."

"But many widows have *affaires* with gentlemen, do they not?"

"Some," admitted Maggie grudgingly, "but you would do best to ignore her, Clare, whether she and Alex are having an *affaire* or not. Wait right here and I shall bring you some lemonade and when you are sufficiently composed we will rejoin the party." Maggie stalked off, her own perturbation apparent in the authority with which she cleared a path for herself through the crowd and the manner in which she ignored all attempts to draw her into conversation along the way. Honestly, she had thought Alex had given The Summarfield her *congé* months ago. Obviously, he had not.

Clarissa's hand went to the emerald pendant and she clasped it thoughtfully. Was Sarah Summarfield her husband's mistress? Did Alex love her? But no, he had told her only this afternoon that his heart belonged to no lady. Had he lied? Did he love Sarah Summarfield? But if he loved Sarah Summarfield, why had he offered for—? It made not the least bit of sense. Certainly no eyebrows would have been raised had he married the widow of Mr. Summarfield. A good many people, it seemed, had expected him to do just that.

"I should not allow The Summarfield's presence to disrupt your evening," murmured a low voice.

Clarissa looked up to discover a fair-haired gentleman dressed to the nines in white satin breeches, clocked stockings, a waistcoat embroidered with silver hummingbirds, and a deep blue jacket of Bath Superfine gazing down at her with compassionate brown eyes.

"She is not worth the merest wrinkle upon your brow,

m'dear. It is obvious to those of us who know him well that Lex finds you delightful and The Summarfield a dead bore."

"It—it is?"

"Indeed."

"How?"

"How?"

"Yes, how is it obvious?"

The gentleman's lips curved upward in a wry smile. "It is the light in his eyes, my lady, when he looks upon you."

"The light in his eyes?"

"Indeed. You have not yet learned to read Lex's eyes, have you? They are amazing really. They speak volumes and he cannot still them. If you need to know the truth, you must only search those great blue orbs of his and you will find it." The gentleman looked about him and shrugging, grinned. "I expect Mags will return, but lord knows when. May I introduce myself, do you think?"

Clarissa nodded.

"I am your new cousin, John, Viscount Norris."

"Cousin?"

"On the Sinclair side, through my mother. Perhaps second cousin or cousin once removed. We have never sat down and sorted through it actually. When we were children, it was enough just to be cousins. Still is, in fact."

His brown eyes twinkled most charmingly and Clarissa could not help but think him quite handsome. He was, she thought, near Alex in age and though somewhat shorter than her husband, still possessed of broad shoulders and a pleasing form. And, she thought, he reminds me greatly of Edward, Lord Parkhurst.

"Oh no, go away, John," Maggie laughed as she approached the two and placed a glass of lemonade into Clarissa's hand. "I have no intention of protecting Clare from you this evening. If you must maneuver your way into her heart, you must pick another time to do so. And you, dearest sister-in-law, must not speak another word to this rogue until Alex is at your side."

"Poppycock," grinned Norris. "Alex will be more than pleased to have his wife and myself cry friends."

* * *

"You do not truly love that child, do you, Balmorrow?" Lady Sarah asked with a pretty pout designed to steal gentlemen's hearts away. "No, of course you do not. Her family has entrapped you somehow and forced you to marry the chit."

Balmorrow nodded as he swirled her across the floor in a waltz.

"I knew it!" Lady Sarah cried. "I knew that must be the case! Why no one has ever heard of the girl before and suddenly she appears on the town as the Countess of Balmorrow."

"She not only appears as the Countess of Balmorrow, Sarah m'dear. She *is* the Countess of Balmorrow, and you would do well to remember it."

"But surely there is some way—some means by which you may be rid of her."

"I expect there are any number of ways I may be rid of her," replied Balmorrow, his well-placed hand drawing the lady closer to himself than was acceptable. "I might poison her, for instance." His deep blue eyes caught and held Lady Sarah's hazel ones.

"Alex, you are incorrigible," the lady giggled uneasily. "You know perfectly well that *that* was an accident. Simply a case of the fish having gone bad."

"So you have maintained from the first," nodded Balmorrow, an odd light in his eyes. "But I, of course, having been the only victim, find it difficult to accept that no one else suffered any ill effects."

"Alex," gasped Lady Sarah, as the music came to an end, "you do not truly believe that someone in my household *intended* to poison you? You are only teasing me about it, are you not? I could have died right there on the spot when it happened."

"You mistake, madam. *I* could have died right there on the spot when it happened. You, my dear, were simply a bit inconvenienced. I shall cease teasing you about it in a year or two, Sarah. I cannot promise to stop before that. Now, come take a stroll with me upon the balcony."

Lady Sarah plied her fan wistfully. "Should you not be getting back to your wife, Alex? We will raise innumerable eyebrows if we stroll off to the balcony together and she is nowhere to be seen."

"I assumed when you pounced upon me in the midst of the throng that you wished to raise some eyebrows, sweetings. Did I misread your intent?"

"N-no. I expect not. I was—it—oh, Alex, how could you have married her? You have broken my heart."

"Come outside with me and I will mend it again," smiled Balmorrow as he placed her hand upon his arm and escorted her toward the wide open doors leading to the Hoggs' balcony.

Lady Sarah had been correct in her estimation of the crowd. Their exit onto the balcony did raise innumerable eyebrows and in addition set a great many tongues to wagging. So many, in fact, that by the time Clarissa, accompanied by the Duke and Duchess of Corning and Viscount Norris, found her way into the ballroom, nearly everyone was discussing Balmorrow's abandonment of his new bride in favor of his old flame. It was the new countess' entrance, the moment it was noticed, that sent a resounding silence over the entire company.

The musicians, who had taken a short break, returned with haste to their instruments and struck up a tune, but not before the unnatural hush had aroused Clarissa's suspicions and Maggie's hackles. Tugging Clarissa by the arm, Maggie strolled up to a group of ladies and inquired sweetly what great piece of gossip she had missed by being absent from the ballroom. "For nothing of import is being discussed in the drawing rooms, my dears," she said with a threatening frown. "You have all met Lady Balmorrow, have you not? Good. Then kindly include us in your gabblemongering for we do not wish to be behind hand with the latest tidbit. It concerns Lady Balmorrow, I collect, or me or perhaps Corning? Doubtless it is not Norris for he is seldom fodder for the mill."

"Oh, it is nothing," offered Lady Sheffield with a nervous giggle.

"It is something," glared Maggie. "An entire room seldom falls silent when I enter it. Speak, Adrianna, or I shall cut you from my invitation list."

"You would not!" cried Lady Sheffield as the women around her shuffled apprehensively. "Maggie, I am your very best friend."

"Yes, and if you wish to remain so, you will cease speaking behind my back and do so to my face."

"But it has nothing at all to do with you."

"Oh, no, certainly not," agreed several of the other ladies.

"I see. Then it has to do with whom? Corning? or Lady Balmorrow?"

"It is merely that Lord Balmorrow—that he—"

"That he what?" asked Clarissa, freeing herself from Maggie's grasp and placing her hands upon her hips.

"That he has taken Lady Sarah out onto the balcony," squeaked a young lady in dampened muslin.

"Helena, do be quiet," glared her mother. "None of this is any of our business."

"No, it most certainly is not your business," declared Clarissa roundly. "Nor is it mine, nor Maggie's. If my husband wishes to spend a few moments alone with an old friend, it is no one's business but his own."

Maggie's jaw felt very much like dropping, but she would not allow it to do so.

"Surely," Clarissa continued, her emerald eyes sparking dangerously, "if my lord wishes to bid Lady Sarah farewell somewhere far from prying eyes, he may do so with impunity. Our marriage has come as a great shock to that poor woman. She possessed certain expectations of my husband from what I gather. Undoubtedly there will be tears on her part. He does not wish her to shed them before all the world and no one can possibly fault him for that!" Clarissa stalked away from the group and took a seat upon one of the chairs on the far side of the ballroom. "I shall kill him," she mumbled, as Maggie spun down into the chair beside her. "Balmorrow is a dead man."

"Oh, but you put up such a fine defense on his behalf," whispered Maggie. "I was fairly well amazed."

"I am not some simpering milk-and-water miss," muttered Clarissa from behind a waving fan. "Did you think I would faint dead away to hear that Alex had gone off into the dark with his paramour?"

"Sssh! Clare, we have not the least proof that she is his paramour. It is merely speculation."

"Everyone's speculation! But I will not be pitied by a roomful of strangers and I tell you that for a fact!"

Norris and Corning strolled up before the two ladies and invited them to join the set that was just forming, Corning leading Clarissa to the floor and Norris partnering his cousin, Maggie. Within a few moments a smile was back upon Clarissa's face. Though her thoughts were never far from what might be occurring on that infamous balcony, she could not resist the Duke of Corning's gentle goodwill nor Viscount Norris' laughter. It was not, in fact, until she and her new brother-in-law were coming down the line together toward the end of the dance that her smile faded into a thoughtful frown.

"What is it, m'dear?" Corning asked. "I have not trod upon your toe?"

"What? Oh, no, Your Grace."

Corning's gaze followed the direction of Clarissa's and discovered Balmorrow, one shoulder propped against a wall, arms crossed over his chest, watching their every step. "Wishing *he* had claimed you for a partner," the duke murmured in her ear with a smile.

"No, do you think so?"

"Yes, and he is also giving thanks that you are dancing with me and not Jack."

"Why?"

"Because Jack can charm the heart right out of any member of the female persuasion," chuckled Corning, "and well Alex knows it, too. I would hesitate to let Jack partner Maggie, let me tell you, except that I know Mags is the one woman invulnerable to his nonsense. They spent almost every summer together when they were youngsters and Maggie knows every one of the gentleman's advances by heart. She even recited them to me once when I was jealous. That was before we were married of course."

The dance separated them then and Clarissa had to wait impatiently for the duke to return to her before she could broach the question that had popped immediately to mind. "Do gentlemen not get jealous after they are married?" she asked immediately he linked arms with her.

"Eh? What, m'dear?"

"Do gentlemen not get jealous after they are married?"

"Well, some do and some do not. I do not," replied Corning with a rather smug look upon his slightly flushed countenance. "I am positive Maggie's heart belongs entirely to me."

"How do you know?" Clarissa asked.

"How?"

"Yes, does she tell you and you believe her, or is it something else?"

Corning's face flushed a bit more and the tips of his ears tinged with color. "I—I—" The duke was saved from further explanation by the last step of the last figure of the dance and the fact that Balmorrow strolled out on to the floor to escort his bride back to the sidelines upon his own arm. "I must apologize for The Summarfield's astounding display of bad taste," he mumbled.

"And your own?" replied Clarissa through tight lips.

"My own?"

"When I entered the ballroom, my lord, everyone was gossiping about how you had led Lady Sarah out onto the balcony. You did not come back for a prodigious long time."

"I did not? I thought I returned rather quickly." His incredibly blue eyes looked down upon her with pure innocence. "Would you care for some refreshment, sweetings? You and I and David and Maggie will make up a table, eh?"

"And Lord Norris."

"Jack? I had not the least idea Jack was in attendance."

"Oh, no," replied Clarissa with the merest hint of agitation. "You merely stood glaring at him the whole time he danced with your sister."

"Did not. I was glaring at you and Corning. At least—I was not glaring. I was merely observing. Why would I glare? Come along, my dear, and we will raid Artie's sideboard. Corning, gather up Mags and Jack and join us in the refreshment room, eh?"

"He has not the least interest in the chit, Aunt Grace," twittered Sarah excitedly into Miss Gonnering's ear as she adjusted the plunging bodice of her gown before the looking glass in the ladies' retiring room. "He was forced into marrying her. He as much as said so."

"*Did* he say so?" asked Miss Gonnering in a carefully lowered tone so as to keep the conversation from the ears of several other ladies present.

"Well, not in so many words, of course. But he—his every action proved beyond doubt that theirs is not a love match."

"His every action? Sarah, what on earth did you allow him to do on that confounded balcony?" gasped Miss Gonnering.

"Merely kiss me," shrugged Lady Sarah. "But he is such an inordinately good kisser!" She giggled and turned to face her aunt. "Lord Balmorrow is still mine," she declared in an excited whisper. "I have nothing to fear from that child who has managed to sink her claws into him. I am the lady Lord Balmorrow dotes upon, and my wishes will rule him, not that silly chit's wishes. Why after a month or so he will send her off to that dreadful castle of his and we will never see the witch in London again."

Miss Gonnering gulped. Her pudgy cheeks jiggled with excitement. "Sarah, you cannot mean—you have not—you do not intend to become Lord Balmorrow's—"

"Perhaps. Do not scowl so, Aunt. It is not in the least unheard of for a married man whose wife remains in the country to form an alliance with another woman in town. Why, I can name countless such alliances and all of them accepted by the *ton,* too!"

"Sarah, you cannot do it!"

"I can if I must. And I will if it becomes necessary."

"Necessary? But how can it possibly become necessary? Sarah, my dear, you are a lovely woman and there are any number of gentlemen would be pleased to dangle after you and marry you quite properly if you would but give them the least bit of encouragement. It is not as if you were in love with Lord Balmorrow. You are not in love with him, are you, Sarah? You have not lost your heart to that gentleman?"

"Oh, of course not," hissed Sarah, grasping her aunt by the arm and leading her from the room which was becoming inordinately crowded. "And it is not his title nor his fortune nor his consequence that I care for either. Aunt Grace, please do not work yourself up into a tizzy. It is quite likely that within a month or two I shall have no need of Lord Balmorrow whatsoever. But at present, I must be seen to dangle upon his sleeve, which I will do, be he wived or be he not."

"You are completely mad," muttered Miss Gonnering. "Summarfield's death has sent you completely 'round the bend."

Chapter 10

"Damnation, Clare, you have got it wrong!" Balmorrow had stalked into her chambers, sent Kate scurrying off and now paced about the small boudoir avoiding the least flicker of an eyelid toward where Clarissa sat, scowling, upon the small bench before her vanity. "The Summarfield is not my paramour. I do not have a paramour. And if you do not believe me, you may ask Maggie."

"Maggie says that you are devilish discreet about your *affaires.*"

"A pox on Maggie! And what do you know about *affaires* at any rate? A veritable innocent like yourself?"

"I know that gentlemen have them!" Clarissa exclaimed vehemently. "And everyone thinks that you are having one with Lady Sarah. Because of it, I am become an object of their pity!"

"Well, I am not having an *affaire* with The Summarfield!"

"Do you swear so?"

Balmorrow's pacing came to a halt.

"Do you? Do you swear on your honor?" Clarissa spun around to stare upward into his eyes. "Do you, Alex?"

"Yes," growled Balmorrow in a low, angry tone. "I swear on my honor. Are you satisfied now?"

"No!"

"Botheration! Clare, you are being impossible!"

"No, *you* are impossible!"

"Me?"

"Indeed. If Lady Sarah is not your paramour, why does she act as though she is and why did you lead her off to waltz and then escort her onto that balcony? Did you not think for one moment that everyone would take note?"

"Of course I knew that everyone would take note."

"But you did so regardless!"

"Yes."

"Why?"

"Sweetings," Balmorrow's tone grew soft and he came to her, kneeling before the little bench and taking her resisting hands into his own. "I desire certain people to think that Sarah and I have an understanding between us."

"You what?" Clarissa snatched her hands from his, rose and dodged adroitly around him and into her bedchamber, slamming the door behind her. Of all the addlepated, audacious boors! How dare he! He *desired* people to think that Lady Sarah was his paramour? Why? Did Lady Sarah inflate his consequence in some unique manner? Well, if it was so very important for people to think of him and Sarah Summarfield together, why had he not married the woman? Tears started to Clarissa's eyes. She was so very angry and confused as well. All the way home Balmorrow had sat across from her in silence. She wished now with all her heart that his silence had continued. Every word he had said since then had made the situation more and more unbearable. Clarissa threw herself across the bed and began to punch the pillows and the counterpane as hard as she could. Tears streamed down her cheeks and heat and heartache prickled her face, turning it red and puffy.

Balmorrow rose from his knees and began pacing again. The little gudgeon is jealous, he thought. Jealous! Of me and The Summarfield! Madeline would never have been jealous. I could have set up any number of ladybirds and Maddy would not have said a word. Any one of a hundred public courtesans might have clung to me and plied me with sweet attentions and Madeline would never have blinked an eyelash.

But then, Maddy did not love me, he told himself. She

merely pretended to love me until the vows had been taken and then reveled in being the Countess of Balmorrow and looked upon me as a mere necessity to that end.

Still, she was a decent wife, he reminded himself. She gave me Brandy and Zander and did not begrudge me either one of them—at least she did not overtly begrudge me. And it was not her fault that she could not love me. No, and it was not her fault that I loved her and was so bitterly disappointed when things came clear to me.

"A pox on love!" he muttered. "It is nothing but a path that leads direct to Hades!" And a pox on Clare, too, he added silently. If she did love me instead of merely imagining it, she would take me at my word and not doubt me.

Balmorrow's brow puckered in confusion. Maddy had always taken him at his word and had not loved him. Was he mistaken in what he thought love to be? Perhaps Clarissa did love him. Perhaps women loved differently from men. No, that was absurd. If someone loved you, they trusted in you and stood beside you no matter what the cost to themselves. And they were certainly not so insecure as to rail over a slight flirtation. Balmorrow sighed and came to a halt before Clarissa's bedchamber door.

Why was he suddenly so damnably concerned with love? Little over a month ago, when he had been struggling over marriage settlements, devising the means to rescue Malcolm and Clarissa from penury, no thought of love had entered into it. And it need not enter into it now. His actions this evening, despite his opinion that they should not have done so, had embarrassed Clare and set her to sobbing. All without knowing, he had been a brute. And if he were to have any peace of mind at all, he must make things right with her. He turned the china knob and was relieved to find that she had not thrown the lock against him.

"Go away," Clarissa sobbed as she felt him sit down upon the bed beside her. But Balmorrow did not go away. Instead she felt his hand gently stroke her back. "Go away!" she sobbed more fiercely. "If you do not go away, I shall hit you!"

"You will?"

"Y-yes!"

"With what?"

Clarissa turned over upon the bed and stared up at him.

"With what? What on earth difference does it make with what?" she asked sitting up and swiping at her tears with the sleeve of her nightgown.

Balmorrow immediately placed a linen handkerchief at her disposal and gazed around the room thoughtfully as she made use of it. "Well, it must be something solid and heavy enough to hurt me," he murmured. "If you only use your fists, I will not even know I have been hit. You might use that water pitcher. It will make me bleed, of course, when it shatters. But then I expect you would take great joy in spilling my blood, no?"

"No," hiccoughed Clarissa. "I d-don't want to sp-spill your blood."

"Oh, well, then perhaps the candlestick. That is solid brass. One good blow to my jaw and I shall go down like a dead man. Probably crack my jawbone, of course, but then, you do intend for me to suffer."

"I do not wish to crack your jawbone," gulped Clarissa as Balmorrow's fingers brushed her wet, sweaty hair back from her face.

"You do not? Well, I suppose it will need to be the coal bucket then. If you bring it down upon the back of my head, I guarantee I shall fall, dazed, at your feet. Of course, then you must either step over and around me until I recover my senses, or send for Mackelry and Jonson to carry me off to my own chamber."

Clarissa stared at him agog. "I do not at all wish to make you lose your senses, Alex."

"No? You do not wish to make me bleed, nor break my jaw, nor lose my senses? You did say you wished to hit me, Clare. And a person does not hit another person unless they intend to do them some damage. Precisely what kind of damage did you have in mind?"

"I—I—" Clarissa swiped at one last tear that lingered at the corner of her eye and sniffed. "I do not wish to do you any damage."

"No? Well, I expect we can dispense with the hitting part then. Clare, I am most heartily sorry that I upset you. Believe me, I did not at all intend to embarrass you. It did never occur to me that you would give a fig whether I wandered off with The Summarfield or not."

"Why—why would I not give a—a—fig?"

"Well, because it ain't fashionable for married people to live in each other's pockets. Husbands and wives generally do go their separate ways at parties."

"But n-not generally out onto dark balconies with—with alluring members of the opposite sex."

"Well, no, not generally. But you see, I had to do that. Sarah Summarfield is—well, she is very important to me."

"You *love* her."

"No, no, no! I *need* her. Clare, listen to me very carefully. I am *not* having an *affaire* with The Summarfield. But I must continue to lead her on as long as is necessary because without her I am quite likely to lose my head."

"Lose your head?"

"Yes, sweetings. Lose my head—have it separated from my body by aid of an axe and a chopping block."

"Alex, what are you saying?"

"I am saying that if I am found guilty of subversive and treasonable acts—"

Clarissa's mouth dropped open. "You? Alex, no! You are not—you would not plot rebellion against your King!"

"No, most certainly not now, my dear, when the war against Napoleon is going so well."

"Alex!"

"No, Clare," Balmorrow chuckled. "I would not. But there are some who believe I would. And others who hope to make it appear as if I do."

"But how? Why?"

"Well," sighed Balmorrow, "the how is very complicated, but the why of it is easy enough. You see, Clare, not one Earl of Balmorrow has ever been renowned for his—ah—complacent membership in the fold of the British aristocracy."

"Not one?"

"No. Balmorrows have been very indiscreet over the centuries. One or another of them fought for Charles I, helped to restore Charles II, argued in defense of James and the Catholics, attempted to dislodge the Hanovers and place Bonnie Prince Charlie upon the English throne. And not very long ago, my own father took up against Farmer George in Parliament and argued in favor of giving the American colonists their independence. He pressed for passage of the Roman Catholic Relief Act as well, my papa."

"You are—Catholic?" asked Clare, aghast.

"Do not look quite so horrified, sweetings. Certainly I am not Catholic. I should not have near as much power as I wield at the moment if I were. Actually, most of the Sinclairs are quite likely Presbyterians by now. But they are yet in Scotland. The land of the Balmorrows became English, my dear, by virtue of treaty and the whimsy of the River Tweed sometime during the reign of James the First. And when The Balmorrow at that time accepted James' alteration of the Scots title to an English one, he also chose to become Anglican. I expect it seemed more important to him to hold a powerful voice in Lords where one might work to bring about change than to lose all power by quibbling over religion. It seems that way to me. We Earls of Balmorrow have always been a very pragmatic lot."

Clarissa's discomposure over Balmorrow's brief escapade with Lady Sarah was fast falling from her mind. "But you are not a rebel like your ancestors, are you Alex?"

Balmorrow's eyes twinkled. "I am," he whispered conspiratorially, "a radical. When I speak what I believe on the floor of the House of Lords, Clare, all of Westminster Palace shakes and the rumblings are always heard clear to Carlton House. One of the very first things I did when I took my seat, and one of the things I am proudest of, too, was to help push The Act of Union through the English and Irish Parliaments. That did not prove to be the answer to the problem, of course, only a first step. I must continue to speak out for the obliteration of the Test Acts and for Roman Catholic Emancipation."

Clarissa was at a loss. Certainly her education was grievously lacking. "I do not understand," she murmured. "I confess, I know little of what you speak."

"Well, never mind then. Maddy did never understand it either. I expect it is only girls like Maggie and Michaela and Brandilynn, whose fathers are likely to get them killed over it, who are taught about laws and loyalties and causes."

"I shall learn," declared Clarissa with a worried frown. "Your wife shall stand beside you in these things."

"Yes, well, I would appreciate that, but you need not worry overly much. I am not so very deep in the briars. It is merely that there are rumors of a plot by the nonconformists to bring themselves into power and already the Prime Minister's finger is pointing at me."

"Oh, Alex, no!"

"Yes. I can see myself being set up to take the fall if their planned rebellion fails, but I do not know by whom. Sarah Summarfield is involved in it."

"Oh, no!"

"And that, my dear, is why I am obliged to cultivate The Summarfield. You must not take anything I say or do with Lady Sarah to heart. She is someone's cat's paw, doing whatever she is told. But I must discover whose cat's paw she is."

"But why would she allow herself to be used in such a way?"

"To save herself from penury, my dear. Summarfield cut up cold. She had to find some way to support herself and the little Miss Gonnering. I am the way. As long as she appears to hold my attention and is able to report my thoughts and pry particular secrets from me, she and Miss Gonnering are taken care of."

"Oh!" Clarissa stared at her husband with open mouth and wide eyes.

"I must discover who is at the bottom of this conspiracy and put an end to it, Clare. At the moment, my relationship with Lady Sarah provides me the only hope to do so."

"And what must I do?" Clarissa asked breathlessly. "How may I help, Alex?"

Balmorrow looked down at the eager little face and chuckled. "Why, you must pretend to be my wife."

"I *am* your wife."

"No, really?" He twirled one of her long curls about his finger and grinned down at her. "Prove it," he whispered huskily.

On Monday morning a number of packages arrived upon the Countess of Balmorrow's doorstep from Madame de Bonnette's little shop in Mayfair and all Clarissa's anxiety over Balmorrow, though it did not disappear, was submerged in the excitement of touille and muslin and cherry-striped satin. All of the gowns, of course, were not completed, but the three that had arrived had necessarily to be tried on and posed in and waltzed about the sitting room. Clarissa could not recall when she had felt so completely beautiful. Her looking glass reflected the image of a highly fashionable young matron, and she could not twirl far from it but she must turn back to reassure herself that she indeed appeared as she imagined herself to appear. Alex would be entranced with her. And if, as he so stubbornly held, he did not love her, well, the sight of her in these dresses would at the very least urge him to the very brink of love.

And then I shall kiss him and hug him and tease him and tip him right over the edge, Clarissa thought with a smile. For I do love him, despite what he says, and he will love me, too. I vow he will.

"Oh, my lady," sighed Kate, helping her to change from one gown into the next. "Ye'll be all the rage!"

"Do you think so, Kate?"

"Yes, my lady, an' his lordship will be overcome at the sight of you!"

Though Balmorrow, much to Clarissa's disappointment, did manage to keep from being completely overcome, he nevertheless drew up a chair in Clarissa's dressing room when he returned from Tattersall's and demanded to be shown just what his blunt had bought. He pronounced each of the gowns "just the thing," gave Clarissa's cheek a kiss when the show of fashions had ended, and then led her out to the stable to introduce her to a most exceptional gray filly with a white blaze and two white stockings. "Her name is Windsong," he drawled, his arm protectively around Clarissa's shoulders. "You may change it if you wish. She is merely three and will adjust to another name easily."

"Oh, no. It is a lovely name."

"I thought so when I gave it to her, but I am a bit fey when it comes to naming horses."

"You named her?"

"Indeed. Three minutes after she was breeched. Born at the castle, she was. But I sold her to Lord Clarendon when she was a yearling. When I heard he had stock for sale at Tat's I had hoped Windsong might be among them. I was at *point non plus* when she was not."

"She was not among them? Then how—?"

"I took Clarendon aside and admitted I had to have her back—at any price. He, of course, was pleased to oblige."

"For goodness sake," Clarissa replied as Windsong nudged at her shoulder, "at any price? I am not an outstanding horsewoman, Alex. You might have settled for any hack."

"Any hack? I think not. Besides, I—she—well, she has the same spark and determination in her eyes that you do yourself. I thought of her immediately when I laid eyes upon you. You share a rare and special look and are meant for each other."

"Our eyes have the same spark and determination?" Clarissa stared up at him amazed. "My eyes and a horse's, Alex?"

"Um-hmm. And she is a sweet-goer as well. And once we go back north you will enjoy her even more. We can ride the Likely Run together, you and I. It is beautiful in the summer and autumn—and in the winter and the spring, too," he added as he turned and led her from the stables. "There is nowhere as lovely and mysterious in all of England as the Land of the Balmorrows and at last I will have someone to share it with."

"Certainly you share it now with Brandilynn and Zander."

"Only a bit. They are too young, Clare, to ride out along the Likely Run and through the forests and up into the hills. It is not a place for children. Which makes me think—I need to visit my cousin Alden this evening, but would you like to put your new morning dress on display tomorrow? We can pay a visit to the Tower. I have not been there since I was a boy and I should like to see it again. And I shall ask Maggie and Corning to join us, eh? We will make a day of it."

Alden Sinclair, Bishop of Leeds, settled into his chair with a glass of brandy in one hand and stared down into the fire. Equally as large and intimidating as his cousin, he possessed an enormous amount of power as well. But he was highly uncertain at this point whether his power—even combined with Alex's—would serve to protect Balmorrow from the insidious rumors and suspicions that had begun to permeate the Court and Parliament. Even Canterbury was aware of them and had flown up into the boughs, demanding that Leeds exercise some control over his outspoken cousin—preferably lock him up in one of the Castle Balmorrow towers—until the war on the continent had ended and the discontent at home could be dealt with adequately. Alden had sought to dismiss the rumors as groundless and Canterbury's fears as groundless as well, but the Archbishop of Canterbury was not one to be got 'round lightly. He wielded substantial power of his own and unless Alden could discover some way to placate him, Alex's goose would be thoroughly cooked.

"Not to mention my own," he muttered gruffly.

"Your own what?"

Alden's gaze went quickly to the door. "Alex? What? Have all my staff deserted me?"

"No, I just told Bennington I was expected. He trusts me to find my own way, you know. May I come in?"

"You are already in, Alex. Pour yourself a brandy and join me over here."

Balmorrow did exactly that. "What were you muttering about, Alden, when I strolled in?"

"Cooked geese, Alex—you and I and Jack as well."

"No, not Jack. He will come off with not a whisper against him. And no one will blame you, Alden, of any involvement if only you cut ties with me immediately if I am taken up."

"The devil I will!"

"I know, but you truly ought to do so. Of course, we are going to stop the thing before it occurs, so I shall not be taken up at all, so it does not bear thinking about. I take it Canterbury is aware of the plotting?"

"And thinks you are at the root of it. He ordered me to take you in hand."

"Fat chance of that."

"Yes, but he does not know it, Lex. The Court of St. James is boiling, by the way, and like to erupt. And you know in which direction their venom will flow. Now that we have given Liverpool evidence of the collusion between the nonconformists and the Luddites, can we not call a halt?"

"Soon. But not yet. We have got to see it through to the end, Alden. It is not enough to know the threat. We need to discover who stands at the bottom of the thing and to put an end to it. Besides, it is a fine adventure, is it not?"

"Yes," sighed Alden, taking a sip of his brandy. "But we are not halflings any longer, Lex. You and I and Jack have a great deal to lose if we should fail in this. Never mind that

Liverpool knows the truth. Who is to say that Liverpool can protect us from anyone—or that he will?"

Balmorrow's brow puckered in thought. "Do you wish to withdraw, Alden? I had not considered, but you are a bishop now and if we were to fail why— Perhaps there is another way. A way in which Jack and I can succeed without you."

"Devil a bit! I am only wishing for the thing to come to an end soon and the three of us to be victorious, Lex. I am not about to pull out of it."

"Did you discover anything to the point at Canterbury's?"

"Merely a list of names. I doubt it is anything important but the seal was recognizable so—"

"You snabbled it!"

"I wish you would not use precisely that term," grinned Alden.

"You did, though, did you not?" rejoiced Balmorrow, his eyes gleaming with triumph. "I knew you would, Alden! You are the best of all cousins!"

"Well, there are not many cousins who would rob the Archbishop of Canterbury for a featherwit like you," laughed Alden. "But, like it or not, I appear to be one of them. Happened that I needed the back of something to make notes upon and searched about his clerk's desk until I found it. Canterbury thought me a blazing lunatic for refusing to accept a clean sheet. But I only said, as I pawed through paper after paper, that it was my parsimonious Scottish blood, and he smiled and let me search. It is stowed in my Book of Prayers. A fitting place, I think. I shall give it to you in a moment or two, but first you have things to tell me."

"I have?"

"Indeed. If you think that I intend to let you run off without being told the truth about this hasty marriage of yours, you are incredibly mistaken, Coz. You do intend to remain married to the girl, do you not? It is not all some harum-scarum plot to get her to accept your support and then abandon her? I am not going to be entreated to help bring a bill of annulment before Parliament, am I? Because I will not do it, you know. You are well and legally hitched to that little filly."

* * *

"But I do not in the least understand," protested Clarissa, staring down at the list of names before her. "We know none of these people. And yet here is Malcolm's name and mine as plain as can be. Oh, and Lord Parkhurst!"

"Do you know Lord Parkhurst well? He was the one kissed you in a garden somewhere. Was it a true kiss, Clare? Or catch as catch can?"

Clarissa stared up at her husband in surprise. He had remembered her one mention of Edward. He had remembered both name and circumstance. And she had thought at the time that he had not even been truly listening to her. "He—we—I thought at one time, before my father died, that Edward would offer for me."

"But he did not."

"No, he could not, Alex. He could not afford to marry a young woman of no means."

"I see. And you have no idea why he and your brother and yourself should be included upon a list along with all of these other people?"

"No. I have never heard of—oh! here is Lady Sarah's name!"

"Yes. Do you at all recognize the seal on the thing, Clare? Might you have seen it before?"

"This—this has something to do with the nonconformists and the riots, has it not?" asked Clarissa excitedly, studying the partially destroyed seal. "It—it looks oddly like a bell, do not you think?"

"No, a bell? Do you really think so? I thought perhaps a candleholder or a vase of some kind, but that makes no sense."

"Well, perhaps I am looking at it upside down."

"Or perhaps I have been," mused Balmorrow, eagerly leaning down over Clarissa's shoulder. "Yes, I see what you mean. It could be a bell from this angle."

The very nearness of him as he lounged over her staring at the damaged seal made Clarissa's heart leap and increased the burning in the pit of her stomach. Never had she expected that the very proximity of a gentleman could light such a fire within her. Even Edward, Lord Parkhurst, when he had taken her into his arms for that one swift kiss had not aroused her to such a degree as her husband did merely by standing over her in such an easy fashion. Oh, most certainly Alex was mistaken. What stirred within her at this moment was neither desire nor passion nor lust. It was love.

True, she could not account for it exactly—how it had come to be and in so brief a time—but it was love nonetheless and the day would come when she would convince her husband of it. "It does have to do with the plot against you, does it not?" she whispered up at him, her green eyes deadly serious.

"We think the man at the bottom of the thing—we think he uses that seal. I have seen it on documents at The Summarfield's and it has appeared on certain papers we have been able to liberate from known agitators. The last paper we liberated mentioned the Archbishop of Canterbury's clerk, so Alden requested an audience with Canterbury concerning his wayward cousin—me—in order to see if he could discover anything about the clerk's desk with the same seal upon it." Balmorrow shrugged. "It may all turn out to be a wild goose chase in the end. As a crest it belongs to no one."

"It is some secret sign, then," murmured Clarissa, noticing a most rapid fluttering of wings in her stomach as Balmorrow's arms came down beside her own and his smooth-shaven cheek brushed against hers. He was staring at the paper, of course, and taking not the least notice of how the alignment of his body with her own was affecting her. He was deadly serious as he gazed at the list of names. Clarissa held her breath as his cheek brushed against hers again. And then he was gone, pacing about the study with long strides, his hands behind his back, his head lowered.

"Who are we?" she asked, turning in the chair to watch him as he paced.

"Hmmm?"

"You said 'we. We think.' Who are we?"

"Just me and my cousin Alden, and—"

"And?"

"Ah, no one. Just myself and Alden."

"You fear to confide in me?"

Balmorrow's head came up swiftly. "No. It is merely that

the fewer who know of the third person involved, the safer he will be. And he must remain safe, Clare, for if I am sacrificed in this thing, Alden will not hold his tongue and his head will roll right behind mine and—and Jack will needs be your saviour."

"Jack?"

"Yes, but it is of no moment now, Clare, for I am not about to go down as yet. I have no intention to go down at all."

"Jack who?"

"You do not wish to know."

"Yes, Alex, I do wish to know. Who am I to turn to if you and your cousin Alden are—are—?"

"Arrested, m'dear, is the word. Taken up. Gaoled. And you have already met the gentleman, so he will come to you and not the other way 'round."

Clarissa's eyes lit with a most determined fire. "You do *not* trust me," she declared in a low growl. "First you do not love me and now you do not trust me. What sort of marriage is it we are to have, Balmorrow? One based upon shared premises and nothing more?"

"Mad Jack Docker," Balmorrow said, taking her hands into his own and tugging her up into his arms. "If the need should arise—which it will not, mind you—you are to await the appearance upon our doorstep of Mad Jack Docker. And even though you did not see his face well at all, you will recognize him, Clare, because he will present you with your ruby bracelet to identify himself."

Chapter 11

Clarissa, her eyes sparkling with excitement, stood in the bow of Corning's yacht as it made its way up the Thames toward the Tower. "I did never know one could sail to it, Alex!" she exclaimed excitedly. "Alex? Alex?"

Balmorrow, his uncovered curls blowing in the wind, his hands thrust deep into the pockets of his breeches, stood silently beside her and stared straight ahead. His deep blue eyes sober, his fine, seductively-drawn lips formed into a hard, tight line, he appeared not to have heard a word she had said.

"Alex," Clarissa cried more loudly, taking his arm and giving it a tug. "Are you all right? What is it? Are you getting the *mal de mer?*"

"No, I am fine, my dear," he replied after a long moment. "What was it you said?"

"That I did never realize one could sail to the Tower."

"They were accustomed to take a barge."

"Who were?"

"The traitors. Ahead of us there, where we will land, is known as the Traitor's Gate. I cannot help but wonder if this is not Corning's subtle way of pointing out to me my presently perilous position. But of course it is not. Corning would never think to be so subtle."

"His Grace knows you are suspected of treason?"

"Indeed. His Grace was one of many present at Carlton House that evening when Perceval had the gall to bellow out that I was involved in the thing. It is more than likely that Maggie knows about it as well. Corning is defenseless against her. She discovers from him his every secret."

"Do the two of them know about Lady Sarah, do you think?"

Balmorrow's lips twitched up into a smile. "The Summarfield? No. I am certain not. Last Season the entire *ton* knew her to be my flirt and betting was heavy that I would step into the parson's mousetrap with The Summarfield this Season. Maggie went so far as to warn me against it. You are the only other person knows of the game I play with Sarah—Oh, and—"

"And?"

"My cousin Alden, but he may be trusted to keep mum on the subject, and Mad Jack, of course."

"Again the highwayman? Alex, are you certain the man is so very trustworthy? How can you know?"

"I have not the least doubt of him."

They disembarked at the bottom of the stairs, Corning lifting Maggie gingerly to the quay and Balmorrow offering a hand to Clarissa.

"Where to then?" Corning inquired.

"The Lion Tower!" replied Maggie enthusiastically.

"And the jewel house," requested Clarissa. "I have never seen the crown jewels. I have heard that one may see them if you give someone a penny."

"She is an old crone," laughed Corning. "And though it once took only pence, now she wishes to have her palm crossed with silver."

"The Lion Tower first then," grinned Balmorrow, "for it is not a pleasant smelling place once the heat of the afternoon hits it. And then the jewels."

"Not fond of animals?" Balmorrow asked Clarissa in a quiet whisper as they stood behind a spellbound Maggie considering the lion.

"It is very big for a cat, is it not?" Clarissa replied, wishing it were appropriate behavior to hold her nose. The animals were cared for as well as possible, but the need to keep them confined and the heavy humidity of the air did nothing to improve the smell of the place.

Balmorrow chuckled at the look upon her face. "Fond of animals," he concluded, nodding. "Not fond of the smell. It was you, no, who complained about horses being smelly? Yes, indeed it was. Maggie, Corning, come away. I think Clare has had enough of the lion for a time."

"Whew, myself as well," nodded Corning. "About to expire. Mags, come, out into the fresh air."

Maggie laughed and took his arm. "Very well," she agreed. "I just love to watch it, is all. On to the jewels, gentlemen?"

"Oh, Alex," sighed Clarissa, slipping her arm through his as she stared at the royal trappings of state, "how wonderful it must be to be a queen!"

"Fond of jewels, are you?" Balmorrow asked. "Have to get you some, I expect. But not any like these. Nor any of the Balmorrow cache—except the sapphires. Everyone will expect you to wear the sapphires at Court. Tradition, you know. But you would look like a troll in fancy dress if you wore any of the rest of them."

Clarissa squeaked at the exact moment that Balmorrow's hand went to cover his lips and his ears reddened. "Wh-what I meant to say," he gulped, stepping away from the look in Clarissa's eyes, "was that you are much too delicate for such enormous gems, sweetings."

Clarissa thought she would burst into whoops at the mortification on Balmorrow's countenance but she forced herself to keep a perfectly straight face.

"Actually," drawled Corning, attempting to rescue his brother-in-law, "these tidbits are more in Maggie's style. Your beauty, my dear Clare, is the tender beauty of the budding rose. These geegaws were meant for more full-blown blossoms."

Maggie's eyes sparkled mischievously at Clarissa. "So I am a full-blown blossom, am I, David? Tell me, have the beetles begun dining upon my petals yet?"

The Duke of Corning's ears turned quite the same shade of red as Balmorrow's.

"I think that you and Alex had best withdraw from this topic before Clare and I push you both straight out of a window," drawled Maggie in fine imitation of a bored Corinthian.

But Corning caught the teasing glint in her eyes and his laughter echoed about the room drawing a number of questioning glances from the other visitors. Balmorrow, induced by Clarissa's sudden grin and Corning's overt glee, lost all embarrassment and laughed as well. "I believe you are correct, Maggie," he chuckled. "This is definitely an instance when retreat is the answer. Let us please abandon the field, Corning." His kidskin-gloved hand took Clare's and he strolled with her from the room, Maggie and Corning close behind. They descended the narrow stone steps in merry conversation.

"Where else shall we go?" asked Clarissa over her shoulder as she and Balmorrow reached the bottom of the stairs. "Your Grace? Is there something in particular you should like to see?"

"Wakefield Tower, if Balmorrow don't mind."

"Oh," sighed Maggie. "I am not at all certain, David. It is an old ruin. And damp and dingy besides. And the stairs are wretchedly pitted."

"Are you making excuses for me, Maggie?" asked Balmorrow quietly. "I am not afraid if you are not. Have you never wished to see the place?"

"Yes, but it will bring back memories of Papa and Grandpapa and—"

Balmorrow shrugged and raised an eyebrow. "We will not go if you object, Mags, but I will not mind."

"Are you certain, Alex? It is you who see the ghosts."

Clarissa's ears fairly perked at the statement. "Ghosts?"

"Yes," nodded Corning. "Do not tell me that you have not yet discovered it, m'dear? Balmorrow sees ghosts."

Clarissa gave a tentative grin, but she read Maggie's partially-hooded gaze with accuracy. This great hulk of a man she had married seriously believed in ghosts! And she could tell that the Duke of Corning, though he joked at the moment, was somewhat loath to add fuel to Balmorrow's imagination.

"Bosh," declared Balmorrow abruptly. "I may see them, but I am not afraid of any of 'em. And I should like to see where Papa was detained, Mags. Wakefield Tower it shall be." Balmorrow's hand went snugly against Clarissa's waist and he guided her to Wakefield, held a brief conversation with one of the warders and then escorted her up the narrow steps with the Duke and Duchess of Corning close on their heels. They peered in at one floor after another until they reached the top of the tower and Balmorrow strode into the first chamber and gazed about him, something very close to wonder in his eyes.

"Was Papa truly confined in this dismal place? How devastating it must have been for him," Maggie murmured.

"Uh-huh," agreed the earl, wandering about the room which had been divided into two by a partial brick wall and a wide arch.

"Of course, it was not quite so old as it is now," Maggie offered, watching flickers of awe, anguish, and anger rise and fall upon her brother's countenance.

"And I expect it was not so damp and moldy as this then," Corning added, running one finger against a wall and grimacing at the chalky, wet substance that came off upon his glove.

"Why you can look straight down into the Thames from here!" Clarissa exclaimed, taking up a position before a long, narrow slit in the wall. "That is exactly where we landed, is it not?"

Balmorrow came to stand behind her, placing his strong hands upon her shoulders, and stared down through the window. "There are men's bones beneath those waters," he whispered. "Almost my father's bones joined them. Ghosts," he added hoarsely, "are everywhere here."

Clarissa thought her heart would break at the sound of his voice. She turned and put her arms around him and rose on tiptoe to bestow a tender kiss upon his pale cheek. "But your father did not join them, my dear," she murmured, giving him the tightest, most consoling hug she had ever given anyone. "Your papa and your grandpapa were freed and sent home to their family, were they not? Most certainly they must have been."

"Yes," he answered, pulling back and looking down into her eyes. "And it was your grandfather who brought the thing off. Did you not know it was your grandfather who saved them?" he asked as disbelief flew to Clarissa's eyes. "Your grandfather, my dear, roused the noblemen and the gentry of southern England and threatened old Hanover with even greater rebellion than he had already seen if my father and grandfather were not set free. He promised that not only all of Scotland would rise against the King, but that every self-respecting gentleman in the south of England would rise as well if a drop of Balmorrow blood was shed. It was an outstandingly courageous thing for him to do, Clare. He was merely a viscount after all. He might well have lost his head on the spot to spout such blasphemy. And your father, who was barely thirteen, stood beside him, promising that even the youngest of the gentlemen were willing to die if the King did not order the Duke of Cumberland to sheath his sword and cease retribution against the failed Jacobites."

"*My* grandfather? *My* father?" Clare asked, awe-struck.

"Aye. We Balmorrows owe them everything. There would have been no more Balmorrows—at least not in our line. My father was merely a lad then, no older than yours, and the next generation not so much as a gleam in his eye. I would never have been born, nor Mags, nor Michaela. In our family, your grandfather and father are great heroes—verging on sainthood."

"That is why you married me!" Clarissa gasped.

"Indeed. How could I let you suffer the degradations of penury and let Malcolm sink into indigence when I would not have been born without your family's intervention? Surely whatever I have is yours and Malcolm's as well. I—I did not know how else to go about it but to marry you, Clare. It seemed the most expeditious way and the least embarrassing for your brother. I could not offer Malcolm charity. I feared he would scorn it and despair even more."

Clarissa studied the haggard face above her. For the very first time she noticed how deep were the lines across his brow and at the corners of his mouth.

"I promise you shall never regret that we are wed, Clare," he whispered. "Never."

"No," she smiled, tucking a dark curl back behind his ear, "you are dear and sweet and precious, and I shall regret nothing."

"Precious? Me?" His eyes lit with mirth and his lips curved upward. "I have been called many things, sweetings, but never precious. I thank you for the thought," he added, planting a kiss on the tip of her nose. Then he disentangled himself from her and wandered into the tiny chamber at the rear of the cell, leaving Clare to follow if she wished. She followed, to find him stomping heavily with one boot upon the stone floor in the far corner.

"What are you doing?" she laughed. "Is it a new dance?"

"I am searching."

"For what?"

"The right place. There is a loose stone. Not very loose, but if you stomp hard enough—ah, here!" With a triumphant glow in his great blue eyes, Balmorrow swept a gleaming blade from his boot and knelt down, forcing the blade beneath the stone. Clare, joined by Corning and Maggie, gazed in awe as the stone tilted up and Balmorrow's gloved fingers probed beneath it.

"Oh, my goodness," breathed Maggie as he tugged a large and formidable-looking horse pistol into view.

"W-what?" stuttered Corning in disbelief. "Alex, how did you know such a thing would be there?"

"Ghosts," Balmorrow replied with an enigmatic smile. "Ghosts told me of it. A few moments ago. At the window."

Balmorrow passed the weapon to Corning and replaced the stone. The blatantly proud look on his face sent both Clare and Maggie into laughter.

"The thing is positively ancient," murmured Corning, examining the weapon. "I expect the ghosts told you whose it was, eh, Alex, as well as where to find it?"

Balmorrow nodded. "It was my grandpapa's and before that the second Duke of Buckingham's."

"Then it is near two centuries old," muttered Corning, studying the weapon.

"Oh, David, you do not believe him!" exclaimed Maggie. "He is bamming you!"

"Could have belonged to The Buck. Old enough. And the Sinclairs knew him well, did they not? The wretched thing is still loaded, Alex."

"Do you want it?"

"Well, I—we cannot just take it."

"Of course we can. It was my grandpapa's last, so now it is mine. It has been here forever, Corning, and no one else even thought to look for it. I do not see why it is not mine to do with what I will. Especially since the ghosts have told me to take it along with me."

"I should like to have it," sighed Corning, "but the Warders will definitely think we are stealing the thing."

"No!" exclaimed Balmorrow chuckling. "Not scruples, Corning! Besides, the thing is mine. M'father told me of its existence years ago. It was smuggled in to grandpapa in case he must needs fight his way to freedom."

"Well, but how can we get it out past the Warders?" Clarissa asked, interested. "It is very kind of you to wish to give His Grace presents, but how do you expect him to carry this horrendous weapon home? He cannot simply walk out dangling it from his hand. The Warder will wish to know where he acquired it and will insist upon placing it in the museum."

"I shall stuff it in my waistband and button my coat over it," declared Balmorrow.

"But it is loaded!"

"The powder is useless, so damp that I cannot get it out without a cleaning rod," he replied, prodding at the weapon with the tip of his knife. "Even the ball is stuck."

Returning the knife to the inside of his boot, Balmorrow thrust the weapon into the waistband of his pantaloons and then discovered that the fashion for shorter, tighter coats would not cover the thing at the front and had to ask Clarissa to help him ease the pistol into the small of his back. He then left the buttons of his coat open so that the back of it would not cling tightly against him and expose the shape of the weapon.

"Oh, that cannot be at all comfortable, and you are going to have to be very careful how you descend the steps. Perhaps we ought to leave it behind," sighed Corning.

"Uh-uh. Be all right. It is cold, though. We are going to ride home in a carriage, are we not?"

"Yes, our coach is to meet us at the entrance," Maggie nodded.

"Good, I shall stuff the thing under the seat."

"I should hope so," giggled Clarissa, "for else you will not be able to sit down."

The Warder standing guard at the entrance to Wakefield noted that the Earl of Balmorrow was somewhat dishevelled. "Something happen, y'r lor'ship?" he asked gruffly. "Ye're walkin' a bit ginger-like."

"Slipped on the steps," mumbled the earl as all three of his companions gazed stoically ahead. "Wrenched m'back."

"You'll want to go home at once," commiserated the Warder. "I can summon a hackney for ye, if ye wish."

"No, I shall be fine. Walk about a bit. Do me good," smiled Balmorrow, artlessly. "We thank you for the privilege of exploring Wakefield. Shall we stroll along the moat as far as the Bell Tower, m'dears, and then cross to the green?"

Clarissa took his proffered arm and nodded. The four strolled from the Tower, Maggie and Corning taking the lead.

"You will not have a sudden attack of scruples and betray him, David?" Maggie asked, the lilt in her voice bringing laughter to his eyes.

"No, of course not. He is doing it for me after all. The thing will make an exceptional addition to my collection. But how on earth does he do it, Mags? *Does* he talk to ghosts?"

"Of course not. Papa told him it was there. There are no such things as ghosts."

"Indeed," nodded Corning with a quick glance over his shoulder at his brother-in-law. "And I expect it was your papa told him where lay that battered chest filled to the brim with bullion that we dug up that night in the middle of Hyde Park."

"Well, no, I expect if Papa had known of that, he would have dug the thing up himself."

"Exactly. This is the fifth time I have been with Alex when he has recovered something ancient—and it is only the first time, Mags, that he has provided a logical explanation for how he learned of its whereabouts."

Clarissa, who had overheard this last bit of conversation, gazed wide-eyed up at her husband.

"What?" he asked.

"Do you, Alex?"

"Do I what?"

"Speak to ghosts?"

Balmorrow grinned down at her—a secretive and curious grin. "At times, yes, I expect I do. Most especially when I am at the castle. Should you like to meet one or two ghosts yourself? It is not at all frightening, I assure you. They live in old diaries and paintings and pieces of music, scribbles on the walls and cracks in the floors and, in one case, in a ceiling beam. And especially, they live on the outside of the castle. You have seen several of their homes already, Clare, though you most likely thought them only gouges in an ugly pile of stone."

Clarissa's brow knit at his words. "Oh!" she exclaimed after a few more steps. "The outer walls of Castle Balmorrow!"

"Indeed. And I will bet you thought me a pinchpenny, too, when you saw how chunks had fallen here and there and spilled across the ground and then had been left as they had fallen."

"I—I did," Clarissa admitted with a tiny smile. "I wondered, that is, if you might be—clutchfisted."

"Well, I am not. I did think to repair the stonework, you know. But I could not bring myself to do it. Because there is pride and courage and spirit in each one of those scars, Clare. I can tell you to the day and sometimes to the hour when each gouge came to be and by whose armaments and who defended from within."

"And he will, too," Maggie tossed back over her shoulder, "if you allow him the opportunity. Zander will tell you as well," she added with a chuckle. "And Brandy."

"And Maggie," inserted Corning, coming to a halt at the wall that wound beside the River Thames. "There is not a Sinclair alive who does not know the history of those battle scars," he explained, leaning back against the wall. "Nor, may I add, a man or a woman married to a Sinclair, except for you m'dear. And you will learn them all soon enough, I think. Alex, look out!" Corning exclaimed as a bedraggled pieman came dashing down the pavement. Corning's cry came just a moment too late however. The man smacked straight into the earl sending Clarissa staggering aside. The pies tumbled everywhere and Balmorrow plummeted to the ground.

Corning quickly steadied Clarissa then hurried forward as the pie seller exclaimed in dismay and bent over Balmorrow, clutching at the earl's lapels in an attempt to pull him from the ground. Once he had Balmorrow upright again, the man began to dust at Balmorrow's coat and waistcoat with great sweeping motions.

"I am fine," mumbled the earl, pushing aside Corning's extended arm and bidding the pieman be off in a loud, exasperated voice. "Devil a bit!" he exclaimed as the man backed away amidst a series of short bows accompanied by guttural words of apology. "If I were not smuggling a pistol, I would box the fellow's ears! The last I looked this was not a race track."

Corning gave his brother-in-law a most bewildered stare. "Alex, that bloke nipped something from you."

"He what?"

"He did, Alex. I saw. He reached his hand inside your coat just as you went down," Clarissa exclaimed in agreement.

"You had best check, Alex," suggested Maggie. "If he has snabbled something out of your pocket we must tell the Warders. It is likely he can still be found."

"Not likely he did," muttered Balmorrow, checking from the corner of his eye to see if the well-disguised John Norris had gotten cleanly away or if someone had followed the man. "Had nothing in that pocket. Still don't," he added, checking. "But I thought sure certain the blighter was going to jolt our pistol into action. Perhaps you ladies have seen enough for one visit, eh? I would feel a deal better in your coach, Corning, with this barker safely disposed of."

"Are you certain you are all right?" Clarissa asked, preceding her husband into the house. "You did fall rather hard."

"I am fine, Clare. It was nothing at all."

"It was something."

"And what does that mean?" Balmorrow asked, handing his gloves to Jonson and turning to escort his wife up the front staircase.

"It means that I saw the man's hand reach into your coat, Alex, immediately he bumped you. And if you had had anything at all in your pocket, it would have been gone."

"Yes, well, there are pickpockets all over London, m'dear."

"Such very forward ones?"

"Forward ones?" Balmorrow ushered her into the morning parlor, a wide grin gathering upon his face.

"Yes, forward ones. Ones who come running directly into you. I would have thought they were more—more—subtle."

"Well, perhaps he was not very good at it."

"Most certainly he was not very good at it. Are you certain he stole nothing, Alex?"

The Earl of Balmorrow seated his bride upon a brocade sopha and strolled across the room, returning moments later with two glasses of brandy in hand. "Sip it very slowly if you please," he instructed with a twinkle in his eyes as he handed one of the glasses to Clarissa. "I do not wish to have a drunken little hoyden upon my hands this evening."

Clarissa accepted the glass with a smile. "You are sharing your brandy with me. Does this mean that you intend to share something else as well?"

"Like what?" asked Balmorrow, gazing down at her.

"Like secrets."

"I have no secrets."

"Bosh! I have seen that pieman before, my lord, and though I cannot quite place his face—it was so very dirty, you know—still if I think on it long enough, I am certain I shall recall."

"Well, you do not need to think on it," sighed Balmorrow, slumping down onto the sopha beside her. "I have been thinking on it all the way home. And I have decided."

"Decided?"

"Yes. Decided to tell you. It was Mad Jack Docker. But you are not to tell anyone else, Clare, not even Maggie."

"M-mad Jack Docker? But why? I mean—he is a highwayman, is he not? Why is he in London? Why pick your pocket? And you never did explain, Alex, just how that madman comes to be your friend and is to be my saviour should it become necessary."

"No, and I am not about to explain the whole of it now, either. I only thought you ought to know because—because—"

"Yes?"

"Well, because it is the truth, Clare. And if we are to stand the least chance of happiness, the two of us, there had best be truth between us. I have thought about it all day long. You are to know the truth of everything so far as I am free to confide in you and I would be greatly relieved if you could see your way to speaking truth to me as well."

"I would not dream of lying to you, Alex. I lo—"

A smile replaced the serious frown upon Balmorrow's countenance. "You lo?"

"I was going to say I love you, but then you would tell me again that I do not, and since I do not wish to hear that lecture another time—"

"Oh. Well, I will not spout off about it then. Do you remember, Clare, when it was your mama died?"

"M-my mama?" Clarissa gazed at him amazed. "Why should you wish to know about my mama?"

"I cannot say, exactly. It is something vague that puzzles me. I met her once, you know. She came with your father to the castle. She died of a fever did she not?"

"Yes."

"Was she ill for a very long time?"

"No. That is, I do not think so. It happened here in London, you see, and Malcolm and I were at Halliard Hall. And it felt to me as though one day we had a mama and the next day we did not."

"You were very young."

"Two."

"Very young," mused Balmorrow, settling back and stretching his legs out before him. "Malcolm would have been?"

"Merely four."

"Indeed. And your father never remarried. Did you and Malcolm attend her funeral?"

"No. Mama was not buried at the Hall but here in London. Papa and the physician feared the fever to be contageous and wished to bury her as soon as possible."

Balmorrow's dark curls bounced as he nodded. "It would certainly make sense then not to carry her body to Newbury. Do you know where her grave lies, Clare? Have you been there?"

"Why, no. I—I—I only came to London one time. For my Season, you know. And that was when Papa died. We did never go to mama's grave. We took papa home to be buried."

"I am sorry for it, Clare," Balmorrow murmured, placing one arm gently about her shoulders. "Zander never did know his mama, but Brandy did and was crushed when Maddy died. And you have lost two parents you loved."

"But so have you," Clarissa replied, sipping at the brandy and wondering what in all the world had brought this topic to her husband's mind. "We all do, you know, lose our parents to death. It is a part of life, is it not? And must be accepted."

"Indeed. Is she buried at the chapel in St. Mary's Lane, your mama? There are a number of Beresfonts buried there. Your papa was used to attend services at that chapel."

"I—I have not the least idea. Alex, it does not truly matter. It is near twenty years since my mama died."

"But would you not like to know where she is buried—to once visit her grave?"

"Well—well—"

"I shall see if I can discover where she lies, shall I? Then we shall go, you and I, and bid her a proper farewell."

Clarissa could not put that conversation behind her. She and Alex had dined at home and she had played for him upon the pianoforte for an entire hour afterward, gladdened by the peaceful smile upon his face. And then he had simply arisen from his wing chair, given her a quick kiss upon the cheek and taken himself out into the night with not the least explanation. And at the hour of—she gazed at the ormolu clock upon her mantle—at the hour of two he had not yet returned! Clarissa paced the brightly-colored carpet of her sitting room restlessly. She had been to bed twice already. She had a mind to try for sleep a third time. But she lit another brace of candles instead, set them upon the vanity, and then opened the draperies so that she might peer down into the street to see if even now Alex was approaching the front door. He was not. Clarissa sighed and began to pace again.

What had caused him to ponder so seriously her mother's death? What had put it into his mind that they must locate and visit her mother's grave? Was he compulsively drawn to thoughts of the dead, this perplexing gentleman she had married? He had spoken of ghosts at the Tower. Spoken *with* ghosts if the Duke of Corning were to be believed. And though Alex had intimated that it was merely history and records with which he conversed, perhaps there was a dark, morbid side to the gentleman. Perhaps he did think he could communicate with the dead.

No, that was stupid, and she was stupid to even consider it. He had simply been thinking for a moment of his first wife and his daughter. And his compassion for them had led him to an empathy for herself and her own loss. And certainly, the abruptness of his departure this evening had had nothing at all to do with that earlier conversation.

Clarissa wondered for the very first time if Balmorrow were a gamester. Did he play cards? Did he bet on races and mills and how many cats would cross the street? Or was it something more sinister that had possessed him so suddenly and drawn him off? Lady Sarah for instance? Clarissa gave a sigh and settled herself upon the settee before the casement. It came to her quite clearly how little she actually knew of this man who was her husband.

"But I will never again believe him to be clutchfisted or a savage or a boor," she whispered to herself as she tucked her legs up beneath the skirt of her nightdress and rested her head against the back of the settee. "No, and I will not think him morbid, either. There is some reason he wishes to visit my Mama's grave that has nothing at all to do with death and ghosts. Most likely," she yawned, her eyes growing heavy, "it is his sense of family and history and he thinks it only fitting that I should pay poor Mama proper respect. Yes, that sounds quite like the Alex I am coming to know."

Chapter 12

Balmorrow dismounted before the cemetery gates and, tying the reins of his mount to the limb of an elm, knelt to light the lantern he had carried with him from home. It shone brightly amidst the darkness and the gathering mist as he stood and pushed his way through the gates and into the hallowed ground behind the chapel in St. Mary's Lane. It was all foolishness, of course. What he was thinking could not possibly be true. Except—except that The Summarfield possessed a ruby necklace that matched perfectly the bracelet and earbobs that had come to Clare through her mother.

There might be any number of explanations for such a thing as that, of course. The elder Halliard or Malcolm when he acceded to the title might well have sold the thing to pay off some of the overwhelming debts. One of the unknown conspirators might well have bought it and given it to The Summarfield in payment for her services. There, that was certainly a reasonable explanation. And what he had thought earlier—what had come swirling into his mind as he had sat conversing with Clare that afternoon—made no sense at all. Unless one considered the list Alden had snabbled from Canterbury's clerk. It was that list, he decided, that gnawed at him most and sent his thoughts flying in a totally unreasonable direction.

The entire evening he had been most uneasy—the fear that he was not mistaken nibbling over and over at his mind. And when he had given Clare a quick kiss upon the cheek and taken himself off, he had been fearful that a faint glimmer of truth clung to his notion of the afternoon. The need to prove himself wrong had literally driven him into the streets. Because if he were not wrong then it made perfectly good sense that Clare's name and Malcolm's should be upon a list composed by seditionists.

Balmorrow was not at all certain where the Beresfont family members were laid to rest but it was a small cemetery compared to most of the London boneyards and even if he must stop and peer at every marker, he would be home well before the sun came up. He raised his coat collar against the damp and began with the first of the stones to his left, leaning down to peer at the inscription in the lantern light. Collingwood. Not Beresfont. He went on to the next and the next and the next.

"Well, what the divil is 'e doin'?" whispered a man who stood amongst the trees lining the outside of the graveyard. " 'E's stoppin' at ever' grave, the bloke is!"

"Looking for someone."

"Aye, but who?"

"I am certain I have not the vaguest idea, Henry. It is merely one of his queer starts I should think. The man speaks with ghosts, you know. Comes of living in a wretched old ruin of a castle for the most of his life. Ghosts everywhere at Castle Balmorrow they say. His lordship is most likely seeking out some particular spirit with whom to converse this evening." The gentleman who spoke was immediately forced to stifle a laugh as he watched his companion blanche beneath the misty starlight.

"G-ghosts? S-spirits? Blimey!"

"Shhh, he will hear you, Henry. Must be quiet. It is not the ghosts you need fear but Balmorrow himself should he discover the two of us spying upon him. That, my dear fellow, is why we have tethered the horses so far from this spot. So they would not give away our presence. That short sword Balmorrow wears is not just a pretty trinket, my man. I have seen him put it to good use."

Balmorrow paused with the lantern half way to one of the

markers. Had he heard a whisper over near the gates? He held his breath and listened intently but no sound except the trembling of leaves in the wind reached him. He took one quick look back over his shoulder and saw nothing but his horse tethered to the elm. With a shrug, he continued his search.

It took him the better part of an hour in his organized fashion to discover a bevy of graves all marked with the name of Beresfont. They were congregated at the far right of the chapel around a small fountain and edged about with rose bushes. The earliest marker held a date of 1660 and bore the name Malcolm Thomas Beresfont. The most recent was a marble tombstone with the carving of an angel that bore the name Arielle Beresfont and the date 1748. Balmorrow shook his head and returned to the first of the stones, making the circle again. No, he had missed none. Clarissa's mother, then, was not buried amongst these Beresfonts. Perhaps there were more of the family further along. With a sigh and a quick glance at his pocket watch in the lantern light, he continued his search, moving methodically from one tombstone to the next, always from the chapel outward. His horse neighed as he came nearer the gate and he looked up to see that the gelding was still tied securely to the elm. From the corner of his eye he thought he caught a slight movement and he held his breath, concentrating, attempting to identify what it was that had seized at his attention. But whatever had moved at that particular moment had now ceased to move and he could distinguish nothing out of order, nothing that did not belong.

"Do ye think 'e saw us?" whispered the little man in the catskin waistcoat, wiping his brow with the back of his sleeve as he huddled behind a clump of wild hawthorne.

"No, definitely not," came the hushed reply. "Had he seen us, he would be here now and we would be facing the gentleman's sword."

"Let's go home."

"We cannot go home, Henry."

"But he ain't a doin' of anythin' the least bit sensical."

"All the same, we must wait him out and follow wherever he goes from here. Somehow snatches of our plans have leaked out. Already the Prince has been informed of our support of the Luddites. He does not yet know which of the organizations is at the root of it, but his people will continue to search. It is more important than ever that we know every move Balmorrow makes, Henry. Everything we learn of his movements will make it easier, you see, to lay the blame at his feet should our plans fail."

"No, I don't see," muttered Henry nervously. "I don't see fer a minit how knowin' the earl be wandering about a burial ground in the dead o' night is goin' to help put the blame off on 'im."

"Why, because he is alone, Henry, with no one to swear to his whereabouts. And we know the hour and the day. And I will stand up and testify that I saw him this very evening at this very hour in the back room of the Lion's Head Inn in the company of traitors and thieves. There will be only his word against mine then, you see. And I will be believed, because already rumors are spreading that Balmorrow has sided fully with the nonconformists and turned against the Crown."

Robert, Lord Liverpool chewed on his pipestem distractedly as he stared at the piece of vellum that lay upon the table before him. "I cannot make head nor tail of it, Norris."

"It was all Lex carried in his pocket this afternoon except a note setting our next meeting date. It does have that wretched seal upon it."

"Yes, and it also bears the name of his new bride and new brother-in-law. Why? Who wrote the thing? And how long ago? And how did Balmorrow come by it? Are you quite certain that you raided the correct pocket?"

"Indeed. Always the inside left. We set that rule between us a year ago and Lex has kept to it steadily. He is not likely to mistake this late in the game."

"When do you see him again?"

"Wednesday night."

"Almack's?"

"So his note said. I gather the patronesses have a distinct wish to reacquaint themselves with his new bride."

"Well, I shall see what can be discovered about the other names on this list. You will stop in again before Wednesday night, eh, Norris? Perhaps there is some thread connects the lot of them that will lead to the heart of this plot. Though, if Balmorrow's new bride and his new brother-in-law are embroiled in the thing, there will be Hades to pay and that's a fact."

Norris nodded silently. It was an awe-provoking thought that his cousin might have unwittingly married into the very midst of the conspiracy that they were struggling to uncover. "A good many people will believe Lex involved in the thing if his bride turns out to be one of them," he mumbled with a despairing shake of his golden curls. "Perhaps someone thought The Summarfield unable to enmesh Lex tightly enough and called upon Halliard's daughter."

Liverpool sighed. "And Balmorrow, gudgeon that he is, went and married the chit."

"Well, but he had to marry her, Liverpool."

"He had to marry her?"

"Indeed. It would have looked distinctly odd for him to settle her brother's bills and then set her up in high style without the benefit of marriage."

Lord Liverpool nodded sagely and took another puff upon his pipe. "I see," he drawled. "It was a matter of loyal and honorable recompense, eh? Damnation but your family is honorable beyond belief, John. I would not have done it."

"No, but the Halliards did not save your father and grandfather from the block, neither."

"True, but if Alex's bride is involved in this conspiracy, his head will rest upon that same block."

"But it will not roll," Norris replied, a tinge of frost in his tone. "You will come to his defense and explain the situation, Liverpool, no matter what state secrets must emerge into the light. Lex will no more kneel down and become the Crown's sacrificial lamb than he will lie back and allow The Summarfield and her cohorts to lay responsibility for whatever dastardly plot they have conceived at his feet."

"Well, of course I will come to his defense. But there is no saying, you know, that my testimony will save him. Especially if he is married to one of the villains."

"If Lex's head rolls," Norris growled, "then England will no longer need involve itself with the conflict on the continent. There will be conflict enough at home. The beheading of a Balmorrow is not so uncertain a thing as the placing of a Bonnie Prince Charlie upon the throne, Liverpool. There will be no division of loyalty among the clans if a Sinclair is murdered by the English Parliament, especially if that Sinclair is The Balmorrow. The Greys and the Black Watch will abandon the field before Napoleon and appear in the streets of London instead, and all the gentlemen of all the clans with them. And there are men of Northumberland and Yorkshiremen who will stand for Lex, and gentlemen as far south as—"

"And I need not ask with whom your loyalty lies either, need I, John?" interrupted Liverpool with a fond twinkle in his eyes.

"No, you need not. Lex is my cousin and one of the most honorable men in all the world and I will not stand by and see him murdered, not for any cause under heaven!"

"Well then, it serves us all to bring an end to this conspiracy before anything comes of it. Because I tell you, John, if Balmorrow is called up upon treasonable acts and convicted, I shall be forced to resign as Secretary of War and join with you against my own King, and that would be uncommonly disturbing."

"You would never," murmured Norris, cocking an eyebrow in Liverpool's direction.

"Oh? You think not? When I know the gentleman to be more than innocent? To be, in fact, struggling through a cesspool of plots and machinations on England's account? To be placing himself and his reputation in danger not only to lay bare the plans of a group of seditionists but to discover who they are and capture them as well? What do you take me for, John, a mere politician to be bought and sold on a whim?"

"No, sir," Norris grinned. "Not any longer."

"Good, because I am not, John. We shall find the answer to this despicable dilemma, you and I and Balmorrow, even if I must come down out of my plush little office and wallow in the mud and muck of conspiracy myself."

When Balmorrow entered Clarissa's sitting room at the hour of four intending to peer into her bedchamber and satisfy himself that she was safely asleep, he discovered her upon the settee before the window, all but one candle gutted and the fire upon the hearth flickering palely amidst dying embers. He gathered her into his arms, as he had often gathered his sleeping children, and carried her to her bed, placing her carefully between the sheets and pulling the coverlet up to her strong little chin. Then he simply stood and stared down at her for the longest time by the light of one sputtering candle and a dying fire.

An old thick scar near the region of his heart began to ache and he sighed as he felt it. He told himself he was a fool and attempted to think the very real pain away. But the longer he stared down at the sleeping Clarissa, the deeper and stronger the aching grew until at last it brought the startling sensation of tears to his eyes.

It was hope, he realized. The very real ache of hope was rising through him like an incoming tide and shocking him into the most unsettling emotions. And he could not fend it off. As much as he wished to deny it, to subdue it, to bury it, hope would not be denied. Even the very real fear of crushing blows similar to those with which Madeline had driven him nearly to his knees, even that fear could not force his hope into retreat.

"Could you love me?" he whispered to the sleeping Clarissa. "Do you love me?"

Damnation! He had thought such naive and nonsensical notions ruthlessly laid to rest, but here they were, alive again and stirring. What a fool he was! He had allowed himself to hope for love once before and been bitterly and thoroughly disillusioned. And if Madeline, whom he had loved with all his heart, had discovered nothing in him to love in return, then why should he hope for a moment that a young woman he barely knew might come to love him? He should not. He was being deplorably whimsical and he would suffer for it in the end.

But Clare had been waiting up for him. She had been waiting, watching by the casement window. He could not deny that it was so for he had watched and waited for Madeline by that same window many an evening and fallen asleep on that same settee. "What did you think, Clare?" he murmured, brushing a strand of hair from her cheek with one gentle finger. "Did you wonder where I had gone without you?

Did you imagine for one moment that I had gone to The Summarfield as I was used to imagine Maddy dallying with one or another of her cicisbeos? I ought to have told you where I was bound. If I had known you would worry, I would have said something. But what could I have said? Clare, I am off to the cemetery in St. Mary's Lane to seek your mother's grave?"

Clarissa stirred briefly at his touch and the sound of his voice but she did not wake.

No, of course he could have said no such thing, he thought with a shake of his head. But he ought to have said something. How many nights had he been the one to sit upon that settee, the drapes barely parted behind him, waiting for the sound of an approaching carriage and the sweet smothered trill of Maddy's laughter as she approached the front door? He knew well the feel of it, that waiting. He could feel it still.

Certainly he could have made it far easier for Clare. He could have claimed an appointment, or a long-standing engagement with one of his cronies in which Clare could not possibly be interested. Or even a summons from Prinny. By gawd, that was an excuse he could have used with impunity. She would never have questioned such a summons. But he had not wished to lie to her. And besides, he had not guessed that she would linger at the window awaiting his return.

For a brief moment the hope in him began actually to blaze and he let the amazing warmth of it course through his veins. But then he recalled again, with painful clarity, the great crushing reality that had been his first marriage and he remembered quite lucidly how and why Clare had come to marry him. And with that cold dose of reality rumbling about his brain, he rose from the side of the bed and wandered toward the chamber door.

"Alex?" Her voice was hesitant, a whisper. "Alex, is it you?"

Balmorrow's hand lingered upon the latch as he turned. "Indeed, it is I, Clare. I did not intend to wake you. Go back to sleep."

"No, you did not wake me. It was a dream. I—Alex, are you all right? Nothing has happened to you?"

Clarissa sat up in the bed and swung her legs over the side. He was posed so oddly there across the room. "Alex, what is it? What has happened?" Without the least thought even to don her slippers, she hurried across the carpeting to where he stood and put her arms as far around him as she could reach and hugged him to her. He was forced to release the latch in order to hug her back. And he did hug her back, but most rigidly, without so much as bending at the waist.

That uncharacteristic restraint was not lost upon Clarissa. "Oh, my darling Alex," she whispered, moving her arms upward until they were around his neck and then standing upon tiptoe to bestow a kiss upon his stubborn jaw. "Whatever is wrong? What has happened? What may I do to make it better?"

"Nothing has happened," mumbled Balmorrow, condescending at last to gaze down at her in the faint light—but still unbending, only his glance lowering to meet hers. "And only I can make it better."

"Never," she replied, releasing her hold upon him and stepping from his arms. "Whatever it is, I am your wife, and we shall make it better together. Come and talk to me," she urged, taking one of his hands in both of hers and tugging him toward the bed. "Sit down beside me here and tell me what makes you seem so—so—vulnerable."

"Vulnerable?" Balmorrow sat beside her upon the edge of the heavy four-poster.

"Yes, I believe that is the word."

"Cannot be. Balmorrows are built like great fortresses. Never vulnerable. Never unprotected."

"Oh. Well, perhaps that is not the word, then. Truly, Alex, I do not quite know how you seem. Only different. Very different. As though you have been harmed in some way. Oh! You have not been summoned before the Prince again? They have not accused you further?"

A light began to rise in the great blue Balmorrow eyes that even in the flickering of one candle and a dying fire Clarissa could easily discern. But though she took note of it, she had not the least idea what sort of light it was. "Alex, do let me be of help. I can see that you are upset."

"No, can you? And do you know that at this very moment you are upsetting me even more? Have you no mercy, Clarissa?"

"No mercy? But—whatever are you speaking of?"

"You. I am speaking of you, Clare. I left you this evening without a word of explanation only to return and discover you asleep upon the settee with the draperies open the least bit behind you. Watching for me. Were you watching for me?"

"Yes."

"And now all you wish to know is what has happened to make me—sad. Because that is what I am, Clare, merely sad. You ought to be asking me why I left you and where I have been and with whom. But you do not care, do you?"

"No, not now. Not now that you are safely home."

"Exactly. And that resemblance is even more unmerciful."

"Alex, you are not making the least bit of sense."

"No, I expect not."

"No, and you have not given me so much as a hint as to what I may do to make you feel more yourself."

"I could never feel more myself than I do at this very moment," Balmorrow sighed, his stiffness easing somewhat as he drew her against himself and bestowed a tender kiss upon her brow. "I feel—and see—myself everywhere. It is like being imprisoned inside of a looking glass."

Clarissa brushed his wind-tossed curls aside and placed her hand upon his brow. He smiled and took it down and held it in his lap.

"Well, you speak like a man with a raging fever, Alex."

"The bracelet Mad Jack stole, Clare, you have earbobs to match, do you not?"

Clarissa stared at him, turned away, turned back and stared again. "The bracelet? Earbobs? Alex, from where does this subject abruptly arise? You do change horses so suddenly in midstream. What about the looking glass? Do you realize I have not the faintest idea what you meant?"

"I will explain that to you at a better time. Did the set have a necklace as well? Did your father sell it perhaps? Or Malcolm?"

"No, most certainly not. Malcolm used the monies set aside for my marriage with my permission. But he did never once ask for mama's jewels. That set I had from my papa's hand the moment he returned without Mama. And there never was a necklace."

"Never?"

"Well, never while I had it, Alex. I expect there was a necklace at one time for there was a place for it in the box, but it never came to me."

"And you did never ask your papa about it?"

"No. Alex, whyever are you so worried about a silly necklace?"

"Because I have seen it, Clare, around Lady Sarah's neck."

"Oh." Something terribly heavy tumbled to the pit of Clarissa's stomach and lodged there. "This—this evening?"

"What?"

"The necklace—she wore it this evening?"

"I have not the vaguest idea what—" Balmorrow peered down at her in the dim light and then with a most knowing lift of his eyebrow, shook his head. "No, not this evening, Clare. I was not within so much as hallooing distance of Sarah this evening. I was at the graveyard in St. Mary's Lane."

"You were where?" Clarissa could not believe her ears. "Alex! In the middle of the night?"

"Yes."

"Well, no wonder you seem so—so woebegone."

"I am neither woebegone nor vulnerable. Where do you get all these words? Balmorrows are not bred to be woebegone. It is not in their blood."

"What is in their blood then? Ghosts and ghoulies and graves in the dead of night?"

"Ghoulies?" Balmorrow snickered, the last of the tension visibly draining from him. "Ghoulies, Clare? Do you even know what a ghoulie is?"

"Yes, I do. Well, no, actually I do not."

"A ghoul is a person who robs graves, sweetling."

"Oh! I thought it was some sort of—of—otherworldly being."

"No, it is definitely a thisworldly being, and I assure you, my dear, the Balmorrows do not claim to have mixed their blood with ghoulies."

For a long moment Clarissa enjoyed the smile that spread across his face and the arm that tightened about her and the hand that squeezed her own in his lap. And then the smile fled and his arm loosened and, moving a bit away, he took both her hands into his own and looked down at them as though studying them carefully. "I should not have—" he mumbled at last without looking up. "I did not mean to speak of it so soon. But—"

"But what, my darling?" The vulnerability that he eschewed

was back and quite apparent and Clarissa wished with all her heart to take him in her arms and reassure him. But she could not, because she had not the least idea what he needed reassurance about. "Tell me, Alex. Whatever it is, I shall strive to understand, my dear. Have you discovered my mother's grave in sorry state, Alex? Well, but that is easily rectified. We shall go and fix it up. I did never think to do so before. But we shall do it first thing in the morning if that is what upsets you."

"There is no grave," Balmorrow murmured, raising her hands to his lips and bestowing a kiss upon each palm. "Your mama is not buried behind the chapel in St. Mary's Lane."

"She is not? Well, she is buried elsewhere then. I shall send Malcolm a note to search papa's old records. He will discover the place for us."

"I think the records will say St. Mary's Lane," sighed Balmorrow. "There are other Beresfonts buried there. In three separate sections. I found them all. But I did not find your mama. Still, it would be best to do as you say. Malcolm will not think it odd for you to ask your own mama's resting place."

Clarissa freed her hands from his grasp and placing one on each of his cheeks, turned his head until he must look directly at her. "What is this about, Alex? Why are you so interested in my mama's grave? Why do you care so greatly where she is buried?"

He took her hands back into his own. "I do not know, Clare, if I ought to tell you. I am most likely wrong and—"

"Tell me."

"But if I am mistaken you will think me mad and most likely take me in abhorrence and never wish to speak to me again."

"Never. Tell me, Alex."

"I—I think your mama is alive," stuttered the earl softly. "I think there is no grave because she never died. That is why there was no ruby necklace in your set, because she kept the necklace for herself. And I think that she is in danger and that in the last two years of his life, your papa spent his entire fortune in an effort to rescue her."

Clarissa had the oddest sense that she would awaken at any moment to find herself safely between her sheets and

Balmorrow nowhere in sight. Certainly this was a dream, some nightmare caused by fretting the night away over her husband's whereabouts. Certainly this great clunch of a man she loved was not sitting with her upon the edge of her bed telling her that her mama, whom she had not seen one time since she was two years old, was alive.

"Clare? I knew I should not have said it! Clare? Speak to me. Please."

"My mama is alive?"

"Perhaps. Only perhaps she is alive," Balmorrow whispered, taking the suddenly shivering girl into his arms and hugging her mightily. "I do not know for certain, Clare. I only think it. I only see threads drawing together."

"But—but you said that the necklace—that Lady Sarah wore the necklace—why would she do so if Mama were still—if she had kept it for herself?"

Now it seemed the most preposterous theory he had ever conceived and Balmorrow detested himself for having conceived of it. But he detested himself even more for having mentioned the least part of it to Clare. "I am wrong," he murmured, kissing the perplexed little face that peeked up at him from the shelter of his chest. "I am wrong, Clare. I am a man with windmills in his head and the breeze from them has blown all my wits away."

It was the oddest thing. Even in such dim light as existed she could read alarm and distress in his eyes as clearly as if he were speaking it aloud. It was just as his cousin, Lord Norris, had said. Alex's every thought and emotion displayed itself before her clearly and succinctly. And all his thoughts, all his concern at this very moment were for her. His eyes told her so and she knew it to be true. Well, and she was frightening him, was she not? She was clinging to him and shaking like some puling little infant. And why? Why? Because he had told her something wonderful—something most strange, but wonderful—that her mama might be alive! With a deep breath and a shake of her head and a swipe at the tears that had started, unbidden, to her eyes, Clarissa pulled away from his embrace, sat up straight and squared her shoulders. He reached for her impulsively and she captured his hands and held them securely in her own. "You spoke of threads, Alex," she said, "of threads drawing together."

"I—it is a curse."

"No, Alex, it is not a curse. You have discovered something no one else has noticed, have you not? In the necklace and the absence of my mama's grave, in my papa's reverses and in something else you have not yet spoken of, you have discerned a connection. Is that not so?"

"Yes, but I may very well be wrong, Clare. I was foolish to say a word about it without the least evidence. Yes, and I was totally without sensibility, too, to mention it to you. I am so very sorry. I cannot explain why I did such a thing. I intended not to say a word to you about where I had gone and why."

Clarissa, loosing his hands from her grasp, stood and crossed to the nearest of the windows where she pulled aside the draperies, allowing the first grey light of dawn to filter into the room. She turned and studied him thoughtfully.

Chapter 13

"I cannot imagine for one moment why I have told you all of this," mumbled Balmorrow, his coat and waistcoat long since tossed aside, his neckcloth hanging open and his shirt sleeves rolled part way up his arms as he peered over Clarissa's shoulder where she sat in her nightrail at her little desk, penning a missive to her brother.

"Because you need assistance, Alex, and who better to provide it than myself?"

"Yes, but it is all highly unlikely, Clare."

"Is it?"

"Indeed."

Clarissa ceased her writing and looked up at him. He truly was the most handsome of gentlemen, and the most noble, and the most caring—

"What? Why are you staring at me like that again?"

"Hmmm?"

"The last time you stared at me like that was near three hours ago, Clare, and it caused me to spew forth secrets like a bloody fountain."

"No."

"Yes."

"And do you regret spewing forth those secrets, my lord?"

"Yes."

"Alex, do you truly? Do you think that I am not to be trusted?"

"No, it is not that. It is—Clare, the less you are involved, the safer you will be. I referred to it as a puzzle, but it is much more. Lives may be lost if Alden and Mad Jack and I are not successful in this particular instance."

"I do understand, Alex."

"No, I do not think that you do. *Your* life, my dear, may be forfeit if things go badly and you are discovered to have aided us in any way."

"Oh, Alex, a letter to my brother requesting the location of my mama's grave? However could that lead to speculation that I had the least idea what you were doing?"

"Well—"

"It cannot. Admit it."

"No, the letter cannot, precisely, but if your interest reaches our unknown villains' ears, you are like to come under their scrutiny. I merely expressed a vague suspicion about the Luddites joining with the nonconformists in a conversation with The Summarfield last Season and two days later I was poisoned at Sarah's table."

"That might well have been an accident, Alex."

"It was not."

"How do you know?"

"Because a number of people ate the fish but I was the only one of them to become ill."

"Perhaps it was not the fish?"

"Oh, I am certain it was not the fish, sweetling. It was something placed unobtrusively inside *my portion* of the fish."

"But no one has attempted to—to—murder you since. And if their object is, as you say, to lay all of the blame for their actions at your feet and to keep themselves thus clear of blame, then why would they wish to kill you at all?"

"I have no idea, unless they are madmen. Or perhaps they had not yet decided I could be of value to them and only saw me as someone dangerous. I knew, you know, that something odd was going on and had told Sarah that I had decided to look into it. I was not even certain of Sarah's involvement with them until I was poisoned at her dinner table."

"But you had already deciphered a message that proved

the conspiracy between the Luddites and the reformers in the rioting."

"No, that particular piece of work I did not complete until very recently. I had, though, come across several messages implying such a union and mentioned their existence to Sarah."

"I cannot imagine how anyone can undo a code when they have not the least idea upon what it is based."

"No, neither can I."

"You cannot?" A smile flickered to Clarissa's face. "How odd for you to do the thing and not know how you did it."

"It is inbred," smiled the earl rather sheepishly. "Balmorrows have been sending and receiving messages in code forever. But it is a bit ironic, do not you think, that I was the one to decipher a message which brought Perceval shouting to Prinny about conspiracy and treason and spouting my name in the same breath?"

Clarissa sanded her letter, folded it carefully, placed a seal upon it and set it aside. "Alex? You have explained to me that the book I found in your chambers with all the numbers writ in it was, in fact, the coded message, but you did not tell me how the decoded message came to reach London before we did ourselves."

"I did not?"

"No, my dear, you did not," Clarissa murmured, rising and going softly into his arms. "Did you send one of your grooms ahead with it perhaps?" she asked, snuggling wearily but happily against his chest.

"No. A lone rider headed toward London from Castle Balmorrow might well have been noted and stopped—though Gowan rode cross-country to Larchmont without the least incident. Perhaps we are too suspicious, the lot of us. But when I left London after I was poisoned, we supposed that they—whoever they may be—would be keeping me under surveillance and so we made—special arrangements."

"Special arrangements?"

Balmorrow gazed down at her with a wide grin and kissed the very most top of her dishevelled curls. "You are the nosiest little thing."

"I am not," Clarissa replied softly from the cozy comfort

of his arms. "I merely wish to know everything about everything that has to do with you, Alex, because I lo—"

"No, do not stop. Because you love me. I shall not embark upon another sermon."

"You will not?"

"No. I—you—I—"

Clarissa giggled. She did not truly intend to giggle, but the large and thoroughly charming gentleman stuttering above her drove her to it. How Alex could be so strong, so courageous and so very intelligent, and still sound like a confused six-year-old she could not quite understand, but it was enough that he did. It pleased her remarkably. "Special arrangements, Alex," she murmured, once the giggle had subsided. "You *do* intend to tell me what they are, do you not?"

"Mad Jack Docker," whispered the gentleman into her ear.

"Mad Jack Docker again?"

"I stuffed the book with the decoded message between the coach seats and Mad Jack took it and stuffed it into his pocket when he robbed us."

"But how did he even know that we—"

"Parsons sent a message to one of my cottagers who sent his son to Mad Jack's brothers who rode off to tell Mad Jack. It is one of the reasons we spent the night at Larchmont Abbey, so that word had time to reach Mad Jack. He rode a good fifty miles cross-country to rob us, you know. It was not an easy task. And then he rode all the way to London to deliver the book to Lord Liverpool."

"Lord Liverpool? The Secretary of War?"

"Yes. I did not begin by searching for this conspiracy amongst the nonconformists and the Luddites, Clare. First I offered Liverpool my assistance in decoding communications seized from French agents and then in encoding them again with altered information and passing them on. I would much rather have joined in the fighting, but it occurred to me that I might do more good here at home. It is not so glorious as a commission in the cavalry. It is not glorious at all, in fact, because no one so much as guesses that I am doing it, but Liverpool swears it is most helpful and has already given the allies a distinct advantage."

Clarissa was amazed at him. Here with his arms securely about her, his dark locks tumbling every which way from the innumerable times he had combed his fingers through them, his clothing in total disarray, and his brilliantly blue eyes weary from lack of sleep, stood a truly unsung hero. And he was her husband. Pride surged through her every vein.

The Duke of Corning had spent a restless night and woke the following morning more discomposed than ever. That pieman *had* snabbled something from Alex's pocket. And the fact that Alex had refused to admit it had made the whole episode a good deal more suspicious than it might have been. Devil it, Corning thought, Alex is involved in something very shady. He must be. Why else would he allow some raggedy, unwashed rapscallion to steal from him? He would not and that's a fact. He would have chased after the fellow and had him down on the ground in the blink of an eye. Yes, and he would have darkened the chap's daylights for him, too.

With a sigh Corning nudged the final perfect crease into his neckcloth and allowed his valet to assist him into his morning coat. With quiet dignity he made his way to the morning room, bestowed a chaste kiss upon Maggie's cheek and accepted a cup of hot chocolate from one of the footmen. He drank it standing, staring out at the increasingly busy street below the morning room windows. Declining any breakfast whatsoever, he observed to Her Grace that it was going to be a very fine Tuesday, indeed, and that he had a notion to take his breakfast at White's and discuss with his cohorts the latest news regarding the progress of the war.

Maggie eyed him suspiciously.

"No, but what it is, Mags, I have not been paying much attention of late and I ought to keep abreast of things don't you know. Collier has returned from the Peninsula and Devon with him. They will undoubtedly be huddled at the club by now. It is nearing one o'clock."

"It is eleven twenty-five, Your Grace," offered Maggie softly.

"Oh."

"And you despise the food at White's."

"Do I? No, I am certain I never said any such thing."

"No, you merely moan and groan for hours around the house every time you agree to dine there with one of your cohorts. What is it, David? You may tell me what is bothering you. We do not keep secrets from each other you and I."

"Only because I do not seem to be very adept at it," sighed the duke, slumping down into a chair opposite her.

"No, is that the reason? And all this time I thought it was because you trusted me, David, and wished me to share in all the facets of your life."

"Well, I do. I trust you implicitly and wish to share everything with you. I love you beyond anything, Mags. And you know so, too."

"Indeed. So it must be something very dire that makes you wish to keep it from me."

"No. It ain't dire at all. The truth is, I am not certain it is anything, and I do not wish to worry you with it for precisely that reason."

"Worry me, David," urged Maggie softly. "I am worried already because you are so hesitant to tell me. Chances are I shall be less worried once I hear what it is."

The duke studied her silently, pondering. Then with a slight shrug of his shoulders and a nod of his head, he rose and began to pace the room. "It is Alex," he said from before the windows. "He lied to us," he blurted out on his way past the fire screen. "I am certain that that pie man at the Tower snabbled something from him," he added as he tramped down the length of the chamber. "Deuce take it, Mags! Why would he lie about something like that? What has he gotten himself into? Somehow, someway, Alex has fallen into the brambles," he sighed, as he completed his route and slumped again into the chair opposite his wife. "You do not for one moment expect that the Prime Minister was correct, Mags, do you? You do not think that Alex has been forced into participating in a nonconformist conspiracy against the government?"

Maggie set aside her own cup of chocolate and the copy of the London *Times* she had been perusing when the duke had entered, and stared at the flowers upon the carpeting for the longest time. "I cannot conceive," she stated at last, "how anyone might force Alex into anything."

"Blackmail?"

"Blackmail? What would anyone have to blackmail my brother with? A person must have secret sins that he does not wish revealed in order to be ripe for the plucking, David. And all of Alex's sins are hugely public. Why, some of his sins have become legendary. Alex never did a wrong thing in his life that was not immediately fodder for one rumor mill or another."

"But his pocket was picked nonetheless, Mags, and he assured us left and right and up and down that it was not. It is his lying about it that disturbs me. You do not think that he has chosen of his own free will to join in some conspiracy?"

"Never. You are quite certain his pocket was picked, David? I did not see it."

"Quite certain."

"Well," Maggie sighed, "if it is so and Alex has lied about it, then that great clunch somehow *has* fallen into the soup. You and I shall need to 'rouse the troops, David, and fish him out of it."

Lady Sarah plumped down wide-eyed upon the silver lustre sopha in the front parlor and allowed the elegant and truly handsome Lord Parkhurst to possess himself of her hand and to kiss the back of it gallantly.

"You were not expecting me, I think," he smiled as he freed the little hand and took a seat in the wing chair to Sarah's right. "Your aunt is not at home?"

"She has the headache," murmured Sarah.

"She is upstairs lying down then?"

"Indeed."

"Just as well," nodded Parkhurst slowly. "Just as well. I am come, my lady, to discuss with you your further association with the Earl of Balmorrow."

"What?" Sarah's eyes grew rounder at his words and her cheeks blushed a faint pink. "I fail to conceive, my lord, how any association between Lord Balmorrow and myself can be of interest to you."

"Oh, but it is of great interest to me, my lady."

"It—it is?"

"So great, in fact, that I have come to offer my services on your behalf."

"You have?" Lady Sarah could not keep her heart from beating in the oddest rhythm, nor could she manage to keep her hands from fidgeting about witlessly in her lap. She had never before spoken to this suave and most cultivated dandy except to nod in acknowledgement of his presence at a soirée or a ball or a musicale. Though he had seemed always to attend the same gatherings as she since her return into Society, still, he had never before taken any undue notice of her. And of a sudden, this very afternoon, he had come knocking upon her door with the head of his malacca cane.

"I can see you are somewhat bewildered, Lady Sarah," Parkhurst droned, relaxing comfortably and crossing one knee over the other. "Let me explain it to you. Before old Viscount Halliard died, I was in the way of courting his daughter."

"M-miss Beresfont?"

"Indeed. I courted the gel from the day she entered Society until she was so sadly forced to go into mourning on her father's behalf."

"You were in love with her," Sarah murmured, her hands clasping and unclasping, all of their own accord.

"No, my dear. No more in love with her than you are with Balmorrow."

"I—"

"Do not protest, my lady. I know precisely how much you love the Earl of Balmorrow. You love that gentleman not at all. He is your meal ticket, much as Miss Beresfont was mine. Although, I did not have the added burden of attempting to drain information from the chit as you must from Balmorrow. I was simply to keep her under my thumb and to make a great show of winning her heart within her father's sight. Halliard had discovered by then, I understand, all that was intended in their plan and they had threatened that I would ruin his daughter if he broke his silence."

"Who are they?" Sarah blurted before she could stop herself.

"You do not know? No, what am I thinking, of course you do not know. I am not quite certain myself. It is a gentleman name of Quigley who sees I am regularly paid. And yourself?"

Lady Sarah nodded. "He is a gentleman of medium height with light brown hair and fierce eyes and a tiny scar upon his chin and his voice is deep and hoarse as though he spends his entire day shouting at people."

"That's the gentleman," agreed Parkhurst. "Made me an offer I could not refuse. About to go under the hatches until he appeared upon my doorstep. I snapped at his offer, let me tell you. Now, of course, my position has been altered."

"It has?"

"Yes, my dear, as has yours—by this fool marriage between Balmorrow and the gel."

"Oh, of course. Yes. But I shall still be able to uphold my end of the bargain with Mr. Quigley. Alex is not at all in love with the girl, you know. He told me so himself. He vows this marriage will not force him to abandon me—though we must be very careful for awhile."

Parkhurst smiled his most beatific smile. "And that is just why I have come, my dear. To offer my services. Clarissa Beresfont cannot be happy, you know, in a marriage of convenience with a Philistine like Balmorrow. What woman would be happy? The man is a northern barbarian at best and a provincial bumpkin at worst. Why Balmorrow made her an offer in the first place, not even the astute Mr. Quigley can understand."

"Alex said it was a matter of a previous debt to the family."

"Yes, so you informed Mr. Quigley and he informed me. It must have been an incredible debt for him to go from a marriage with the incomparable Madeline to marriage with a green little gel from Newbury. At any rate, Sarah. May I call you Sarah? I am instructed to reestablish my connection with Miss Beresfont—pardon me, Lady Balmorrow—and to draw her off from the earl so that you will be free to resume your relationship with him to its fullest extent."

"To its fullest extent?" Lady Sarah's cheeks turned positively rosy.

"Oh, I do not think they meant precisely that, my dear," snickered the elegant Lord Parkhurst with a knowing leer. "They meant only that I should set you free to live in Balmorrow's pocket again as you did last Season. Once he sees that his new little wife is occupied and does no longer require his constant attention he will be pleased enough, I think, to leave her to my ministrations and to continue his *affaire* with you."

Lady Sarah did not quite know what to reply. Neither she nor her Aunt Grace could possibly carry on without the income Mr. Quigley provided. And Lord Parkhurst's proposed participation would prove most helpful. But she had never much liked Mr. Quigley with his gravelly voice and air of command. And of late, she had begun to grow fond of Balmorrow. Perhaps he was a Philistine as Lord Parkhurst suggested—whatever a Philistine was—but he was a genuinely nice person and she was beginning to feel badly whenever she must betray his confidences. Still, Summarfield had left her nothing but a mere pittance and even with Mr. Quigley's generous payments, she was finding it difficult to maintain herself in anywhere near an acceptable style. One could not, she was learning, always choose with whom one did business or what that business involved. Perhaps Lord Parkhurst felt likewise.

"You are very quiet, my dear," drawled Parkhurst. "Do you not wish to continue in Balmorrow's pocket then? Shall I tell our Mr. Quigley that he must find himself a new widow to gain the earl's confidence?"

"No," murmured Lady Sarah most thoughtfully. "I was merely considering—will you go so far as to make Lord Balmorrow's bride fall in love with you again? I expect that would be the thing to do. Alex does not care for her, you know. And if you set out to capture her heart, then she will not care a whit whether I am keeping her husband company or not."

"I shall conquer the maiden's heart with a whispered word, an aspect of melancholy, and one lift of an eyebrow," chuckled Lord Parkhurst. "She was in love with me once and will be again, I promise you, my dear. Anything to further the cause."

With another well-bred snicker of laughter and a tug at his sleeves, Parkhurst rose from the chair, took Lady Sarah's hand into his own and kissed the back of it quite regally. "I shall see myself out, dear lady. It has been a most pleasant visit, I assure you. And I do envy Balmorrow his part in this little charade. I only wish my role paired me with such an exceptional beauty as yourself."

Clarissa, who had slept the remainder of the morning and a good bit of the afternoon, emerged from her chamber bedecked in a Clarence blue walking dress with a matching riband threaded through her curls and matching kid slippers and hurried down to the long drawing room. Alex had sent a message by one of the footmen that she was to join him there as quickly as possible. Why she was to join him there as quickly as possible he had not said and a tiny frown played across Clarissa's brow as she pondered over it. Alex had franked her missive to Malcolm and placed it upon the table in the hall before they retired. That, certainly, was safely upon its way by now. His summons could have nothing to do with the letter.

Her heart stuttered the merest bit as she reached the bottom of the staircase on the first floor and turned toward the rear of the house. Never in all their married life—though, she reminded herself, that had not been very long at all—had her husband sent anyone to fetch her to him. Perhaps he was ill? Perhaps he had had some sort of accident? Oh, God forbid, perhaps the King's Guard had come to arrest him for treason! Clarissa's dainty little slippers seemed to increase speed of their own accord at that thought and she veritably flew down the corridor and spun around the door frame into the long drawing room and smack into a tall, heavily-muscled gentleman who threw his arms about her immediately to keep her from falling at the impact.

"Good heavens," he chuckled, setting her firmly upon her feet again and gazing down upon her with eyes almost as blue as her husband's own. "Do you have permission to fly in this house, little bluebird?"

"She needs no permission, Alden. This is her house. Do cease grinning at her like some twit with his upper stories to let."

In less than the time it took Clarissa to note that the gentleman who had steadied her possessed the same dark curls as her husband as well, Balmorrow was beside her, one hand possessively about her waist and drawing her close. "You will not remember my Cousin Alden, Clare, because he looks human today, but it was he married us."

"I do take offense, cuz. I look human every day."

"No, you do not. When you are floating about in your blasted robes you look most inhuman. Yes, and unapproachable, too. And do not go kissing his ring, either, Clare."

Clarissa felt the merest twitching of her lips upward. So this was the Bishop of Leeds. And Alex was correct. She had not recognized the man—would not have recognized him even had he worn his vestments—because she had paid him only the vaguest attention the last time they had come together. Though she would have guessed immediately that he and her husband were related.

"But I ought to kiss his ring, Alex. It is the appropriate thing to do," she murmured, her eyes catching the gleeful look in Alden's.

"Balmorrows do not kiss rings," replied her husband.

"Never?"

"Never. Most especially never Alden's ring because he puts pepper on it."

"I only ever did that once, Lex, and well you know it."

"No, I do not know it. I only ever kissed it once and it had pepper on it! It was the very day he was made bishop, Clare," grinned Balmorrow fondly. "I thought to make an exception, you know, because he was my cousin. I truly thought I ought to do the thing up right and proper and kiss the deuced ring and—"

"—he came up sputtering and cursing like a drunken sailor!" finished the Bishop of Leeds with a most engaging laugh. "Come, my new Cousin Clare, and let me kiss your hand instead," he added, bowing grandly. "Lex tugged me from the chapel so rapidly that evening that I did not even have the opportunity to welcome you properly to the family. Oh, and I have brought you a present," he added as he straightened up again. "Now where the deuce has it got to?"

Looking about him and running his fingers at the same time through his dark locks just as Alex always did, Clarissa thought the Bishop of Leeds pratically a twin of her husband. She studied him very closely. He had the same height, the same coloring, even their smiles were similar.

"But my nose is much more classic than Lex's," chuckled the bishop, turning back to her in time to catch her thoughtful gaze. "That is what you were doing, eh, my dear? Comparing the two of us? Lex's nose turns to the left at the tip."

"Only because you punched me and broke the thing," Balmorrow countered, urging Clarissa to a seat near the windows and settling down beside her. "How you ever came to be a bishop, Alden, I still cannot comprehend."

"Do not change the subject, Lex. His ears are larger than

mine as well, and his lips are puffier, and his eyebrows—well, there really are no words for Lex's eyebrows. And his cheeks are a good deal chubbier, you must admit that."

"Yes," giggled Clarissa. "And his chin is a deal more stubborn."

"Indeed. You are a discerning woman, cousin. You recognize stubborn when you see it. Ah, there it is," the bishop interrupted himself, striding toward the brocade sopha and then stooping down to reach under it.

"What on earth?" gasped Clarissa, darting a laughing glance at her husband.

"A wedding present," sighed Balmorrow. "He says it is a wedding present because he knows that then we cannot decline to accept the thing."

"You are just lucky, cuz, that I did not think to pawn them all off upon you," mumbled the bishop, pushing his way even farther beneath the sopha.

"What is he doing?" Clarissa asked with a quiet giggle. "Why is your cousin the bishop crawling about under our furniture?"

"He is fetching our present, dearest."

"Indeed. In fact, I have fetched it!" announced Alden, rising again and approaching Clarissa with a tiny ball of fur clinging to one sleeve of his coat. "Happy, ah, wedding, my dear," he added, placing the fur ball upon Clarissa's lap. "It is one of the Archbishop of Canterbury's cats," he explained as Clarissa stared at the kitten hesitantly.

It was a very small cat, barely bigger than a rat, with bright green eyes and black fur that puffed in every direction and what must once have been a most becoming red bow now unraveling itself from about its neck.

"Say thank you," prompted Balmorrow with a chuckle as he watched Clarissa survey the kitten. "You do not have to mean it, but you do have to say it. I already did."

"Th-thank you," laughed Clarissa.

"Quite proper," nodded Alden. "You are most welcome, my lady. In fact, you are most welcome to five more of them if you wish."

"Ah, but that would be greedy of us," inserted Balmorrow rapidly before Clarissa could reply. "You would not approve of my being greedy, Alden."

"I would just this once, Lex. I am stuck with them and it is your fault that I am, too."

"My fault?"

"Because Canterbury has heard of this conspiracy business and decided that having to dispose of the kittens is just punishment for my having the audacity to be related to you. Oh, I ought not to have said that."

"Why not?"

"Because, well—" The Bishop of Leeds' gaze fell solidly upon Clarissa who had taken the kitten up to hug it.

"Clare knows all about it, Alden."

"She does? All?"

"Everything. Well, not precisely everything."

"I do not?" asked Clare. "I thought I knew everything."

"No, you do not know who Mad Jack is, remember?"

"Oh, yes. I do not know Mad Jack," Clarissa repeated, meeting the bishop's astounded gaze complacently. "I did see him when he robbed our coach, but not well. Still Alex said that the fewer people who recognized him the safer we all would be, so I allowed him to keep Mad Jack's identity a secret. But I do know that you are involved, Your Grace, and that you snabbled that list of names from the Archbishop of Canterbury's residence."

"Clare is aiding me with a theory I have about that list, Alden," added Balmorrow helpfully.

"Well, I'll be whiskered," murmured the bishop, studying the two of them together. "Well, I'll be whiskered."

Chapter 14

"I expect it is not quite the thing," whispered Clarissa, one hand upon the bannister and the other clutching nervously at her gown as she came to a halt upon the third stair from the bottom in the vestibule. "I—I—"

Oh, how she wished that she knew what to say. She had not expected such a reaction. Alex was standing frozen at the bottom of the staircase staring up at her as though she were a perfect spectacle! "You do not like it. I shall go back up and change immediately."

"No!"

"But I have other perfectly lovely gowns, Alex, and they are likely more appropriate for Almack's. This one, you see, is in the Grecian mode, but it is cut quite low and it does cling so. I thought to look more like a young matron than a schoolroom miss and have gone too far. I will change. Kate will help me and I shall be ready in a cat's whisker. I only wore it to please you. I did not think—"

"You do please me," interrupted Balmorrow hoarsely. "The gown is beautiful and you are beautiful in it. It is—the trim—m'dear, that will raise eyebrows."

"The trim?"

"Yes, and that—riband—that dangles down the front. You do not realize."

"What do I not realize?"

"That it is the tartan of the Sinclairs."

Clarissa nodded. "I asked Maggie to be certain it was the correct weave. I am a Sinclair now and—Oh, I ought to have asked your permission to wear the tartan!"

"No. You require no one's permission to wear it and it pleases me no end, Clare, that you wish to do so. But—the wearing of the tartans was outlawed in England after the Jacobite rebellion."

"Outlawed? Patterns of weave were outlawed?"

"The wearing of the tartans of all Scots clans," he nodded. "And only now since the Scots have joined with England against Napoleon have Scots soldiers been permitted the wearing of their tartans on English soil. But for those who are not soldiers to wear them in public—all the quizzing glasses in Almack's will be raised in your direction, sweetling. You cannot wish to be the object of such scrutiny."

"Nonsense," Clarissa protested, stepping down the last three stairs and going into Balmorrow's arms to hug him tightly. "As if I give a fig. It is merely that if you would be embarrassed—"

"I would be proud no end. As a matter of fact—"

"As a matter of fact, my lord?"

"Jonson," grinned the earl, catching a most unbutlerlike gleam in that worthy's eyes as he waited patiently to hand the earl his hat and gloves and cane, "watch over this budding renegade until I return." And bestowing a quick kiss upon Clarissa's upturned nose, Balmorrow literally dashed up the staircase all the way to the second floor.

Lady Cowper's eyes widened. The Countess Lieven's jaw dropped. And Sally Jersey's mouth snapped shut as her fan fluttered spastically.

"I knew it!" cried the Duchess of Corning, who had literally dragged the duke to Almack's that evening. "I knew he would do it once he saw Clare's gown!"

"Do what, Mags? Is it Alex has silenced Silence?" he asked,

turning to see what had bought Sally Jersey's constant and annoying chattering to a halt.

"Indeed. Alex and Clare together. He is wearing it, David!"

"Wearing what? Oh, lord! The waistcoat!"

"Yes, the waistcoat! Oh, David, what a joy to see him in it in public! And can you see it, the trim on Clare's gown? She chose it especially for Alex."

"S'Blood," groaned Corning, slipping closer to the spot where his brother-in-law bowed over Lady Cowper's hand. "The tartans ain't proscribed no more, but he ought not be wearing that waistcoat here, Mags. He is already suspected of treason."

"Well, but to support the Scots now is not to be a traitor, David. Scots are falling upon foreign battlefields on behalf of King George and England at this very moment. And it is time they were acknowledged for it, too. If Alex is not a Scot because of the boundaries, he is a Scot by ancestry and proud of it, too. I might have been born in the Highlands myself if the first Sinclair of Balmorrow had not wandered south. Would you have scorned me, David, had I been born a Highlander?"

"Never, but Mags, this is a time when Alex needs to—to—"

"To what?"

"Remain as inconspicuous as possible."

"Alex? Inconspicuous?"

Corning's reply faltered upon his lips as, at the far end of the chamber, word of the sheer audacity of Balmorrow's waistcoat and Lady Balmorrow's gown had reached the Scot orchestra leader, Neil Gow, and that gentleman's violin gleefully burst into "Auld Lang Syne".

The laughter in Balmorrow's eyes was contageous as he broke free of the patronesses and escorted Clarissa through the crowd to where his sister and brother-in-law stood.

"Gow has thrown in his lot with us," he chuckled. "He is going straight from Robert Burns into a Scottish reel. Do not look so very serious, Corning, at least I am not wearing my kilt."

"Could not have gotten past Willis at the door if you had," offered Viscount Norris as he came to a halt beside them. "Knee breeches or nothing at the marriage mart, Lex. May I, do you think, dance with my beautiful new cousin?"

"To this reel?" asked Balmorrow with a cock of an eyebrow. "Norris is not fond of reels," he explained with a wink to Clarissa. "Tends to get his feet all tangled up."

"Must be to this reel or not at all," sighed Norris. "I have promised every dance but this and the one precedes the final waltz. That is to be a cotillion. I despise cotillions and shall hide in the card room until it is done."

"Take her then," nodded Balmorrow, "if she will have you."

Clarissa had the oddest thought. From the slight trembling in Balmorrow's hand where it touched her waist and from an almost imperceptible twitch near Norris' eye she thought for a moment that a message had just flickered between them. But that was nonsense of course. What message could be contained in such innocent words as Norris had just spoken? And why would Viscount Norris be sending secret messages to Alex in the first place? They were cousins after all and might speak freely to each other whenever they wished.

With a bow and a grin Viscount Norris led Clarissa to the floor and set about dancing the Scottish reel with a great deal of enthusiasm and absolutely no polished grace. He did indeed entangle himself in his own feet from time to time. But his grin was so very infectious and his observations on his own performance so very amusing, that Clarissa enjoyed every moment of it and was smiling broadly as he returned her to her husband and took his leave.

"Enjoyed dancing with Norris, did you? All the ladies apparently do. He is not much on style, my cousin, but his enthusiasm is without bounds—except when the dance is a cotillion. They are to play a waltz next. Do you waltz, Clare? I do not even know if you waltz. Will you waltz with me?"

He led her onto the floor and when the music began, swirled her into the dance. The great sapphires of his eyes smiled proudly down at her as he twirled her about the floor. In the midst of one turn, his hands tugged her gently toward him, rearranging themselves until she fit more comfortably in his arms. In the midst of another she found herself shifted again, brought even closer, so close that when she lowered her gaze, she could distinguish each facet in the diamond stickpin that graced his cravat. Clarissa leaned back against his arm and grinned up at him. "You are wicked, my lord."

"Indeed. Tonight I am truly disgraceful. You have loosed the rebel in me. You do not loathe to be held so closely? You are not afraid that we shall be censored?"

"Well, of course not. We are husband and wife."

"Yes, and that is another thing. Husbands are not expected to dance with their wives. I shall be ragged about this for at least a week by every gentleman I know. Norris and Corning and the rest will call me a mooncalf and grin at each other behind my back. But I do not care a whit."

"You do not?"

"No, not a whit. They may bait me to their hearts' content, but they shall not get a rise out of me. It is worth all of their barbs to hold you so close in my arms as the music plays. There is something magical in it."

Quite inexplicably a pang shot through Clarissa's heart.

"I thought you would never come," sighed Norris, falling into step beside Balmorrow as he entered the card room.

"You did say the cotillion before the final waltz, Jack."

"Yes, but I thought you would come *before* the music began. I have been standing here since the last set ended."

"Oh. Well, I could not just abandon Clare. I waited until some gentleman came forward and requested a dance."

"Some gentleman?"

"Lord Parker. I did never meet him before but Clare apparently knew the gentleman."

"Parker? Lex, there is only one Lord Parker in London and he is eighty-five years old if he's a day."

"Well, perhaps it was not Parker then. There is so much jabbering goes on in there that I cannot always hear clearly."

With the lift of a finger, Norris turned on his heel and marched from the card room to return minutes later with the information that the gentleman dancing with Lady Balmorrow was Lord Parkhurst, not Lord Parker. "Parkhurst was used to dangle after her, Lex, for the brief time she was on the town."

"By Jove, he was the one kissed her!" exclaimed Balmorrow, heading for the door.

"Not now, Lex," snickered Norris, quickly grabbing his cousin's arm. "What do you intend? To dash out there and drag your lady from the dance floor?"

"Well, but I thought he said Parker. I would not have given him permission if I had—"

"It is merely a cotillion, Lex. He is not going to kiss your wife in the midst of a cotillion at Almack's," Norris grinned, tugging his cousin toward one of the card tables. "Damned if you ain't jealous."

"I am not. It is merely that—"

"Good, if you ain't jealous then sit down and deal. We have things to discuss. Liverpool is thoroughly confused," he murmured, studying the cards Balmorrow dealt him. "Except for the seal, that list Alden discovered might be any invitation list."

"I think it is not meant for invitations, Jack."

"Well, of course it ain't. And the fact that your wife and her brother are upon it makes Liverpool extremely nervous. He thinks that it might well be a list of those involved in the conspiracy and—well, your new bride and her brother being upon it—well, Liverpool is no end worried about you."

"I have a theory about the thing, Norris. I think it is not exactly a list of conspirators."

"Not exactly? What does that mean? You are going to enlighten me, ain't you, Lex?"

"Yes, but not until you cease spouting ain't as though it were a real word," muttered Balmorrow, taking a trick from his cousin. "You have been playing at Mad Jack Docker too long, Jack. That wretch begins to creep into your everyday life."

"I rarely have an everyday life of late, but I shall make a stab at proper English for your sake, cuz. What do you mean it is not exactly a list of conspirators?"

"I think the list is of people who are to be kept free of blame when whatever is to happen happens, Jack, but that they are not necessarily all in on the thing. Clare has not the least clue as to what is in the wind."

Norris' bright hazel eyes looked up from his cards abruptly. "How do you know?"

"I asked her about the list before I gave it to you. She knows no one upon it except Malcolm and this Lord Parkhurst fellow and The Summarfield whom she had just met at the Hoggs."

"You showed the list to your wife?"

"Yes."

"But Alex!"

"Ssshhh. Settle down, Jack, do."

"But Alex," Norris began again more quietly, "how do you know you can trust the woman?"

"I cannot explain exactly. She is a Beresfont; she is my wife; I do trust her."

"You barely know her."

"I know her better and trust her more with every day. She has a right to know how things stand with me, Jack."

"Oh, fine," grumbled Norris, discarding an ace of spades, "and suppose she *is* one of them? You will confide everything in her and all our efforts will be for naught."

"But she is not one of them. That is why I am certain the list is not a list of conspirators, Jack—because Clare is not one of them and yet her name appears upon the thing."

Norris stared at his cousin as though Balmorrow had completely lost his mind.

"Play your hand, Jack, or someone will come to see what goes on between us. I have not got it all settled in my mind, but there is something more havey-cavey than we thought happening and I think that Clare's mother is somehow involved in it. Last Thursday, on my behalf, Clare wrote to Malcolm requesting the location of their mother's grave. His reply came this morning. According to the records he possesses, Viscountess Halliard was buried behind the chapel in St. Mary's Lane."

"You think a dead woman wrote that list?" Norris' eyebrows rose almost to his hairline.

"No. She is not buried in St. Mary's Lane, Jack. I have been to every grave in the place."

"You think she is alive!" Norris gasped.

"Very much alive and one of the conspirators. Because then, Jack, it makes perfect sense that she would include her children's names upon a list of those she wishes to protect if the effort fails. No mother would wish her children—even children she had not seen in years—to be implicated in a rebellion against the Crown."

* * *

Clarissa stood wondering where Alex had gone. The cotillion had come to an end and the beginning strains of a waltz were floating about the room and still there was no sign of her husband. Edward, Lord Parkhurst stood beside her, his bright hazel eyes reminding her vaguely of someone else's, his golden curls not the merest bit disarranged by the efforts of the dance they had just completed.

"You have been abandoned, eh?" Parkhurst ventured with a slow smile. "Your new sister-in-law and her duke are already on the dance floor and your new husband has apparently taken himself off to the card room. I wonder, Clarissa, if you would think it presumptuous of me to ask you for this waltz?"

"But we have just danced, Edward."

"Yes, but it will not be noted if we dance again. You are a married woman, after all. No one will look askance at us."

"No, I expect they will not." Clarissa could not quite account for it, but the thought of waltzing with Lord Parkhurst did not thrill her as it once had done. She remembered other Wednesday nights at Almack's when her greatest wish had been to be swept about the dance floor in Edward's arms. Her heart had fluttered and dipped at the mere anticipation of it. But this evening her heart stirred not at all. Where was Alex? Why did he not appear? She had seen him wander off when Edward had led her to the floor. Was her husband fond of gaming? Was he so caught up in the cards that he did not realize she would be waiting for him now? Really, it was exasperating the things she did not know about the man she had married.

"Shall we?" Lord Parkhurst asked, offering his arm to lead her to the floor.

Clarissa placed her hand upon it and allowed him to do so.

"I have missed you most dreadfully, my love," Parkhurst murmured as he swept her into the dance. "You have not the least idea, Clarissa, how devastated I was to hear that you had married that Scots barbarian. I thought my heart would break to think of such a lovely blossom as yourself crushed beneath Balmorrow's old muddy topboots."

Clarissa looked up at him, her eyes wide. "P-pardon me, my lord? Crushed beneath Balmorrow's old muddy topboots?"

"Well, you know what I mean, my dear."

"No, I do not think that I do."

Parkhurst stared down at her, a font of sympathy apparent in his gaze. "It is common knowledge, Clarissa, that Balmorrow is fond of having his own way and not loath to trample upon others to obtain it. Only look how he has forced you to trim your gown in bits of that dreadful tartan of his. Does he care one bit how embarrassed you must be by it? Did he give one thought to what you must feel appearing amongst your peers sporting that hideous and nearly treasonable plaid? But you are not to worry, my dear. I know the sort of tyrant he is and I do not at all blame you for it. Indeed, I pity you."

"Oh!" gasped Clarissa in disbelief, almost missing a step.

"And you are not to think for one moment that anything Balmorrow does or bids you to do will ever reflect badly upon you, my dear. Your friends realize that you were forced by circumstances to marry that devil and we will stand by you in spite of him."

Clarissa could not believe her ears.

"I did wish to marry you myself, Clarissa," Parkhurst purred softly, pulling her more closely to him. "I longed to marry you more than anything. And had you not accepted Balmorrow so quickly, I would have discovered some way to go about it, too—some way to overcome my lack of capital and your lack of fortune. You do realize that, do you not, my dearest?"

"I realize," hissed Clarissa, struggling to reestablish the accepted distance between them, "that you told Malcolm that you could not marry me and that you *did not* marry me, Edward. And that Alex did!"

"You are angry with me," drawled Parkhurst, "but it is plain truth I speak. I loved you. I love you still. I will always love you. And you love me. You know that you do. Ow!"

"Oh, I have stomped upon your foot! How clumsy of me, Edward."

"No, no, not at all. My fault. Should have been paying more attention. Ow!"

"Oh my goodness! I have done it again! And to the very same foot, too! Perhaps we ought to sit down, Edward."

"No, no, I shall manage, my dear one. Ouch!"

"Now what did I do?"

"You kicked me in the ankle. How did you manage to kick me in the ankle when we are waltzing?"

"Why, I have not the faintest idea. I meant to kick you in the shin. I expect my aim has gone quite sour."

"What?" Parkhurst's glorious hazel eyes widened in astonishment.

Balmorrow swung back out the door he had just entered and burst into whoops in the corridor.

"What? What is it, Lex?"

"My darling bride just came close to crippling Parkhurst upon the dance floor."

"She what?"

"I—I—she is waltzing with Parkhurst and kicked him in the ankle."

"Oh, surely not," murmured Norris, peeking in around the door frame.

"Yes, she did! And on purpose too!"

"But why would she do that? She is out and out glowering at him now. Must be something he said."

"Good. I hope he says it again."

"Lex!"

"Well, well, I do," gasped Balmorrow, fighting to control his laughter. "And here I was worried that I had been gone much too long and that Clare would be falling under that popinjay's spell again."

"Again under his—? Do you mean to say, Lex, that things had gone so far between your new bride and Parkhurst that she—"

"Would have married that gentleman if he had requested it of her. Yes. I was a fool to have granted him permission to dance with her, but I had to meet you, you know, and I did think he had said Parker and not Parkhurst. He kissed her once in a garden," the earl added much more quietly.

Viscount Norris stared at his cousin with a most outrageous twinkle in his changeable hazel eyes. "You told me that he kissed her when we were in the card room."

"I did? Yes, well, he did kiss her. But it was before Clare and I ever knew each other, so it is of no account."

"Of course not."

"And you are not to bandy it about, Jack, that he kissed her. Sprung upon her no doubt from the shrubbery, before she knew what was coming."

"No doubt," murmured Norris, stifling a snicker.

"You are not to go bandying that about, Jack, that bit about the kiss, or you will find my fist connecting with your mouth."

"I would not think of bandying that about."

"Well, you are thinking of something. I can see it in your eyes."

"Merely observing, coz."

"Observing what?"

"You. You are jealous of Parkhurst, Lex."

"I am not."

"Yes, you are."

"I have no reason to be jealous. Clare is my wife, not his, and she has just kicked him in the ankle besides. She would not kick him in the ankle if she were bewitched by him, would she, Jack?"

"I highly doubt it. But you are jealous nonetheless."

The carriage ride home from Almack's had been a silent one. Clarissa had done her best to chatter about this and that, but when no response whatsoever was forthcoming, it was most disconcerting and did tend to bring even the merest twittering to a halt. Was Alex angry with her? No. How could he be? There was no reason. But something had certainly sent him into a brown study.

With a sigh Clarissa slipped out of her gown and into the pretty primrose robe that Kate held for her. Would she ever come to understand Balmorrow? Perhaps he had lost a good deal of money in the card room. But that could not be, she thought seriously, because all of the gentlemen complained that the play at Almack's was for chicken stakes and deadly dull. Clarissa was not quite certain what chicken stakes were, but certainly it meant that her husband could not have lost anything worth frowning over. She settled thoughtfully upon the little bench before her vanity and allowed Kate to unpin her hair.

"Did you have a pleasant time, my lady?"

"What? Oh, yes Kate, most pleasant."

"And did his lordship waltz with you?"

"He did," smiled Clarissa into the mirror.

"His lordship waltzes so excellently," Kate murmured on a breath of a sigh.

"You have seen my husband waltz?"

"Oh, yes milady. Always at Christmas time there is a ball at Castle Balmorrow and his lordship does insist that the musicians play at least two waltzes. Last year he waltzed with Lady Brandy and with Mrs. Beal."

"Yes, and this year I will waltz with my lady and with you, Kate," declared Balmorrow as he entered the chamber. "But only if you wish it, of course. Off with you, Katie. I am quite capable of unpinning Lady Balmorrow's hair, I think. Quick, fly away, it is already past two and you need your sleep."

With a hurried curtsey and a wide grin, Kate left them.

Clarissa watched in the glass as her husband, true to his word, deftly finished unpinning her hair and began to brush it. "I have come to beg your pardon for being so silent in the carriage," he murmured after a time. "I was thinking is all."

"I assumed you were thinking."

"Oh? Did you? How kind. Some people would have assumed I was sulking."

"You had no reason to sulk."

"No, none at all. Did you enjoy yourself, Clare?"

"Indeed."

"Even when you kicked Parkhurst?"

"Oh! I had no idea you had seen."

"I was entering the door from the card room when you did it. The two of you were passing right before me."

"It is really too bad that you did not enter sooner, my lord."

"Why?"

"Because you could have watched me step upon that gentleman's feet."

"You did not."

"I did. I was dreadful to him. He made me so very angry!"

"But why, Clare? What was it he said to make you treat him so shabbily?"

"He called you a barbarian and a tyrant. He s-said that I

was a blossom and that you were trampling upon me or some such nonsense," Clarissa replied, one look at her husband's reflection in the glass sending her into a giggle. "No, truly, Alex. Do not look at me like a veritable halfwit. And that man had the sheer audacity to suggest that you had forced me to wear the tartan trim! And then the pompous ass declared that he still loved me and told me that I loved him as well! Honestly, do all men wander about telling women whom they do and do not love?"

"Apparently."

"Well, I will have you know, Alexander St. John Sinclair, that I know very well who it is that I love and I do not require to be told it by any man. Alex, do not make such ridiculous faces at me. I am serious!"

"Yes, I can see that by the way you are giggling, my dear."

"I cannot help myself. You look like a lunatic with your eyes crossed so."

"Crossed? My eyes are crossed? No wonder all I can see is my nose! Oh, but this is dire, Clare. Truly dire!"

"What? What is dire?"

"My eyes being crossed. It is a family curse. I did never tell you about it. I feared you would flee from me directly."

Clarissa could not help herself and went from giggling into laughter.

"No, I am serious, woman!"

"Of c-course you are. W-what is the curse, Alex?"

"Once a Sinclair gentleman's eyes are crossed, they stay that way."

"They stay that way?"

"Forever."

"F-forever?" Clarissa turned upon her bench to blink up at him, chuckling.

"Well, forever unless—"

"Unless what, Alex? Tell me."

"Unless the poor fellow is kissed directly upon the lips by a beautiful woman."

"I see. Well, I have no idea where you will find a beautiful woman to kiss you at this hour, Alex. I expect you will need to go searching for one the very first thing in the morning."

"Baggage," laughed Balmorrow, tugging her up and into his arms. "You know perfectly well whose kiss I require. Give it to me please or I shall not get a wink of sleep. It is near impossible to sleep with one's eyes crossed."

For the very first time Clarissa's eyes remained open as she kissed her husband, focussing intently upon his eyes. The very moment their lips met, those marvelous blue orbs of his uncrossed and laughed down into her own.

"Magic," Balmorrow whispered, his lips remaining upon hers.

Clarissa laughed without drawing away.

Chapter 15

Malcolm Beresfont, Viscount Halliard stared uncomprehendingly at his brother-in-law. "You rode? All the way from London? You did not bring Clare with you? Is there something wrong? Clare is not ill?"

"No, no, nothing like that, Halliard," droned Balmorrow, accepting a glass of port which he hoped would wash the dust of the road from his throat. "I merely had an idea and thought you might be of help to me. You are not all that far from London, you know. I left at nine this morning and here it is merely one in the afternoon. I shall be home well before dinner. I have my own cattle at the posting inns so I need not depend upon just one mount."

"I used to have cattle," sighed Malcolm. "Now I have one cart horse and two saddle horses."

"Ah, but they are all yours and not likely to be sold up, Halliard."

"True, and Halliard Hall is free and clear and I have invested a tidy sum to put the land on a paying basis. In a year or two, Charis and I shall come about royally."

"I hope so. You need not hesitate to say, you know, if there is some way I can be of help. We are family now. And speaking of family"—Balmorrow thought it was a most awkward transition, but he was in the devil of a hurry—"I wondered if there might be a miniature of your mother and father about somewhere that I could borrow."

"A miniature of my mother and father?"

"Um-hmm. Clare mentioned to me last night that she thought there might be one of each of them, but she could not remember. I wish to have a portrait painted of the two together for Clare—as a surprise for her birthday. Lawrence has already agreed to do the thing but he must have something from which to copy their features."

"Sir Thomas Lawrence?"

"You know of him, do you?"

"He is the painter to the King!"

"Yes, well, but he is at loose ends at the moment—with Farmer George locked away and Prinny not yet thought to take advantage of him. Do you have the miniatures? Will you let me have them for a time? I promise to return them, Halliard, undamaged."

"Of course! I should be more than pleased. Only think, to have a portrait of Mama and Papa done by Lawrence!"

"But you are not to let on, eh? It would spoil my surprise. I should not even mention it to your wife, Halliard. They correspond, you know, Clare and—"

"Charis. Yes, I will refrain from any mention of it."

"I thank you. Truly I do."

"The miniatures are upstairs in my chambers. I shall get them for you. Drink up, Balmorrow, and pour yourself another. I shall find some paper to wrap them in and bring them to you directly."

Balmorrow downed the remainder of his port and poured himself another glass as his brother-in-law disappeared into the upper regions of Halliard Hall. For the first time that day the tension drained from him. He was not at all adept at lying and already he had lied to Halliard three times. Clarissa knew perfectly well that he had come to fetch the miniatures. It had been her idea. And Lawrence had not agreed to do a portrait. He had not even approached that gentleman on the subject. And most certainly none of this had a thing to do with Clare's birthday.

* * *

"I cannot imagine where Alex has gone," Clare murmured, most uneasy because she had not expected to be faced with the need to lie to her new sister-in-law. "He rode out very near nine this morning and has not been heard from since."

"And he did not tell you where he was bound?"

"Well, well, I did not ask, you see. I expect he has gone to one of his clubs."

"How odd."

"Odd? Why would that be odd? Do not gentlemen often go to their clubs to wile away the time?"

"Oh, indeed they do. But Alex is not a member of any of the clubs."

"He is not?"

"No," laughed Maggie. "Do you know you are blushing the brightest pink, Clare? Come, there is no need to be embarrassed. You are newly married. The topic of gentlemen's clubs, I take it, has not yet arisen between you."

"N-no, it has not. But I thought all gentlemen belonged to one club or another."

"No, not all of them. Not even the majority of them. The clubs are most exclusive, you know, and a considerable number of gentlemen are not given entrance."

"Alex was denied entrance? To *all* of them?"

Maggie laughed again and smoothed a crease from her emerald-striped walking dress with one hand. "Well, he is a notorious figure, my brother, but not quite that notorious. He was not blackballed by any of them. He just did never apply to any in the first place."

"But why not? I thought that it was most prestigious to belong to a gentlemen's club. I thought all gentlemen longed to do so. And Alex is an earl besides. Surely he is expected to belong to one or the other of them."

"Yes, so David says over and over again. Alex is expected to belong to one or the other of them. But he will not join because—because—"

"Because why, Maggie? Oh, do tell me," urged Clarissa, somewhat spellbound by the humorous glint in the duchess' eyes and the quiet gurgle of laughter that once again escaped her.

"You do know that Alex is the most generous person in the entire world, do you not, Clare? Well, no, most likely you have not discovered that as yet. But he is. He will contribute to funds to save the orphans and funds to save some old church and funds to save the destitute and funds to save the funds if it comes to that. But—"

"But what?"

"But he will not sport the blunt to join any of the clubs! He is as clutchfisted as he can be when it comes to paying the membership fees. 'What, pay to be put in the way of losing my blunt to Brummell and the like?' he will say to David. 'I think not, old man.' And then David will tell him that a great many things occur at the clubs other than gambling and will expound upon the great political debates that rage at White's and Watier's. And Alex will merely shrug his shoulders and say that he has enough debating in the House of Lords and at Lady Holland's and at Carlton House and practically at every entertainment he attends, and he can well forego paying for gentlemen to deride his ideas because they are all quite willing to deride them for free elsewhere."

"My lady," interrupted Jonson coming stiffly into the room to present Clarissa a calling card upon a silver tray. The corner was bent down, indicating that the gentleman was calling in person.

Clarissa read the name upon the card and sighed. "I expect you must bring him up, Jonson. And send word to the kitchen for another cup, another pot of tea and a plate of scones as well. He will expect tea, I think."

"Who is it?" Maggie asked, curious.

"Lord Parkhurst. I cannot imagine why he has come."

"Did you not dance with him last evening at Almack's?"

"Yes, but—"

"He is merely paying you a morning call then. A great number of gentlemen do, you know—visit for a time with each of their partners of the evening before. Though generally they do so only with the unmarried ones."

Edward, Lord Parkhurst entered the parlor with a bright smile upon his face and bowed most politely over Clarissa's hand and over Maggie's. "I thought to find his lordship at home as well," he declared, lowering himself into a lyre-backed chair between the two women. "Perhaps he has not yet arisen?"

"What? At two in the afternoon?" smiled Maggie. "Surely you mistake my brother for one of Mr. Brummell's dandies, my lord."

"Alex has gone out," provided Clarissa quietly, wondering what on earth had possessed Edward to appear upon her doorstep after the way she had treated the man last evening.

"Ah, to Tattersall's perhaps?"

"I have no idea. Did you wish especially to see him?"

"No, no, not at all," protested Parkhurst quickly. "I only came to pay my respects and to, ah, apologize, Cla—my lady—for last evening."

"Apologize?" The Duchess of Corning's lovely eyebrows rose significantly at this hint of some altercation.

"Indeed. I fear I was most aggravating to your sister-in-law, Your Grace, though I have not the least idea why. I have thought about it all morning. It was, I fear, some slip of the tongue. And I do apologize for it, whatever it was, Lady Balmorrow," he added with a knowing gaze at Clarissa.

Maggie did not for a moment miss the flash of spirit in Clarissa's eyes that answered him.

"I take it I said something quite unpalatable," continued Parkhurst. "My words did not come out at all as I intended, I assure you."

Lord Parkhurst lowered his gaze to the floral carpeting then raised it again in expectation of forgiveness. He knew the look that appeared upon his handsome countenance was a perfect mixture of confusion, apology and petition. He had practiced it most of an hour this morning before his looking glass. No young lady had ever held out against that look. Certainly Clarissa Beresfont would not be the first to do so.

"Well, I expect you are forgiven, Lord Parkhurst," Clarissa sighed. She did not for a moment forgive him, but with Maggie present it was the polite thing to say. Certainly she could not rail against the man and send him packing with Maggie as onlooker.

"I thank you, my lady. What's this? Oh, no, though I thank you for the kind thought, I cannot stay for tea," Parkhurst drawled as a footman entered with the requested refreshments. "I must be off. A previous engagement, you know. Your Grace, a pleasure to see you again. And my lady, I thank you for your forgiveness. I shall do better the next time we meet." And with that Parkhurst was up and out the door and hurrying down the front staircase.

He retrieved his hat and gloves and cane from Jonson and gave a heavy sigh as he paused on the walk at the bottom of the front steps. Which way? St. James's? Bond Street? The Summarfield's? Yes, The Summarfield's, he decided. Damnation, but he could murder Henry! Stupid man had had the sheer audacity to step in front of a hack and get his leg broken last night and had not sent word until noon and now they did none of them have the least idea where the Earl of Balmorrow might be. But he knew Balmorrow belonged to none of the clubs. Perhaps they would be lucky and discover that he had gone to refresh himself at the fount of Sarah. They were due for some luck, the lot of them.

"What on earth was that all about?" queried Maggie, walking to the window to note Parkhurst's progress toward Russell Street.

"Nothing."

"Do not tell me it was nothing, sister-in-law. I saw the sparks in your eyes. You may tell me, however, that it is none of my business. I shall accept that."

"Very well then, it is none of your business."

"Lord Parkhurst is a very handsome gentleman, is he not?" asked Maggie.

The question was so unexpected that it came close to taking Clarissa's breath away. "Yes, he is. I was used to think him quite handsome," she replied with hesitation.

"And now?"

"And now? Well, he is quite handsome still."

"You are not in love with him, are you?" Maggie left the window to take a seat in the high-backed chair directly across from Clarissa. "I only ask," she continued hurriedly, raising her hand for silence, "because Norris informed me that you and Lord Parkhurst had become something of an item before you were forced into mourning and—"

"And?" queried Clarissa.

"Well, devil take it, you said once that you were in love with Alex. If you have now decided that you were mistaken about your feelings and that you are truly in love with Lord Parkhurst and you intend to carry on an *affaire* with the man, I do not give tuppence how discreet you are, I shall shoot you in cold blood."

Miss Grace Gonnering peered near-sightedly from the window of the town coach. "I do not for a moment understand, my dear, what it is we are doing. Oh, my heavens! We are not driving down Bond Street! Quickly, Sarah, alert the coachman. We cannot be seen driving down Bond Street in the middle of the afternoon! Why, everyone will think we are fast to go parading before all the dandies and the loungers. Oh! He *is* turning into Bond Street. Hurry, Sarah, pull the shades!" Miss Gonnering followed these exclamations with a most futile attempt to pull down all of the shades at the same time and was bounced quite heavily to the floor of the coach. "Oh! Oh!" she gasped excitedly from the floorboards. "Sarah, pull the shades, do!"

Lady Sarah merely smiled at her aunt and held out her hands to help that ancient back up to her seat. "I am quite certain that no one will so much as take note of us, Aunt Grace. And we cannot possibly discover if Lord Balmorrow is on Bond Street if we do not look out the windows."

"Is that what we are doing? Looking for Lord Balmorrow?" squeaked Miss Gonnering, lowering the shade nearest her to the very bottom of the window frame.

"Indeed. Did you not hear Lord Parkhurst? It is imperative that he discover the earl's whereabouts."

"Well, I did hear that," nodded Miss Gonnering, huddling into the corner of the coach and taking a quick peek out from behind the edge of the shade. "Sarah, dear, really, we must pull all the shades or your reputation will be a shambles! See, one may look out and not be seen oneself. You must just pretend to be a little mouse with a cat near by."

With a sigh, Lady Sarah did as her aunt bid and lowered the rest of the shades in the coach, then peered around the edge of the one closest to her. "I do not think, Aunt, that this is the answer. We shall need to ride the entire length of Bond Street and then turn around and ride back in order to see who is on the other side."

"Oh no! No! Not twice through Bond Street. Why could Lord Parkhurst not come here himself? There is no danger to a gentleman's reputation to be in Bond Street of an afternoon."

"Because Lord Parkhurst has gone to search for Lord Balmorrow in Tattersall's, Aunt Grace. You certainly do not want me to go wandering on foot through Tattersall's amongst all the gentlemen there, do you?"

"No, most certainly not. But we might have sent Jemmy."

"No, we might not have sent Jemmy."

"Why not?"

"Because we do not wish Lord Balmorrow to know that we are searching for him, Aunt."

"What? We are risking our reputations searching for the gentleman but we do not wish to find him?"

"Honestly, Aunt Grace, how can you see anything at all this way? I vow I shall grow squint-eyed before we reach the end of the street. We *do* wish to find him, but we do not wish him to know he has been found."

Miss Gonnering grew most discomposed at this information and lost possession of the strings of her reticule letting it tumble to the floor. Lady Sarah bent to retrieve it for her just as the shade nearest Miss Gonnering snapped open. Miss Gonnering jumped at the sound and her knee quite unavoidably hit Lady Sarah in the chin. "Ouch!" cried Lady Sarah, straightening hurriedly.

The trouble was that she straightened so hurriedly that she smacked an elbow into the shade closest to her and it snapped open with an enormous pop that startled the coachman who jerked on the reins which set his horses to rearing in protest.

This alone would have elicited little attention had not Lady Sarah's coach been immediately before Jackson's Boxing Saloon when the horses began to rear and had the Duke of Corning's curricle not been awaiting him at that exact spot. But as it was, Corning's team thought themselves entirely too close to the other horses' flailing hooves and bolted, dragging his tiger, shrieking wildly and clinging to the harness, all the way up the street.

At those pitiful shrieks gentlemen thundered from Jackson's in varying states of undress to see what all the commotion was about. Miss Gonnering took one glance at Mr. Tom Bedlow without his shirt and slipped from the seat to the floorboards in a dead faint while Lady Sarah, her lower lip bleeding because she had bit it when Miss Gonnering had knocked her in the chin, stared out at the gentlemen in a stunned and wretched state.

Lord Worth, in his shirtsleeves, ran immediately to the coach horses' heads and brought them under control. Viscount Norris, with one boot off and one boot on, leaped into the saddle of the closest hack and took off after the duke's curricle, and Mr. Tom Bedlow and Mr. Harry Chisolm and Sir Ralph Forthingate opened the coach doors and piled inside. Mr. Bedlow tugged Miss Gonnering to the seat. Mr. Chisolm pawed energetically through Miss Gonnering's reticule for a bottle of salts to wave under that poor woman's nose. And Sir Ralph, who was the only gentleman dressed enough to be in possession of one, pulled his handkerchief from his pocket and pressed it forcefully against the astounded Lady Sarah's lip. Artemus Hogg, glancing up the street to satisfy himself that Norris had captured the duke's team and saved the tiger, burst into whoops and turned back inside the building to fetch Corning who was just then stepping from the ring.

"Only The Summarfield would be caught driving up Bond Street in the middle of the afternoon," chuckled Mr. Edwin Daws upon hearing the cause of the commotion.

"In search of a new beau now that Balmorrow is leg-shackled," responded a young Lord Bedford. "Shouldn't mind taking her on myself, I'll tell you that."

"Aye, shopping for a new gentleman," laughed Captain Carly McCallogh. "Devil of a way to go about it, but that's The Summarfield. Never was one for convention."

"The woman is fast," gasped Lord Ornesby, wiping tears of laughter from his eyes, "but not quite fast enough today."

The Duke of Corning, however, was not amused as he struggled hurriedly into his clothes and rushed out into the street. His first thought was for Teddy, the little tiger who was merely ten and might well have been seriously harmed. But Norris was riding back toward him with the boy up before him and leading the team behind. "All in one piece," Norris shouted, "the lad, the team, and the curricle."

That set Corning's mind somewhat to rest. He poked his head in through the open door of The Summarfield's coach and stared up into Lady Sarah's shocked hazel eyes. Sir Ralph was still pressing his handerkerchief against her lip and on the seat across from them, Miss Gonnering, under Bedlow's and Chisolm's ministrations, was groaning into awareness.

"What the devil is wrong with you?" Corning shouted into Lady Sarah's amazed face before he once thought what he was doing. "Are your attics to let? You have near killed my tiger, near lamed my horses and near destroyed my curricle! Are you completely bonkers, madam? And what in Hades are you doing in Bond Street in the middle of the afternoon at all?"

This minor tirade was interrupted by a piercing shriek from Miss Gonnering which would have sent the coach horses into a veritable frenzy had not both Worth and the coachman been holding them. "Help! Help! Naked gentlemen are upon me!" shrieked Miss Gonnering and fainted dead away again.

Bedlow and Chisolm could no longer help themselves and roared into laughter. Sir Ralph with admirable aplomb choked back his own guffaw and fell to coughing. The Duke of Corning forced himself to continue glowering at Lady Sarah even though it was a battle to keep the corners of his mouth from twitching upward. And with Sir Ralph's handkerchief now in her own hand, Lady Sarah stared wide-eyed at the gentlemen around her, great glistening teardrops rolling silently down her pale cheeks.

"Well, I am not Madeline," declared Clarissa with some vehemence. "I did not marry your brother simply to revel in the use of his fortune and his title. I have not the least intention to play Alex false no matter what the circumstance—not with Lord Parkhurst nor with any other gentleman."

"No, I can see now that you have not," mumbled Maggie, staring down, embarrassed, into a cup of newly-poured Bohea. "And I ought to have known so, too. It was just the way Lord Parkhurst looked at you, Clare, with those sheep's eyes of his. And the way your own eyes sparked at him. It gave all the appearance that you had had a lovers' quarrel. And then you would not tell me what it was all about. I do beg your pardon for making a most appalling assumption. Honestly I do."

"And well you should, too," Clarissa smiled. "Do not look so woebegone, Maggie. I think it is very kind of you to wish to protect your brother. And I am certain Alex would be pleased to know that you care so much about his happiness that you would shoot me rather than allow me to be unfaithful to him."

"Oh lord, do not tell Alex that! He will fly up into the boughs and not come down for a month."

"No, I will not tell him." The smile on Clarissa's face faltered and Maggie was quick to notice.

"What is it, Clare?"

"Only that I wish Alex would give his heart to me as thoroughly as he once gave it to Madeline. I would take so much better care of it."

Maggie did not quite know what to say and was relieved to see Jonson entering the chamber. For a moment or two—at least until the butler had departed—she would not need to say anything. Her relief, however, was replaced immediately by surprise as her husband tramped into the chamber upon Jonson's heels, supporting a trembling, sobbing Miss Gonnering with one arm and a strangely pale and silent Lady Sarah with the other.

"I know full well I ought to have sent them home," grumbled Corning, pacing restlessly about Clarissa's parlor with a glass of much neglected sherry in his hand. "But I sent Teddy home with the curricle instead and escorted them here in their own coach. And I do not know why!" he added before the duchess could so much as form a word. "It is just that Miss Gonnering was in such a state and The Summarfield staring at me so totally witless. Well, and I knew you would be here, Mags, so here is where I came."

The duchess, knowing full well that this was not an opportune time to point out to her husband that he had delivered the woman suspected of being Alex's paramour into the arms of Alex's new bride, merely nodded.

"Well, what was I to do?" muttered Corning. "You know as well as I that there is no one but that half-witted little boy-of-all-jobs and that ancient cook at Summarfield House these days. They would not have been of any use to the ladies."

"No, they would not," agreed Maggie.

"No. And they were in need of assistance, Mags. Why, you could see that for yourself."

"You did exactly as you should, Your Grace," announced Clarissa, sweeping into the parlor, the skirts of her new willow-green striped walking dress swishing around her ankles. "I have tucked the both of them into bed, each in one of the guest chambers, and Kate has given them a bit of a potion to help them sleep. Once they have rested and are more composed I shall send them home in charge of one of our footmen. Thank heaven you thought to bring them in their own coach. Imagine if anyone should see Lady Sarah in a vehicle sporting Alex's crest."

"Oh, blast!" exclaimed the duke spinning down onto the brocade sopha beside his wife. "Slipped my mind. Deuce of a thing to do, bring The Summarfield here! Apologize," he muttered with a shake of his head in Clarissa's direction. "Not thinking."

"Oh, I am not in the least discomposed by it, Your Grace," smiled Clarissa. "They were both so wretchedly overset. I am certain you only wished to get Maggie to help them and did not once consider where you were bringing them. Besides, Alex is not in the least enamored of Lady Sarah, you know, despite what everyone imagines."

"He is not?" asked Maggie, her eyebrows rising in surprise. "Oh, well, I know that Alex is not actually *in love* with her, but he did allow her to sit in his pocket all last Season—and during the Little Season as well."

"Yes, he had to do that," nodded Clare.

"He *had* to do that?" The Duke of Corning's eyes fastened upon his sister-in-law with the most speaking look. "What do you mean, he *had* to do that?"

"He who?" asked a familiar voice from the parlor doorway. "Had to do what?" Balmorrow, covered in dust so thick that even his curls had grown light with it, stood in the parlor doorway with hands on hips grinning in at them.

"Alex, wherever have you been?" Clarissa, so signaling that she had not confided his expedition to his sister and Corning, rose from her chair and hurried to him.

"No, do not even think to touch me, sweetings. I am nothing but dirt from top to toe. One step closer and you will ruin your gown. And that I could not bear," he added with a cock of an eyebrow. "What a charming gown it is. And you look a veritable vision in it. I knew I ought to have stayed at home today."

"You don't know the half of it," sighed Corning.

"I do not? But you will tell me, will you not, David? I rather think I had best not set foot on the Persian carpet, though. Come up and tell me what I have missed while I clean up. Yes, do, David. You will save me from Mackelry's scathing remarks upon the manner in which I treat *his* clothes and I will be eternally grateful."

"Very well," Corning agreed, rising, "but the tale I have to tell will likely send shivers up your spine, Alex."

"It will?" Balmorrow asked, leaning carefully forward to bestow a kiss upon the tip of Clarissa's upturned nose. "Hurry then. I can barely wait to hear it."

"Boys," laughed Maggie. "I expect we shall need to invite ourselves for dinner, Clare. I know those two. They will not be down again until the first course is on the table."

"Good!" bellowed the earl from the corridor. "Company for dinner! Shall we have them boiled or roasted, dear wife?" he laughed, poking his head back around the door frame.

"Shhh, Alex, you will wake our guests."

"Wake our guests?"

"Indeed," offered Maggie with a lift of an eyebrow. "You and David must be especially quiet while you are upstairs. You will not wish to disturb Lady Sarah and her aunt after the vile afternoon they have had."

Balmorrow's jaw dropped so suddenly that even Clarissa burst into whoops.

Chapter 16

Clarissa collapsed gratefully onto the small sopha in the drawing room and giggled.

"And well you may giggle, you minx," chuckled Balmorrow, aimlessly pacing the room. "Of all the unwieldy situations to toss me into completely unaware."

"You were not unaware, Alex. I am quite certain that His Grace told you all about it. I heard you laughing upstairs while you dressed for dinner."

"Yes, but Corning did not tell me that Sarah and Miss Gonnering would be joining us at table. Truly, Clare, it was abominable of you to put Sarah on my right and Miss Gonnering on my left."

"Well, but it was your laughter woke them. They would have slept right through dinner else. I thought it served you right. Besides," Clarissa grinned, "you, yourself, were wonderful to see. Neither Maggie nor I could keep our eyes from you. How you could appear to be so spellbound by Lady Sarah's conversation and all the while take complete charge of Miss Gonnering's plate. It was sheer artistry. More pheasant and more jugged hare and more creamed peas and onions and more wine made its way to her on the instant she required it. How did you know she required it, Alex? I have never seen our footmen's eyes so very wide as when you signalled Jacob to provide Miss Gonnering with a fourth portion of the beef tremblant and Gerald to pour her a third glass of the claret without ever once looking in her direction. And she finished every bit of it too!"

"Well, but I did look, my dear, out of the corner of my eye every time I took a bite of my own dinner. Poor little Miss Gonnering was famished. And not for attention either—simply for some decent food. I do not think that little Miss Gonnering ever gets enough to eat."

"She got enough tonight," giggled Clarissa.

"Yes, indeed, and I was pleased to be the means of it. I have got the miniature of your mother, Clare." Balmorrow slipped the tiny portrait from his coat pocket and carried it to her. "I gave Kate the one of your father to place in your bedchamber. I had to ask Malcolm for both. I did not wish him to become suspicious."

"No, asking for both was best. What did you tell him?"

"That Lawrence was going to do a portrait of the two of them together for your birthday. He was pleased as punch to hand them over. She was a beautiful woman, your mother."

Clarissa studied the tiny portrait beneath the glow of the candelabra upon the table beside her. Her smile faded. A sad, thoughtful frown took its place. "I cannot quite believe that Mama may still be alive, Alex. It seems so very farfetched. Why would Papa pretend that she had died? And why would he not confide in Malcolm and myself when we grew older? And why would Mama—why would she agree to—to leave her children? Why? For what reason?"

Balmorrow, his ear quickly catching the melancholy in her tone, sat down beside her and put a steadying arm about her, drawing her to him. "Perhaps," he sighed, as Clarissa rested her head upon his broad shoulder. "Perhaps there was some circumstance prevented your mama and papa from staying together. Perhaps there was a grave illness in her own family and she was forced to return to them to—"

Clarissa straightened and pressed one long, slim finger against his lips to silence him. "It is kind of you to make the attempt, Alex," she murmured. "You are very sweet. But if Mama is alive, there can be no acceptable excuse for her not to have contacted Malcolm and myself at all. Perhaps she and

Papa had a terrible fight and she walked away from him—but she walked away from us as well. She could not have loved us, Alex. We were her very own children, but she did not love us."

For the very first time Balmorrow sincerely wished that he had not come to discover these wretched maneuverings of the Luddites and the nonconformists. His precarious position, the possibility that whatever happened might easily come to be laid at his feet, meant nothing. But the sadness and confusion that at the moment cloaked his young bride brought his heart up into his throat and he cursed himself silently for ever having deduced that Clarissa's mama was alive and involved in the thing. It was his fault—his fault—that this lovely and very kind young woman sat baffled and dejected upon the sopha beside him.

"I was wrong to confide in you," he mumbled, bestowing a chaste kiss upon Clarissa's brow. "I ought to have kept my theory to myself. It brings you nothing but pain and doubt and you are deserving of neither. I am a stupid man."

"No, no, you are not stupid, Alex!"

"Unfeeling then. Insensible to your needs. I have brought you grief you did never deserve by speaking to you of this fool idea of mine at all. And I could very well be wrong, Clare. Your Mama may very well be dead and buried just as you were raised to believe and all your—your—anguish of this moment—may well be for naught."

"But her grave is not at the chapel in St. Mary's Lane. You said so yourself. And yet, that is exactly where the records claim she was laid to rest. No, I believe you are correct, Alex. I believe my mama is alive. And I am pleased that you thought to share your suspicions with me as an equal—as your wife—and did not assume me to be some child unable to deal with an unpalatable subject. I do feel terribly dismal and angry, too, Alex. I think now that my mama abandoned me. Until I have discovered her true reasons for doing so, I shall go on feeling that she could not possibly have loved me—or Malcolm—to do so vile a thing. But I shall not let the thought of it ruin my life or yours. Especially I shall not let it ruin yours. No, nor shall I shy away from aiding you in your quest to unearth those who plot against the government and blacken your name as they do so.

"But I doubt Mama will look at all as she does in this miniature, Alex. It was painted so long ago. You rode all the way to Halliard Hall for nothing, I think."

"Perhaps not," replied Balmorrow softly, taking the tiny portrait into one large hand and studying it while he hugged Clarissa tightly against him. "She will have grown a deal older but there is a certain look about her—a most distinctive set to her jaw and those marvelous high, sharp cheekbones and there is a unique cast to her eyes as well if the artist was true to his subject. You, my dear, never told me how much you resemble her."

"Oh, do you think so? I never once thought that to be the case. She is so very beautiful."

"And so are you," offered Balmorrow quietly. "Are you certain you wish to continue to help me in this, Clare? I shall show this miniature to Alden and to Mad Jack and they will set themselves to searching. I shall not be at it all alone. It is not vital that you involve yourself further."

"Of course I wish to help you, Alex. I am not such a poor-spirited thing as to sit brooding over circumstance. Besides, she is my mama. And if she is indeed alive, I wish to find her. There are a good many questions I wish to ask her."

"Then study this portrait well, Clare. You must keep your eyes peeled for that face grown eighteen years older wherever you go—to the shops, to Hatchard's, to balls and soirees, even to the opera."

"But, Alex, it does not make sense that my mama would yet be in Society. Certainly she has withdrawn from participation in the *ton* or Papa could not have convinced everyone that she was dead."

Balmorrow nodded. "That would be true at the time. But that was eighteen years ago. By now your mama may well have come back into the fold under a different name. No one would suspect, you know. She might say she was related to the—to her family in some distant fashion and chanced to look like her second cousin or her great aunt or some such. What, by the way, was your mother's family name? I do not think I ever knew."

"Mama was a Bellingham—Miss Daphne Bellingham before she married Papa."

Balmorrow's eyebrow cocked. He straightened it immediately then gazed down at his wife to see if she had taken note. Obviously she had not. She was staring at the miniature, her thoughts for the moment a million miles away. Bellingham! And the seal that marked all the nonconformists' communications a bell! Was her mama's family name indeed the link? It appeared through most of the communications he had deciphered that the owner of the seal was the person who directed the efforts of the entire group—but it could not be Clare's mama. That would be entirely unacceptable. Why, he could no more turn over his new bride's mama to Liverpool as a traitor than he could hang Brandy and Zander by their thumbs from one of the castle towers.

At a most inappropriate hour of the morning two days following the impromptu dinner party at Balmorrow House, the Bishop of Leeds slipped the miniature that Balmorrow had sent him hurriedly beneath the folds of his robes and turned with a bright smile to welcome the Duke and Duchess of Corning. "You are out and about early, the two of you," he chuckled, taking Maggie into his arms and giving her a hug. "Corning, good to see you. It has been awhile," he added, extending his hand.

"Only because you are so rarely in London, Alden," drawled the duke, taking the hand and giving it a firm shake.

"Yes, well, the business of being a bishop keeps me away. Come, sit down. Early for tea, but if you would care for—"

"No, we are not come for tea, Alden," interjected Maggie, smoothing the sprigged muslin of her walking dress across her lap. "We are come to recruit you."

"Recruit me?" The bishop's face took on a most puzzled expression as he took a seat across from his guests. "Recruit me for what, Mags?"

"To help us rescue Alex. We have already recruited Jack."

The bishop's eyebrows rose in surprise. "Rescue Alex? From what? If it is from that kitten, I will not. I gave it to him and to Clarissa as a wedding gift and therefore they are required to keep it, you know. Only polite. Not about to take it back. Speaking of which," he added, standing and moving to the bell pull. "I have a gift for you as well, Mags. Meant to drop it around later in the week, but since you are here."

"If it is a kitten and you dare touch that bell pull, Alden, you are a dead man," offered the duke quietly.

Alden, entirely unaffected, chuckled and tugged on the pull. "I am not in the least frightened of you, Corning," he grinned. "It is Maggie frightens me. Her threats are much more likely to be carried out. She threatened once to toss me into the River Tweed. And she did, too."

"It was an accident," smiled Maggie.

"Yes, that is exactly what you said at the time. Now what is all this about rescuing Alex?" asked Alden.

"Well, we do not know for certain," drawled Corning, leaning back comfortably in the over-stuffed chair and crossing one knee over the other. "It is just that some rough fellow picked his pocket at the Tower and then Lex claimed the man had taken nothing. That his pocket had not been picked."

"Perhaps it had not."

"That is exactly what Jack said, but it had," insisted Maggie before her husband could reply. "David saw it and his observations are certainly to be depended upon. Alex is in the briars, Alden. His name has already been mentioned in connection with an expected uprising."

"I know," nodded the bishop. "I have heard that."

"Yes, and if the great clunch actually has been forced in some way to involve himself in the thing," sighed Corning, "we have got to fish him from the soup before it begins to boil. We are his friends, Alden, and that is what friends are for."

"Indeed. But can we fish him from the soup? Oh, Bennington, something to drink for my guests, I think. Sherry? Yes, sherry all around and Her Grace's gift. You know which gift I mean. But do not bring that until we have finished with the sherry."

"Yes, Your Grace," acknowledged the bishop's butler with a bow. "I shall see to it immediately."

"Now," stated the bishop thoughtfully once the butler had departed, "how shall I go about setting your minds at ease on this matter? Jack did not, I assume."

"No," sighed Corning with a shake of his head. "Jack did not and you cannot. I had all I could do last evening to keep from confronting Alex with what I know at his dinner table the other night. Had Lady Sarah and her aunt not been present, I would have done so with out the least hesitation."

"Lady Sarah? At Balmorrow House? For dinner?"

"It is a long story, Alden, and not worth repeating. You change the subject as quaintly as Alex when you are attempting to avoid the point."

"No, I do not. I, at least, attempt to switch to a topic that has been put upon the table. Lex would have attempted to begin discussing the color of the draperies or some such thing."

"Nevertheless," Maggie protested, "we have come here for a specific purpose and we will not be put off. You do wish to help Alex, do you not, Alden? You are not thinking to abandon him?"

"Never. Ah, here's our sherry. Now we shall have a civil discussion. Close the door, Bennington, on your way out."

The bishop's butler set the silver tray containing the sherry and three glasses upon the oval table nearest His Grace, and strode quickly and quietly from the room, closing the door behind him. The click of the latch sounded firm and decisive.

"Now, my dears," began the bishop, rising to pour them each a glass of the reddish liquid, "let me set your minds to rest, eh? Someone did pick Lex's pocket at the Tower. And did a wretched job of it, too, I gather, because no one was meant to notice."

"I could not help but notice," offered Corning as the bishop took a seat upon a chaise longue. "I was in precisely the spot to see the blighter's hand slip inside Alex's coat."

"Well, there you are. The best laid plans of mice and men oft do gang agley, do they not?"

"Alden, do you propose to tell us that you know all about this?" asked Maggie, her eyes narrowing with suspicion.

"Well, I did never intend to tell you that I knew anything about it, Mags, but apparently I must confess a bit of what I know or the two of you will run off full tilt at the windmill and ruin everything."

"Tell us all of it," frowned Corning.

"No, not all of it, Your Grace. Lex would have my head should I confess all of it."

"All of it," demanded Maggie, rising to stand over her cousin and glare down at him.

"If you do not cease to be so demanding, the both of you, I will tell you none of it," replied the bishop, smiling up into Maggie's frowning countenance, "and then where will you be?"

Clarissa stared down at the wildly fluffy black kitten in her lap and sighed. "Aphrodite," she murmured.

"Aphrodite?" chuckled Balmorrow. "I rather think not, thank you very much. How do you expect me to reprimand that beast if I cannot get past its name without snickering? Besides, she does not look at all like an Aphrodite, Clare."

"But Alex, we have gone through hundreds of names, and we can agree on none of them. We must call her something—and very soon, too. She has been running about without a name for much too long already."

"Yes, and chewing upon my slippers and carrying one of my stockings all over the house and scratching upon the settee in your sitting room, which she may not do—scratch upon the settee, I mean. She may keep the slippers and the stocking now she has them. We are very lucky, you know."

"Lucky?"

"Indeed. At least it is only a cat and not one of our children we cannot name. Now that would be awkward."

Clarissa blushed very prettily. It was the first time thoughts of their own children had been spoken aloud and though she could not think exactly how to reply, she was pleased to note a certain gleam in Balmorrow's eyes as he smiled down at her.

He reached down and snatched the kitten from her lap, holding it up before his eyes and studying it carefully. A pink tongue stretched out eagerly toward his nose. "Oh, you are all sweetness and light, are you not, cat, when I have you face to face? But once let me put you down and look the other way and you are the devil incarnate."

"Meow," replied the bit of fluff so addressed and realizing her tongue could not quite reach his nose, batted that slightly left-leaning appendage tenderly with a paw instead.

"Goblin," suggested Clarissa, enjoying immensely the sight of her large husband in conversation with the delicate little kitten.

"Imp," Balmorrow offered, staring into the wide green eyes that came near to matching the color of Clarissa's own.

"Terror."

"Demon."

"Upstart."

"Trouble."

"Trouble?" Balmorrow grinned and brought the kitten against his chest where it happily occupied itself with one of the brass buttons upon his riding coat. "Trouble is most apt."

"Yes, I think so as well. She is always in trouble or causing trouble or about to cause trouble."

"Trouble. Yes, exactly right. Trouble you are," he laughed, freeing his button from between the kitten's paws. "And Trouble you shall continue to be."

He set the kitten down and it attacked one of the tassels upon his Hessians and then scampered under the chair in which Clarissa sat and peeked at him from behind her skirts.

"I have a notion to abandon Trouble to the staff and ride through Hyde Park at this most unfashionable hour," he said. "Will you join me, wife?"

"Wife?" Clarissa grinned. "You have never addressed me quite so quaintly before, Alex."

"Ah, but now I have a new outlook. I see trouble and I call her Trouble. I see my wife and I am pleased to call her wife."

"Are you, Alex?" asked Clarissa as she took the hands he offered and allowed him to tug her from the chair.

"Are I what?" he grinned with a cock of his eyebrow.

"Are you pleased that I am your wife?"

"Immensely pleased. Inordinately pleased. Beyond anything pleased. Will you ride with me?"

"Yes."

"Good. Run and change into your habit. I will send to have the horses brought around."

Hyde Park was nearly empty in the morning. Clarissa was amazed at it. "Does no one come then except at the fashionable hour?"

"Oh, people come at all hours," replied Balmorrow astride Donadee who had only three days before appeared in town healthy and in the care of one of the grooms from Castle

Balmorrow. "But it is a great relief to be here so early and not need to deal with all those vehicles. Is it not, Donny?" he added, giving the great horse a pat. "London is a dead bore for Donadee. Confined to a slow trot in Rotten Row is not his idea of a good time."

"Nor yours," observed Clarissa from Windsong's back.

"Nor mine most usually. But it is a pleasure to have you beside me and that quite makes up for the pace."

"Ho!" cried Clarissa, brimming with laughter. "If that was not a left-handed compliment, my lord!" And with a nudge of her heel and a loosening of the reins, she set Windsong into a canter and then into a gallop and then into a run, taking the fence at the side of the Row and setting out across the green, the sound of Donadee's hooves pounding loudly behind her.

"Steady, Don," Balmorrow murmured, leaning down to speak into the horse's ear. "We do not wish to catch them yet."

The truth was that he had no wish to catch Clarissa and Windsong at all. The lovely sight they made—Clarissa in her Spanish fly riding habit as lovely as a wood nymph in perfect harmony with the agile little grey—came near to steal his heart away. She does ride, he thought joyfully. She rides like a huntress. She will like to ride with me through the forests and along the Likely Run and up into hills once we are home again!

He could not account for the inestimable joy this thought provided him. It would not have been such an enormous thing after all if Clare had proved to be a lackluster rider. It would not have altered his steadily-strengthening regard for her. It would not have diminished the ache of hope in him that seemed to grow more intense with each passing day. But the fact that she did ride with such enthusiasm and exhilaration and skill and might be expected to do so with him in his most favorite place, sent his spirits to soaring and his heart to leaping with jubilation within his breast.

As Clarissa and Windsong neared the far end of the green, Balmorrow at last gave Donadee his head and the great black closed the distance between them, bringing him up beside his wife in a matter of seconds. "Enough!" laughed Balmorrow. "I am humbled. I shall never again mention pace in your presence so long as I live!"

"I hope," replied Clarissa primly, "that you and Donadee are not all done in, my lord. Windsong and I realize, of course, that the two of you are older—"

"Older?" grinned Balmorrow. It was the precise grin that lit his entire countenance and set Clarissa's heart to pounding.

"Indeed," nodded Clarissa, attempting to maintain a serious expression. "Older. And so we shall attempt from now on not to press the two of you beyond your capabilities."

"Minx!" laughed Balmorrow, and before Clarissa could guess his intentions, he drew Donadee up even closer beside her and sliding from his saddle transferred himself in the wink of an eye to Windsong's back, wrapped his arms around Clarissa and kissed her soundly upon the lips. "Older, indeed," he chuckled, and kissed her again. "I will be most pleased to demonstrate, wife, how age has limited my capabilities the moment we return home."

Clarissa giggled and kissed his nose. "I love you, oh ancient one," she murmured demurely. "And in deference to your age, I feel we ought to return home at once."

Edward, Lord Parkhurst paled at the sight. It was not the impropriety of Balmorrow up behind his wife kissing her soundly that upset him. It was the fact that the earl was kissing her at all. What was the man about? Balmorrow had already confided in Lady Sarah that he cared not at all for Clarissa, and yet, he kissed her in full view of every lounger and stroller in the park, as if to declare that theirs was a love match. Great heavens! Had the dullard actually lost his heart to the gel? And had Clarissa lost her heart to the earl as well? That would make for a difficult time of it. How could he be expected to occupy Clarissa and give Lady Sarah more opportunity to be private with Balmorrow if that was the case?

But that could not be the case. It had been merely a marriage of convenience. Everyone knew that to be so. Some debt or other to be paid on Balmorrow's part and Clarissa's unexpected penury had driven them both to it. No, his worry was for nothing. This impetuous eccentricity on the earl's part could be neither as impetuous nor as eccentric as it appeared. Balmorrow was planning something, attempting to deceive Clarissa into believing that she had won his heart. Perhaps it was an attempt on the earl's part to give his bride a confidence in him that would set him free to visit The Summarfield whenever he desired.

"Well, and that is all well and good," mumbled Lord Parkhurst to himself. "If it works, that will eliminate the need for me to keep the gel out of his way and we will continue to gain information from Balmorrow without the least inconvenience."

Besides, it will make my life a great deal calmer, he thought. For how they can expect me to occupy Clarissa and still know every moment where Balmorrow has gone and what he is about, I cannot think. Now that I have lost Henry's assistance, simply keeping track of Balmorrow is near impossible.

Parkhurst turned his horse's head toward the West Gate and followed the pair at a stately pace and a considerable distance, not once taking note of the smallish woman in black bombazine who strolled along a footpath in the opposite direction, though she had stopped to gaze open-mouthed at the spectacle of Balmorrow and Clarissa much as he had himself.

Daphne Beresfont, the Dowager Viscountess Halliard, had never been so stunned before in all her life. That after eighteen long years she should at last gain sight of her daughter! And to see that daughter laughing and joyous in obviously loving arms, in arms that encircled her with goodwill and passion! Strong arms, dependable arms, protective arms! She had not been prepared for it. Her heart, which the interminable years had hardened into dull, unresponsive flint, began to flutter and beat again within her breast. "Clarissa," her lips said without her mind even knowing that they did so. "My dearest little Clare."

Chapter 17

"Well, I have not had a chance to study it myself as yet," murmured the Bishop of Leeds, withdrawing the miniature of Clarissa's mother from his robes and offering it to the Duke and Duchess of Corning. "But this is the woman Lex wishes to locate, though she is eighteen years older now and likely has changed a good deal."

Corning, peering at the tiny portrait over Maggie's shoulder, shook his head. "I cannot say as I have seen her anywhere about. Do you recognize her, Mags?"

"No. That is, she does look somewhat familiar, but—why does Alex wish to locate her, Alden? Did he give you a name to go with this face? Perhaps if I knew her name."

"She is the Dowager Viscountess Halliard."

"Never!" exclaimed Maggie. "Clare's mama? Why the viscountess has been dead for years. I was still in the schoolroom when Papa told Mama that she had died. But that explains why she looks familiar. Clare is much like her."

"Is she? Let me see. I have not so much as looked at the thing as yet. I was just about to do so when you and Corning appeared upon my doorstep." The Bishop of Leeds strolled over behind the settee and peered down over Maggie's shoulder. "Oh, great goblins!" he exclaimed, taking the miniature from her hand and hurrying with to the window to gain more light. "Great goblins, Maggie, I know exactly who this woman is and where she is to be found as well."

"You do?" asked Maggie and Corning simultaneously.

"Indeed," nodded Alden excitedly. "I spoke to this very woman only two days ago. I had not seen the miniature then, so I did not remark much upon her. But this is the very woman. I would swear to it. This soup is getting much too salty for my taste, let me tell you!"

"Well, but who is she?" asked Maggie. "Where is it you saw her, Alden?"

"Yes, spill it out, Alden," urged Corning.

"I will. Yes, I will," nodded the bishop somewhat mystified and still staring at the tiny portrait. "I will swear to it. She is the Archbishop of Canterbury's housekeeper!"

Clarissa watched her husband wistfully from the open window of her sitting room as he mounted Donadee and turned the horse's head toward Westminster. Assuredly Alex was the most wonderful gentleman in all the world. Had she searched forever, she could not have found a more considerate, loving husband—whether he would admit to loving her or not. With a gladdened heart, she noted that he turned in his saddle to gaze back and upward to the window of her sitting room and spying her there, waved farewell. She smiled and waved back. Oh, surely, surely he loved her! He had chosen of his own free will to confide in her, to trust her, to make her an equal and integral part of his life. And if he did not vow to lay all of the stars of heaven at her feet, if his words were not endlessly sprinkled with flowery compliments, if he did not wear his heart upon his sleeve for her, what did that matter? Anyone might speak pretty words and promise the impossible and gaze soulfully into her eyes and sigh.

She knelt upon the settee, her elbows resting upon the sill, her chin upon her hands and her gaze fastened upon Balmorrow as he moved off up the street at a sedate canter. She took pleasure in the mere sight of his strong, broad-shouldered form so very composed, so very much in control of the beautiful Donadee. And then she imagined how elegant and how very impressive he would look once he had reached

Westminster and had donned his robes in the antechamber and strolled into the House of Lords in all the glory of his earldom. "And in all the rebellion of your earldom, too," she whispered, remembering all that he had told her of his political leanings. "How I wish I could go with you and watch you and listen to you speak."

And that was the precise moment that Balmorrow turned the corner and rode from her sight and she turned her gaze down to the square beneath her window and noticed a woman in black bombazine staring up at her. The woman turned away immediately and proceeded up the square. Someone's housekeeper most certainly, decided Clarissa, her eyes following the woman for a moment longer. What a hoyden she must think me to be leaning upon a window sill waving a gentleman goodbye. Well, and I do not care one bit what she thinks. He is my husband and I may bid him goodbye however I care to do so. And with that she pulled the window closed and went off to tell her maid that she would be bound for Hatchard's shortly and would require Kate's company upon the expedition.

The little scene that had just been played out before her cracked open even further the flint that armored Daphne Beresfont's heart. She had not expected it. She had gone to Leicester Square because she knew that Lord Balmorrow's residence was there and having gotten a glimpse of her daughter early that morning, she found that she longed to have another. Perhaps she would see Clarissa mounting into one of Lord Balmorrow's vehicles to go shopping, or perhaps she might catch sight of her as she sat before one of the windows plying her needle. But to see Lord Balmorrow riding sedately off and stopping to wave his wife goodbye, and to spy Clarissa leaning upon the window sill above, waving back to him as if she were a little farm girl sending her beloved off into the fields—it sent a pang through Daphne's heart and into her very soul that she could not ignore.

Oh, most certainly John and Nathan both had lied to her! They had assured her that this liaison between the Earl of Balmorrow and her daughter had been strictly a marriage of convenience; that there would be no need to alter their plans; that any harm which might befall the Earl of Balmorrow because of them would cause Clarissa not the least pain. But they had lied! Most certainly any harm that befell Lord Balmorrow would hurt her daughter grievously for it was quite obvious, even to a woman so hardened as herself, that Clarissa loved this gentleman and that he loved her in return.

"Attempting to pull the wool over my eyes," Daphne Beresfont muttered to herself as she trudged slowly off in the direction of the Archbishop of Canterbury's London residence. "Both of them. How dare they! After all I have sacrificed, how dare they! Well, and I will not sacrifice my Clarissa's happiness for anyone or anything. I will not! The plans will need to be changed."

"She is where?" asked Balmorrow, a most perplexed look upon his face.

"At Canterbury's residence."

"In Kent?"

"No, no, at his residence here, Lex. I saw her," insisted Alden in a low voice as he and Corning and Balmorrow huddled together in the lobby of the House of Lords.

"And you are positive it is she?"

"Well, no, not positive."

"How can he be positive?" queried Corning. "The lady in the miniature is near two decades younger."

"Exactly," nodded Alden. "But she resembles it greatly, Lex. I shall stop in at Canterbury's for a chat tonight, eh? And see if I can catch sight of her again."

"Yes," agreed Balmorrow. "And perhaps Jack might find a way into the kitchen there, eh?"

"Jack?" Corning's eyebrows raised. "Do you mean to tell me that Norris is in on this already? When Mags and I approached him about you, Alex, he played the astounded innocent to the hilt. Am I the only one has been left out then?"

Balmorrow gazed at his brother-in-law with the most amazed countenance.

"What? Do you think that just because I am a duke, I am adverse to a bit of adventure?"

"No, never," murmured Balmorrow and Alden together.

"We, ah, just thought to keep it in the family, you know," offered the bishop.

"I *am* in the family," Corning pointed out with a glare.

"Yes, and we are all pleased that you are, too," offered Balmorrow.

"Right."

"No, truly, David. And we did not actually plan to have this much of an adventure. I merely offered to decode intercepted French messages for Liverpool, and Jack and Alden offered to carry them for me. So that I would not be always seen going into the war office, you know. Except for Jack getting to sport about as a highwayman—Mad Jack Docker we named him—it was considerably boring work until we came upon this conspiracy. Mistook one of the nonconformist messages for a French one, we did. Pure accident."

"Discovered that they planned to overthrow the government and lay the blame for everything at Lex's feet if they should fail," added Alden. "That was the very first moment that things began to get interesting."

"And that was only last Spring," supplied Balmorrow.

"You have known about this since last Spring?" cried Corning accusingly.

"Sshhh. Settle down, David, do, or everyone will be wandering over here," Balmorrow whispered. "We have had bits and pieces of it since last Spring, but no actual proof of what they were about to do until early this year. You are practically in at the beginning of it. You have only missed the boring parts."

"Then I am to be a part of it?"

"Yes, well, provided you can keep Maggie under control," nodded Balmorrow with a glance at Alden. "You know how Maggie is, David. She gets every last secret out of you."

"Yes, Corning, very much as Cousin Clarissa gets every last secret from Lex," observed Alden drolly.

"She does?" Corning's eyebrow cocked significantly. "Your new bride knows all, Alex?"

"Well—she does not know who Mad Jack truly is. She thinks Mad Jack Docker to be a member of the Great Unwashed."

"But that is all she does not know?"

Balmorrow sighed and began to move into the chamber, the other two close upon his heels. He knew perfectly well what both Corning and Alden were thinking. "Clare is concerned in it," he offered quietly. "She has a right to know."

"Indeed," responded Alden with a wide smile.

"Well, she is!"

"And you trust her enough to share every secret with her—except for Jack. You will most likely share Jack with her shortly," grinned Corning. "Admit it, Alex, you are in love with the gel."

"Yes, well, she is an exceptional person."

"Exceptional," Alden and Corning repeated, chuckling. And the both of them giving Balmorrow a pat on his shoulder, they moved off to take their seats in the hall. Balmorrow slumped down into his own place and immediately proceeded to ignore all that went on around him as he began to ponder.

Clarissa could not comprehend what had come over her husband. No sooner had he appeared in the summer parlor after returning home from Westminster than he took the book she was reading from her hand, tugged her to her feet, swept her up into his arms and carried her, laughing, up the staircase to the second floor and down the corridor into her sitting room where he deposited her upon the settee, spun into her dressing room, spun back out again with her gold silk opera dress upon his arm, and informed her that they were going out to dinner at Grillon's and then on to a special entertainment.

"And you will wear this one, will you not, Clare? For me? You have not worn it anywhere as yet and it is the most beautiful thing. You looked like an angel in it when you tried it on for me last week."

"An angel?" Clare asked, smiling.

"An angel," Balmorrow repeated with a determined nod.

And then he took himself off to his own chamber, calling at the top of his voice for Mackelry to produce his very best evening clothes and in the devil of a hurry, too, because he intended to spend the entire evening with his wife and he intended the evening to begin as soon as possible.

"His lordship be most exuberant, my lady," giggled Kate as she scurried into Clarissa's presence. "Caught me in the hall, he did, and steered me into here, all the while callin' for Mackelry."

Balmorrow wore a forest green coat of elegant cut over the most amazing golden waistcoat shot through with forest green threads, and buff knee breeches with clocked stockings. His black half-boots gleamed. His neckcloth was tied flawlessly in an Osbaldestan. His dark locks were brushed until they glowed and his great blue eyes sparked and glistened as he waited upon the checked tile of the front hall and watched Clarissa descend the staircase in her golden gown, a tiny tiara bedecked with emeralds in her upswept hair and the emerald pendant he had presented her, sparkling at her throat. "You take my breath away," he declared quietly, helping her down the final step. "You are surely the most beautiful woman in all the world."

Clarissa felt a protest rise to her lips, for most certainly she was not the most beautiful woman in all the world and well she knew it, but the protest died before it slipped into the air between them. It was the honest openness of his countenance and the proud look in his eyes, and the truly beguiled grin he grinned at her that stopped it. "What a lovely compliment," she said instead. "Thank you, Alex."

He took her off in the town coach to a private dining room in Grillon's Hotel and fed her on baked apple soup and garden chowder, stewed eels, a leg of lamb, lobster with green peas, and broccoli in sweet cream sauce. Apricot fritters and plum pudding also made an appearance and once the cloth was removed, an extravaganza of fresh fruit presented itself.

Clarissa was certain that once she rose from her chair her gown would burst at the seams. But she said nothing, protesting not a whit even when he signalled the waiter to refill her wine glass for the third time. She could not bring herself to say one word against the magnificent meal because Alex was actually eating it. He was not picking at one thing and taking a tentative taste of another, but eating as though he had not been fed in months. Which, she thought, is quite the case. Has he at last overcome his fear of being poisoned again? Yes, she thought. He has. Perhaps that is what we are celebrating. For we are certainly celebrating something. That much is obvious.

"What?" asked Balmorrow, grinning at her across the table. "What brings such a satisfied smile to that lovely face?"

"It is merely that I have just divined that this is a celebration, Alex. It is, is it not?"

"Yes," nodded Balmorrow enthusiastically. "A celebration."

"Are you going to confide in me, my lord, what it is that we are celebrating?"

"No," Balmorrow replied with a gleeful shake of his head. "Not yet. Later."

"But how much later, Alex?"

"I am not quite certain," he chuckled. "Perhaps in the midst of Madame Catalini's *Semiramide.*"

"Oh!" cried Clarissa in joy. "We are truly going to the opera! And to hear Madame Catalini! What a pleasure, Alex."

"I guessed you would enjoy it. You play so beautifully, as though music is an inborn part of you. Did you not suspect the opera when I pleaded for the opera gown?"

"I, well, I did not think. It is such a wonderful gown, Alex, and perfect for almost any entertainment. Oh, how wonderful to hear Madame Catalini! She is a veritable legend! I have heard hers is the most magnificent voice ever to grace any stage in all the world."

"Have you never heard her sing?" asked Balmorrow in surprise.

"No, never. I was to hear her two years ago but—"

"But what, my dear?"

"Well, there was—that is to say—my father slipped, you know, outside the theatre and—" Clarissa stuttered to a halt. The bright smile upon Alex's face had fled. "Alex, what is it?"

"What a dunce I am!" he exclaimed, rising from his chair and going to kneel at her side, his hands taking hers, his lips kissing one palm and then the next. "Forgive me, Clare. I have been utterly stupid. It was in Haymarket your father was killed. I did not remember. If you would perfer not to—"

"Oh, Alex, no! It was not Haymarket nor the King's Theatre at fault for the thing. It was an accident. Papa slipped from the walk and fell beneath the wheels of an approaching coach."

"And you will not feel sad to see the place again?"

"Well, I expect I shall remember him with a sigh and

perhaps a tear, but, no, Alex, I shall not feel sad to go there. I shall love at last to see the inside of the King's Theatre—which I never did—and to hear Madame Catalini sing."

The enormous crowds in Haymarket were quite as Clarissa remembered them—boiling, vibrant, exciting. All of London appeared to have converged upon the King's Theatre. Vehicles of every description jostled for position upon the cobbles. Horses neighed and whinnied and pranced in their shafts. Group after group of elegantly gowned ladies and exquisitely dressed gentlemen spilled out of coaches and cabriolets, landaus and curricles and drags, and made their way into the lobby, from whence they floated apart like tiny glowing bits from one enormous rainbow into the grand horseshoe of the auditorium, becoming colorful, shimmering stars amidst the five tiers of boxes, the pit, and the gallery.

"Oh, it is the most beautiful thing I have ever seen," declared Clarissa as Balmorrow settled her in the box he had borrowed from Corning for the evening. "Just look at all the colors, Alex! It is like—like—"

"Like what, my dear?"

"Why do you know," said Clarissa thoughtfully, "it is not the most beautiful thing I have ever seen. It is much like your wonderful flutterby room in the castle, except that these flutterbys do not float about and rise and fall in waves. Yes, I am certain, *that* is the most beautiful thing I have ever seen. But this, Alex, is a very close second."

Balmorrow grinned and put an arm carefully upon the back of her chair, almost but not quite around her shoulders.

Clarissa, though enthralled by Madame Catalini from her first appearance upon the stage, could not quite lose herself in the splendor of that incredible voice. No, she could not. And it was not a lack of appreciation for the talented performer either. Each time she floated away upon the music, she was called back to earth by her husband. Alex, apparently, could not be still. Though he gazed at the stage in apparently rapt attention, his legs and arms and hands fidgeted. One moment he was motionless and the next moment one of his fingers was teasing at the nape of her neck. Then his knees pressed against her own. Then he shifted in his seat and appropriated one of her hands, his thumb traveling in tiny circles upon the back of it while he held it in his lap.

"Alex, whatever are you doing?" Clarissa whispered upon a giggle as he shifted once more and began to trail a finger along the path between her bare shoulder and her ear.

"Doing?" he whispered back, turning his gaze from the stage and bestowing upon her his most innocent and inviting grin. "Why I am reveling in Madame Catalini's talent, my love."

"No, you are not," smiled Clarissa. "You are fidgeting about like a—like a gentleman seated upon hot coals."

"Oh?"

It was the most unlikely thing she could have imagined. Alex stood up directly, turned about and stared down at his chair. "No," he informed her, running one hand across the seat. "No coals, hot or otherwise."

"Alex!" she gasped, suppressing with all her might the urge to burst into whoops as innumerable heads turned questioningly toward them from the other boxes.

"Hmmm?"

"Alex, sit down. Everyone is looking at us."

"No, not everyone," he informed her. "But everyone will if you give in and burst into laughter. This is a very serious part of the music, you know, and the entire theatre will think you shatterbrained if you laugh." His eyes fairly bubbled with goodwill as he stared down at her. Except for Madame Catalini and a few dandies in the pit who were without seats, Alex was the only person standing in all of the great auditorium. Clarissa had not the least idea what was going on in his mind, but the look upon his face and the marvelous light in his eyes forced her to sputter a bit of laughter despite her every attempt not to do so.

"I knew you would," nodded Alex smugly.

"Alex, do sit down. I th-think you have had a smidgeon too much wine."

"No, I have not," announced the earl, quite abruptly going down upon one knee before her. "I have not had near enough wine. Not near enough."

"Alex, what *are* you doing?"

"I am asking you to take my heart," he declared softly beneath the Catalini's awe-inspiring aria as he took one of Clarissa's hands into his own. "I did never propose to you properly, Clare. But I am proposing to you now. Not a marriage of convenience, but a new marriage. A love match."

"Alex!"

"I find that you are always on my mind, Clare, and that having you there fills me with joy. You stir every wonderful passion in me, body and soul. And I love you, Clare. There is nothing I cannot share with you and nothing in which you do not offer me support. What a dolt I am, then, not to entrust you with my heart."

"Alex!"

"Will you take it, Clare? Will you take my heart? You have filled it with hope and made it ache to be whole again. Everything I have is yours. Can my heart not be yours as well? I will love you for all time, if only you will say yes."

"Yes," whispered Clarissa, all thought of laughter fled. "Yes."

"Thank you," murmured Balmorrow, raising her hand to his lips and kissing it tenderly. "I hoped that you had not changed your mind, that you had not decided that you had made a mistake when first you said you loved me. That is what we are celebrating, Clare—that my old fears have succumbed to the hope you sparked in me. And we are celebrating now besides because you have told me yes."

He took his seat again beside her and his arm went about her shoulders and he drew her to him, pressing his lips softly and then hungrily against her own as Catalini soared onward toward a high C and any number of eyes in the boxes surrounding them stared agog and any number of ladies in their most beautiful gowns hid their smiles behind their fans and tittered.

He had said he loved her. In no uncertain terms, without any ifs, ands, or buts. He had begged her to take his heart—bruised and battered though it had been. Clarissa's joy was overwhelming. She held tightly to his arm as they descended the staircase. Once, as they waited for an opportunity to continue their journey through the lobby, she even leaned her head upon his shoulder and he bent down and kissed her. She knew thousands of people surrounded her, but she felt so completely alone with him, as though they stood in the room full of flutterbys sharing the most awe-inspiring feelings. It was the oddest sensation, to feel so alone amongst so immense a crowd. But she delighted in it. He had said he loved her. He loved her. He loved her. Clarissa stepped out upon his arm to the beat of that single phrase. Through the lobby and out onto the flagstones she marched to the tune of his declaration. And he stepped along beside her, his great blue eyes beaming down upon her in the glow of the torch boys' flambeaux and the new gas lamps, and the coach lanterns. He loved her. He loved her. He loved her.

And then, most suddenly, as they neared their own coach, Balmorrow's step faltered from that most wonderful beat. There was a slight hesitation and an odd sound and his arm jerked away from her and began to make the oddest windmill motion and then he was lurching forward into the street and falling—falling—

Clarissa screamed. Her arms reached out to grab at the tails of his coat. It was the nightmare of her father's accident all over again. Only this time they were leaving the theatre, not entering it. And this time she could see the team of bays that was just passing plunge and rear at the abrupt and frightening intrusion of a tumbling body catapulting into their midst. And this time—this time—it was not her father. It was Alex!

The horror that had frozen her two years ago upon the walk threatened to turn her into stone once again. Alex's coattails slipped from her grasp. Her fist went to her mouth and her eyes widened in fear. And then she was tossing her reticule to the ground and lifting her skirts and shoving aside any number of people who were queueing up around her and she dashed after her wildly toppling husband into the vehicle-clogged street.

Chapter 18

"You saved his life. Everyone says as much. He would surely be dead this very moment if you had not dashed after him and grabbed him about the waist and pulled him back." Maggie sat staring at Clarissa in the summer parlor with a most admiring glow in her eyes. "You are a heroine, Clare."

Clarissa colored prettily under the duchess' reverent gaze. "But I did not pull him back, you know," she murmured shyly. "My added weight merely altered the direction of his fall."

"You were immensely brave to run into the midst of all those horses and carriages," Maggie continued, overriding Clarissa's demure diminishing of her deed. "I owe you my brother's life. There is nothing you can ask of me that I shall not give you."

"Nothing?" asked Clarissa with the lift of an eyebrow.

"Nothing. I vow it."

"Are you very certain, Maggie? Because there is something I wish to ask of you, but—"

"Only ask," urged Maggie.

"Well, Alex is confined to his bed, you know, for at least another day, because of that great lump he got upon his head when he hit the cobbles, and I do not think I ought to wait for another day. I think I ought to go at once."

"Go?" The Duchess of Corning sat up straighter in the lyre-backed chair, her pretty blue kid slippers planted firmly upon the Aubusson carpet. "Go where?"

"To the Archbishop of Canterbury's."

Maggie's eyebrow's rose.

"Maggie, a woman who resembles my mama is housekeeper there. Alex muttered about it all the way home in the coach last night. It took me a great while to make sense of what he was saying, but I did at last comprehend it all. He thinks my mama is not dead, you see."

"Yes," Maggie nodded. "I know he does. David and I pried as much out of Alden yesterday. We were with Alden, in fact, when he studied the miniature and thought he recognized the woman."

"Oh, it was Alden? I wondered who had told Alex of her. Well, but it does not matter who it was. What matters is that this housekeeper may be my mama. I must go to her, Maggie. I must discover if it truly is she. And I wish you will accompany me, because I shall be very nervous to go alone."

"Well, of course I will accompany you," declared Maggie. "But do you not think that you ought to wait until Alex can do so himself?"

"No." Clarissa rose and began to pace the chamber, the skirts of her cherry and cream morning gown swirling about her ankles. "How much do you know, Maggie? Do you know that Alex suspects my mama's involvement in this bit of treason that threatens him?"

The duchess nodded. "David and I were very worried about Alex," she offered by way of explanation. "We confronted Alden in his chambers and forced him to tell us what game was afoot."

"Good. Then I have no need to explain to you what has gone before. I need only tell you this. Alex says he did not simply slip last evening. He says he was pushed."

"Oh, no, surely not! He was jostled in the crowd."

"Pushed," repeated Clarissa. "And pushed hard, too, for he spun off into the street very violently. He did not mean to tell me he was pushed, I think," she added with a shake of her head. "But he was so very addled that it came out despite his best intentions not to upset me further. And if he was pushed for some reason to do with the nonconformist plan and my mama is indeed alive and involved with them, then I must certainly find her and speak to her. She cannot, no matter what sort of woman she is, go about attempting to have my husband murdered. And I will tell her so, too!"

Maggie's eyes sparkled. "You are thoroughly intrepid," she said on a short bark of laughter. "Alex has got himself a true and loving and noble wife at last, despite his reluctance to accept it."

"Oh, but he is no longer reluctant, Maggie," Clarissa breathed, abruptly starry-eyed. "Last evening he declared he was genuinely in love with me and begged me to take his heart. Oh, it was the most romantic thing! I thought I should leap for joy at his every word! Did you—did you not think he would come to love me?" she added hesitantly.

"I knew he ought to love you," replied Maggie, rising from her chair and going to engulf Clarissa in a pleased hug. "And I prayed with all my might that he would put Madeline behind him and be brave enough to give his heart again. Oh, Clare, I am so very happy for you! And yes, I will accompany you to the Archbishop of Canterbury's residence. At once, if you wish it."

Daphne Beresfont, Lady Halliard, in the prim and proper black bombazine that proclaimed her to be a mere Mrs. Quigley, answered the summons to the Archbishop's library without the least trepidation. His Grace, she knew, had gone out for the day, and she assumed that some problem with the household had arisen with which the Archbishop's assistants did not feel equipped to cope. Normally, of course, they would have summoned Mr. Quigley, the butler. But since Mr. Quigley had departed the premises early that morning she, as his second in command, was the person to be consulted in any immediate household matter.

She sailed into the room, a competent and efficient woman of sober demeanor, and came to a foundering halt at sight of the two exquisite young ladies who met her gaze. Her lower lip began to quiver, but she stilled it. One of her hands began to shake, but she thrust it nonchalantly into the pocket of her gown. "Yes, Mr. James," she asked the Archbishop's senior assistant who stood beside the ladies, "how may I be of service?"

"The Duchess of Corning and Lady Balmorrow have asked for a word with you, Mrs. Quigley," replied that gentleman quietly. "Your Grace, my lady, may I present our housekeeper, the intrepid Mrs. Quigley." He said this with a shy smile and then, giving the ladies a tiny bow, departed the library and closed the door behind him.

The click of the latch reverberated like a cannon shot through Daphne Beresfont's mind. Her pale face colored the slightest bit as she lowered her gaze from the ladies' faces to the tips of her sturdy black shoes. "How may I help, Your Grace and your ladyship?" she asked quietly.

"Mama?" whispered Clare, clutching unconsciously for support at the long sleeve of Maggie's carriage dress. "Mama? Oh, it cannot be! Mama?"

Daphne Beresfont raised her own lovely green eyes to meet those of her daughter. The color that had risen to her face drained away again. "I do not understand, my lady," she whispered hoarsely. "How may I be of service?"

Clarissa's lips parted, then drew together without a sound. In silence she studied the worn face, the wrinkled brow, the proud yet submissive stance of the woman before her. Tears started to her eyes. Her knees began to feel quite like *blancmange.* She took a deep breath which ended in a tiny shudder. And of a sudden Maggie's arm was around her and lowering her into one of the red leather chairs scattered about the room.

"Oh, what a fool I am," Clarissa mumbled, raising one prettily-gloved hand to cover her eyes. "My heart beats like a veritable tympani and some great beast roars about in my head. And all because I have seen what I have come to see! And I feel so vile, too, Maggie," she murmured. "Just as I did after we drank the brandy. I am going to be ill."

Maggie searched hurriedly through her reticule for the vial of smelling salts she carried there. The lady who called herself Mrs. Quigley, more to the point, hurried to the hearth and tipped the coals from their scuttle and rushed with the bucket to Clarissa who made prompt use of it, over and over again.

By the time she leaned back, exhausted and sobbing, into the comfort of the heavy chair, a footman was there to carry the evidence of her breakfast from the room, Maggie was dabbing at her brow with cool lavender water and Mrs. Quigley was pouring her out a cup of chamomile tea.

"Shhh," Maggie whispered as Clarissa opened her mouth to apologize. "You must just be still, dearest. You have had a great shock."

"Try to drink some of this, my dear," urged Mrs. Quigley, placing an elegant bone china cup into Clarissa's hand. "It will soothe your nerves and your stomach as well. I promise you will feel more the thing once you have finished it."

"No," sighed Clarissa with a tiny shake of her head. "I shall never feel better—not until I understand. Mama, how can it be that Papa lied to us, that he has lied to us for years and years? Why did he pretend that you were dead? Why did you leave us? What are you doing *here?*"

Daphne Beresfont turned away to check that the library was empty again of all but the three of them. She walked to the door, opened it, stared out into the hall, then closed the door quietly and returned to Clarissa's side where she sank down upon a footstool and buried her face in her hands. For a very long time she sat just so, in silence, without the least movement.

"D-do not deny that you are my mama," pleaded Clarissa at last in a voice no louder than the breath of a breeze. "I have only just studied the miniature of you a few days ago. I know I am not mistaken. You have not changed, Mama. You are older is all, as you should be."

The woman on the footstool did not so much as look up. Instead she seemed to crumple into herself in an attempt to become invisible. A faint groan was the only sound that escaped her.

"Please, Mama, look at me," urged Clarissa, one hand clutching Maggie's and the other reaching out to touch the housekeeper's arm. "Whatever it is that happened so long ago, it has all ended. It is over, Mama. I know now that you are here and alive, and I shall tell Malcolm that you are, too."

"It is not over," murmured the woman, straightening stiffly and removing Clarissa's hand from her arm. "It will not be over until there is justice for all of the citizens of Great Britain, not just the privileged few. I am not your mama, Clarissa. I declined to be your mama years and years ago and I do not wish to begin being your mama now. I am Mrs. Quigley, the Archbishop of Canterbury's London housekeeper. And when the Archbishop returns to Kent, Mr. Quigley and I shall be in complete charge of this premises once again. And then Nathan and John and I—and the others, of course—shall devise a new plan and carry on."

"D-devise a new plan?" stuttered Maggie, sinking to a seat on the arm of Clarissa's chair.

"Mr.—Mr. Quigley? There is a *Mr.* Quigley?" Clarissa asked, appalled.

"I cannot understand," sighed Daphne Beresfont with a shake of her head, "how you have come to discover me. After all these years—and with Thomas dead. He did not leave you some message in his will? He vowed he would not. He vowed he would bury me from Malcolm and from you forever."

"He attempted to do so, Mama. He told us you were dead and for almost twenty years we believed him."

"Then how—why—?"

"Alex noticed that my ruby bracelet and earrings and Lady Sarah's ruby necklace were of a set, Mama. And he also noticed that there was no gravestone with your name upon it in the chapel yard at St. Mary's Lane. And, of course, he knew of the nonconformist conspiracy and had seen the list with Malcolm's and my name upon it."

"My list?" cried Daphne Beresfont excitedly, rising from the footstool and beginning to pace the library, her hands fidgeting at her breasts. "Lord Balmorrow has seen my little list? But this cannot be. However did he come by it? I left it in John's care."

"My brother has come by a good many more papers than just a list, ma'am," offered Maggie quietly. "And since very early last Spring, they have all apparently been concerned with an attempt at making him—"

"Yes, yes, I know!" exclaimed the woman. "Do you not think I know he was to be our scapegoat? I struggled and struggled over it. His father and grandfather both fought for us and he as well in his way. But someone must take the blame if we fail. And Nathan cannot be spared. And John—no, it could never be John. And Lord Balmorrow is truly the most believable of the lot from which we were forced to choose. And he is noble, you know. He believes in the cause of religious freedom and equality within the government. I was certain he would not mind."

"Not mind?" gasped Clarissa, her eyes widening with every word her mother spoke. "You thought that my husband would not mind to lose his head over a rebellion in which he had no part whatsoever?"

"Well, but he was not your husband then."

"But Mama, even so!"

"Hush, never mind," murmured Daphne Beresfont, crossing to the chair where Clarissa sat and once again sitting upon the footstool before her. "You are not to worry, Clarissa. That plan has been called off. No one will blame your husband for the revolution. I have set myself against it and Nathan understands and agrees with me. We will go about it another time in another way. Lord Balmorrow will not be troubled further."

"Oh no, he will not be troubled," glared Clarissa, longing to despise this person before her, but constantly pricked by the notion that she could not despise a woman she did not know anything at all about, especially not her mother. "He will not be troubled at all," she mumbled angrily. "He will merely be murdered."

"Murdered?"

"Indeed," frowned Maggie. "Last evening my brother was pushed into the midst of the carriages in Haymarket after the opera."

"Oh!" exclaimed Clarissa's mother. "Oh, it cannot be! He was not—not—killed?"

"Only because Clarissa dashed after him and caught him 'round the waist and caused him to fall back instead of forward."

"Thank heaven," sighed the older woman. "Thank heaven you were there, Clarissa. And thank heaven you did not freeze as you did when your papa was pushed. I should have known," she muttered then. "I ought to have warned Nathan to be on guard."

"Papa was pushed?" A great shudder weaved its way up Clarissa's spine. "Papa was murdered?"

"Murdered," Daphne Beresfont nodded. "Murdered."

* * *

The Earl of Balmorrow put the final crease into his neckcloth, spun on his heel and started for the door into the hallway. "You will be sure to tell her, Mackelry, that I have gone to Westminster. It is the final debate upon Holloway's bill in Commons and I have had a mind to hear it since first the thing was brought up. Everyone is concerned over it. You will tell Lady Balmorrow that I awoke right as a trivet and took myself off in the care of John Coachman, eh?"

"I will tell my lady so," nodded Mackelry, "and then she will box my ears for allowing you to escape your bed. You ought not to be walking around, my lord, much less going off to Westminster."

"Yes, so I have been told ever since I opened my eyes. But I am perfectly well, Mack, honest. It was merely a knock in the head. I did not split my thick skull wide open, you know. Why there is barely a lump there now."

Mackelry nodded, knowing it was useless to attempt to keep the man abed once he had decided against it. The valet watched him down the stairs, then returned to the earl's bedchamber to begin clearing things away. He was in the midst of folding Balmorrow's nightshirt when he paused before the window at the sound of the earl's coach being brought 'round and watched as his master ascended into the vehicle and it pulled away. He was just turning to set the nightshirt upon the bed and pick up his lordship's slippers when something moved at the very corner of his vision. Mackelry turned quickly back to the window.

"The devil," he breathed, staring through the glass. He, too, had heard his lordship mutter and mumble about being pushed last evening. And he had been privy as well, from the very first, to the aspersions cast against his employer's character. Rumors of treachery and conspiracy had flashed through the underworld of *ton* servants like lightning. And though many of their masters and mistresses had not yet been apprised of Perceval's accusations against Balmorrow at Carlton House, there was not an upper class servant in Grosvenor Square, Mayfair, or Leicester Square who had not discussed it and agreed that the Earl of Balmorrow was being set up somehow to take a mighty fall.

And now there was a gent on a flashy bay riding out of the square at a circumspect distance behind the earl's coach. And it was no one who lived on the square either. Mackelry was certain of that. "The devil," he breathed again, and tossing both nightshirt and slippers aside he dashed into the corridor and down the front staircase, whipping open the front door as soon as he reached it and sailing out onto the top step.

The gent had reached the far corner of the square and was standing in his stirrups, gazing in the direction that the earl's coach had taken. Then he sat back down upon the saddle and gave his horse the office to follow at a dignified trot.

"What is going on?" asked Jonson, stepping out beside Mackelry and pulling the door closed behind him.

"That gent. You do not know him, do you, Jonson?"

"Well, I cannot say, Mack. I can see nothing much of him from here. Why?"

"Because he is following his lordship. I am certain of it."

A worried scowl made Jonson's fine grey eyes squint and numerous wrinkles appear upon his generally placid countenance. "Following his lordship? You don't say? Well, but his lordship is bound for Westminster and Parliament. There cannot anything happen to him there, Mackelry. And John Coachman will keep his eyes peeled. He'll not have the master come close to being trampled again on his way to the coach. He will drop him directly at the bottom of the steps and take him up there as well. I am confident of that."

"The cabriolet," murmured Mackelry. "I can drive one horse. Have the cabriolet brought 'round, Jonson, and I will go after his lordship and warn him. Or if I cannot catch up with him, I will warn John outside Westminster and wait with him and see do I catch sight of the gent again."

"Her ladyship has the cabriolet. She and Her Grace went off in it over two hours ago."

"Damnation!" muttered Mackelry and Jonson's eyebrows rose considerably at the word.

Mackelry, rubbing energetically at the back of his neck with one hand, spun around to reenter the house and then came to a halt at the sound of a horse's hooves upon the cobbles.

"A piece of luck, Mack!" cried Jonson. "Her ladyship has just now turned the corner."

Clarissa's mind was all ajumble. She could not quite sort out the meaning behind all the words she had had from her mother. Her heart ached and her mind whirled and she had driven home in silence with Maggie beside her, thoughts tying themselves into knots inside her brain. She did not notice Mackelry and Jonson standing upon the steps of the townhouse until she had brought the cabriolet to a halt and Donnie had run to the horse's head and she had stepped down herself onto the flagway. And then it was Maggie who exclaimed at the servants meeting them outside the front door and who asked them if something were the matter.

In moments Clarissa was back in the vehicle with Maggie beside her and she was turning the little horse's head toward Westminster. Up behind, Mackelry had replaced Donnie and clung with great trepidation, but still bravely, to the undersized perch at the rear. The streets were becoming so very crowded that Clarissa was forced to come to a halt several times as she searched for a way through the throng. Still, it was less than ten minutes before she could clearly see her husband's coach drawn up near the main entrance to Westminster Palace and not very far from it, a flashy bay tied to one of the posts. "There, Mack," she called over her shoulder, pointing at the animal. "Is that the horse, do you think?"

"Aye, it appears to be, my lady. I do remember that spot upon its rump and the odd color of its tail."

"I shall pull to the curb here, then, Mack, and Her Grace and I shall walk the remainder of the way to the coach to warn John and then we shall go into the palace to see if we can gain sight of his lordship. I have never seen such a press of people. Why there are more here than last evening in Haymarket!"

That announcement sent a shiver down the valet's back. The two women had no gentlemen to accompany them and the flagstones were thick with people, anyone of whom might take advantage of them. "Here, boy!" he called, swinging down from his perch. "You, halfling, take this horse in hand until we return and there will be a shilling in it for you."

The urchin thus addressed ran immediately to the horse's head.

Thinking to protest that they could easily proceed without him, Clarissa nevertheless thought better of it. Perhaps Mackelry was correct. Perhaps his escort would be helpful. Truly, she thought, as she tucked her arm through Maggie's, she had never seen any street in London so crowded as this small space outside Westminster Palace, and everyone appeared to be shouting and running about quite wildly. Whatever was going on? Oh God, she prayed silently, her grip upon Maggie's arm tightening. Oh God, please do not let anything have happened. Let it be just ordinary for so many noisy people to be here. Please let it be just ordinary.

Balmorrow, stunned, knelt upon the cold stone floor of the lobby of the House of Commons. Around and above him gentlemen bellowed and roared. Running footsteps, the sound of a scuffle reached his ears but did not penetrate to his mind. Knees jostled against him; shoe toes and boot toes shuffled in and out of his vision as with a badly shaking hand he brushed sweaty wisps of hair from a pale brow and mumbled hoarse and useless bits of encouragement to the gentleman in his arms. A dry, rattling gasp for breath and the dismal damp of the gentleman's blood soaking through to Balmorrow's skin at last roused him to action and he placed an arm beneath the gentleman's knees, kept the other about the gentleman's shoulders and taking a deep breath, gained his feet with the dying man clasped tightly against his chest. He swung around, stared dazedly through the throng. Bodiless arms urged him first in one direction and then another, until at last a firm hand caught at his elbow and led him toward a tiny antechamber and directed him into it, pointing out an ancient plum-colored fainting couch.

Not until Balmorrow had lowered his burden to that couch and covered the shivering man with his own coat did he actually hear the tumult and cacophony just beyond the archway. Shrieks, howls, curses pummeled the air. A great tide of humanity surged toward the antechamber from the crowded corridor, but it retreated again in an instant, unwilling to pass the figure who stood steadfast beneath the arch. For an instant the Duke of Corning turned to stare at the earl and give him an encouraging nod, and then he turned back to the business of keeping the crowd at bay.

"What is it?" cried Clarissa, as the milling throng around herself and Maggie increased a hundredfold, a swarm of men excitedly exiting the palace. "Here, sir," she demanded, grabbing a gentleman by the sleeve and swinging him around to face her. "What has happened?"

The dead white face that stared down at her sent her to shuddering.

"Edward!" she gasped, noting his dazed expression and the way his hand tugged at the perfect knot of his neckcloth. "Lord Parkhurst, what has happened?"

"Sheer madness," mumbled Parkhurst, attempting to free himself from her grasp. "Fired off a pistol."

"Oh, great heavens," gasped Maggie, seizing upon Lord Parkhurst's other arm. "The Duke of Corning and Lord Balmorrow—are they inside? Are they all right?"

"Dead," Parkhurst mumbled, picking first Clarissa's hand from his arm and then Maggie's. "Dead. Must be. Blood everywhere."

"Who is dead?" Clarissa nearly screamed, visions of Alex and the Duke of Corning lying stiff upon the floor exploding into her mind. "Who, Edward? Not Alex?"

"Huh? Oh, no, not Balmorrow."

"Not D-David?" stuttered Maggie.

"Perceval," mumbled Parkhurst unsteadily. "Prime Minister Perceval. Quigley must have gone berserk. Not in the plan. I am certain 'twas not in the plan. Fired a damned pistol in the midst of all that crowd."

The two young women looked at Lord Parkhurst, then at each other. "Come, Mackelry," Clarissa commanded, abandoning Lord Parkhurst and taking the valet's arm.

Maggie quickly took the other. "We must get inside Westminster," she told the valet, her eyes blurred by a mist of tears. "The duke and your master may be in serious trouble and have need of us."

Mackelry thought to mention that the gentleman to whom the ladies had just spoken was the same gent who had ridden after his lordship upon that flashy bay, but he thought better of it. It was not the time to bring that bit of knowledge to their attention. At least he knew now who the gentleman was.

He centered all his energy and ingenuity upon assisting her ladyship and Her Grace to enter the palace as they wished. At one point the crowd grew so thick and rowdy that Mackelry feared he could get the two young ladies no nearer, but he kept on, shaking their hands from his arms and instead grasping each of them tightly around the waist, keeping them upright and mobile amongst the pushing and shoving of the mob, part of which flowed in the direction of the tiny antechamber just off the lobby of the House of Commons. Behind them whistles began to blow, announcing the arrival of a number of constables. Before them, the Duke of Corning stood, his feet spread, his arms akimbo, right in the center of the antechamber archway. "Mags! Clare!" he bellowed upon first sight of them. "Mackelry, what the deuce are you about to bring my wife and sister-in-law in here?"

"I told him he must," explained Clarissa breathlessly as Corning stepped aside and she and Maggie and the valet tumbled past him into the room. "Oh!" she gasped, her gaze immediately coming to rest upon her husband as he sat upon the edge of the couch, covered in blood, with Spencer Perceval's head resting amazingly still in his lap.

"Did you come in the town coach?" Corning whispered in Maggie's ear.

"No, Clare drove Alex's cabriolet. Why are we whispering?"

"Because I do not wish Alex to hear. We must get him out of here, Mags. Quickly. They have caught the fellow who fired the pistol, but I heard cries of Balmorrow as soon as its echo died. I think that ball was meant for your brother, Mags. He was standing right beside Perceval when they were fired upon, and after what happened last evening—there may be a second gunman."

The Duchess of Corning walked quickly up behind Clare and whispered in her ear.

"No!" exclaimed Clare in hushed but horrified tones. "That cannot be! My mama said—"

"It is what David thinks, Clare. We must get Alex to safety at once."

Clarissa studied the bewildered look upon her husband's face. He is so staggered, she thought, that he does not even realize. "Alex, my darling, Mr. Perceval is dead," murmured Clarissa softly as she stood beside him and brushed an errant curl behind her husband's ear. "Come away from him now, dearest. You cannot be of help to him any more."

Chapter 19

Lady Sarah sat, stunned, upon the sopha in her front parlor and stared openmouthed at Lord Parkhurst. "Mr. Quigley?" she murmured with a nervous shake of her pretty blonde curls. "I cannot believe it."

"Believe it," muttered Parkhurst, tugging distractedly at the knot in his neckcloth. "I followed Balmorrow all the way to Westminster. Followed him inside as well. Can you imagine how difficult it is to trail after that gentleman through the halls of Westminster Palace without drawing attention to oneself? It is deuced difficult, believe you me!"

Lady Sarah nodded in sympathy.

"Yes, well, and who should he meet but Perceval and Castlereagh and Liverpool and the four of them fall into a debate right in the middle of the Commons lobby. And out of nowhere, without the least warning, Quigley leaps into sight and fires a dueling pistol into the midst of them."

"Oh!" squeaked Lady Sarah.

"Brought down Mr. Perceval, he did. Apprehended on the spot, of course," sighed Parkhurst sorrowfully. "Quigley. Hauled off and slapped into irons I have no doubt. And that is the end for us, m'dear."

"The—the end?" Lady Sarah's hand absently pleated the soft muslin of her cornflower blue morning dress.

"Indeed."

"But why do you say it is the end for us, Lord Parkhurst? Surely Mr. Quigley was not in charge of everything. Why would those remaining not continue to require our services?"

Parkhurst's hazel eyes flashed with cynicism. "I cannot think, my lady," he muttered snidely, "unless of course it is because Quigley will name every one of them and they will be arrested and sent to the gibbet."

"Oh, he would never tell!" exclaimed Lady Sarah.

"Of course he will name names," sighed Parkhurst in exasperation. "He will attempt to buy his own way off the gibbet by doing so. He will tell everything he knows, now, to save his own neck."

"Everything?" Lady Sarah's face grew even more pale. "Everything, Lord Parkhurst?"

"Indeed!" And then Parkhurst, seeing the panicked expression upon Lady Sarah's adorable little face, comprehended for the first time—everything. "Oh, my great Uncle Hiram!" he gasped. "He will open his budget and spill everything he knows, including my name!"

"And—and mine."

Lord Parkhurst, with a shake of his bright golden curls, stood and bowed over Lady Sarah's hand.

"Where—where are you going?"

"I have just remembered, my lady," mumbled Lord Parkhurst. "I have a—a previous appointment. I must be gone immediately." And without another word he took himself from Sarah's presence.

"Oh, has Lord Parkhurst departed already?" queried Miss Gonnering, gazing back over her shoulder at the sound of the front door closing. "I did so hope he would stay to tea. He is quite nice, do you not think so, dear? And most handsome. And I do believe he is quite eligible, Sarah."

Lady Sarah stared flabbergasted at her aunt but then she recalled that Miss Gonnering was only just entering the room and had not the least idea why Lord Parkhurst had come to call or what he had said, and she gave an uneasy little giggle.

* * *

The Bishop of Leeds swirled from his coach, up the steps of Balmorrow House, and in past Jonson without once breaking his stride. "Where is he, Jonson?" he called back over his shoulder on the way to the first floor.

"In his chambers, Your Grace. But the others await him in the long drawing room."

Alden nodded and swept up the staircase and down the first floor corridor to the rear of the establishment.

"Alden!" exclaimed Maggie, rushing to him as he entered the chamber. "Do you know what—"

"Everything," declared the bishop. "I know everything, Maggie. Corning, you must discover pressing business in the provinces at once. That pistol ball was intended for Lex and he will not seek shelter unless we force him to do so. And you must stand watch over him until Jack and I send word that all is safe in town."

"I am not traveling even so far as the outskirts of London," drawled Balmorrow from the drawing room doorway, his arm securely around Clarissa. "The man has been captured, has he not, Alden? Then where is the danger?"

"You do not understand, Lex," Alden growled, turning his wide blue eyes upon Balmorrow. "Apparently your unexpected marriage to this young lady has run all our villains' plans amuck, forged a rift amongst them. Canterbury's clerk has lost his mind entirely I think."

"Canterbury's clerk?" Balmorrow escorted Clarissa to a seat beside Maggie on the sopha and then stomped across the room to pour out cognac for the lot of them. "What has the Archbishop of Canterbury's clerk to say to it, Alden?" he asked, his hand shaking just the slightest bit as he poured from the decanter.

"That was John Bellingham who brought down Perceval this afternoon," growled Alden, accepting a glass from Balmorrow's hand and then beginning to pace the room.

"Bellingham?" gasped Clarissa, her gaze meeting Maggie's in astonishment. "The archbishop's clerk is a Mr. Bellingham?"

"Aye," nodded Alden. "John Bellingham. Took the position only last year. Canterbury claims he had not the least indication that the man was bonkers. But he is bonkers, Lex. And when they dragged him out of Westminster Palace, he was raving that you, personally, had strangled a glorious revolution in its infancy and for that you deserve to die. Lord Liverpool wants you out of town immediately, before someone else involved in this dreadful little conspiracy attempts to rectify Bellingham's bad shot. Liverpool and Castlereagh are already passing around word that Bellingham had a long-standing grievance against the government, and that he is mad as a hatter, hoping to keep your name out of the thing as much as they can."

"Clarissa's mama is a Bellingham, Alden," Maggie said quietly, drawing her cousin's attention to the young woman who sat silently beside her upon the couch. "It is quite likely that John Bellingham is also a relation of Clare's."

"I am—I am sorry. I did not intend to—it is nothing against you, Clarissa," the bishop stuttered. "It is only that I wish to impress upon Lex the danger involved. Where there is one madman, there are quite likely others."

Clarissa nodded slowly. "I know there is one other," she whispered. "Oh, Alex, I know there is one other madman involved. At least—she is a madwoman. She is my mama. Maggie and I have been to see her."

"You have been to see her?" Balmorrow and Corning and Alden all set their glasses aside and moved closer to the two young ladies on the couch.

"You have been to see your mama, Clare?" asked Balmorrow, pulling up a footstool and settling at Clarissa's knee, his hand covering her own in her lap. "Why did you not tell me? How brave of you to seek her out, and yet, how sad it must have been. Could you not have waited, my love, until I could accompany you?"

"N-no, I could not, Alex. Because someone had attempted to kill you, you see, and I feared mama might well be involved in it. That is—I thought, perhaps, that she might know who was involved in it. And oh, Alex, I do believe my mama is quite as mad as ever this Mr. John Bellingham may be."

With an angry swipe at a teardrop that rolled unbidden to her cheek, Clarissa stared from her sitting room window down into the shadowy street below. Across the square a large gentleman leaned against a lamppost. She could not make out so much as the color of his coat in the failing light, but she knew him to be a Bow Street Runner. And she knew there were other runners lingering about Leicester Square as well, keeping watch—keeping watch over Alex and herself. The Duke of Corning had sent them shortly after leaving Balmorrow House, because even knowing all that Clarissa's mama had said to her, Alex had still refused to depart London for the safety of the provinces.

"We are surrounded," announced Balmorrow, his voice making Clarissa jump because she had not at all heard him enter the chamber. "Our every movement is under surveillance."

"Oh, no, Alex. They are here to protect you, not to spy upon you." Clarissa smiled weakly as he knelt upon the settee beside her, put his arm around her and stared down into the street.

"Perhaps, but the effect is the same, you must admit. I am so sorry, Clare."

"Sorry? You are sorry?"

"Indeed. I did never intend that any of this nonsense should touch you and instead, here you are in the very midst of murder and mayhem."

"As I chose to be," Clarissa whispered.

"Yes, and why you chose so, I cannot comprehend. You, at least, might have gone safely home to the castle. Maggie would have been pleased to accompany you, had that been your choice."

"And leave you here alone to face the unknown? I think not, Alex. 'Whither thou goest, I shall go' and whither thou stayest, I shall stay, too!"

"Only provided," Balmorrow murmured, noticing a tear clinging to her cheek and wiping it gently away with one long slim finger. "Only provided the whither I goest is not to the gallows. I forbid you to follow me there."

"The gallows?"

"Yes, dear heart. There are yet those who believe I am in this nonconformist plot up to my neck. Alden confessed before he took his leave that Liverpool and Castlereagh are spreading those rumors about Bellingham because word took flight immediately that I was responsible for Mr. Perceval's being in the lobby of Commons and had set him up for Bellingham to shoot down."

"Oh, Alex, surely no one will believe that now! Certainly Lord Liverpool and Lord Castlereagh will quash such nonsense."

"Well, I do hope so," murmured Balmorrow. "I shall place my trust in them, shall I and not worry overly much about the matter? Unless a mob appears outside our door and I am dragged off kicking and screaming into the night, of course."

His arm tightened around her and Clarissa looked up to see a smile mounting to his eyes.

"What? What can you find in this situation that brings mirth to your eyes, Alex?"

"Why, the vision of myself being dragged off kicking and screaming, Clare. Cannot you see it? A great clunch like myself? It would take at least ten strong men to do the thing and they would be tripping over each other every step of the way. And I would look a veritable twit, would I not?"

"Alex, it is *not* funny. And it will not happen," Clarissa added with a tiny gulp. "You are not to be the nonconformist scapegoat any longer, either. Mama promised me as much. She said they would begin on a new plan and that it would not involve you. Oh, Alex, to think that my own mama could be so evil!"

"Is that what has you crying?"

"I am n-not c-crying," Clarissa wailed suddenly, burying herself against Balmorrow's chest.

Picking her up in his arms, he turned from the window and sat down upon the settee, setting her on his lap like some forlorn child. "Sshhh, sweet girl," he murmured, kissing one hot little cheek. "Hush, my little love. Your mama is not evil. I am nearly certain of it. There is much goes on here that we do neither of us understand, Clare."

"But my mama knows all about the nonconformists' plot," she sobbed. "She speaks of herself and a Nathan and a John as though they were in charge of all—Oh! Oh, Alex! John! Mama was speaking of Mr. John Bellingham!"

"Did she say she was speaking of Mr. John Bellingham?"

"No, but—"

"We ought not leap to conclusions then, dearest. Perhaps

there is another John. And perhaps not. Perhaps John Bellingham is at the bottom of everything, eh? Perhaps he is your mad uncle who has kidnapped your mama and kept her in his power for years and years. Do you not remember your mad Uncle John, my love?" he teased, nibbling at her ear. "I remember my mad Uncle Angus vividly. He was accustomed to walk about with a mouse in his pocket and the most pleasant smile upon his face."

"A mouse in his pocket, Alex?" asked Clarissa, straightening and wiping at her cheeks with the backs of both hands.

"Uh-huh," nodded Balmorrow, smoothing wisps of hair back from her burning brow. "A mouse named Argyl which he kept on a golden chain and brought out in the midst of every dull entertainment to frighten the ladies into liveliness."

"Oh, you are telling the biggest clanker," hiccoughed Clarissa, a faint smile edging in through her tears.

"No, I am not. He was well over six feet tall."

"The mouse?"

"No, Uncle Angus, you rascal, and he was broad as a bull and daft as a loon, believe you me."

"But he—he never—shot—anyone."

"Let me think. Did he? Yes, as a matter of fact, he did. He shot my father. Right in the posterior. With a crossbow."

"Alex, you are making all this up."

"No, no. My papa had to sit on a pillow for weeks and weeks afterward. Carried it around with him everywhere. Even to Lords."

"To Lords?"

"Yes, indeed. Most uncomfortable benches in Lords—especially when one has been—well—significantly injured."

"Balderdash," gurgled Clarissa wetly, leaning her head upon his shoulder.

"There, that is a great deal better," observed Balmorrow, hugging her soundly. "Perhaps a mad relation who shoots a Prime Minister is no one to brag to our children about, my love, but he is also no one for you to be concerned over either. What John Bellingham did this afternoon cannot reflect upon you, Clare. No, and you are no more responsible for him than I was responsible for my Uncle Angus and his mouse and his crossbow. You are much less responsible in fact because you did not even know you had an Uncle John Bellingham—if you do—we do not even know the truth of that as yet—whereas I always knew I had an Uncle Angus."

For the longest while Clarissa lost herself in the comfort of her husband's strong and very protective arms. Now and then she felt him kiss her ear or rub her back or rest his chin upon her head. But he said nothing more, only held her and rocked her a bit as if she were no more than a child.

It was nearing nine o'clock when they heard a carriage draw up before the house and then the sound of the knocker and Jonson opening the wide front door. There were snatches of voices from the ground floor, then the tapping of a footman's shoes upon the staircase and along the corridor, and finally the soft rap of knuckles upon the sitting room door.

Balmorrow stood, gave Clarissa one more encouraging hug, and made his way across the carpeting to answer the summons. "What is it, James?" he drawled as he swung the sitting room door inward.

"Visitors, my lord." James presented to Balmorrow two calling cards upon a small silver tray.

"Lady Sarah?" Balmorrow murmured. "And little Miss Gonnering?"

"Jonson has put them in the summer parlor, my lord."

"Yes, well, say that her ladyship and I will be down presently, James, eh? And be certain the fire is lit for them. It is a bit nippy this evening."

"Yes, my lord," nodded James, departing.

"Lady Sarah and Miss Gonnering?" Clarissa had crossed to her husband and now took his arm in both hands. "What can they want with you at this hour? Oh, do not go down, Alex."

"Do not go down? But why should I not go down, Clare?"

"B-because Lady Sarah works for the nonconformists. Perhaps she has come to—to—"

"Shoot me?" Balmorrow's eyes crinkled with mirth. "Oh, my sweet girl. Do you actually think that The Summarfield has come to shoot me? And where would she carry her pistol, in her reticule?"

"Do not laugh, Alex. Mama said that all their plans would need to be changed and changing the plans made Mr. John Bellingham so desperate as to attempt to kill you—twice! Perhaps Lady Sarah has also become desperate!"

* * *

"Alex!" cried Lady Sarah, rising quickly from a lyre-backed chair and racing across the summer parlor to throw herself into Balmorrow's arms. "Oh, Alex, I am in such terrible trouble!" she exclaimed, completely ignoring the fact that Clarissa stood nonplussed beside them. "You must help me. Oh, please say you will help me. I have not the least idea what to do. I am desperate!" Her lovely, changeable hazel eyes overflowed with tears as she fell to sobbing against Balmorrow's chest.

"Yes, well," mumbled Balmorrow, one hand going tentatively to pat Sarah's back. "Good evening, Miss Gonnering. And are you desperate as well?"

Miss Gonnering's round little mouth opened, and her plump little cheeks quivered, and her chunky little hands danced in her lap. "Oh, my goodness," she whispered in utter disbelief. "Sarah what *are* you doing? Lady Balmorrow, I am—I cannot—oh, goodness gracious!"

"Clare, go to Miss Gonnering. She is most discomposed," Balmorrow whispered over the top of Lady Sarah's head. "There is some sherry on the sideboard. You had best pour her some. And some for Sarah as well. And do not look quite so upset, my love, Sarah's reticule is way over there on the table."

The sly reference to Lady Sarah's having come to shoot him and the startling twinkle in his eyes dissolved Clarissa's sudden discomposure and a faint smile mounted to her countenance.

"Will you have some sherry, Miss Gonnering?" she asked, crossing to the sideboard and opening the decanter. "It is most efficacious for settling one's nerves."

"I—I—I—" stuttered Miss Gonnering, her hands now twisting and tugging at the stiff brocade of her gown.

"You must not be so very upset, Miss Gonnering," continued Clarissa, pouring out four glasses of the sherry and once again catching her husband's mirth-filled eyes upon her. "I am quite certain that Lady Sarah would not be in my husband's arms if she had not a very good reason for it."

"Exactly so," offered Balmorrow still standing near the doorway with a whimpering Lady Sarah plastered against him.

"Drink up, Miss Gonnering, and Clare shall ring for tea and cakes as well. You would like some cakes, would you not?"

"I—I—I—" stuttered Miss Gonnering.

"Sarah, you are distressing your aunt exceedingly," whispered Balmorrow into one of Lady Sarah's shell-like ears. "She is not even rising to the offer of tea and cakes. And she will not do so either until you are out of my arms. Come and sit down with me just there and try to compose yourself, eh?"

The earl helped Lady Sarah to a seat upon the wicker couch and sat down beside her, keeping a strong arm about her shoulders. "There, that is much better," he observed, offering her his handkerchief.

"Oh, Alex, I am come all a-a-part," sobbed Lady Sarah.

"Well, here is Clare with some sherry, sweetings. That is just the stuff to put you back together again. Now you must dry your tears, Sarah," he continued as he took the glass Clarissa handed him. "Take a sip of this, my dear." He held the glass gently to the lovely Lady Sarah's perfect bow lips. And she did take a bit. The tiniest swallow.

"That's my girl," nodded Balmorrow. "Now wipe your eyes and blow your nose and take another sip and then tell me how I may be of service."

"Oh, Alex," sniffed Lady Sarah once she had dried her eyes and swallowed the remainder of her sherry at a gulp, "I am a horrible, dreadful person."

"Never," declared Balmorrow with a speaking glance at Clarissa who had gone to sit beside Miss Gonnering.

"Yes, yes, I am. And I have betrayed you. Not just once, but over and over again."

"You have?" asked Balmorrow, the corners of his lips quivering upwards.

"Oh, yes. I am not madly in love with you, Alex. I only pretended to be because they paid me."

Lady Sarah glanced at him sideways, like a shy little girl, and Clarissa nearly giggled as Alex's quivering lips hastily curved downward into a sad frown.

"You *are* hurt! Oh, I knew you would be, Alex," sighed Lady Sarah. "I should not have done it. I knew from the very first it was a bad thing to do. But Summarfield died at the very worst time. He was in debt, you know, and we had already spent all of my inheritance from Papa. And ugly old Cousin

Roger who inherited Papa's title and estates would not give me anything further. He is a terrible, awful man, Cousin Roger! He told me straight out that Aunt Grace and I might ply our wares in the street for all he cared. He said that that was what I deserved. A daughter of an earl, he said, had no business throwing herself away upon a mere mister and I could expect no help from him nor he would not help Aunt Grace either."

Beside Clarissa, Miss Gonnering gave an astounded gasp.

"What was I to do, Alex? When Mr. Quigley came to me and suggested that I might earn the money I required and gave me a hundred pound note and a perfectly gorgeous ruby necklace as the first payment, what was I to do? He said, you know, that he only wished me to sit in your pocket and relay your thoughts to him upon certain subjects. It did not seem such a terrible thing at all. I did not know that he meant to—to shoot the Prime Minister! Honestly, I did not!"

"No, of course you did not," offered Balmorrow, his arm still firmly about Lady Sarah's shoulders. "Who is Mr. Quigley, Sarah?"

"Why, he is the man who murdered Mr. Perceval this afternoon. Lord Parkhurst saw him do it."

"No, that was a Mr. Bellingham, my dear. And he did never intend to shoot the Prime Minister, Sarah. Mr. Bellingham intended to shoot me."

"Eek!" squeaked Miss Gonnering, her glass of sherry tumbling from her hand. By the greatest of good fortune it was already empty. Clarissa bent to lift it from the carpet and placed it upon a small cricket table.

Lady Sarah's eyes began once more to fill with tears. "Then he lied to me about his name, Alex. Oh, he lied to me about everything!"

"No, do not weep again, Sarah," commanded Balmorrow rather forcefully.

"But I am a—a—murderess!" wailed Lady Sarah loudly.

"Oh, for heaven's sake," declared Clarissa abruptly, "you are no such thing. Cease this Cheltenham tragedy at once. You are frightening your aunt more and more."

"I am not a murderess?"

"No," repeated Clarissa, catching the laughter in her husband's glance and finding it hard to maintain a somber countenance. "You are simply a spy. And not a very good one at that, because Alex knew all along what you were doing."

"You did?" asked Lady Sarah wide-eyed.

"Indeed," nodded Balmorrow, "from the very beginning."

"And you led me on?"

"Well, I did not want you to lose your income, Sarah. And you passed on a good deal of information which was false for me, you know. Though I cannot think now that any of it was quite what your employers hoped to obtain. What did they hope to obtain?"

"I am sure I have not the vaguest idea," murmured Sarah. "Mr. Quigley—I mean, Mr. Bellingham—never once said. But I was not a spy! I would not have accepted Mr. Bellingham's offer had it had anything to do with the Frenchies. I despise the Frenchies—except for their fashions, of course, which one cannot truly dislike no matter how hard one attempts to be loyal. I would have tossed Mr. Bellingham out into the street if he had said my work had anything at all to do with helping the French. Aunt Grace and I would have gladly starved rather than do that!"

The appalled look upon Miss Gonnering's face at this last remark set Balmorrow off into roars of laughter and Clarissa was not far behind.

It was baffling. Clarissa knew with shuddering awareness how close Alex had twice come to death in the past two days and how close he might yet come again. She had been in tears over it only moments ago. And she knew she ought to be most put-out with Lady Sarah over the part that woman had played, but still, she could not help but laugh. Perhaps it was simply because Alex was laughing and that incredibly precious sound was most contagious.

Lady Sarah gazed at both Balmorrow and his bride as if they had gone mad. And poor little Miss Gonnering, apparently still hearing the words 'Aunt Grace and I would have gladly starved' sat gulping in a significant amount of air.

"I—I am sorry," offered Balmorrow as he chuckled to a stop. "I should not have laughed, Sarah. It is truly a serious matter." But then another wave of laughter rolled over him and he stood, while attempting to smother it, and strolled over beside Clarissa and bent down to bestow a tender kiss upon her cheek. "I know you lied to me and misled me,

Sarah. But I have done the same to you. I do not love you, Sarah, nor I never have. I like you well enough, but it is my wife I love."

"But you said—" protested Lady Sarah on a tiny gasp.

"It was a frightful bouncer. You are not the only one who knows how to lie, my dear."

"Ahem," breathed Jonson from the doorway.

"Yes, Jonson?" Balmorrow asked with a cock of his eyebrow.

"There is a gentleman to see you, my lord. He is out of calling cards, my lord."

"Well, who is it, Jonson?"

"It is Lord Parkhurst, my lord."

"Parkhurst?" Balmorrow's eyes met Clarissa's. "Are you quite certain I am the one he wishes to see, Jonson? Not Lady Balmorrow?"

"The gentleman asked for you, my lord. A matter most urgent, he said."

"Lord Parkhurst?" cried Lady Sarah. "He is here? Oh, Alex, he is one of them! He, too, worked for Mr. Quigley—I mean, Mr. Bellingham. You do not think he has come to shoot you?"

"Ssshhh, Jonson does not care to hear such things, Sarah. He has quite enough to worry about already, do you not, Jonson?" He took Clarissa's hand tightly into his own and kept it there. "Apparently this is a night for surprises. Show the gentleman up, then. Oh, and check to see if he is carrying a pistol with him, eh, Jonson? It will most likely be under his shirt at the back.

"Under—under his shirt? At the back, your lordship?"

"Yes. Just give him a pat, Jonson. You will feel it if it is there." Balmorrow, his eyes lit with good humor, took the hand he held so tightly in his own and placed a gentle kiss upon it. "We know about smuggling pistols, do we not, my love?"

Chapter 20

"I fail to understand," sighed Balmorrow, his gaze riveted upon the quaking gentleman before him, as he took up a stand before the fireplace. "What do you expect of me, Parkhurst?"

"Nothing," muttered Parkhurst with a sad shake of his golden curls. "I know I can expect nothing of you but disgust and condemnation. It was unconscionable of me to sell myself to such a cause. It was unforgiveable."

"Well," murmured Balmorrow with a shrug of his broad shoulders, "the cause is not unforgiveable, Parkhurst. I have been striving to eradicate the Test Acts since first I set foot in Lords. Yes, and my father did likewise and his father before him and any number of honorable gentlemen over the years. But you—you do not even know what the Test Acts are, do you?"

"No," mumbled Parkhurst, staring down at the toes of his boots.

"No. And yet you join up with revolutionaries."

"Revolutionaries!" The word escaped Lady Sarah's lips in a great gush of surprise.

"What did you think this was all about, Lady Sarah?" asked Clarissa with a frown. "Had you not the least idea that these people you helped were planning to overthrow the government?"

"Oh, no, never!" squeaked Sarah.

"Actually, I do not think she did know," offered Parkhurst quietly. "I knew because they set me to following you, Balmorrow, and I pressed them to know why. But I do not think Lady Sarah had the least inkling."

"And I expect you took the position from the very beginning because you were dreadfully short of funds, eh, Parkhurst?"

Lord Parkhurst nodded his golden curls and Clarissa could not help but wonder how she had ever found those golden curls at all alluring.

"How short of funds are you, Parkhurst?" Balmorrow asked.

"Extremely."

"So short that you cannot arrange for a long voyage in distant climes? For your health, I mean."

"Oh, are you ill, Lord Parkhurst? I knew you did not look at all the thing, but I thought perhaps it was just upset over all of this—"

"Sarah, be quiet," ordered Balmorrow, running his fingers through his hair, sighing disgustedly and glaring at Parkhurst. "Well, Parkhurst? Are you as short of funds as that?"

"I departed Lady Sarah's establishment this afternoon with just such a voyage in mind, but I found I could not accomplish it. I have not quite enough money to manage the thing. Besides, even if I did have the funds, my man Henry has a broken leg and cannot possibly tolerate such a voyage at this point. And I cannot abandon Henry."

"Why not?"

"Well—well—because Henry is the only person cares anything at all about me," whispered Parkhurst hoarsely. "He taught me to ride my first pony and saw me through all the worst of the hubbub that was m'life when I was a halfling. And when I lost everything and had to lease out my little estate and put myself up in wretched chambers here in London and exist upon almost nothing, only Henry stood by me. I have not paid him one penny for almost two years. I have got him mixed-up in treason. And now he vows he will spend his meagre life savings to help me pay for passage upon one of the ships to India. But I cannot take his money. No, nor I cannot abandon him either."

"And you have come here to ask me to—?"

"To defend Henry should it come to that," declared Parkhurst, his glance rising from the toes of his boots to meet Balmorrow's eyes squarely. "And to provide him a position if you can. He is a very good groom. He will prove a decidedly good investment for your stables. I shall likely hang when Quigley mentions my name, Balmorrow. And I am deserving of it, too. I have played a most dishonorable and despicable part in this thing. And I have no excuse for it. Money is not an excuse. I see that now. But it was none of it Henry's decision. He did never even meet Mr. Quigley."

"That fiend's name is not Quigley!" exclaimed Lady Sarah. "That fiend's name is John Bellingham! Alex has told me so."

"Bellingham?" Parkhurst cocked an eyebrow. "He is a relation of yours, Clarissa?"

"Do not call my wife by her Christian name, Parkhurst."

"No, no, sorry. He is a relation of yours, my lady?"

"I do not know," responded Clarissa with a searching look at her husband. "I expect he may well be."

With a great sigh Parkhurst spun down into an overstuffed chair and resting his elbows on his knees, buried his head in his hands. "It is all such a muddle," he groaned. "And I am to blame for all of it."

"Never say so," pouted Lady Sarah, going to kneel beside him and patting him upon the arm. "That dreadful Bellingham person is to blame for it. And he is a relation of Balmorrow's new bride. You heard her say so."

"Sarah, do go sit back down and be quiet!" growled Balmorrow. "You are very far out if you think to blame any of your troubles upon Clare."

"Oh! Oh! I do not mean to do that! I only mean to point out to Lord Parkhurst that neither he nor myself would be at all in the briars if this villainous relation of your wife had not shot the Prime Minister and then gotten caught!"

Clarissa heard Miss Gonnering take a great gulp of air beside her and she glanced at the elderly lady from the corner of her eye. Poor little Miss Gonnering's chubby cheeks were red as hot pokers and her eyes were squinted tightly shut and she was, by all appearances, attempting to hold her breath. It was a most pitiful and heart-rending sight and Clarissa could not help but put a comforting arm about Miss Gonnering's shoulders and whisper encouragements into her ear.

"All I ever wished to do," sighed Miss Gonnering, exhaling at last, "was to have a gown of bottle green taffeta with carmine piping and a small, just a very tiny, flounce at the front—and perhaps a turban to match. That is why I did not press Sarah about her agreement with Mr. Quigley. I ought to have discovered what it was all about, but I could only think that at last there would be money again and that perhaps if Sarah did well, there might even be enough money to buy myself that one new gown. It is all I ever thought to wish for in my whole entire life and now see where my greed has got me—I am become a seditionist!"

"No, you are quite wrong there," hissed a voice from behind Jonson, who had chosen just that moment to enter the room. "I am a seditionist, dear lady. You are merely a fat, fuzzy-headed featherbrain."

"Oh, come now," drawled Balmorrow, as though strangers appeared in his summer parlor with pistols in his butler's back every evening. "That was uncalled for. Miss Gonnering is none of those things. Does this person have a name, Jonson, or simply a firearm between your shoulder blades?"

"He is a Mr. Quigley, your lordship," replied Jonson stoically. "He did insist upon seeing you, sir."

"So I gather," sighed Balmorrow.

"You cannot possibly be Mr. Quigley," advised Lady Sarah confidently, settling to the floor beside Lord Parkhurst's chair, her skirts plumping out around her. "There is no Mr. Quigley. There was a Mr. Quigley but he was not Mr. Quigley. *He* was Mr. Bellingham."

The rather elderly self-proclaimed seditionist, with thinning blond hair and a cherubic though wrinkled face, scowled as he stepped out from behind Jonson and leveled his pistol directly at the earl. "Where do they all come from?" he muttered, a most perplexed look in his deep brown eyes. "I vow the entire aristocracy is full of twits and featherbrains."

"No," sighed Balmorrow, "not the entire aristocracy, but my summer parlor is certainly filling up with them this evening. And now you are arrived, Mr. Quigley," he added with a distinct cock of an eyebrow as he studied the gentleman.

The older man studied him in return. Studied him very carefully. Clarissa watched in silence as the smaller, thinner man ran his eyes over every inch of her husband. She knew she ought to do something. Whoever this man was, he was certainly dangerous. Perhaps, she thought, I shall be able to signal the Runners outside. But how on earth am I to do that?

"You look the devil of a lot like Leeds," drawled Mr. Quigley suspiciously as he continued to study Balmorrow. "Look exactly like the Bishop of Leeds as a matter of fact."

"No, not exactly," replied Balmorrow, stuffing his hands into his pockets and leaning his shoulders back against the mantlepiece. "I am a good deal more handsome than his nibs. Ask my wife if I am not," he added, his great blue eyes catching at Clarissa's with a most speaking look.

If only I knew what that look means! thought Clarissa in a bit of a panic. It is obvious that Alex wishes something of me, but what?

"I *am* a good deal more handsome than Alden, am I not, m' dear?" Balmorrow repeated, his eyebrow cocking.

"Oh, yes, most certainly," agreed Clarissa on an intake of breath as she thought she understood. "And you are taller as well. And—and—your feet! Your feet are much bigger than the bishop's!"

Quigley's gaze traveled from one to the other of them. "His feet are bigger?" he asked, confounded. "His *feet?* You ain't Balmorrow at all, are you?" he accused, staring back at the earl. "What did you do with your cousin, Y'r Grace? Smuggle him out to the country?"

"Not at all, Quigley. I am m'cousin. That is to say—"

"No, you are not," frowned Quigley worriedly. "I ought to have known the moment I walked in, except I have never before seen you without all your paraphernalia. Still, I recognize your voice, now I think on it."

"Well, but Alden and I do have similar voices."

"Prove you are not the Bishop of Leeds," growled Quigley.

"How?"

"Kiss the gel."

"Which gel?"

"Why your wife, of course."

"Oh. All right," nodded Balmorrow nonchalantly. "Of course I shall need to walk over there to do it. You will not shoot me, will you, for crossing the room? Come, Clare, meet me part way," he grinned, holding out his arms to her as he halted before one of the windows.

Clarissa rose immediately and rushed to him and he buried his chin alongside her cheek and whispered into her ear. Then Clarissa flung her arms around his neck and stood on tip-toe and he whispered into her ear some more. And then he pressed his lips over hers, swung her around and they both stumbled most inauspiciously into the draperies, caught their feet in the long folds, and brought the heavy velvet crashing down, rods and all.

Miss Gonnering screamed in surprise and, literally erupting from the settee, fled in bumbling panic directly into the arms of Mr. Quigley. Mr. Quigley's pistol dropped to the floor and fired. Lord Parkhurst jumped up, grabbed Lady Sarah and tugged her out of the way behind the chair in which he had been sitting. And Jonson sped out of the room and dashed wildly down the staircase.

Balmorrow, laughing, assisted Clarissa from the tangle of fabric.

"You *are* the Bishop of Leeds," cried Mr. Quigley accusingly, attempting to free himself of Miss Gonnering's panic-stricken hold and retrieve his pistol. "I never saw such a mad stab at kissing in all my life! Release me, you featherbrained woman! I am not your saviour!"

"No, I am," declared Lord Parkhurst, sprinting out from behind his chair and grabbing Mr. Quigley by an elbow, separating him from Miss Gonnering and then bestowing upon that gentleman a swift jab to the stomach and a right cross to the jaw.

Mr. Quigley dropped directly to the carpet and did not rise again.

With great delicacy, Lord Parkhurst escorted the quivering and shivering little Miss Gonnering back to her seat upon the settee, then helped Lady Sarah to a seat beside her.

Balmorrow, still laughing, gave Clarissa a quick kiss on the cheek. "Excellent, my love," he chuckled. "And even if the Runners did not see the draperies fall, Jonson will be urging them in through the front door even as we speak."

"No, he will not," announced a voice of great authority from the corridor. "Your butler, Lord Balmorrow, is incapacitated at the moment. Tripped upon the staircase. And the Runners have all gone rushing off in pursuit of our frightening mob who gave the impression that they meant to gather outside your front door."

"Mama!" cried Clarissa, as the woman in black bombazine with the flashing emerald eyes strolled into the room.

"I do wish you would refrain from calling me that," sighed Daphne Beresfont, "but it is all so very new to you that I expect you cannot help yourself. Is he dead?" she queried, gazing down upon Mr. Quigley.

"No, he is not," replied Clarissa. "Lord Parkhurst merely hit him with his fist."

"In the jaw, no doubt. Nathan has never been able to withstand a solid pop upon the jaw."

"This is Nathan? The man who understood and agreed that the plan must be altered? Mama, he came here with a pistol!"

"Well, and I am not at all surprised," nodded Daphne Beresfont, rummaging about in her great black reticule and producing a matching pistol which she pointed steadily at the little group of people across from her. "When I heard what your Uncle John had done at Westminster, Clarissa, I knew very well that Nathan's wits would go abegging as well. He is not a well man, you know. He has suffered through any number of dreadful experiences in his life and for John to lose his mind and murder Mr. Spencer Perceval was not at all conducive to Nathan's stability."

"No, I expect not," nodded Balmorrow as he stood behind Clarissa, wrapped her in both his arms and rested his chin cozily upon her head. "Good evening, my lady. I have been longing to make your acquaintance. You are my mother-in-law, are you not?"

"No, I am not!" declared Daphne Beresfont with an oddly youthful and very angry stomp of her foot.

"Well, but if you are Clarissa's mama, you are most certainly Alex's mama-in-law," declared Lady Sarah. "That is how it works. Anyone with half a brain knows that!"

On the carpet, Nathan Quigley groaned.

"He will be awake shortly," Daphne Beresfont said. "Pick up that pistol and hand it to me, my lord Balmorrow."

"It has been discharged," offered Balmorrow, remaining in place.

"I do not care. Pick it up and hand it to me. And very carefully, too."

"Well, I would," murmured Balmorrow, "if it were my mother-in-law ordering me to do so. But since you are not—"

"Oh, very well! I am your mother-in-law! You are just as obstinate as Clarissa! Now do as I say, or I shall shoot you through the heart."

Giving Clarissa a kiss upon her curls, Balmorrow released her from his embrace, stepped around her and went to hand over Mr. Quigley's pistol.

"Now, pick up Nathan and come with me."

"Pardon me, madam?"

"Pick Nathan up and come with me. You are being abducted, my lord Balmorrow."

"Mama! You cannot!" gasped Clarissa.

"Yes I can," declared Daphne Beresfont. "That is precisely what I can do. And do not one of you attempt to stop me, because I shall shoot Lord Balmorrow directly if you do."

"I do think you ought to call me Alex," grunted Balmorrow as he lifted Nathan Quigley into one corner of the coach and then took the seat across from the unconscious man. "I am your son-in-law after all."

"You are my prisoner, Lord Balmorrow."

"No, madam, I am not," frowned Balmorrow as the coach began to move forward. "And we would do best to admit that between ourselves now."

"You do not think that I will shoot you?"

"No."

"Then why did you come with me?"

"Because you could not carry Mr. Quigley down the staircase and up the street to this coach by yourself. Is this the Archbishop of Canterbury's coach? It is quite magnificent."

"It is his old town coach. He does not often require it," sighed Daphne Beresfont, keeping her pistol pointed directly at Balmorrow's heart. "He allows me the use of it from time to time. But I had to get one of Nathan's little congregation to drive the thing. He is not very competent, but apparently he can get the team to move forward when necessary. Nathan preaches, you know, whenever the Archbishop is from town."

"No, I did not know. He is—?"

"A Calvinist. And he is a fine man as well."

"My butler is not dead, I take it?" Balmorrow asked, sinking back against the squabs. "Nor my footmen? Nor any other of my staff? I saw none of them when we departed."

"Your butler did trip upon the staircase—he was that surprised to see me ascending, you know, and he was racing so very fast—but he is not dead. I locked him into the front parlor. And the others of your staff are locked away as well, I expect. Nathan would have done that. He was determined to come to you. He thought that he could force you to have John released."

"And John is your brother?"

"Yes, but I do not want John released. I want him confined to Bedlam for the rest of his days. He murdered my children's papa. And after all Thomas did for him, too! John got very angry because Thomas had no more money and could not contribute to our cause and he went and pushed my Thomas into traffic, just as he did you. And I shall not forgive him for that even if he is mad. He was not used to be mad, you know. It was being held for ransom in Russia that damaged his mind."

"John was held to ransom?"

"Indeed. Taken by French sympathizers and held in some horrible dungeon. It cost Thomas everything he had to bring John home again."

In the corner of the coach Nathan Quigley groaned, and Daphne Beresfont reached out and patted his shoulder sympathetically, though the pistol she aimed at Balmorrow did not waver in the least.

Clarissa fairly flew to the stables, Lord Parkhurst close behind her. "They entered a coach at the corner. They turned to the left," she said breathlessly, fastening her skirts in a most unacceptable manner up around her legs and then hurriedly leading two unsaddled horses out into the yard.

"You must ride to the Duke of Corning and to the Bishop of Leeds and tell them all that has happened, Edward, and send them after me! I trust you to do it. Alex cannot help you or your Henry, you know, if he is dead."

Clarissa clutched Windsong's mane in frightened hands and swung up astride the little grey as she and Malcolm were used to do when they were children and playing at being performers in Astley's circus. Then she turned the little mare's head toward the street. She did not wait for Lord Parkhurst. She waited for no one. She kicked her heels into Windsong's sides and charged up the cobbles at full tilt.

She could not be far behind them. She had watched from the window as Alex, with the unconscious Mr. Quigley tossed over his shoulder, had escorted her mama to the corner of the square and the coach that waited there. The coach had not sped away at top speed. It had moved very slowly. Very slowly. As if someone who knew little about horses were driving it, Clarissa thought. But of course that was nonsense. Why would anyone but an experienced coachman be driving such a large coach with four horses in the traces? No, they had most likely gone slowly at first so as to attract no attention.

But once they are clear of the neighborhood, the driver will give the horses their heads, Clarissa thought with some trepidation. It is very late and most of the streets will be deserted and, oh, I shall never be able to come up upon a four-horse rig. Not with my little Windsong. I ought to have ridden one of Alex's geldings. They are much larger and stronger and undoubtedly they would be able to carry me farther at a faster pace. But I cannot turn about now. I shall never find Alex if I turn back now.

The streets were indeed nearly deserted and Clarissa, who had hoped to glimpse the coach some distance ahead of her, could see very little at all. Wisps and strings and fountains of fog were rolling in along the ground and trellising up the streetlamps, dimming the lamplight. And the faithless moon was hiding behind a great bank of clouds. Still, she knew that the coach had turned left, and in the distance, the rumble of wooden wheels over the cobbles echoed back to her. She urged Windsong onward, trusting blindly that the coach she heard was the coach she sought to find.

"Oh please, God," she whispered into the humid night.

"Please, God, do not let Alex be harmed. Mama is mad. Mama is mad. Oh please, God, do not let my mama murder my husband!"

The vague sound of the coach wheels ahead of her led Clarissa east toward the Thames where the fog grew thicker and the warren of streets closer together and more pressed about with buildings. Often she was forced to draw Windsong to a halt to listen for the sound. They are going directly to the river, she thought. What if Mama intends to shoot Alex and dump him into the Thames and then escape upon one of the barges anchored at the wharves!

And then, as she turned the corner onto New Bridge Street, she saw the coach meandering in and out of a rolling tide of fog ahead of her. It had not attempted even once to bolt over the cobbles at top speed as she had expected, but it continued traveling at a comfortable trot. Why, Mama is so certain that no one has followed her, she has not even told the coachman to spring his horses, Clarissa thought in surprise. How can that be? And tapping her heels urgently into Windsong's sides, she urged the little mare again into a full-out run. The distance between herself and the coach was closing fast when Windsong twisted beneath her, stumbling over a missing cobble in the street and coming near to tossing Clarissa clear over her head. The little mare fought to keep her balance, did not go down, but came to a stuttering halt, holding one hoof tenderly off the ground.

Clarissa's heart, which had just begun to rush in triumph to her throat, plunged instead to the very pit of her stomach. She eased herself to the ground and patting the mare's neck, whispered softly to the animal and stared after the coach as it began to disappear into the deepening fog. Tears of frustration started to her eyes dimming the vision of the vehicle that carried Alex from her into an ever-deepening shadowland—the vehicle that carried Alex from her perhaps forever.

"I telled ye it were not no halfling!" came a raucous shout that pulled Clarissa instantly away from despairing thoughts of Alex and into the present reality. "I telled ye it be a mort!"

"Aye, an' ridin' bareback an' astride, she were! Here, lassie, be ye one o' Astley's gels?"

"Naw, blimey, she bean't no Astley gel. What'd she be a doin' down 'ere if she be a Astley gel? Them what rides fer

Astley makes a bit o' the ready. 'Nuf ta live up near aroun' Basket Lane, I bets."

Before she could think of what to do a dozen or more men were making their way from one of the buildings into the street where Clarissa stood holding tightly to Windsong's mane. She could not see them clearly amidst the shadow and fog, but they certainly did not sound like gentlemen.

" 'Ere now, an' what's amiss wif yer poor li'l horsey, lass? Come acropper did it? Missin' cobbles'll do that now an' again. Come back wif us an' have a drink, lassie, an' I'll sen' me boy ta Cap'n Sutter's stables wif yer filly there."

A number of pale and rather frightening faces bobbed into and out of Clarissa's vision; a peculiar stench began to assault her nostrils; a hand touched her elbow, another her shoulder, and a third her waist. Like a pack of hounds at a treeing, they were baying around her, encircling her, waiting for—"Get your filthy hands off of me!" demanded Clarissa loudly. "Of all the nerve, to come prattling and pawing at me as though I were any paper and pins girl!"

For a moment the men stepped back in surprise at the tone of her voice as well as at her words. But then they began to laugh raucously again and hands caught at her clothing.

"Let 'er be!" roared a voice. "She bean't lyin' to ye. She bean't no ordinary woman, that piece o' baggage!"

Clarissa kicked at one of the men closest to her and spun around to see who it was had bellowed out the command. Surprisingly it was a ruffian on horse back. She had been so overwhelmed by the men who had dashed into the street to confront her that she had not so much as heard the clop of one hoof.

"Who be she then, eh, Jacko?"

"She be mine," growled the villain, bringing his mount up beside Clarissa and leaning down to scoop her up and fling her across his saddle bow. "She be mine an' makin' off wi' one o' me bloods. Ye take that filly ta Cap'n Sutters fer me, Will, an' there be a crown in't fer ye. I be collectin' this li'l filly tanight an' that li'l filly in the mornin'. Ow! Settle down, ye harridan. I ain't be goin' ta let ye 'scape me agin!" shouted the man as Clarissa rammed her fist into his calf in hope of escaping.

Raucous laughter flailed the air as Clarissa pounded harder

and wiggled wildly. But the man simply gave her a whack across her posterior, tightened the hold he had taken on her skirts and gave his horse the office to start, carrying her off as though she were no more than a clutch of dead rabbits.

Chapter 21

Frightened, intimidated, and thoroughly humiliated, Clarissa longed both to scream in fury and weep profusely but she found she could do neither bouncing upside down as she was across a trotting horse. It took all of her attention to keep from plummeting to the cobbles. Indeed, if the villain were not clutching her tightly with one enormously strong hand, she would certainly have fallen directly on to her head immediately the horse began to step out.

But he will bring this cursed horse to a halt sometime, thought Clarissa, steadily growing more angry than frightened, and then I shall pummel him severely. I shall bite him in the knee the moment we cease to move to gain the opportunity to right myself and then I shall box his ears and scratch his face and I shall not cease to do so until he is vanquished!

By the time the man did bring his horse to a halt Clarissa's anger had turned to rage. She did grab him by the leg and did bite him in the knee with great enthusiasm.

"Ow! Damnation, Clarissa, cease and desist at once! Is this the thanks I get for riding to your rescue? And Lex thinks you such an innocent angel, too!"

"What? Who?" cried Clarissa, wiggling from his grasp and lowering her feet hurriedly to the cobbles.

"Do not run off!" ordered the man, leaping from the saddle and seizing her by the elbow. "I realize you are frightened, my dear, but claiming you were mine and throwing you across my saddle bow seemed the most expedient way of extricating you from that little situation. Wait! Here!" he added, fishing hurriedly through his pockets with his free hand as Clarissa strove to tug free of his grasp and aimed a resounding kick at his shin. "Ow! Here! Here! Take this!" and he dangled something before her eyes.

In the faint light that filtered into the street from an open doorway the thing he dangled sparkled just a bit. Clarissa paused in her struggle and stared at it. Then she held out her hand and he placed the tiny falderol into it, but he did not release her elbow.

"My ruby bracelet!" Clarissa gasped. "You are—you are Mad Jack Docker!"

"Indeed. And beneath all this dirt," he added, pushing his wide-brimmed hat to the back of his head to give Clarissa a better look at his face. "Beneath all this dirt, I am Norris as well, though there is no one about this side of town knows me as such. You passed me only a street before Windsong tripped. I recognized her, you know. I was there when she was breeched."

"Viscount Norris? Alex's Cousin John? Oh! Oh, I am so relieved! Alex has been abducted and—"

"Lex? Abducted? That is why you were riding like a hoyden through the city?"

"I was attempting to catch the coach he is in. And I would have caught it had poor Windsong not tripped and gone lame."

"Then we are not far behind? Which way did the coach go, Clarissa? And do you know who has abducted him? How many men must I deal with?"

"Well, there is Mr. Nathan Quigley, if he has recovered his senses, and the coachman of course."

"And how many others?"

"No other men that I saw. But there is my mama."

"Your mama? Lex was abducted by a senseless man, one coachman and your mama?"

Clarissa, adjusting her skirts once again to free her legs and allow her to ride astride, accepted Viscount Norris' help into the saddle and related all she knew of the abduction. Norris, mounting behind her, swore under his breath and urged his horse to a canter in the direction of the Thames.

"There truly is nothing I can do," drawled Balmorrow in answer to Nathan Quigley's dizzily stuttered query. "I do not have that sort of power, Quigley."

"No, and I do not wish John to be set free," declared Daphne Beresfont. "My brother is a lunatic, Nathan. No sane man would have murdered Thomas or attempted to murder Lord Balmorrow. And who knows but that the next time he will not decide to murder you—or me."

"It was your wishing to change our plan that set him off, my love," groaned Quigley. "John was counting upon that plan to gain back his properties. I doubt not but that he thought if his lordship were dead, we would simply discover another likely scapegoat and carry on as we were."

"I do not care in the least what John thought. And I do not care what you think either, Nathan Quigley. You have ruined my life—you and John between you. I will not allow you to ruin Clarissa's and that is that!"

"I think," interjected Balmorrow, gazing lazily out the window, "that your coachman is lost, Quigley. We are going even more slowly than before; the track we are on is overgrown; and we are in the midst of a woods. Where are you bound?"

"Gravesend, I expect," sighed Quigley with a questioning glance at Daphne Beresfont.

"Well, this is not Gravesend. We are somewhere along the Thames, south of the wharves but nowhere near the southern turnpike. And your driver is the merest whipster. Would you like me to drive?"

"You?"

"I can drive four-in-hand, Quigley. I have done so often."

"You?" asked Quigley again. "You, sir, are my prisoner!"

"I am not your prisoner. If I am anyone's prisoner—which I do not concede to be the case—I am the prisoner of this brave woman here. If she had not come so intrepidly to your rescue, you would be in irons by now and I would be home in bed."

"Brave?" asked Daphne Beresfont in a contemplative voice. "Do you think I am brave, Lord Balmorrow?"

"Yes, madam. What? Did you not think yourself intrepid to race into my house, dispose of my butler and hold an entire room full of people at bay with one small pistol? I was rather amazed at it myself."

"You were?"

"Um hmm. And I would be most willing, my lady, to help you reach Gravesend and a ship out of the country if that is your wish. Though I feel no such inclination toward Mr. Quigley."

"You do not?"

"No, madam, I do not. I cannot think why you abandoned Viscount Halliard for this man. That is what happened, is it not? You left your husband for the arms of this gentleman here?"

Daphne Beresfont nodded slowly. "I was seduced, you see, by Nathan's preaching. He was so filled with the spirit of righteousness. Wrath-filled he was at the aristocracy's treatment of the poor and hell-bent to reform all of England. And he was a Calvinist," she added softly, "which my mama was before she married papa. She raised me Calvinist in secret, behind my papa's back. They did not like each other, my mama and my papa."

"No?"

"Not at all."

"And you did not like Viscount Halliard?"

"I liked Thomas well-enough—but then Nathan convinced me that my husband was a greedy, unprincipled devil—one of the unfeeling aristocracy who condemned all the truly noble people of the world to servitude. I was quite stupid then, you know, and believed Nathan's every word. I gave up everything for Nathan and his cause. But I have learned a number of hard lessons since."

"What hard lessons?" grumbled Nathan Quigley from his little corner of the coach. "We have had a few little set-backs is all, my love. We shall conquer in the end."

"I did not at all realize how much Thomas truly loved me and how noble he was until word came of John's capture and I went to beg his assistance. By then, of course, it was much too late to abandon Nathan. Nor did I wish to do so, because

Nathan is not wrong about everything, my lord Balmorrow. There is need for great reform and someone must bring it about."

"You remain with this gentleman only because you believe in his cause? You do not love him, madam?"

"I do not, not any longer. But I have given up my life—my husband, my children, my very existence—I must find meaning for it all in something or I will go mad, and so I strive to bring the dreams of the nonconformists like myself into reality."

"I shall bring your dreams into reality, madam," declared Balmorrow confidently. "But not by some bloody rebellion. I shall bring them about in Parliament with the assistance of an Irish gentleman by the name of O'Connell and the willing aid of Sir Robert Peel and Henry Grattan and Lord John Russell. I happen to know that even Wellesley will cast his lot with us once this blasted war has ended. And Castlereagh—Castlereagh has already won a bit of the battle and is definitely to be counted upon."

"All these gentlemen?"

"And more," nodded Balmorrow. "Corning and Norris and Wright and Abbercombe among them. They do not all speak so loudly as I, but they are committed, madam. The reformists and the nonconformists shall have their rights. And the Luddites shall learn new skills and the poor be given a way out of poverty, and England will be a land of opportunity and freedom for all of its people, not just a chosen few. I vow it!"

"Oh," sighed Daphne Beresfont, lowering the pistol that had so steadily pointed at Balmorrow's heart. "Is that how you speak in the Parliament? So strong and confident and with such passion as that? No wonder Nathan thought you the most likely scapegoat should we fail. And what a stupid thing to do—to think to sacrifice you in our stead when you are much more likely to succeed than we. Nathan Quigley, you are the greatest ninny that ever was!"

"Yes, madam, that is precisely what he is and I cannot think why you do not leave him and throw in your lot with me. I will not abandon the cause, I assure you. And I will take up another on your behalf."

"Another cause?"

"To explain your past actions to your children, my lady. To reunite you with Clarissa and Malcolm. They will like to have their mama back, I think, once they come to understand what happened to separate you from them."

"I could not."

"Only consider it, madam. That is all I ask. That and to allow me to increase the pace of this dratted vehicle and take it in the proper direction."

"They ought to go to Gravesend," declared Viscount Norris in Clarissa's ear as he held her tightly and spurred his mount into a gallop. "If they fear John Bellingham will betray them, they will not attempt to gain passage aboard any ship leaving from the London docks and Gravesend is next nearest. Though how they intend to reach Gravesend along such a track as this I cannot guess. They have already missed the turnpike by a good bit. Good Lord," cried Norris, as a coach drawn by four prime bays raced out of the darkness directly at them. "Hold tight, m'dear!" he shouted, attempting to get his mount hurriedly out of the way of the charging team.

"That is the coach!" cried Clarissa as the vehicle flew past them. "John, that is the coach!"

Norris, considerable perspiration beading upon his brow, brought his animal to a plunging halt, turned the beast and pulled his new cousin tightly back against his chest. "I cannot put you down alone in this place, Clare. Wrap your hands in Barrel's mane and keep your knees pressed tight against his sides and hold on. Barrel is a brute and he will be able to carry us both full-out for the better part of a mile." And then he touched his spurs to the gelding and they were off through the fog and the dark at a most terrifying pace.

But even if we do catch them, thought Clarissa, clinging with all her might to the horse, her eyes squinting against the damp wind for sight of the vehicle ahead of them, how are we going to stop the coach? We did not think of that. How are we going to stop the coach? Mama has two pistols. Perhaps the coachman has pistols as well!

And then it was too late to think of that. The spectre of the coach was rising before them out of the fog, shaking and shimmering eerily before their eyes like a ghost ship upon the sea. Norris, both arms tightening about Clarissa's waist, urged his horse onward, closing the gap until Clarissa could see clearly both rear wheels looming large to either side of her. And then Barrel swerved around and past the outside wheel with but a hair's breadth to spare and they were charging up along the side of the coach, flying past it, hovering level with the outside wheeler. Clarissa felt a shifting behind her, a further tightening of Norris' grip and then the gelding's reins were being thrust at her. "Take the reins, Clare," Norris shouted in her ear. "Take the reins now and do not slow him."

Clarissa gasped in terror but loosed her grip upon the horse's mane and snatched the reins from his hands. And then Norris shifted behind her again and his hold upon her waist was gone and as Clarissa glanced back over her shoulder in sudden panic he launched himself from the gelding's back and on to the back of the outside wheeler.

His load considerably lightened, Barrel fairly soared forward, outdistancing the entire team in moments. It took all of Clarissa's strength and attention to slow him. Fearfully she listened for the sound of pistol shots behind her, but heard none. Fighting Norris' great brute to a standstill, she sat gasping for breath and at the same time attempting to listen to what was happening behind her. Had the team halted? Had it halted? Had Norris stopped the coach with no more fuss than that?

No more fuss than that? What a thought! Why he might have been killed! He might well have slipped beneath those pounding hooves and been trampled to death! Stifling the urge to burst into terrified tears, Clarissa turned the horse's head back the way they had come. Very slowly she rode back, fearing each step of the way what she would come to find in the virtually silent street behind her.

The coach had halted. The horses were standing, quivering and snorting in their traces. Clarissa's eyes widened as she saw Lord Norris still upon the outside wheeler's back—practically lying upon the outside wheeler's back! And a virtual giant of a coachman was leaping down from the box and rushing toward him!

Where was Alex? Clarissa's heart filled with dread. Alex was dead! Alex was already dead or surely he would be springing from the coach to Lord Norris' aid! That was why the coach had taken that almost non-existent track along the river and why it had been returning at such a pace. Her mama had killed Alex and gone to dump his body into the Thames, and now she and Nathan Quigley were attempting to reach the southern turnpike and Gravesend and a ship to far-distant climes! Without hesitation Clarissa thrust her heels into Barrel's sides and rode down upon the coachman, hoping to reach him before he reached Lord Norris and did that gentleman more harm.

The coachman turned at the sound of her approach and ignoring Norris, dashed toward Clarissa instead, grabbing at Barrel's bridle and bringing the horse to a halt. In the blink of an eye he was grasping a shrieking, kicking Clarissa around the waist and dragging her from the saddle and then he was wrapping her in his arms and tucking her against him and kissing her ears and her eyes and her nose and at the very last her lips.

It was Alex! The coachman was Alex! How it came to be so or why, Clarissa cared not. It was enough that he was there, his arms around her, supporting her, his lips pressed lovingly against her own. "Alex," she gasped when at last their lips parted. "Oh, Alex, I thought that you were dead! I thought Mama had killed you! I thought that Lord Norris and I had come too late! Oh, my goodness, Lord Norris!"

"Never mind Mad Jack, my love. Tell me that you are not harmed? I have never seen such a thing in all my life as you and Norris riding up beside me upon that beast of his. I could not imagine what sort of lunatic highwaymen were chasing me. If I had known it was you, Clare, up before him, I would have died on the spot of heart failure!"

"But, but Lord Norris is injured."

"No, he is not."

"Alex, I saw him. He is lying on the wheeler's back."

"Laughing. We recognized each other while we were battling for control of the team, you see, and now he is lying there laughing and gasping for breath. I was just about to go blacken his daylights for him for frightening the wits out of me when you came riding back out of the fog. Are you certain you are not injured, Clare? How did you get here—and with Jack—and why?"

"I came to rescue you," Clarissa smiled, pressing more tightly against him, thankful beyond measure for the solid strength of him upon which to lean and the bracing comfort of his arms around her. "I came to rescue you, Alex, from my mama."

Clarissa curled into Balmorrow's arms beneath the covers of her bed in Leicester Square and closed her eyes. Truly she was exhausted. She could not imagine for a moment where Lord Norris had found the energy to drive them all home, to carry Mr. Nathan Quigley back to the Archbishop's residence so that he might pack a trunk and then to set out again for Gravesend with that gentleman. "And I cannot understand why you gave that hideous man money for passage to the Americas, Alex," she murmured, fighting to keep sleep at bay. "He is a seditionist and no friend of yours."

"No, no friend of mine," agreed Balmorrow, stifling a yawn. "Go to sleep, Clare. You have had enough excitement for one night. We will discuss it in the morning."

"And to invite Mama and Miss Gonnering to remain with us!" Clarissa added, her eyes popping open. "What could you have been thinking?"

Balmorrow sighed, shifted himself to a sitting position and turned up the wick on the new little oil lamp beside the bed. "You are not going to give in to sleep, are you, my love?" he asked, as she snuggled against him. "Well, but little Miss Gonnering did nothing. Merely closed her eyes to wish for a gown. Any gently-bred lady of her age might do the same. She has been through a great deal in her life, Clare. It is hard always to be the poor relation."

"And you like her."

"A great deal. She is such a chubby, dithering little thing. She reminds me of my Aunt Agatha who died when I was twelve and whom I have sorely missed. Can we not keep her, Clare? I assure you, we can certainly afford her upkeep."

Clarissa giggled the merest bit. "You sound as if she is to be a pet like Trouble."

"Do I? Well, perhaps she is, in a way, for I find I should like to take care of her and keep her well fed and happy and purring. Do you not like her, Clare? Can we not keep her?"

"Well, I suppose we can if she wishes it. But we cannot keep Mama, Alex. I do not wish to have my mama in our house, and why you did not send her as you sent off Mr. Quigley and Lord Parkhurst and Lady Sarah, I do not understand. She is a madwoman!"

"She is your mama," Balmorrow murmured, adjusting his arm to a more comfortable position about Clarissa's shoulders.

"No, she is not. She says so herself. She wanted nothing to do with Malcolm and me when we were children. And she wants nothing to do with us now."

"Balderdash. It tore her heart from her breast to turn her back upon the two of you."

"What?" Clarissa pulled away from him and turned to stare disbelievingly into his eyes. "How can you say such a thing?"

"Because I know it to be true, Clare. She was filled with guilt for having done such a thing and over the years she has turned to flint because of it."

"Her heart was flint to begin with or she would not have abandoned us."

"What would you have had her do? Steal you and Malcolm from your father? Carry the two of you off into a life as hard and unforgiving as the cobbles that line the streets? That is the kind of life she has lived, my love—a hard, frightening and unforgiving one."

"That is the life she chose."

"But not for you and not for Malcolm. No mother who truly loved her children could have chosen such a life for them. It would have been truly selfish for her to have taken you with her. And do you think your papa would have consented to let you go? To lose his daughter and his heir to such a one as Nathan Quigley? Was it not terrible enough for him to lose his wife?"

"But—but—"

"Clare," Balmorrow whispered, taking her gently back into his arms, "she is your mama. That is all I could think of for the whole time we were together in that dratted coach. She made one great mistake and perhaps you shall never be able to forgive her for it. I do not know. But she is your mama, and to me that is an argument in her favor that is overwhelming."

Chapter 22

Fully a month later the Duke of Corning's traveling coach pulled to a halt in the circular drive before the main entrance to Castle Balmorrow. Not waiting one moment for the assistance of the footman or any of the outriders, the duke swung open the coach door, hopped down and lifted Maggie to the ground. Like excited children the two then went dashing across the yard and up the steps and in through the open front door.

"Auntie Mags! Uncle David!" Brandilynn and Zander tumbled like ruffians down the staircase and directly into the duke's and duchess' open arms.

"We thought you would never get here!" cried Zander as Corning gave him an enthusiastic hug.

"Aunt Michaela and Uncle Archie are coming, too!" exclaimed Brandilynn, bestowing a most welcoming kiss upon Maggie's cheek. "Aunt Michaela wrote that she did not give a rap about the war with Napoleon, that she and Uncle Archie would sail to England in spite of anything that little Frenchie twit could do!"

"Papa and Mama did not stay in London to 'pear at Court, Uncle David!" cried Zander, as though his uncle's hearing might be somewhat in doubt. "We are in rebellion!"

Corning roared into laughter and Maggie with him.

"We are not in rebellion, scamp," grinned Balmorrow, coming more slowly down the staircase with Clarissa upon his arm. "If anything, we are in disgrace."

"No, we are not in disgrace, Uncle David," insisted Zander. "We are in rebellion! Sylvester says that Papa and Uncle Jack have gone an' smuggled a whole army of seditionists out of the country an' the Prince is very angry. Perhaps our castle will be attacked!"

"You need not say that with such hope, Zan," chuckled Balmorrow, passing Maggie's pelisse into a smiling Parsons' care. "You would not like to be attacked, you know."

"Yes I would, Papa. I am a born soldier! All the Sinclair gentlemen are. Sylvester says so and Duncan, too."

"I see I shall need to strangle Sylvester and Duncan," sighed Balmorrow dramatically while Clarissa took Maggie into her arms and gave her a great hug.

"Malcolm and Charis arrived two days ago and are longing to meet you," Clarissa grinned. "And the Duchess of Larchmont and Cousin John are expected tomorrow. And Cousin Alden is already pouring you each a brandy in the long drawing room."

"And your mama?" asked Maggie, taking Clarissa's arm and starting up the staircase. "Have you made peace with your mama?"

"Grandmama is going to help write papa's speeches against the Test Acts!" cried Brandy from just behind them. "And she is going to teach mama and Uncle Malcolm all about the Acts, too! She is in Mrs. Beal's parlor right now with little Miss Gonnering going over all of the details for the wedding."

"All of the details?" asked Maggie with a glance over her shoulder. "How big of a wedding is it to be?"

"Oh, an enormous wedding," laughed Clarissa.

"A gigantic wedding," nodded Brandy gleefully.

"Everyone is coming," offered Zander, hopping from step to step behind them. "All of the tenants an' all of the villagers an' all of mama's and papa's friends. An' Cousin Alden is goin' to do the deed an' Uncle Malcolm is goin' to give mama away again just like before. Except this time Uncle David and Uncle Jack and Uncle Archie are going to stand up beside papa. And you and Aunt Michaela and Aunt Charis are going to stand up beside mama. And it will not be in the chapel but in the flutterby room, because that is where mama wishes it to be. And there will be music and dancing. And Duncan is to make enough food to fill up three entire chambers!"

"My goodness!" Maggie chuckled. "All of that in one breath?" She turned and took Clare's arm. "I think it is so romantic of you to do it all again, Clare," she whispered as they turned into the corridor that led to the long drawing room.

"Alex begged me to do it again. He said he could not for the life of him remember anything he had said or done the first time. And besides, it is his present to me—a wedding filled with joy and love and family to replace the first which was filled with calculations and trepidations and strangers."

"Grandmama says that mama is in an interesting condition," offered Brandy, "and that is why papa wishes to give her such a wonderful present."

"You are increasing?" asked Maggie, coming to a halt before the drawing room door. "Truly, Clare?"

"Yes, Maggie, she is! Now continue into the room, eh?" growled Balmorrow playfully. "You may not be thirsty, but David's throat is aching for brandy and so is mine."

"So, you are well out of it, Lex," smiled Corning, settling comfortably into one of the chairs and inviting Zander up beside him. "Jack got Mr. Quigley and his man off from Gravesend that night and no one has made the connection between Quigley and your bride's mama and John Bellingham."

"That would have been a settler, would it not?" grinned Balmorrow. "If the connection had been made, there would have been even more suspicions about my involvement in the thing."

"About *your* involvement?" laughed Alden, handing them both snifters of brandy. "Only think of poor Canterbury—his butler, his housekeeper and his clerk all in on it! It was in Canterbury's best interests as well as yours to cover it up. Which is the reason he said nothing when I granted Parkhurst and The Summarfield a special license, drove them to Gretna Green and then put them aboard a ship bound for Archie's little principality. Even gave me the loan of his coach to get them to Scotland, he did, and the price of their tickets."

"Well, but they did promise not to mention a word of it to anyone and not to involve themselves with any more seditionists," grinned Balmorrow. "And Archie will find Parkhurst a position of one sort or another in that principality of his. Parkhurst did turn about at the last, you know. Gave old Quigley one deuce of a leveler. I knew then there was hope for him. And I will send his Henry back with Archie and Michaela when they return home. The fellow will be in good shape by then."

"And Miss Gonnering?" asked Maggie.

"Oh, no. Little Miss Gonnering remains here," smiled Clarissa. "Alex has developed a decidedly protective attitude toward her, you see."

"No."

"Yes. He would adopt her, I think, if she were only fifty years younger. She does not wish to live on the continent, so she is to become a companion to my mama."

"And Liverpool and Castlereagh and I have noised it about for three weeks now that Bellingham lost his mind over some bureaucratic nonsense relating to a land matter," chuckled Corning, taking a sip of his brandy. "I think we have sewn the thing up all right and tight. Prinny seemed quite satisfied with it as long as he was assured that the principals were no longer running free in England. Still, Clarissa's mama is running free, and if that should come to Prinny's ears, Zander may get his war yet. And to think I came all this way without my long guns. I expect I shall have to go back and collect them, eh?"

"No, we will have enough guns," laughed Alden. "Lex's godmama and Mad Jack are bringing all of their weapons to the wedding."

"They are not," Balmorrow growled playfully. "Do cease encouraging Zander, both of you. No one is bringing weapons to the wedding, Zan. And as long as your new grandmama's relationship to a particular Mr. Bellingham does not reach the Prince's ears there will be no troops attacking Castle Balmorrow this week."

"But next week, Papa—" began Zander excitedly.

"Next week you will not have time for a rebellion, Zan. You and Brandilynn will be kept busy entertaining your uncles and aunts and all our guests, because your mama and I will not be here. We are taking a wedding trip to the lake country. Just the two of us. A trip that is not to be interrupted by seditionists or spies or even Mad Jack Docker."

"That will be very dull, will it not?" asked Zander.

"No, scamp, it will not," replied his father, rising and crossing the room to pull Clarissa up into his arms. "It will be the beginning of a great adventure."

Ignoring the company Balmorrow smiled down upon Clarissa and kissed her gently and then more deeply and more deeply still. "It will be a new beginning, Clare," he murmured breathlessly, as their lips parted and Clarissa snuggled comfortably against his chest. "A new beginning to the greatest adventure of our lives. And every day—every day of it—I will show you how I love you and I will never doubt that you love me."

"No," sighed Clarissa, her vision blurred by perfectly happy tears. "No, you will never doubt that I love you, Alex, for I will make it perfectly clear to you that I do forever and ever and ever!"

ABOUT THE AUTHOR

Judith A. Lansdowne grew up in Kenosha, Wisconsin. Following graduation from St. Joseph High School she moved to New York City where she attended the American Academy of Dramatic Arts and spent several years acting and puppeteering. She returned to the midwest to continue her education, and after receiving her BA from the University of Wisconsin-Parkside worked as a journalist, editor, scriptwriter and videographer before turning to writing full time. She and her husband live on the shores of Guntersville Lake, Alabama where they divide their time between fishing and writing.

Judith loves to hear from her readers. You may write to her c/o Zebra Books.